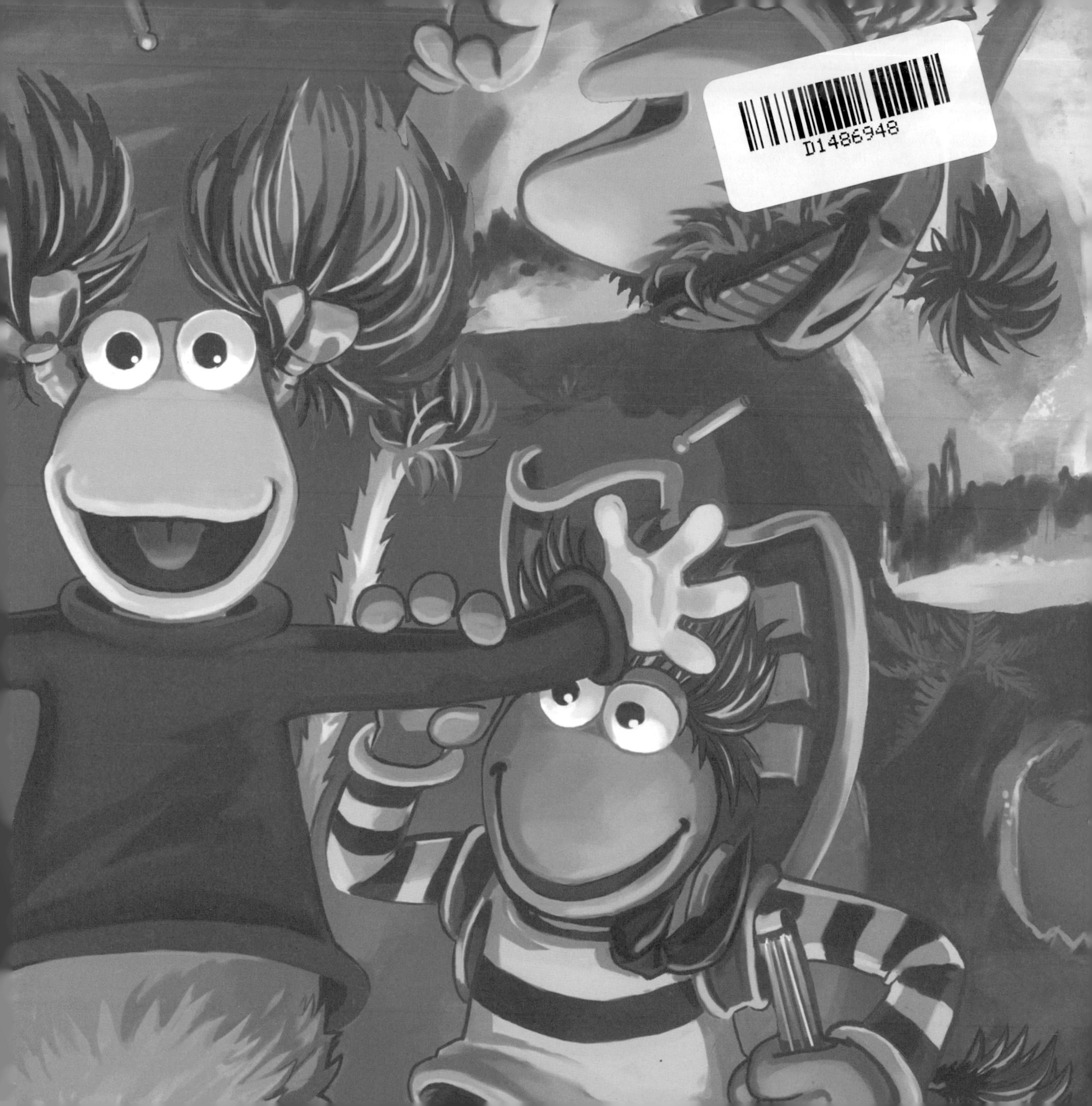

Jim Henson's™

FRAGGLE ROCK™

Jim Henson™
THE JIM HENSON COMPANY

www.henson.com

ARCHAIA ENTERTAINMENT LLC
WWW.ARCHAIA.COM

Jim Henson's™

FRAGGLE ROCK™

Written by Adrianne Ambrose, Nichol Ashworth, Jeffrey Brown, Bryce P. Coleman, Katie Cook, Leigh Dragoon, Sam Humphries, Neil Kleid, Grace Randolph & Heather White

Art by Jeffrey Brown, Katie Cook, Cari Corene, Michael DiMotta, Joanna Estep, Lizzy John, Whitney Leith, Jeremy Love, Jake Myler, Fernando Pinto & Jeff Stokely

Letters by **Dave Lanphear**
Managing Editor **Tim Beedle**
Consulting Editors **Joe LeFavi & Paul Morrissey**
Collected Edition Art and Design by **Scott Newman & Brian Newman**
Collected Edition Cover by **Jake Myler**

Special Thanks to Brian Henson, Lisa Henson, Jim Formanek, Nicole Goldman, Maryanne Pittman, Melissa Segal, Hillary Howell and the entire Henson team.

Published by Archaia

Archaia Entertainment LLC
1680 Vine Street, Suite 912
Los Angeles, California, 90028, USA
www.archaia.com

Jim Henson
THE JIM HENSON COMPANY

ARCHAIA™

FRAGGLE ROCK

August 2010

FIRST PRINTING

10 9 8 7 6 5 4 3 2 1

ISBN: 1-932386-42-4
ISBN 13: 978-1-932386-42-4

Printed in South Korea.

Table of Contents

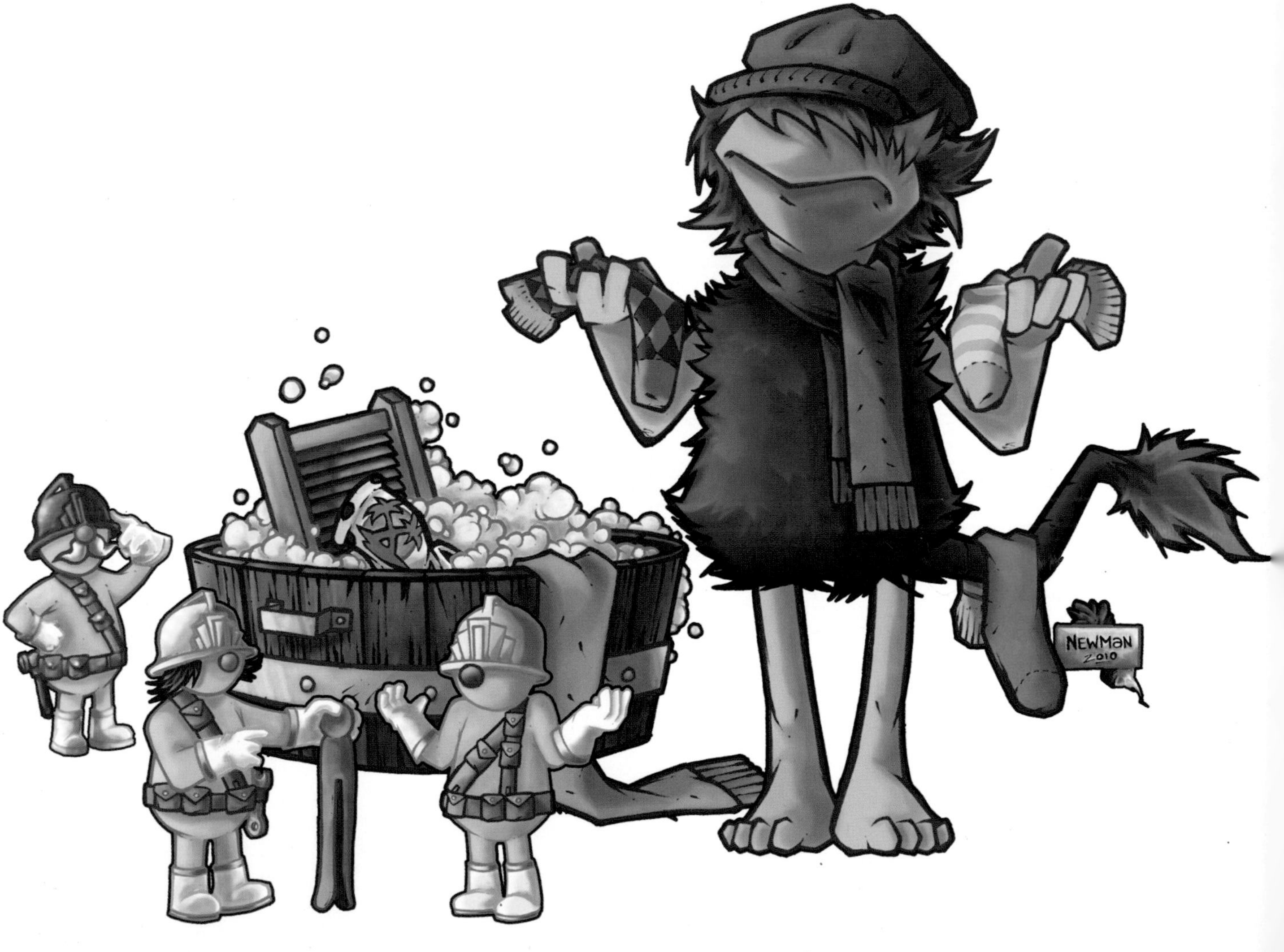
NEWMAN
2010

Foreword

Hey Silly Creatures and Fraggle fans,

I am honored to write this introduction for the first *Fraggle Rock* graphic novel. I, and it seems everyone who had the precious opportunity to work with Jim Henson on the original *Fraggle Rock* television series, continue to be awed by the show's power to inspire. And curiously, at the same time, I haven't been particularly surprised by this either, in a "Well, of course, what else would you expect?" Marjory-the-All-Knowing-Trash-Heap, stating the obvious kind of way.

The ongoing enthusiasm about *Fraggle Rock* is, at its essence, a continuation of the deep, positive force we all felt working on the show. We didn't create that force. It was—and is—a collection of ideals about healthy, responsible, joyful humanity that have been around as long as humans (known to the Fraggles as Silly Creatures) have been around: Explore. Dance. Sing. Laugh. Question. Care. Find strength. Give hope. Take personal responsibility. Dare to truly feel. Appreciate. Share. Use common sense. Empathize. Look past your differences with others and embrace your literal and figurative connections. Don't take yourself so seriously. Think. Love. Have fun. Those ideals—along with the understanding that they can be surprisingly difficult to achieve—resonated with everyone who worked on Fraggle Rock. We simply used the series as a way to wrap those timeless ideals in a new joy that resonated with a new generation.

Many people who were not much bigger than Fraggles when the show first aired are now at an age when they can pass those joyfully wrapped ideals on to their children or anyone else who will find them entertaining and thought-provoking. As an artist and writer as well as a puppeteer, I can appreciate the challenge of gathering up the boisterous energy of the Fraggles and getting them to hold still and lie down flat so that their stories can be passed on in comic book form. A big, thankful "Whoopee!!!" is in order for the artists, writers and the team at Archaia and The Jim Henson Company for their hard work creating these new Fraggle stories. And of course, even bigger thanks are due to Jim Henson, Jerry Juhl, Jocelyn Stevenson, Michael Frith and Duncan Kenworthy, who originally envisioned the world of the Fraggles, and the artists, cast and crew who brought their first stories to life.

I'm writing these thoughts just a short time after the twenty-year anniversary of Jim Henson's passing and the memorial that took place a few days later at the Cathedral of St. John the Devine in New York City. At Jim's request, there was music, color and laughter. At emotional moments in the ceremony, the cavernous hall spontaneously filled with a sea of fluttering rod puppet butterflies that had been given to attendees. Puppeteers, writers, producers, directors, musicians, puppet builders and designers from *Fraggle Rock*, which had finished production just four years earlier, were there. Jocelyn Stevenson, who was one of the show's head writers, talked about each of us who had worked with Jim as being "Jim seeds," to take what we gained from that experience and pass it on, each in our own way. I feel that those who are inspired by *Fraggle Rock* are also "Jim seeds." Whether you grew up with the show or are discovering it for the first time, whether you are a comic book creator or a comic book enthusiast, if the ideals so joyfully presented by the stories, music and characters of *Fraggle Rock* resonate with you, take that seed and, as the Fraggles sang, "Pass It On."

Thank you, Fraggle fans. You rock!

And now, since this introduction has almost certainly violated the Fraggle ideal of not taking oneself so seriously, I will have to remedy that in a most Fragglish way by signing off and balancing a pickle on my nose.

Karen Prell
Puppeteer of Red Fraggle
May 2010

The Residents of Fraggle Rock

c/o Gobo

Gobo is the natural leader of the Fraggle Five. He is an explorer, spending his days charting the unexplored (and explored-but-forgotten) regions of Fraggle Rock. He is highly respected by other Fraggles, although they occasionally find him a little pompous. He is also somewhat egocentric, which can make it hard for him to admit mistakes. As a leader, Gobo often provides his friends with direction, although, since he's a Fraggle, it's sometimes a fairly silly one.

c/o Red

Red Fraggle is a nonstop whirligig of activity. To her fellow Fraggles, Red is often seen as a flash of crimson racing to her next athletic pursuit. She is Fraggle Rock champion in Tug-of-War, Diving while Singing Backwards, the Blindfolded One-Legged Radish Relay, and a number of other traditional Fraggle sports. She is outgoing, enthusiastic, and athletic, but take note--her impetuosity can get her into real trouble.

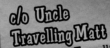

c/o Uncle Travelling Matt

Gobo's Uncle Travelling Matt is the greatest living Fraggle explorer-- the Fraggle equivalent of an astronaut. After completing his exploration of Fraggle Rock, he ventured forth into our world, a place the Fraggles call "Outer Space." He sends his observations back to Gobo on postcards in care of Doc.

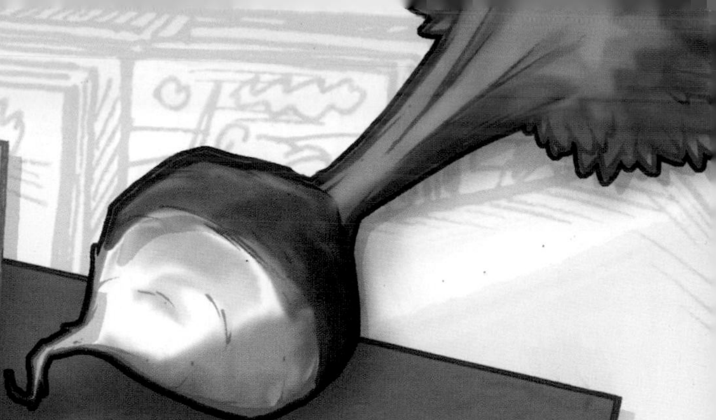

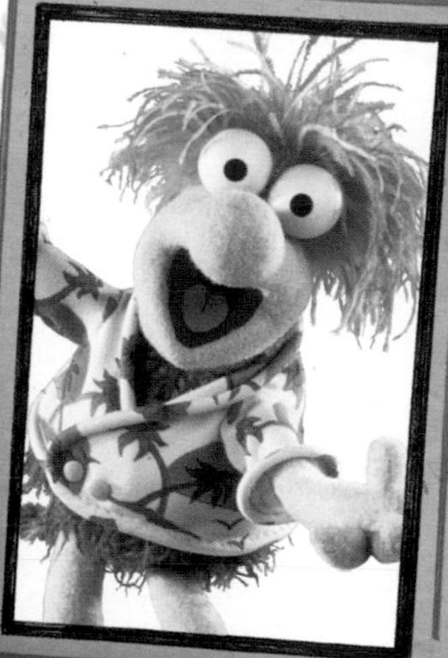

c/o Wembley

Wembley is indecision personified. He only owns two shirts, and both have a banana-tree motif. If he had any other clothes, he'd never be able to get dressed in the morning! Wembley has an uncanny ability to find merit on both sides of any issue. He is steadfast in his admiration for his best friend and roommate, Gobo. It was Gobo who encouraged Wembley to apply for his job with the Fraggle Rock Volunteer Fire Department. Wembley is the siren.

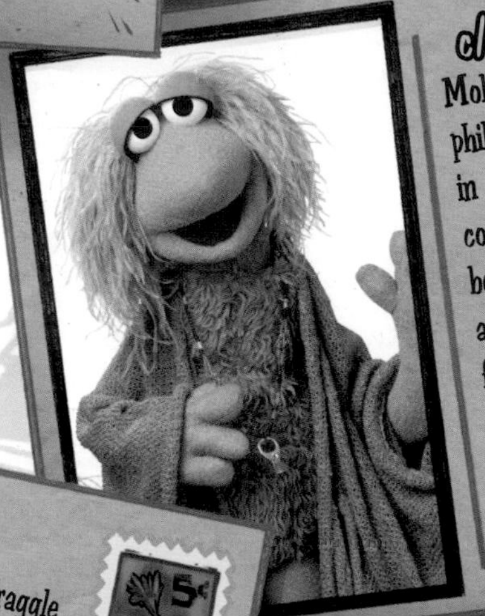

c/o Mokey

Mokey is an artist, poet and philosopher. She seems to be in touch with some sort of higher Fraggle consciousness. Mokey is fascinated by the beauty and intricacy of the world around her, and is always seeking new ways to share this feeling with others. Mokey may have her head in the clouds, but she's also very courageous and resourceful. Her job is to brave the Gorg garden to gather the radishes the Fraggles eat.

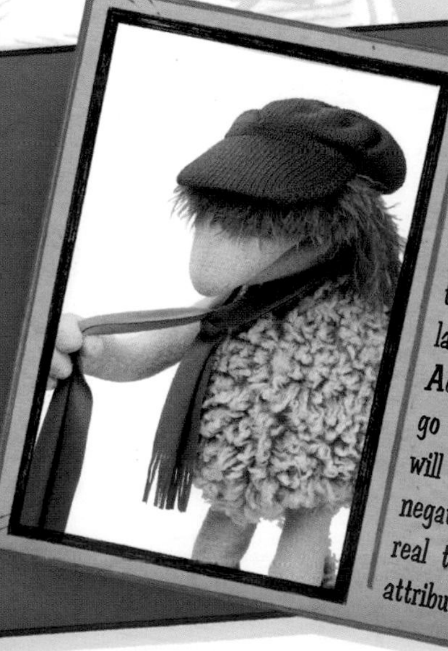

c/o Boober

According to Boober Fraggle, there are only two things certain in this world: death and laundry. Boober is terrified by the former and fascinated by the latter. He is also paranoid and superstitious. According to Boober, anything that can go wrong surely will, and when it does, it will inevitably happen to him. But Boober's negative attitude has a big plus--he can see real trouble coming a mile away, a useful attribute in a land of eternal optimists!

c/o Doc & Sprocket

Doc, the man who inhabits the workshop that contains the hole in the basement that leads to Fraggle Rock, is an inventor and a tinkerer. If it's a wee bit odd, Doc has probably already invented it. Doc doesn't know about Fraggles. Sprocket is Doc's extremely intelligent and expressive dog. Sprocket knows that the Fraggles exist. He's seen them lots of times...but he just doesn't have the words to tell Doc about them. This drives Sprocket crazy!

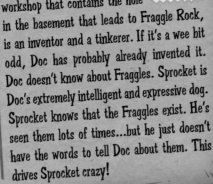

c/o Marjory the Trash Heap

A matronly, sentient pile of compost who acts as an oracle for the Fraggles. She sees all and knows all, but at times her offerings of wisdom go awry in the hands of the Fraggles. Nevertheless, Marjory's advice is usually beneficial. She likes to encourage the Fraggles not just to find temporary solutions to their problems, but to become more self-reliant and work to live in harmony with the other species around them.

c/o Junior Gorg

Sweet, loveable, galumphing Junior is the apple of his mother's eye and the bane of the Fraggles' existence! All he wants to do is "get those Fwaggles." The Fraggles raid the Gorg garden for radishes, and the garden is Junior's pride and joy. But the Fraggles are never really in any danger. Junior isn't very bright or coordinated, and really wouldn't hurt a fly.

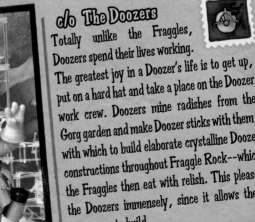
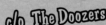

c/o The Doozers

Totally unlike the Fraggles, Doozers spend their lives working. The greatest joy in a Doozer's life is to get up, put on a hard hat and take a place on the Doozer work crew. Doozers mine radishes from the Gorg garden and make Doozer sticks with them, with which to build elaborate crystalline Doozer constructions throughout Fraggle Rock--which the Fraggles then eat with relish. This pleases the Doozers immensely, since it allows them more room to build.

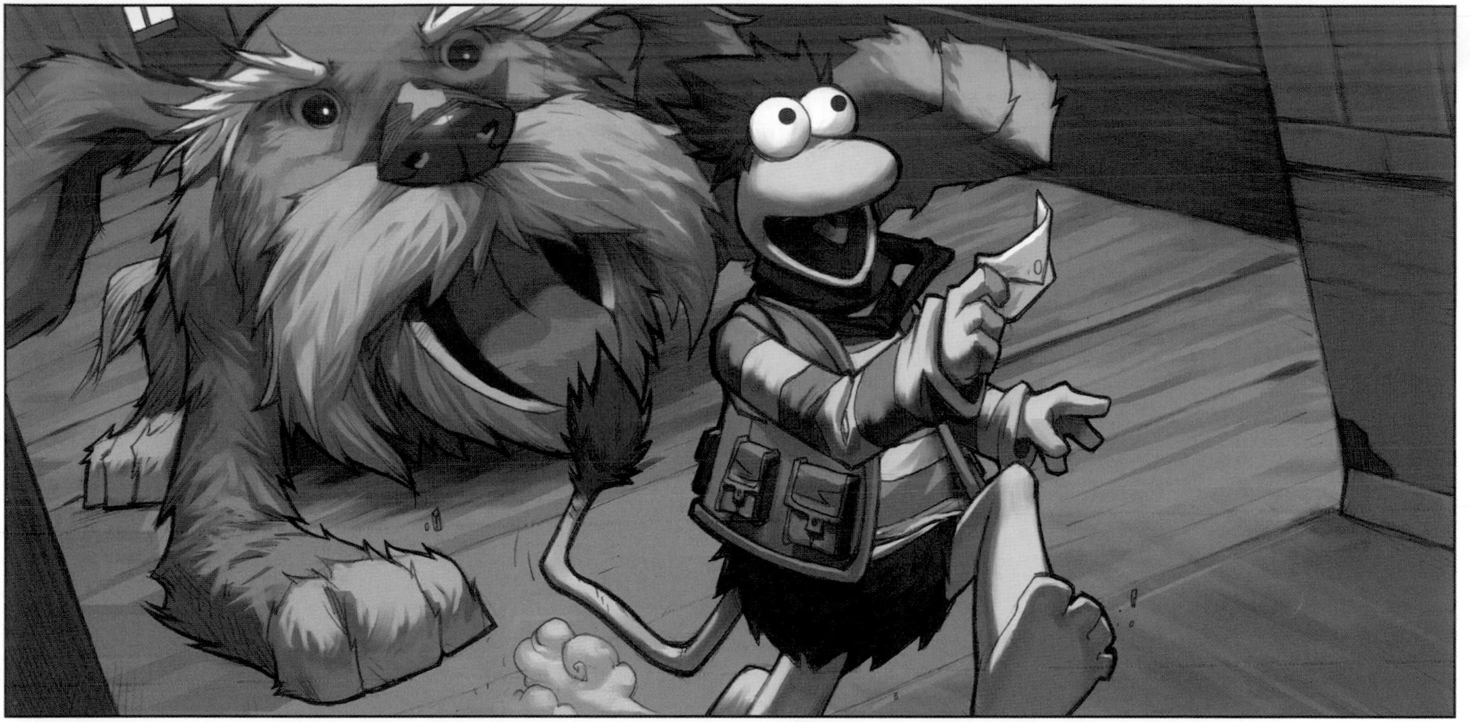

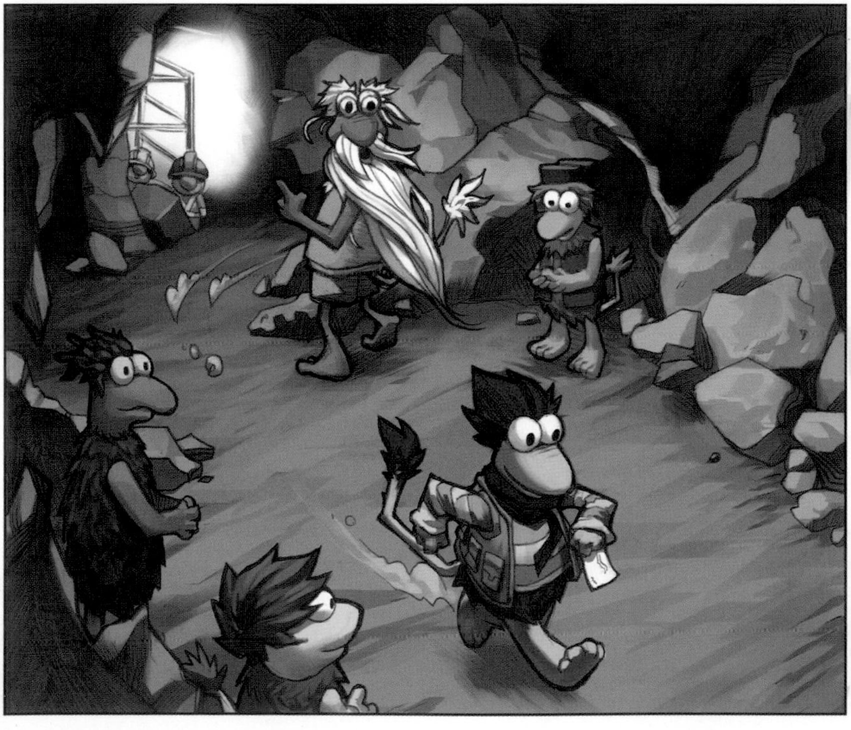

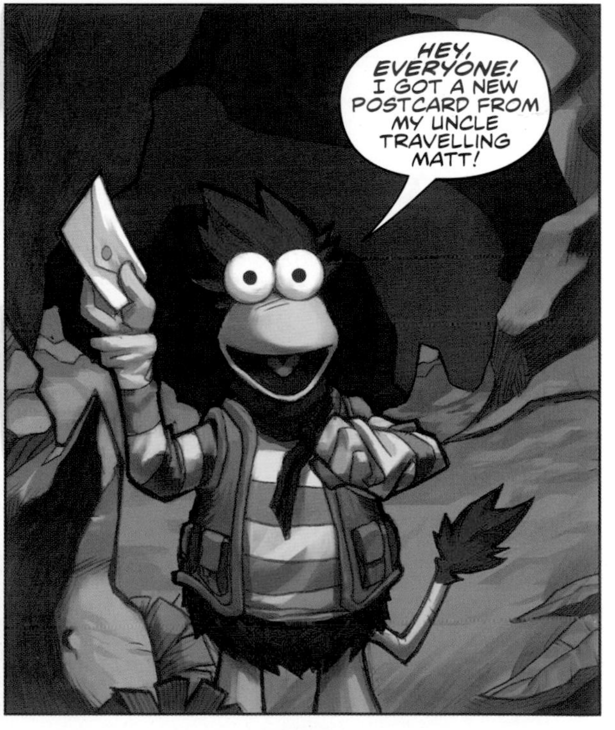
HEY, EVERYONE! I GOT A NEW POSTCARD FROM MY UNCLE TRAVELLING MATT!

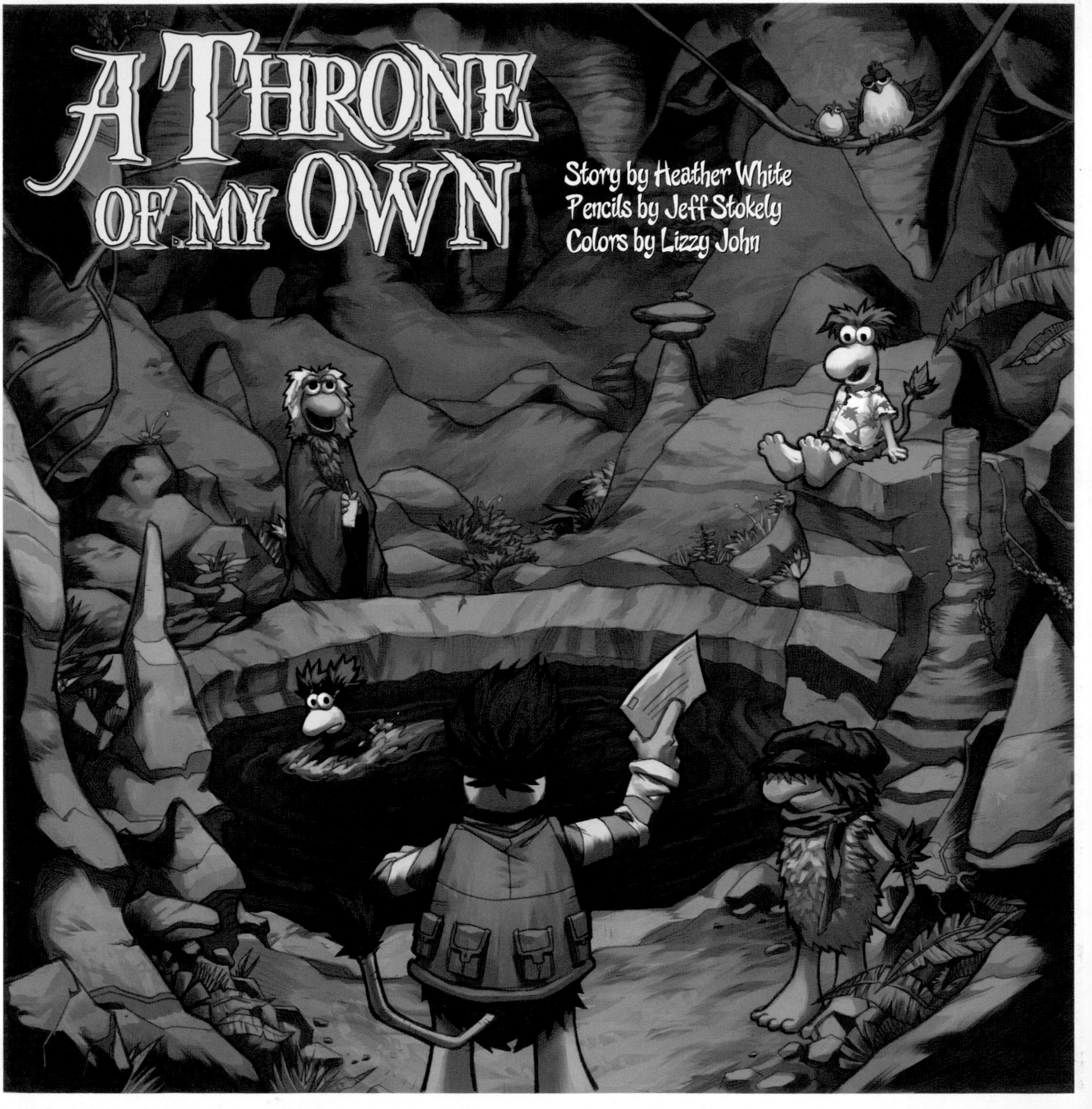
A THRONE OF MY OWN
Story by Heather White
Pencils by Jeff Stokely
Colors by Lizzy John

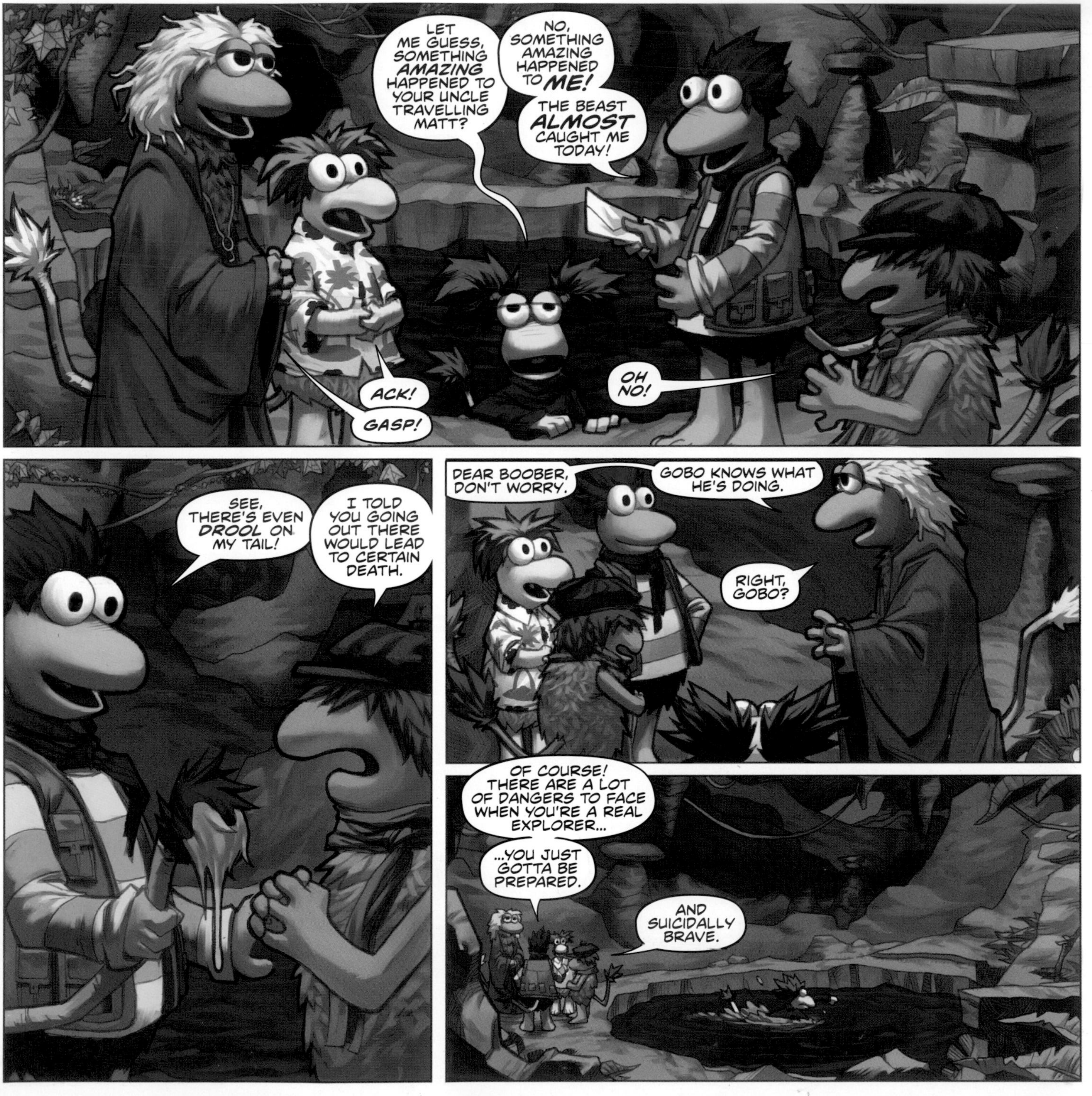
LET ME GUESS, SOMETHING AMAZING HAPPENED TO YOUR UNCLE TRAVELLING MATT?
NO, SOMETHING AMAZING HAPPENED TO ME!
THE BEAST ALMOST CAUGHT ME TODAY!
ACK!
GASP!
OH NO!
SEE, THERE'S EVEN DROOL ON MY TAIL!
I TOLD YOU GOING OUT THERE WOULD LEAD TO CERTAIN DEATH.
DEAR BOOBER, DON'T WORRY.
GOBO KNOWS WHAT HE'S DOING.
RIGHT, GOBO?
OF COURSE! THERE ARE A LOT OF DANGERS TO FACE WHEN YOU'RE A REAL EXPLORER...
...YOU JUST GOTTA BE PREPARED.
AND SUICIDALLY BRAVE.

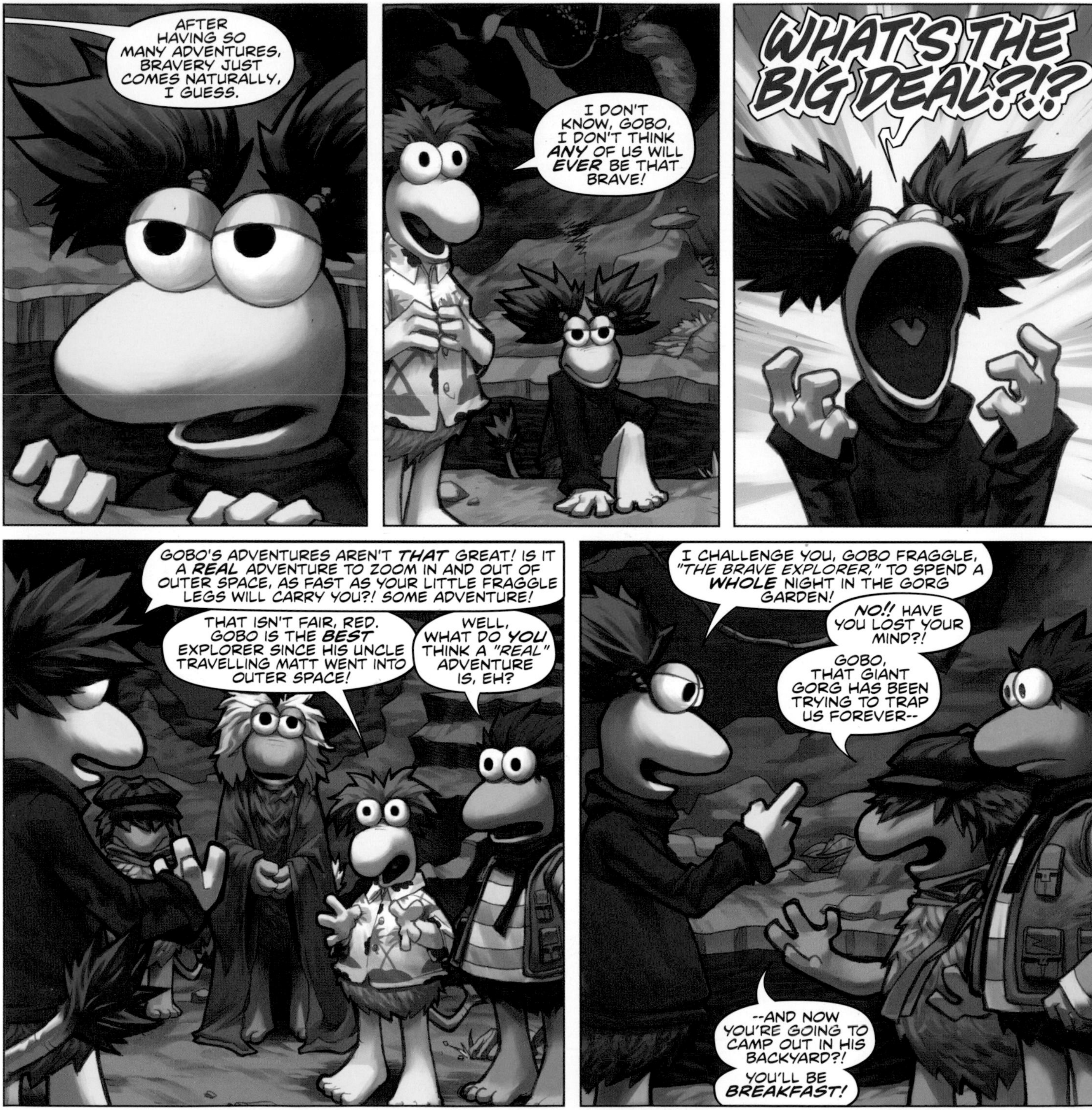

AFTER HAVING SO MANY ADVENTURES, BRAVERY JUST COMES NATURALLY, I GUESS.
I DON'T KNOW, GOBO, I DON'T THINK ANY OF US WILL EVER BE THAT BRAVE!
WHAT'S THE BIG DEAL?!?
GOBO'S ADVENTURES AREN'T THAT GREAT! IS IT A REAL ADVENTURE TO ZOOM IN AND OUT OF OUTER SPACE, AS FAST AS YOUR LITTLE FRAGGLE LEGS WILL CARRY YOU?! SOME ADVENTURE!
THAT ISN'T FAIR, RED. GOBO IS THE BEST EXPLORER SINCE HIS UNCLE TRAVELLING MATT WENT INTO OUTER SPACE!
WELL, WHAT DO YOU THINK A "REAL" ADVENTURE IS, EH?
I CHALLENGE YOU, GOBO FRAGGLE, "THE BRAVE EXPLORER," TO SPEND A WHOLE NIGHT IN THE GORG GARDEN!
NO!! HAVE YOU LOST YOUR MIND?!
GOBO, THAT GIANT GORG HAS BEEN TRYING TO TRAP US FOREVER--
--AND NOW YOU'RE GOING TO CAMP OUT IN HIS BACKYARD?!
YOU'LL BE BREAKFAST!

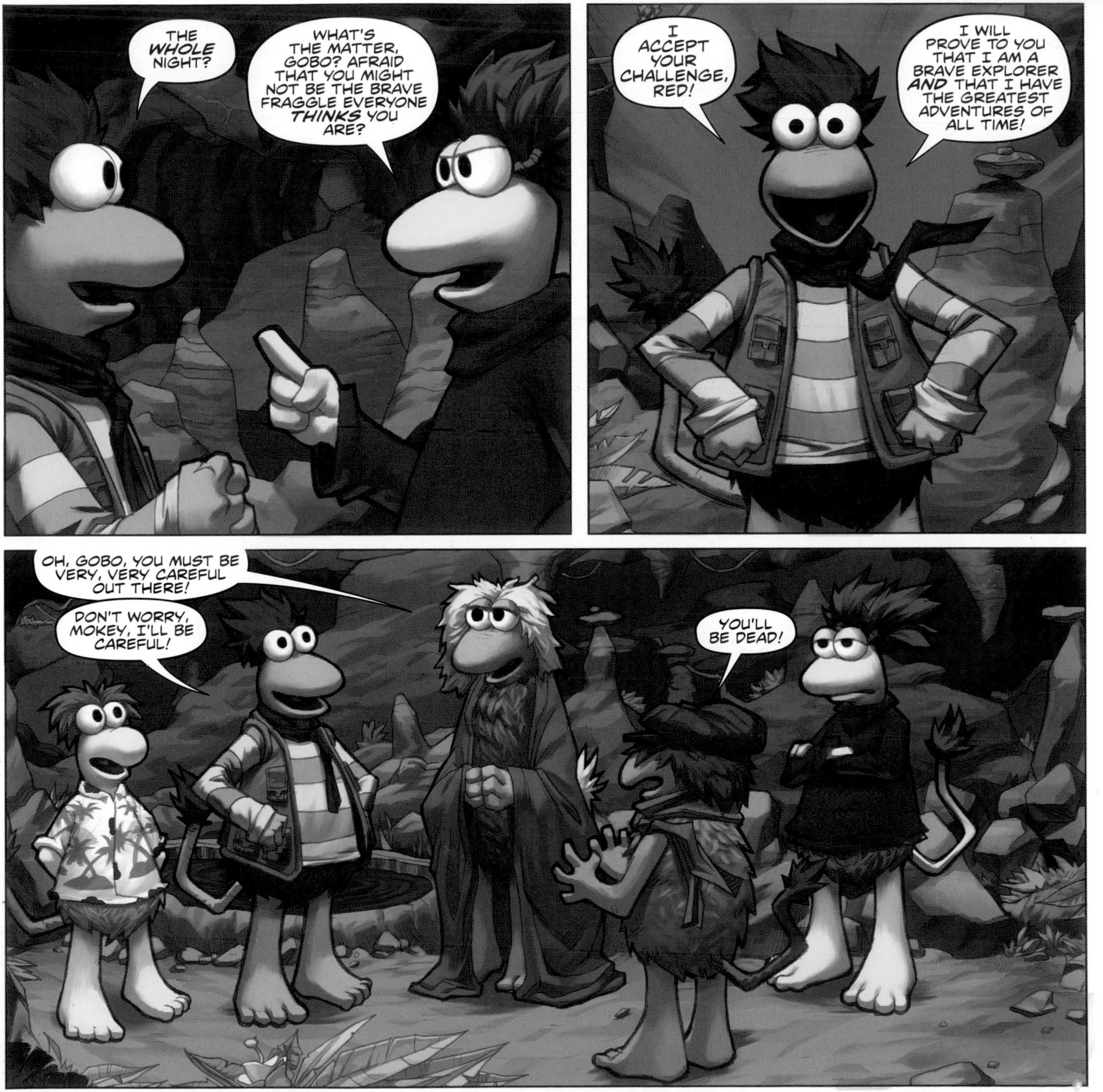
THE WHOLE NIGHT?
WHAT'S THE MATTER, GOBO? AFRAID THAT YOU MIGHT NOT BE THE BRAVE FRAGGLE EVERYONE THINKS YOU ARE?
I ACCEPT YOUR CHALLENGE, RED!
I WILL PROVE TO YOU THAT I AM A BRAVE EXPLORER AND THAT I HAVE THE GREATEST ADVENTURES OF ALL TIME!
OH, GOBO, YOU MUST BE VERY, VERY CAREFUL OUT THERE!
DON'T WORRY, MOKEY, I'LL BE CAREFUL!
YOU'LL BE DEAD!

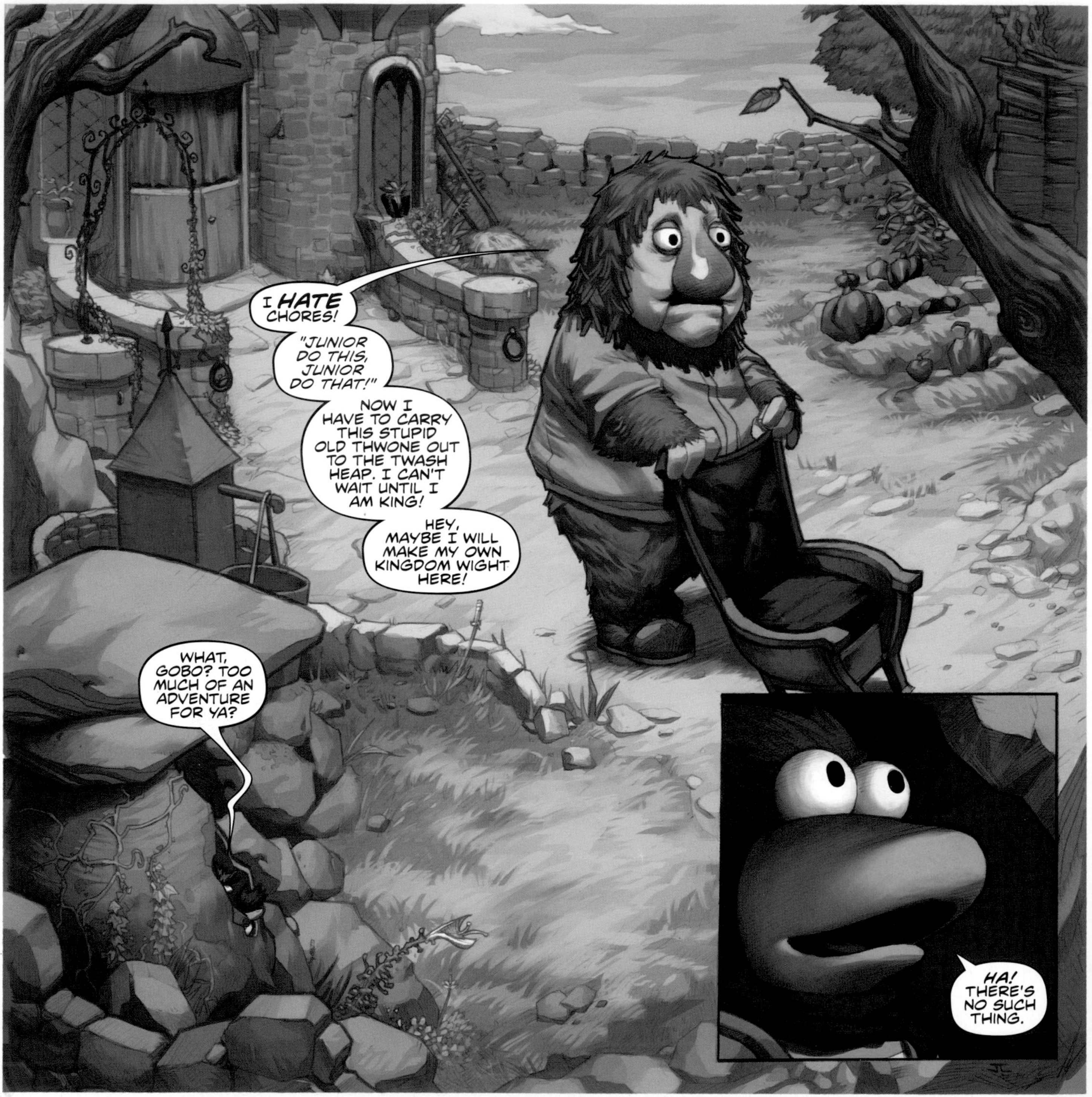
I HATE CHORES!
"JUNIOR DO THIS, JUNIOR DO THAT!"
NOW I HAVE TO CARRY THIS STUPID OLD THWONE OUT TO THE TWASH HEAP. I CAN'T WAIT UNTIL I AM KING!
HEY, MAYBE I WILL MAKE MY OWN KINGDOM WIGHT HERE!
WHAT, GOBO? TOO MUCH OF AN ADVENTURE FOR YA?
HA! THERE'S NO SUCH THING.

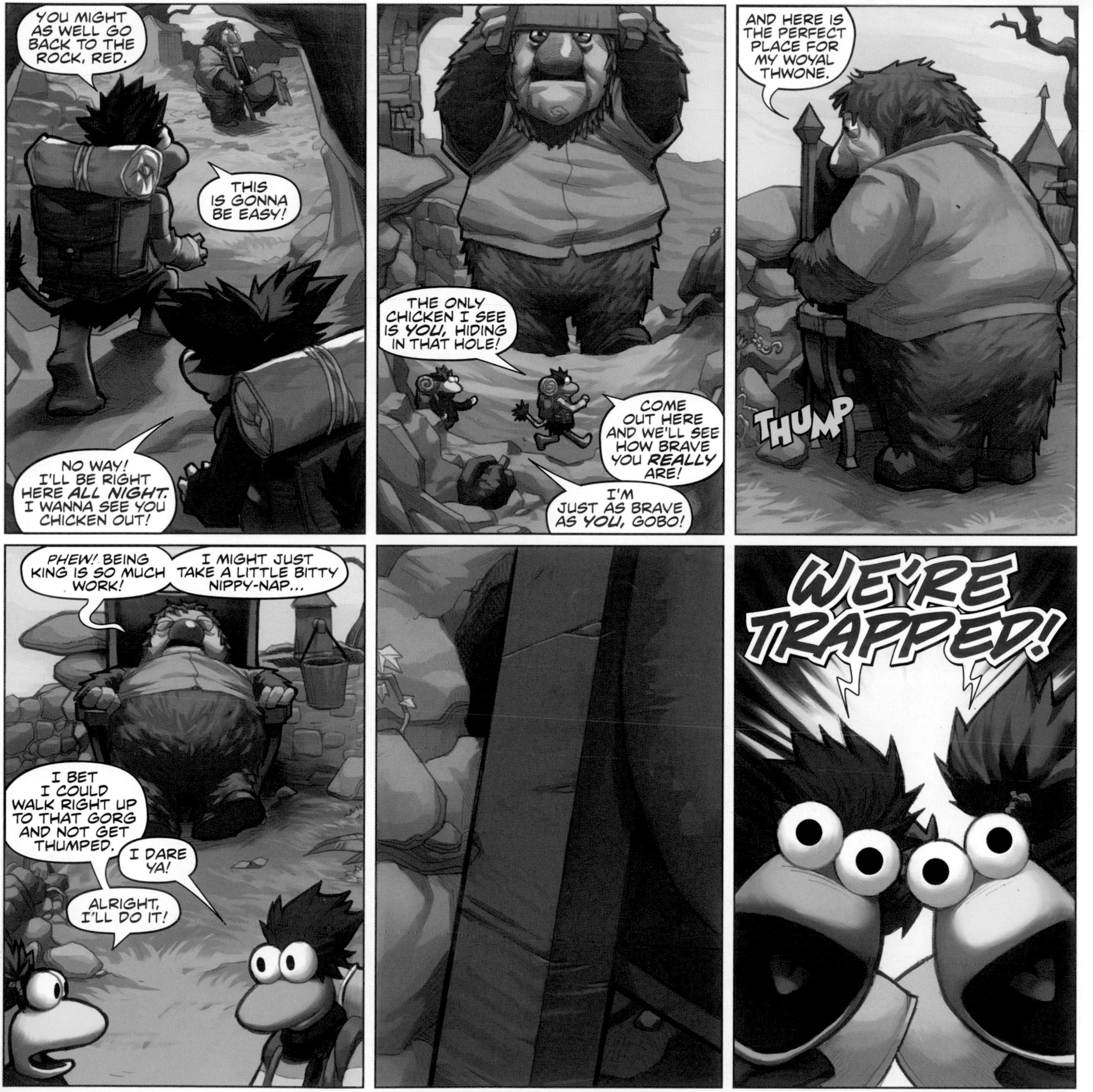
YOU MIGHT AS WELL GO BACK TO THE ROCK, RED.
THIS IS GONNA BE EASY!
NO WAY! I'LL BE RIGHT HERE *ALL NIGHT.* I WANNA SEE YOU CHICKEN OUT!
THE ONLY CHICKEN I SEE IS *YOU,* HIDING IN THAT HOLE!
COME OUT HERE AND WE'LL SEE HOW BRAVE YOU *REALLY* ARE!
I'M JUST AS BRAVE AS *YOU,* GOBO!
AND HERE IS THE PERFECT PLACE FOR MY WOYAL THWONE.
THUMP
PHEW! BEING KING IS SO MUCH WORK!
I MIGHT JUST TAKE A LITTLE BITTY NIPPY-NAP...
I BET I COULD WALK RIGHT UP TO THAT GORG AND NOT GET THUMPED.
I DARE YA!
ALRIGHT, I'LL DO IT!
WE'RE TRAPPED!

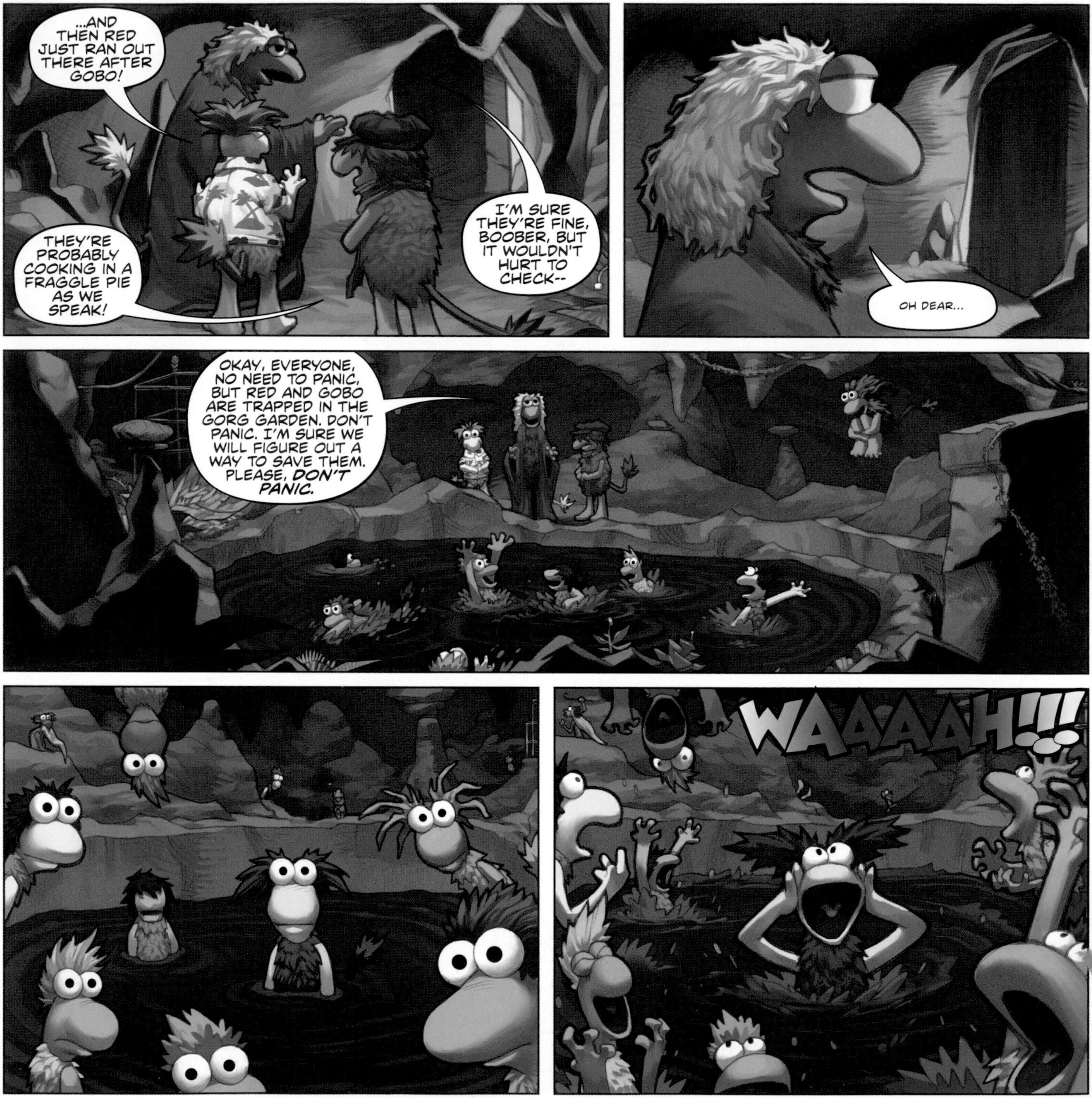
...AND THEN RED JUST RAN OUT THERE AFTER GOBO!
THEY'RE PROBABLY COOKING IN A FRAGGLE PIE AS WE SPEAK!
I'M SURE THEY'RE FINE, BOOBER, BUT IT WOULDN'T HURT TO CHECK--
OH DEAR...
OKAY, EVERYONE, NO NEED TO PANIC, BUT RED AND GOBO ARE TRAPPED IN THE GORG GARDEN. DON'T PANIC. I'M SURE WE WILL FIGURE OUT A WAY TO SAVE THEM. PLEASE, *DON'T PANIC.*
WAAAAH!!!!

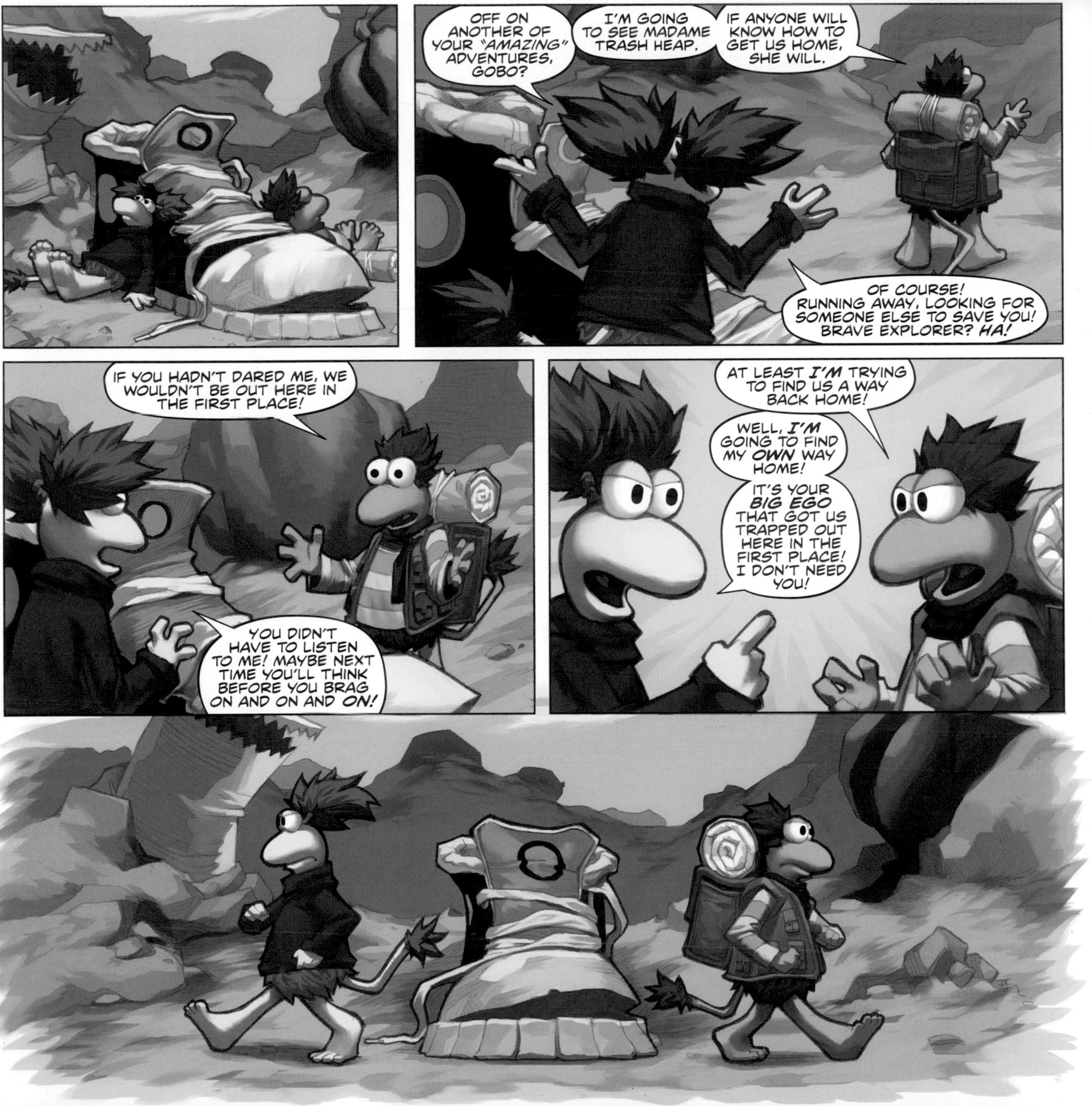
OFF ON ANOTHER OF YOUR "AMAZING" ADVENTURES, GOBO?
I'M GOING TO SEE MADAME TRASH HEAP.
IF ANYONE WILL KNOW HOW TO GET US HOME, SHE WILL.
OF COURSE! RUNNING AWAY, LOOKING FOR SOMEONE ELSE TO SAVE YOU! BRAVE EXPLORER? HA!
IF YOU HADN'T DARED ME, WE WOULDN'T BE OUT HERE IN THE FIRST PLACE!
YOU DIDN'T HAVE TO LISTEN TO ME! MAYBE NEXT TIME YOU'LL THINK BEFORE YOU BRAG ON AND ON AND ON!
AT LEAST I'M TRYING TO FIND US A WAY BACK HOME!
WELL, I'M GOING TO FIND MY OWN WAY HOME!
IT'S YOUR BIG EGO THAT GOT US TRAPPED OUT HERE IN THE FIRST PLACE! I DON'T NEED YOU!

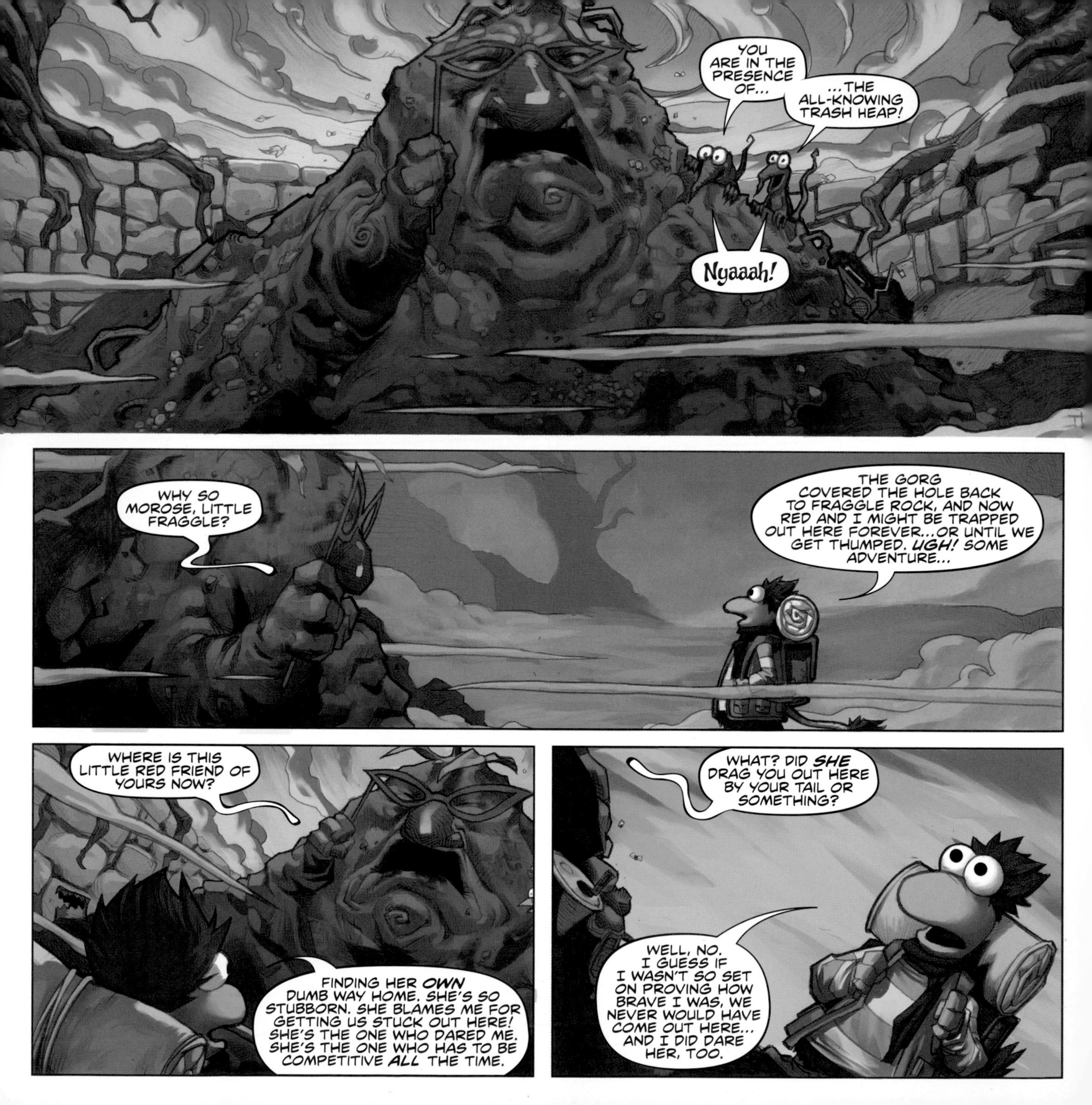

YOU ARE IN THE PRESENCE OF...
...THE ALL-KNOWING TRASH HEAP!
Nyaaah!
WHY SO MOROSE, LITTLE FRAGGLE?
THE GORG COVERED THE HOLE BACK TO FRAGGLE ROCK, AND NOW RED AND I MIGHT BE TRAPPED OUT HERE FOREVER...OR UNTIL WE GET THUMPED. UGH! SOME ADVENTURE...
WHERE IS THIS LITTLE RED FRIEND OF YOURS NOW?
FINDING HER OWN DUMB WAY HOME. SHE'S SO STUBBORN. SHE BLAMES ME FOR GETTING US STUCK OUT HERE! SHE'S THE ONE WHO DARED ME. SHE'S THE ONE WHO HAS TO BE COMPETITIVE ALL THE TIME.
WHAT? DID SHE DRAG YOU OUT HERE BY YOUR TAIL OR SOMETHING?
WELL, NO. I GUESS IF I WASN'T SO SET ON PROVING HOW BRAVE I WAS, WE NEVER WOULD HAVE COME OUT HERE... AND I DID DARE HER, TOO.

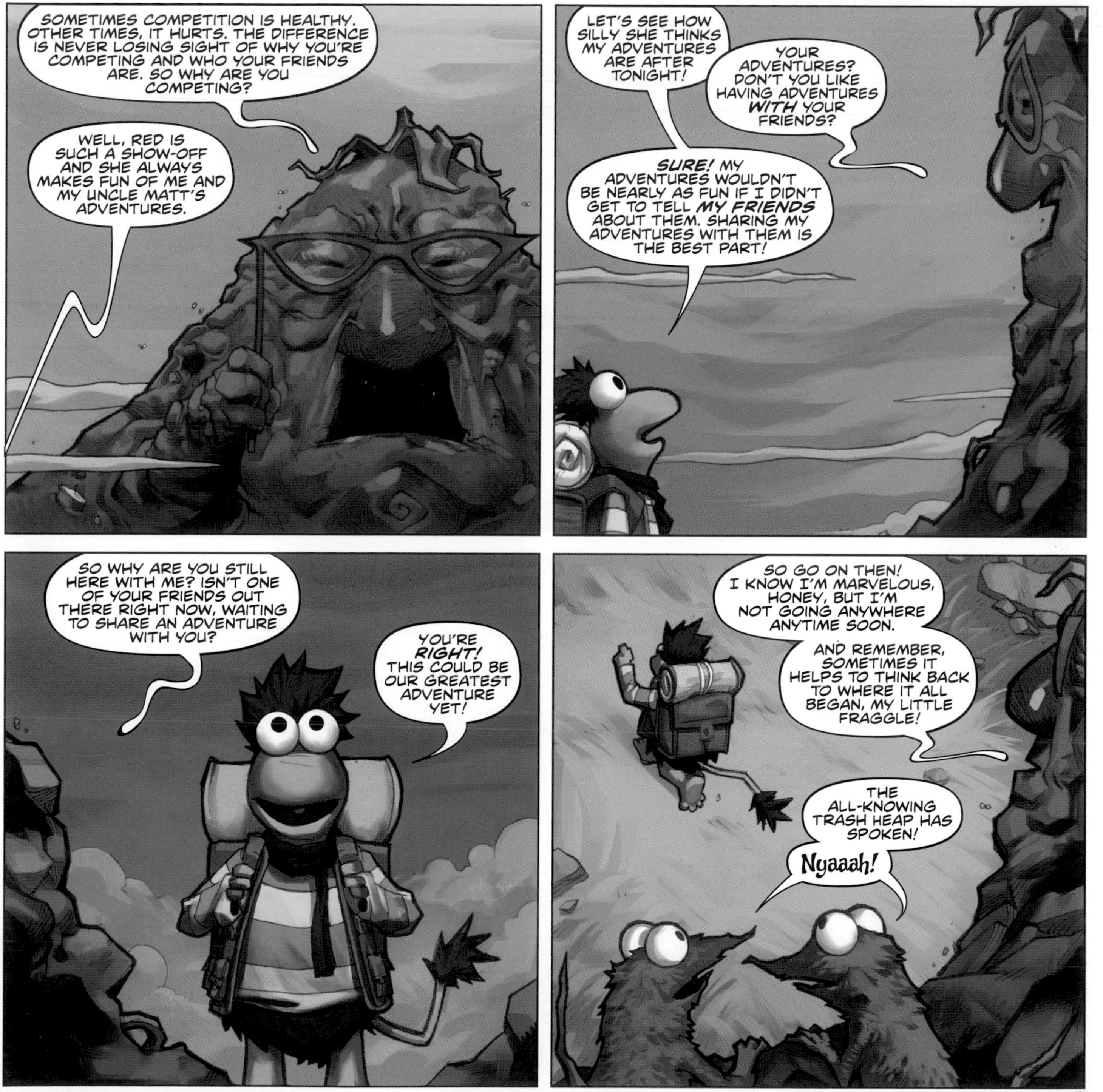
SOMETIMES COMPETITION IS HEALTHY. OTHER TIMES, IT HURTS. THE DIFFERENCE IS NEVER LOSING SIGHT OF WHY YOU'RE COMPETING AND WHO YOUR FRIENDS ARE. SO WHY ARE YOU COMPETING?
WELL, RED IS SUCH A SHOW-OFF AND SHE ALWAYS MAKES FUN OF ME AND MY UNCLE MATT'S ADVENTURES.
LET'S SEE HOW SILLY SHE THINKS MY ADVENTURES ARE AFTER TONIGHT!
YOUR ADVENTURES? DON'T YOU LIKE HAVING ADVENTURES WITH YOUR FRIENDS?
SURE! MY ADVENTURES WOULDN'T BE NEARLY AS FUN IF I DIDN'T GET TO TELL MY FRIENDS ABOUT THEM. SHARING MY ADVENTURES WITH THEM IS THE BEST PART!
SO WHY ARE YOU STILL HERE WITH ME? ISN'T ONE OF YOUR FRIENDS OUT THERE RIGHT NOW, WAITING TO SHARE AN ADVENTURE WITH YOU?
YOU'RE RIGHT! THIS COULD BE OUR GREATEST ADVENTURE YET!
SO GO ON THEN! I KNOW I'M MARVELOUS, HONEY, BUT I'M NOT GOING ANYWHERE ANYTIME SOON.
AND REMEMBER, SOMETIMES IT HELPS TO THINK BACK TO WHERE IT ALL BEGAN, MY LITTLE FRAGGLE!
THE ALL-KNOWING TRASH HEAP HAS SPOKEN!
Nyaaah!

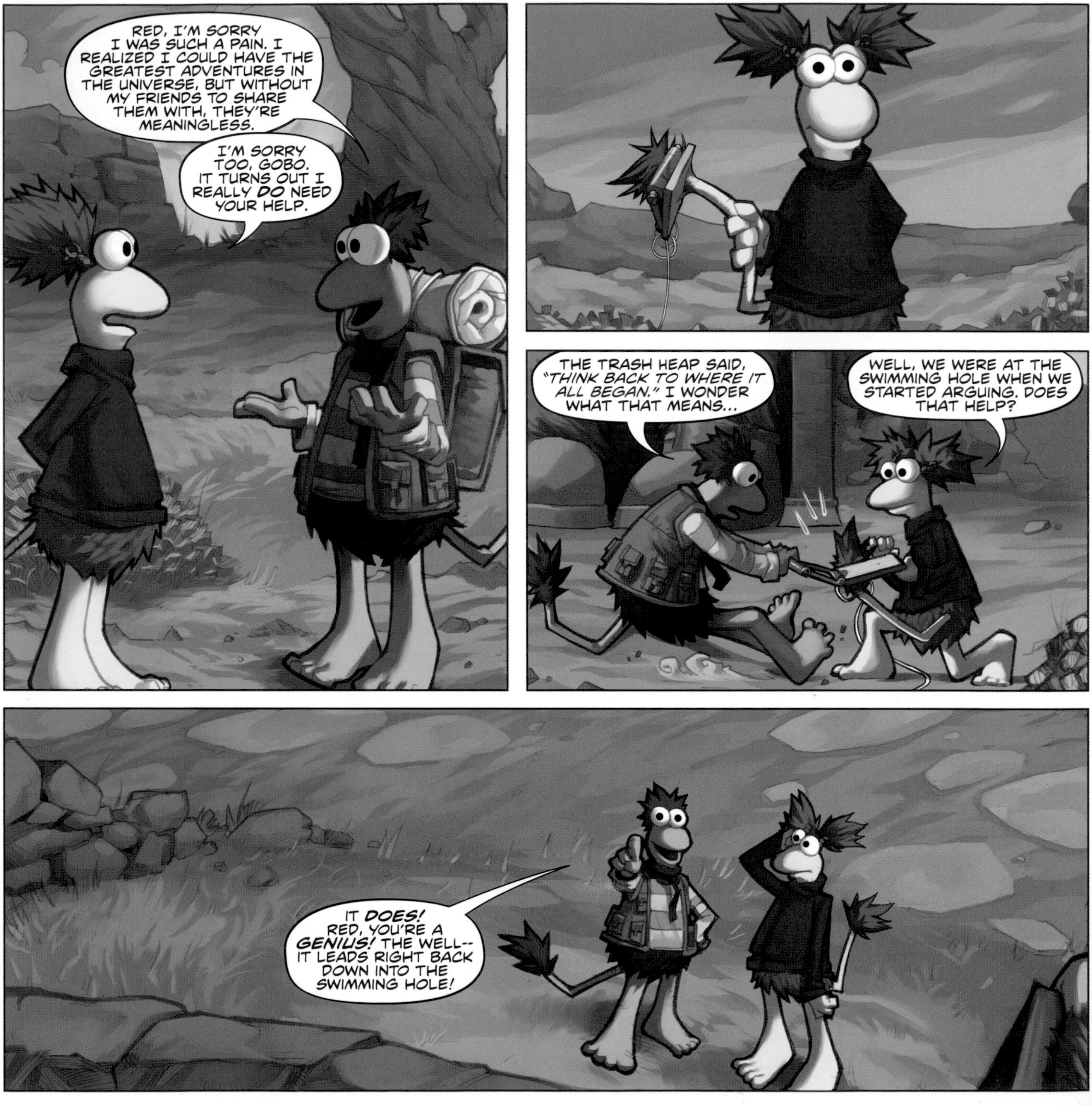
RED, I'M SORRY I WAS SUCH A PAIN. I REALIZED I COULD HAVE THE GREATEST ADVENTURES IN THE UNIVERSE, BUT WITHOUT MY FRIENDS TO SHARE THEM WITH, THEY'RE MEANINGLESS.
I'M SORRY TOO, GOBO. IT TURNS OUT I REALLY **DO** NEED YOUR HELP.
THE TRASH HEAP SAID, *"THINK BACK TO WHERE IT ALL BEGAN."* I WONDER WHAT THAT MEANS...
WELL, WE WERE AT THE SWIMMING HOLE WHEN WE STARTED ARGUING. DOES THAT HELP?
IT ***DOES!*** RED, YOU'RE A ***GENIUS!*** THE WELL-- IT LEADS RIGHT BACK DOWN INTO THE SWIMMING HOLE!

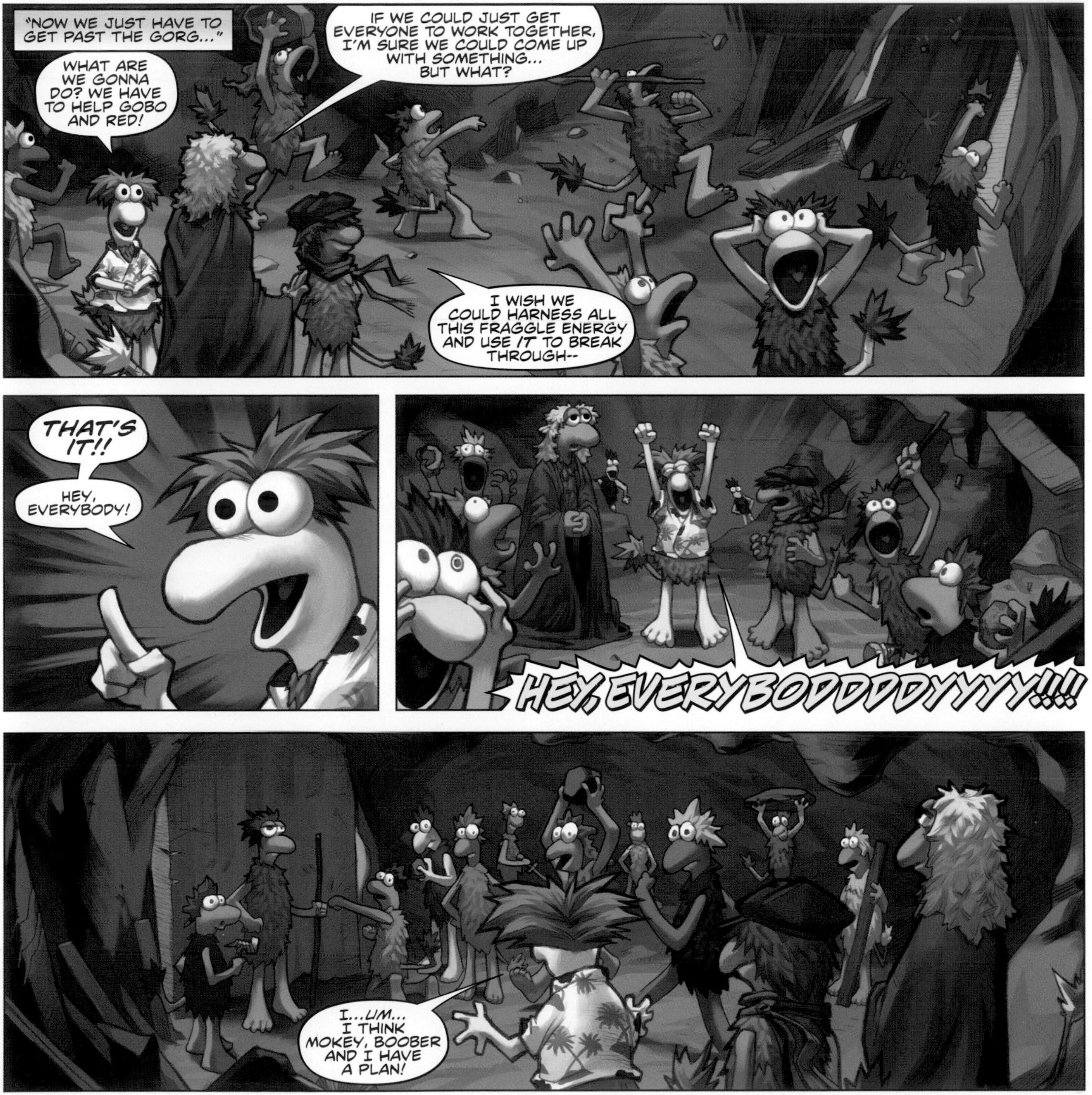
"NOW WE JUST HAVE TO GET PAST THE GORG..."
WHAT ARE WE GONNA DO? WE HAVE TO HELP GOBO AND RED!
IF WE COULD JUST GET EVERYONE TO WORK TOGETHER, I'M SURE WE COULD COME UP WITH SOMETHING... BUT WHAT?
I WISH WE COULD HARNESS ALL THIS FRAGGLE ENERGY AND USE IT TO BREAK THROUGH--
THAT'S IT!!
HEY, EVERYBODY!
HEY, EVERYBODDDDYYYY!!!!
I...UM... I THINK MOKEY, BOOBER AND I HAVE A PLAN!

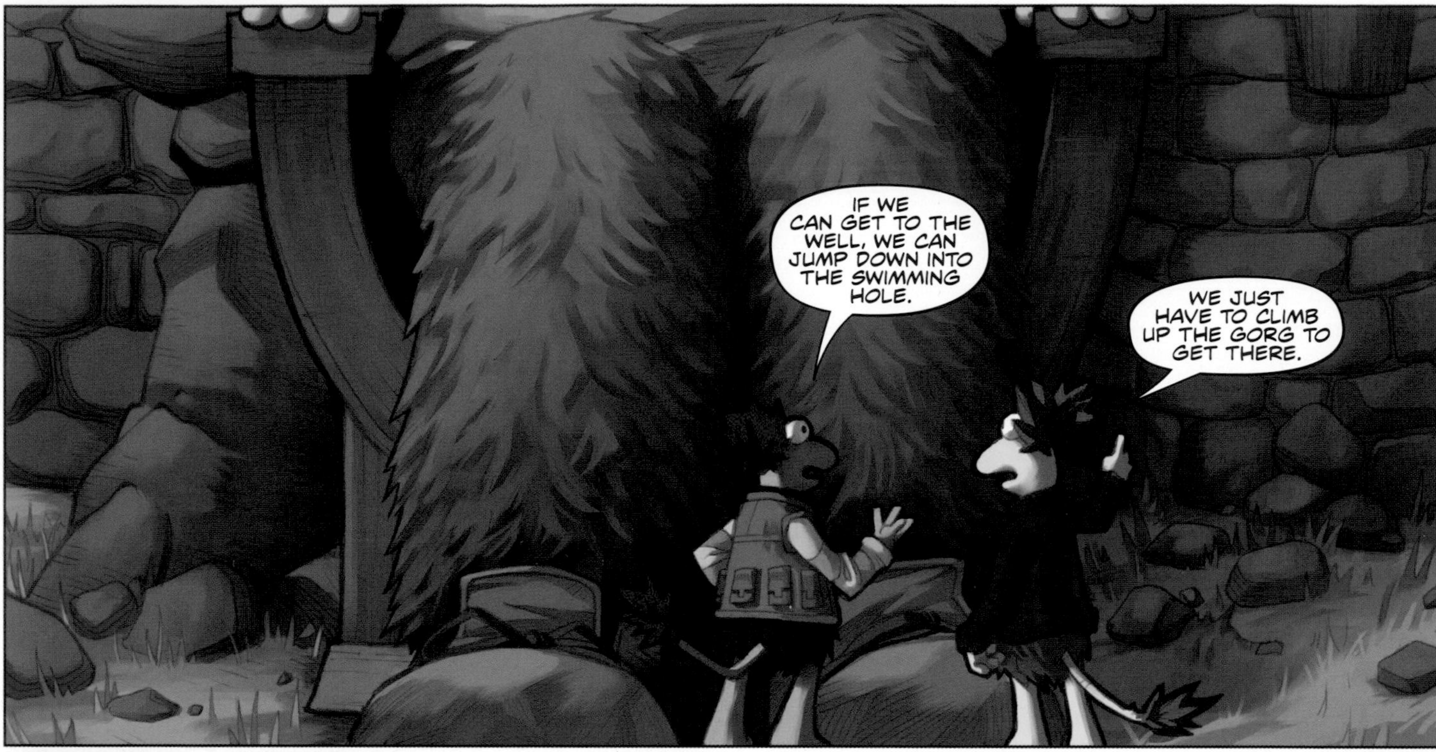
IF WE CAN GET TO THE WELL, WE CAN JUMP DOWN INTO THE SWIMMING HOLE.
WE JUST HAVE TO CLIMB UP THE GORG TO GET THERE.

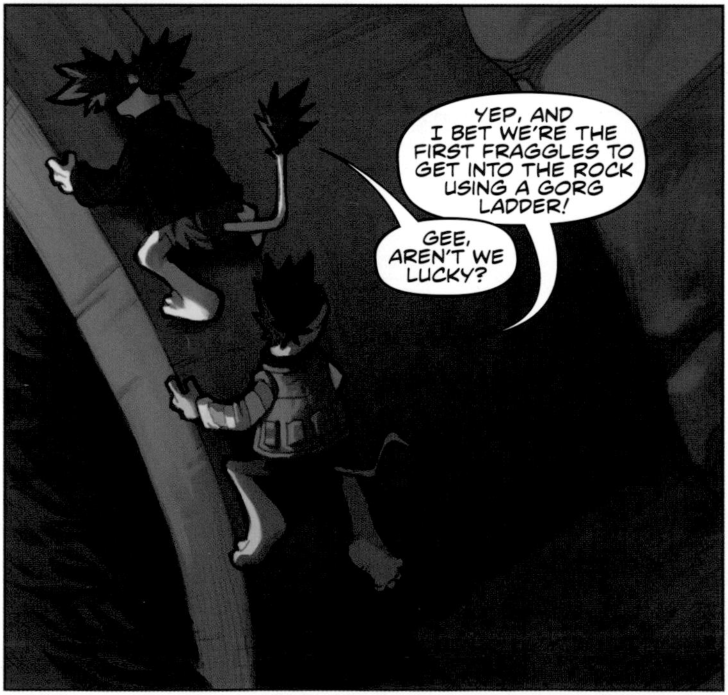
YEP, AND I BET WE'RE THE FIRST FRAGGLES TO GET INTO THE ROCK USING A GORG LADDER!
GEE, AREN'T WE LUCKY?

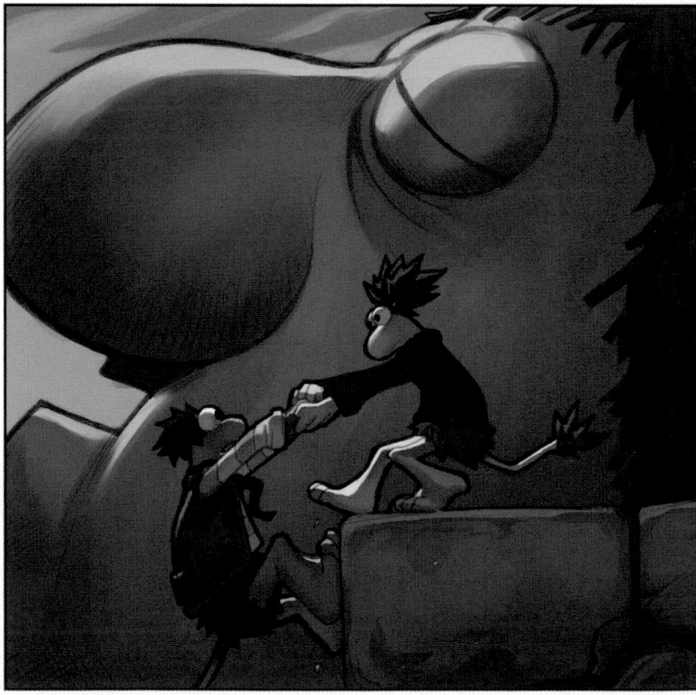

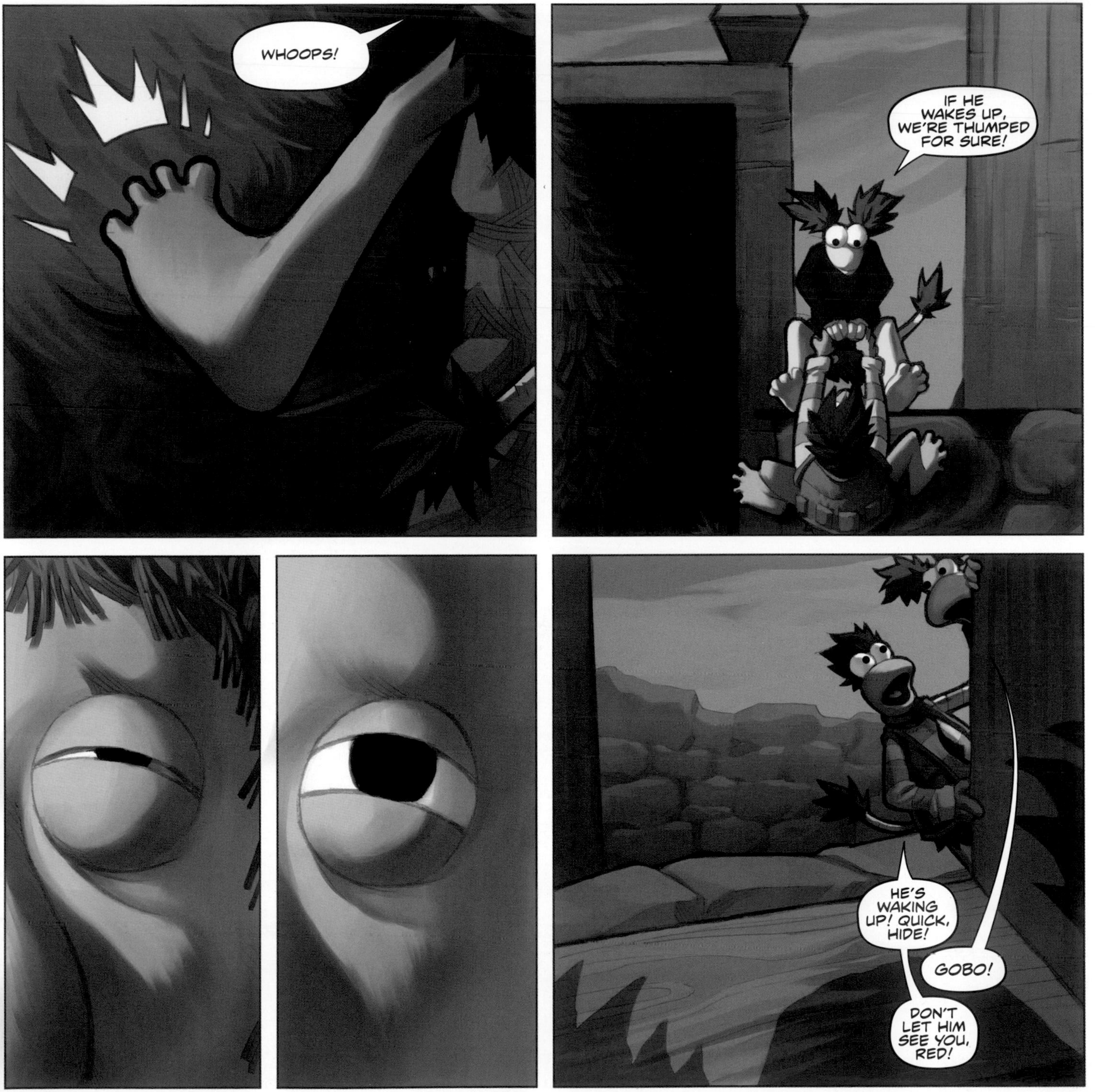
WHOOPS!
IF HE WAKES UP, WE'RE THUMPED FOR SURE!
HE'S WAKING UP! QUICK, HIDE!
GOBO!
DON'T LET HIM SEE YOU, RED!

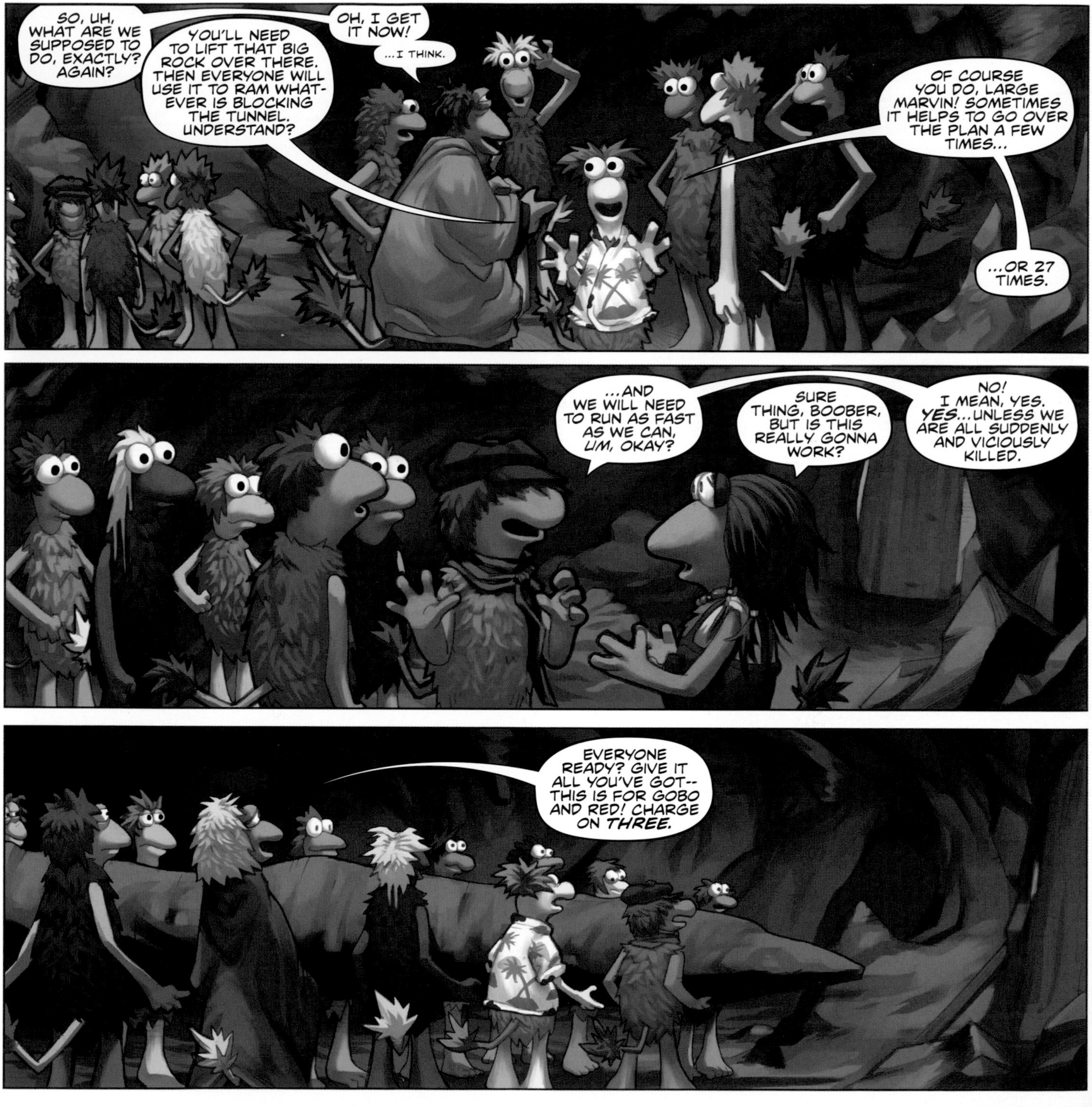
SO, UH, WHAT ARE WE SUPPOSED TO DO, EXACTLY? AGAIN?
YOU'LL NEED TO LIFT THAT BIG ROCK OVER THERE. THEN EVERYONE WILL USE IT TO RAM WHAT-EVER IS BLOCKING THE TUNNEL. UNDERSTAND?
OH, I GET IT NOW!
...I THINK.
OF COURSE YOU DO, LARGE MARVIN! SOMETIMES IT HELPS TO GO OVER THE PLAN A FEW TIMES...
...OR 27 TIMES.
...AND WE WILL NEED TO RUN AS FAST AS WE CAN, UM, OKAY?
SURE THING, BOOBER, BUT IS THIS REALLY GONNA WORK?
NO! I MEAN, YES. YES...UNLESS WE ARE ALL SUDDENLY AND VICIOUSLY KILLED.
EVERYONE READY? GIVE IT ALL YOU'VE GOT-- THIS IS FOR GOBO AND RED! CHARGE ON THREE.

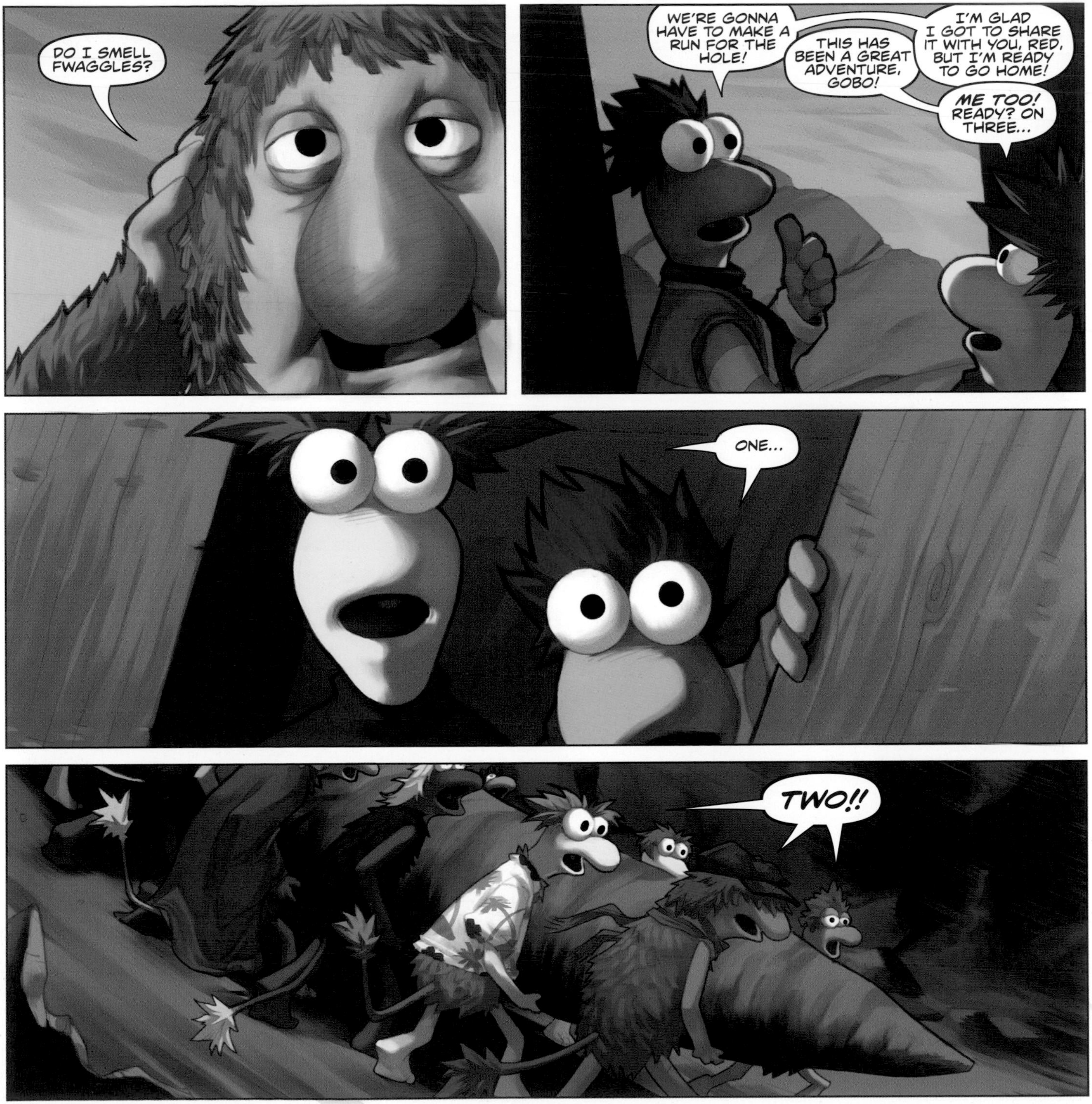
DO I SMELL FWAGGLES?
WE'RE GONNA HAVE TO MAKE A RUN FOR THE HOLE!
THIS HAS BEEN A GREAT ADVENTURE, GOBO!
I'M GLAD I GOT TO SHARE IT WITH YOU, RED, BUT I'M READY TO GO HOME!
ME TOO! READY? ON THREE...
ONE...
TWO!!

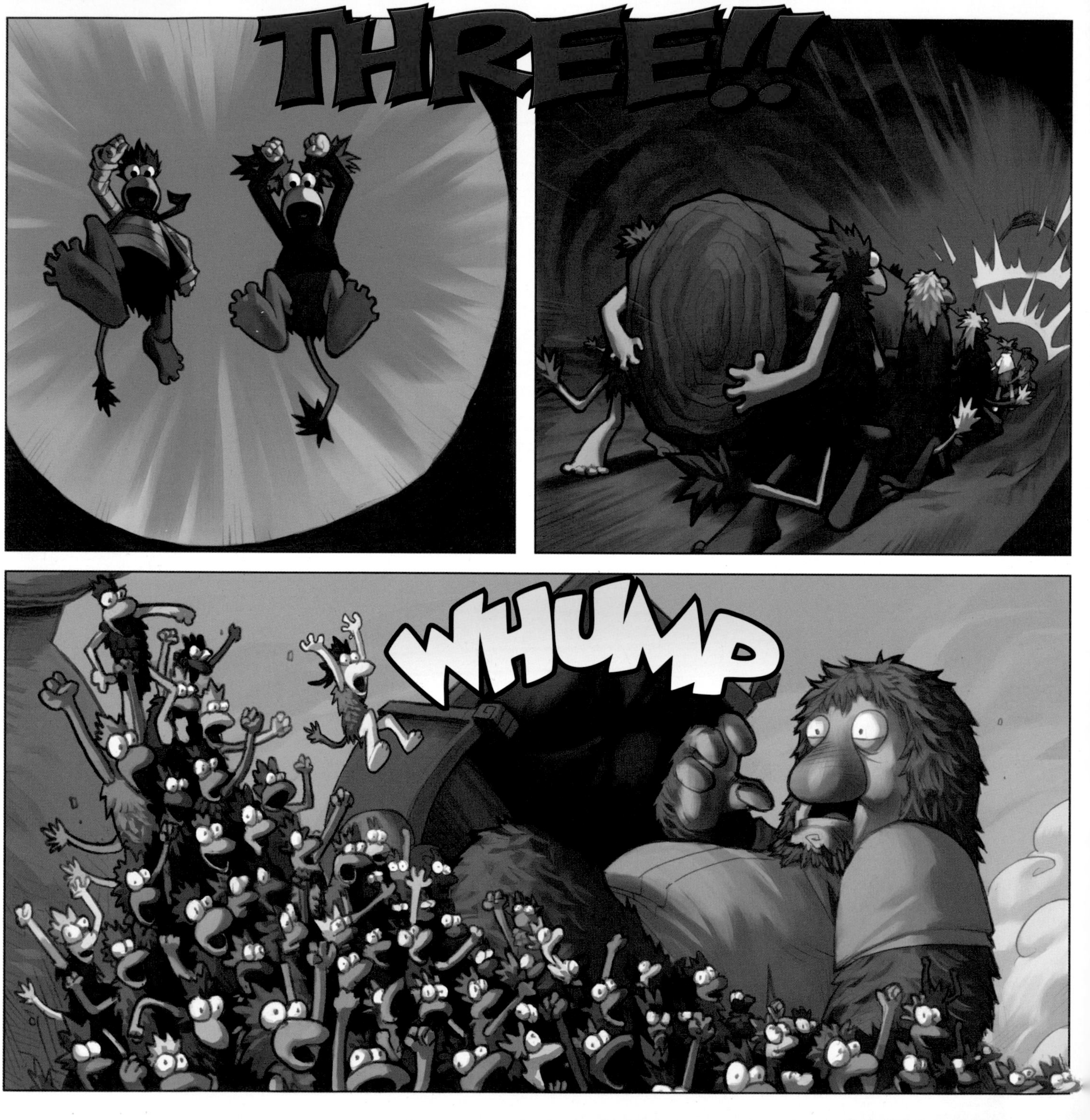
THREE!!
WHUMP

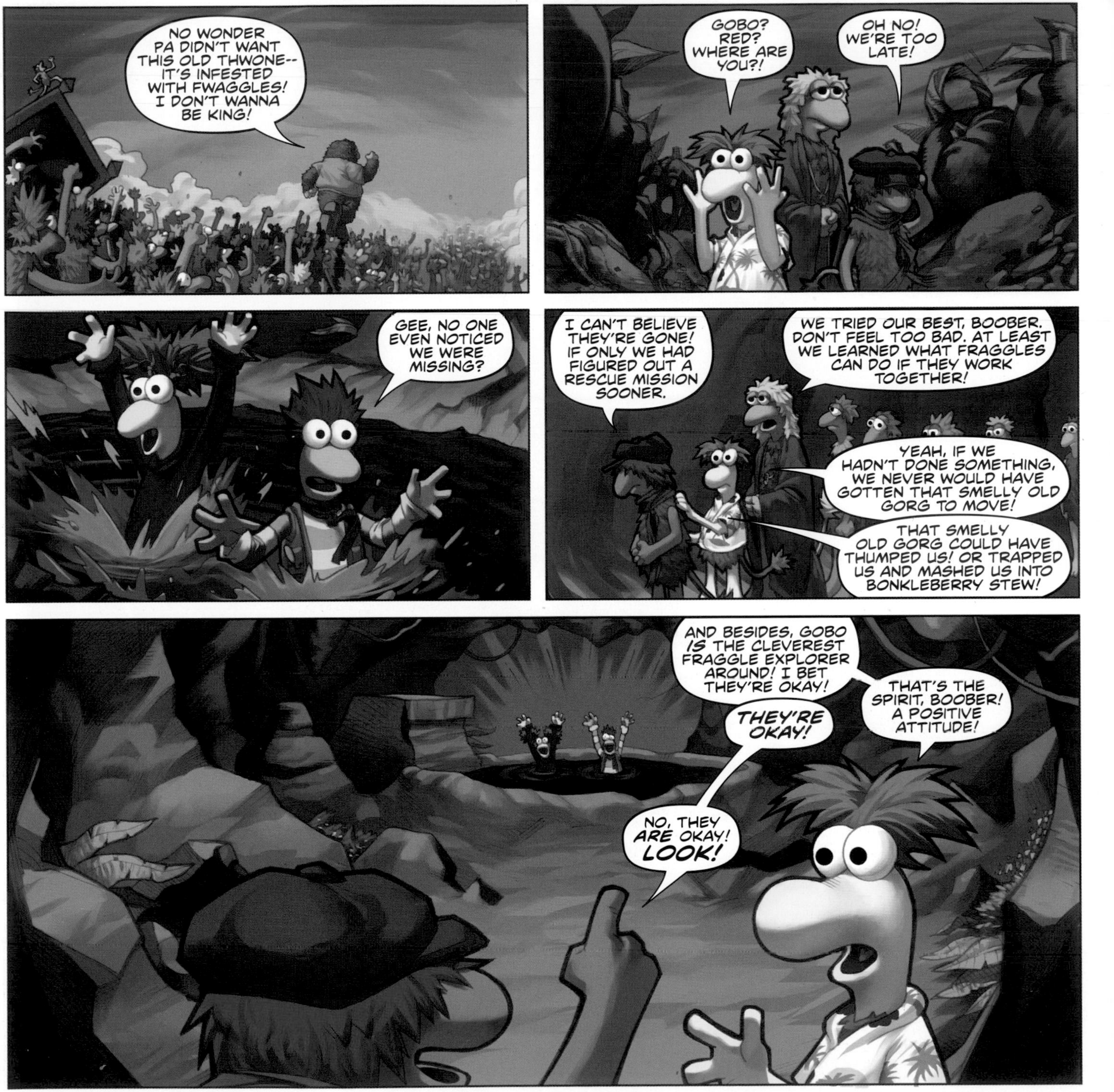
NO WONDER PA DIDN'T WANT THIS OLD THWONE-- IT'S INFESTED WITH FWAGGLES! I DON'T WANNA BE KING!
GOBO? RED? WHERE ARE YOU?!
OH NO! WE'RE TOO LATE!
GEE, NO ONE EVEN NOTICED WE WERE MISSING?
I CAN'T BELIEVE THEY'RE GONE! IF ONLY WE HAD FIGURED OUT A RESCUE MISSION SOONER.
WE TRIED OUR BEST, BOOBER. DON'T FEEL TOO BAD. AT LEAST WE LEARNED WHAT FRAGGLES CAN DO IF THEY WORK TOGETHER!
YEAH, IF WE HADN'T DONE SOMETHING, WE NEVER WOULD HAVE GOTTEN THAT SMELLY OLD GORG TO MOVE!
THAT SMELLY OLD GORG COULD HAVE THUMPED US! OR TRAPPED US AND MASHED US INTO BONKLEBERRY STEW!
AND BESIDES, GOBO IS THE CLEVEREST FRAGGLE EXPLORER AROUND! I BET THEY'RE OKAY!
THAT'S THE SPIRIT, BOOBER! A POSITIVE ATTITUDE!
THEY'RE OKAY!
NO, THEY ARE OKAY! LOOK!

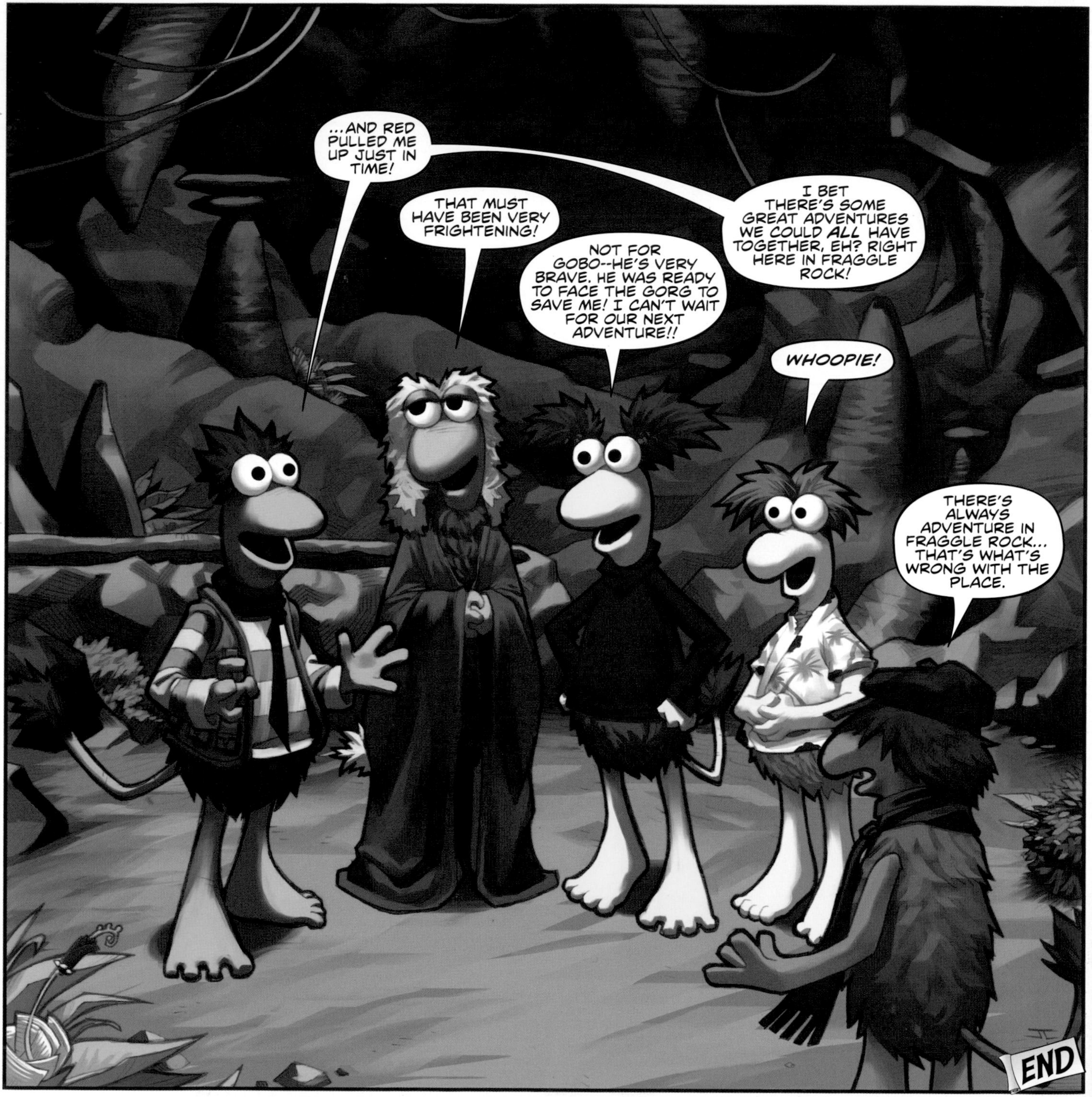
...AND RED PULLED ME UP JUST IN TIME!
THAT MUST HAVE BEEN VERY FRIGHTENING!
NOT FOR GOBO--HE'S VERY BRAVE. HE WAS READY TO FACE THE GORG TO SAVE ME! I CAN'T WAIT FOR OUR NEXT ADVENTURE!!
I BET THERE'S SOME GREAT ADVENTURES WE COULD ALL HAVE TOGETHER, EH? RIGHT HERE IN FRAGGLE ROCK!
WHOOPIE!
THERE'S ALWAYS ADVENTURE IN FRAGGLE ROCK... THAT'S WHAT'S WRONG WITH THE PLACE.
END

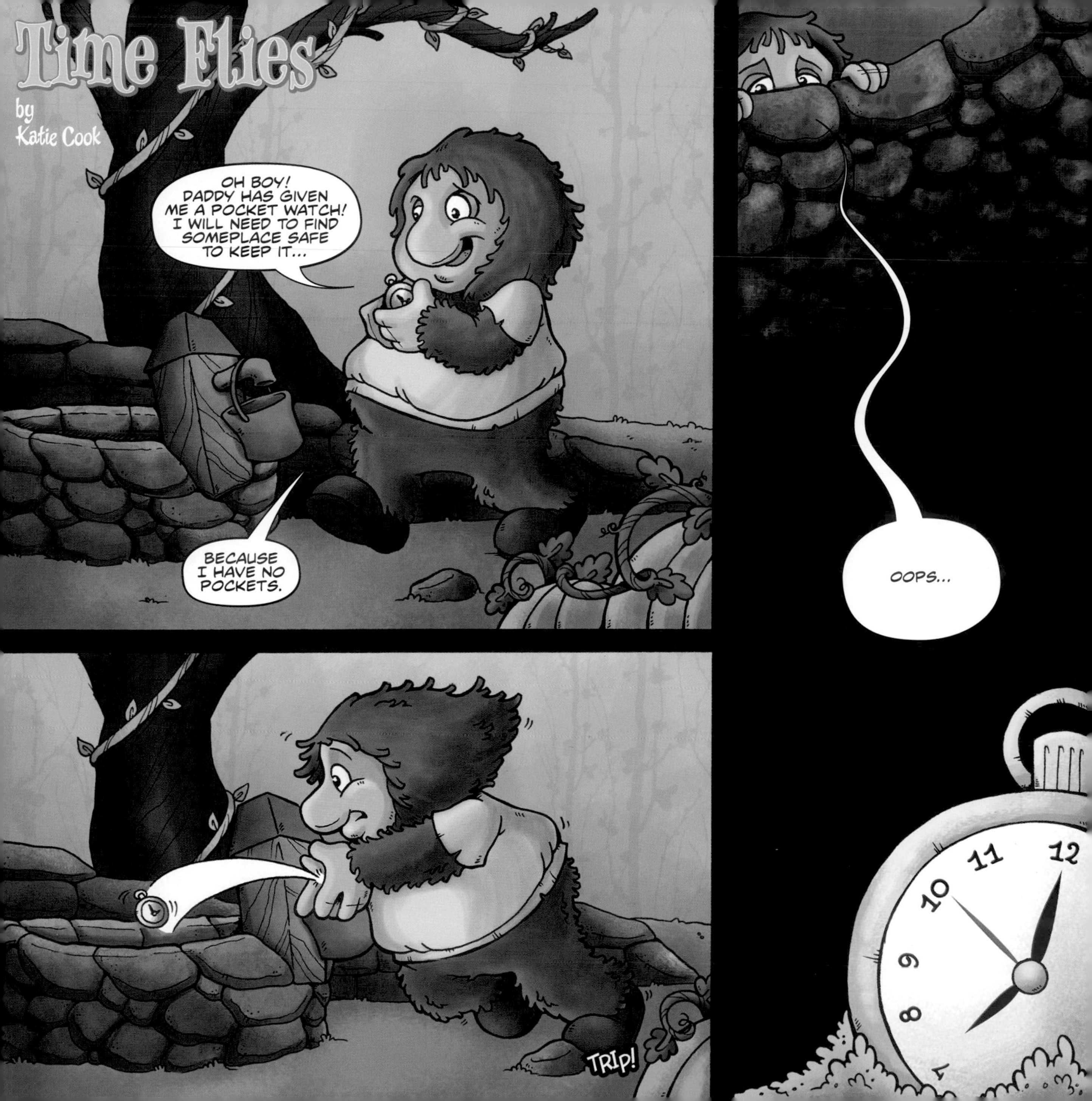
Time Flies
by Katie Cook
OH BOY! DADDY HAS GIVEN ME A POCKET WATCH! I WILL NEED TO FIND SOMEPLACE SAFE TO KEEP IT...
BECAUSE I HAVE NO POCKETS.
TRIP!
OOPS...
11 12
10
9
8
7

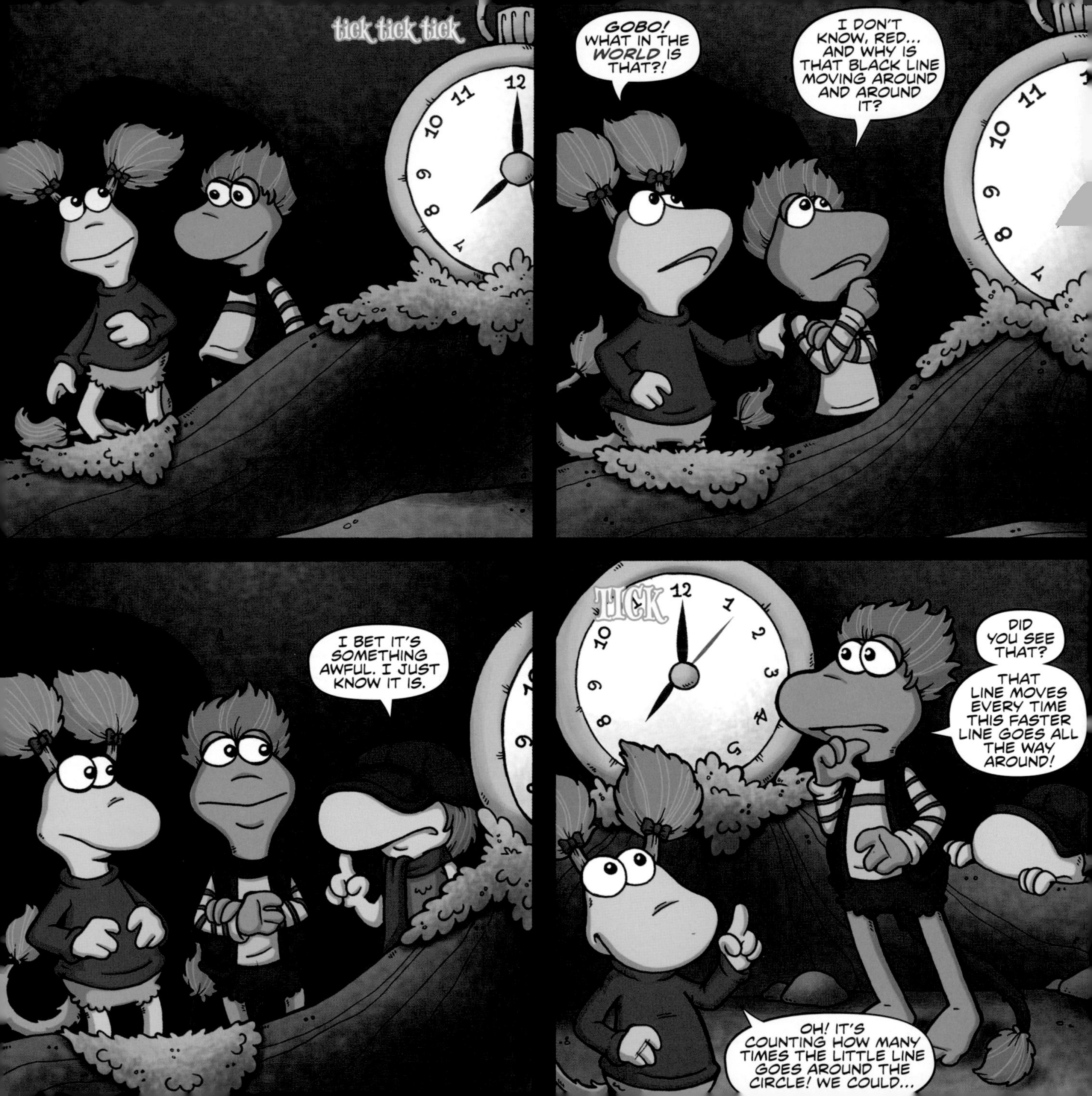

tick tick tick
GOBO! WHAT IN THE WORLD IS THAT?!
I DON'T KNOW, RED... AND WHY IS THAT BLACK LINE MOVING AROUND AND AROUND IT?
I BET IT'S SOMETHING AWFUL. I JUST KNOW IT IS.
TICK
DID YOU SEE THAT?
THAT LINE MOVES EVERY TIME THIS FASTER LINE GOES ALL THE WAY AROUND!
OH! IT'S COUNTING HOW MANY TIMES THE LITTLE LINE GOES AROUND THE CIRCLE! WE COULD...

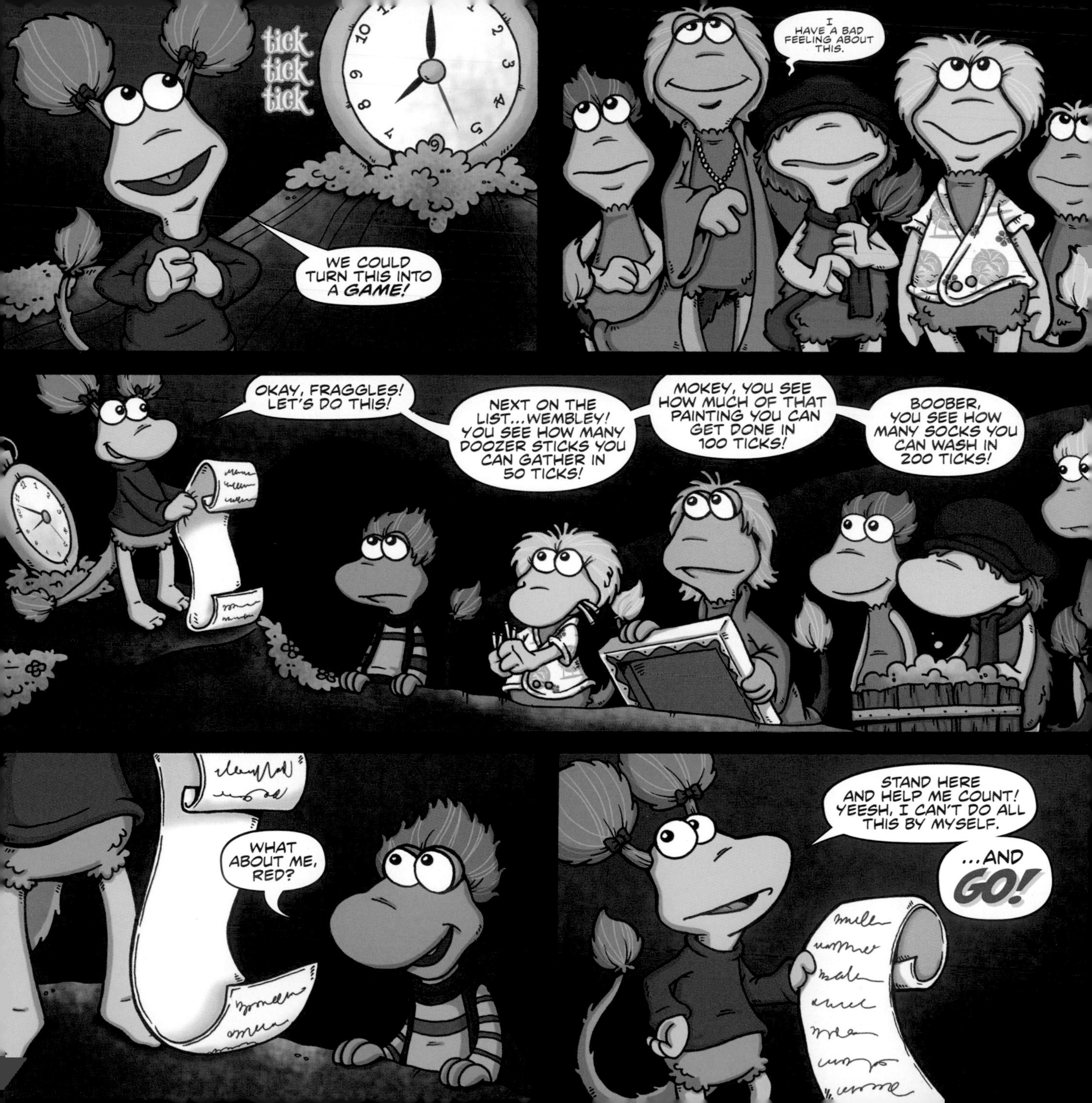
tick tick tick
WE COULD TURN THIS INTO A GAME!
I HAVE A BAD FEELING ABOUT THIS.
OKAY, FRAGGLES! LET'S DO THIS!
NEXT ON THE LIST...WEMBLEY! YOU SEE HOW MANY DOOZER STICKS YOU CAN GATHER IN 50 TICKS!
MOKEY, YOU SEE HOW MUCH OF THAT PAINTING YOU CAN GET DONE IN 100 TICKS!
BOOBER, YOU SEE HOW MANY SOCKS YOU CAN WASH IN 200 TICKS!
WHAT ABOUT ME, RED?
STAND HERE AND HELP ME COUNT! YEESH, I CAN'T DO ALL THIS BY MYSELF.
...AND GO!

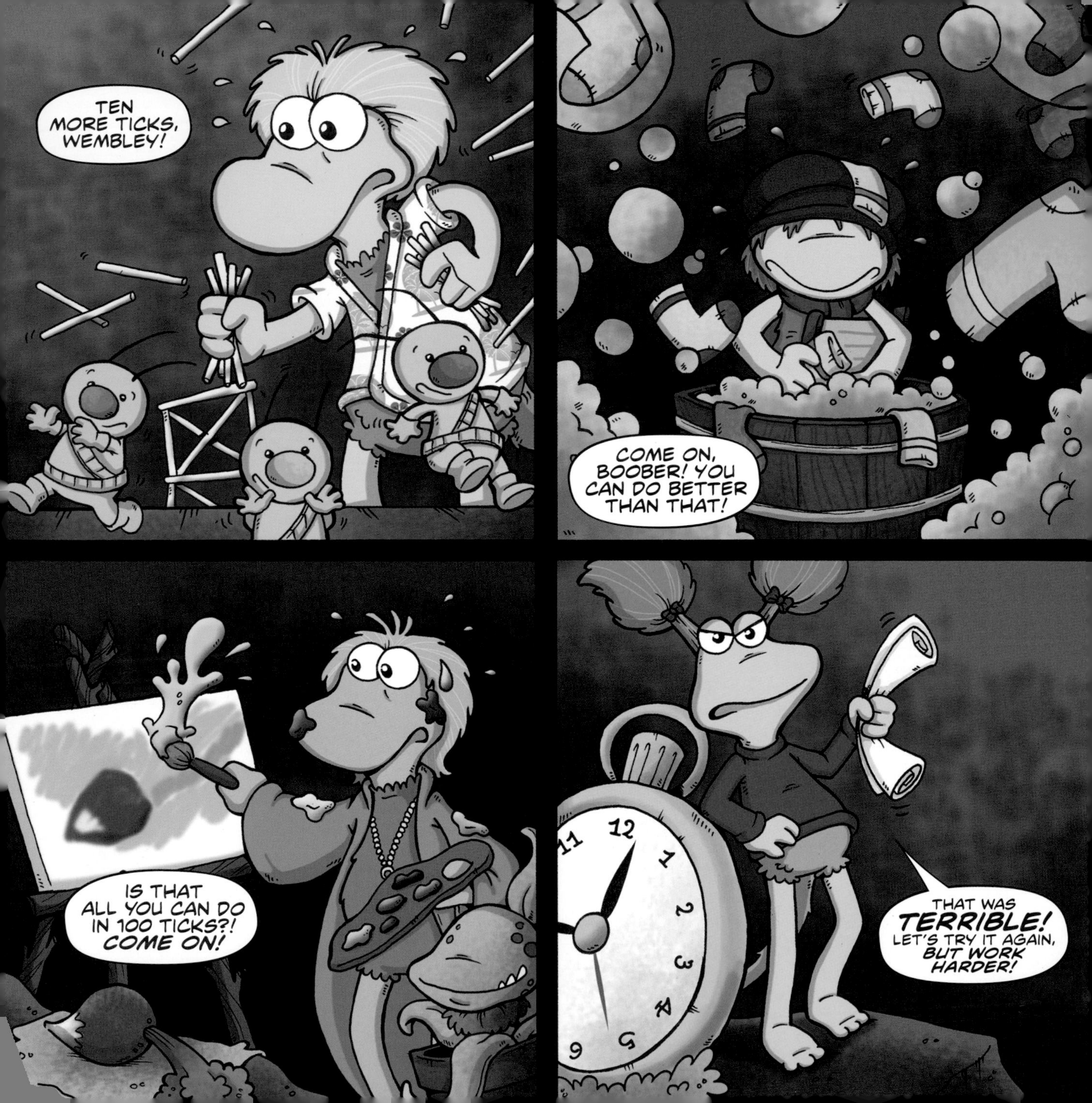
TEN MORE TICKS, WEMBLEY!
COME ON, BOOBER! YOU CAN DO BETTER THAN THAT!
IS THAT ALL YOU CAN DO IN 100 TICKS?! COME ON!
THAT WAS TERRIBLE! LET'S TRY IT AGAIN, BUT WORK HARDER!

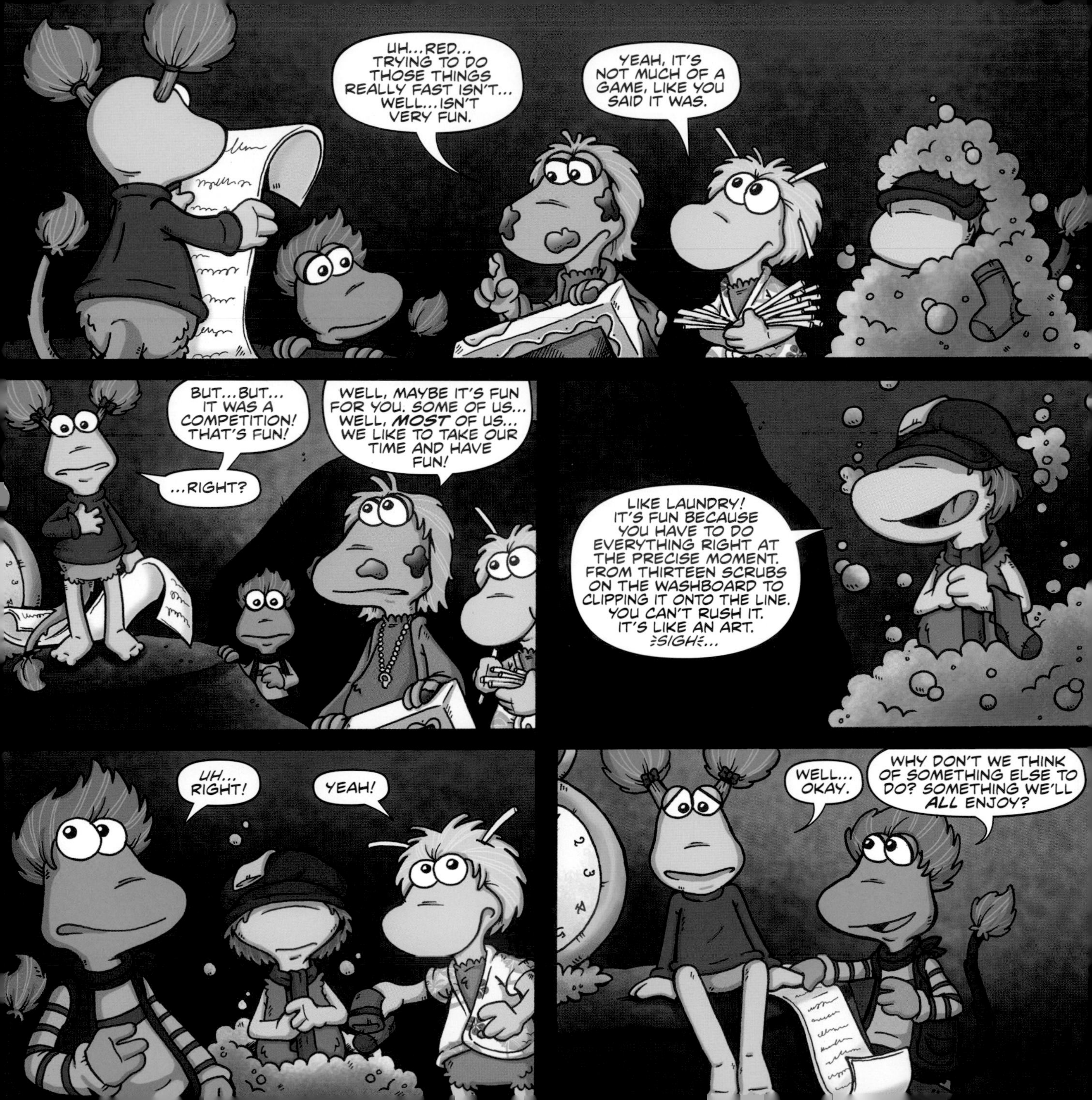

UH...RED... TRYING TO DO THOSE THINGS REALLY FAST ISN'T... WELL...ISN'T VERY FUN.
YEAH, IT'S NOT MUCH OF A GAME, LIKE YOU SAID IT WAS.
BUT...BUT... IT WAS A COMPETITION! THAT'S FUN!
...RIGHT?
WELL, MAYBE IT'S FUN FOR YOU. SOME OF US... WELL, *MOST* OF US... WE LIKE TO TAKE OUR TIME AND HAVE FUN!
LIKE LAUNDRY! IT'S FUN BECAUSE YOU HAVE TO DO EVERYTHING RIGHT AT THE PRECISE MOMENT. FROM THIRTEEN SCRUBS ON THE WASHBOARD TO CLIPPING IT ONTO THE LINE. YOU CAN'T RUSH IT. IT'S LIKE AN ART. *SIGH*...
UH... RIGHT!
YEAH!
WELL... OKAY.
WHY DON'T WE THINK OF SOMETHING ELSE TO DO? SOMETHING WE'LL *ALL* ENJOY?

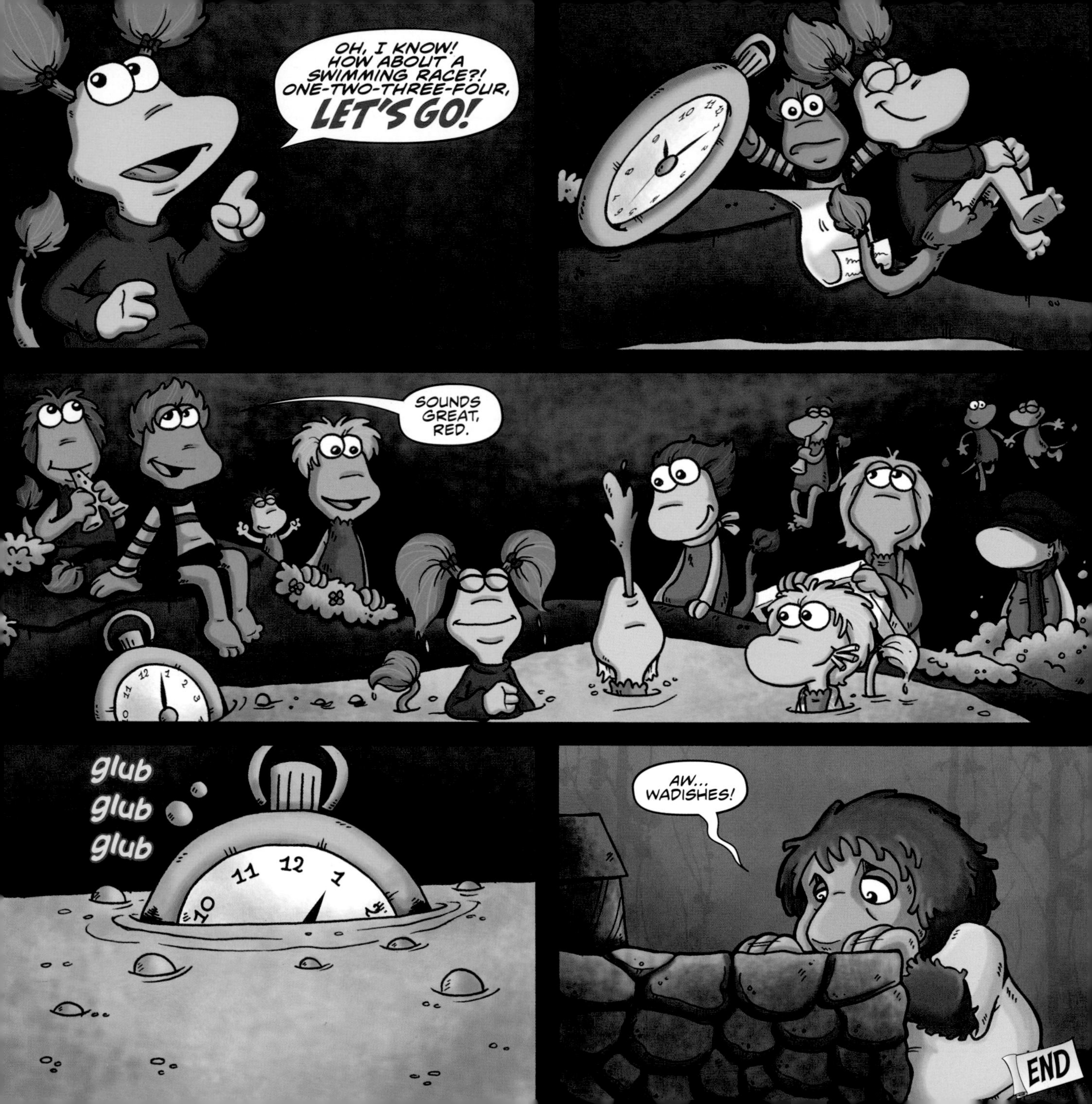
OH, I KNOW! HOW ABOUT A SWIMMING RACE?! ONE-TWO-THREE-FOUR, LET'S GO!
SOUNDS GREAT, RED.
glub
glub
glub
AW... WADISHES!
END

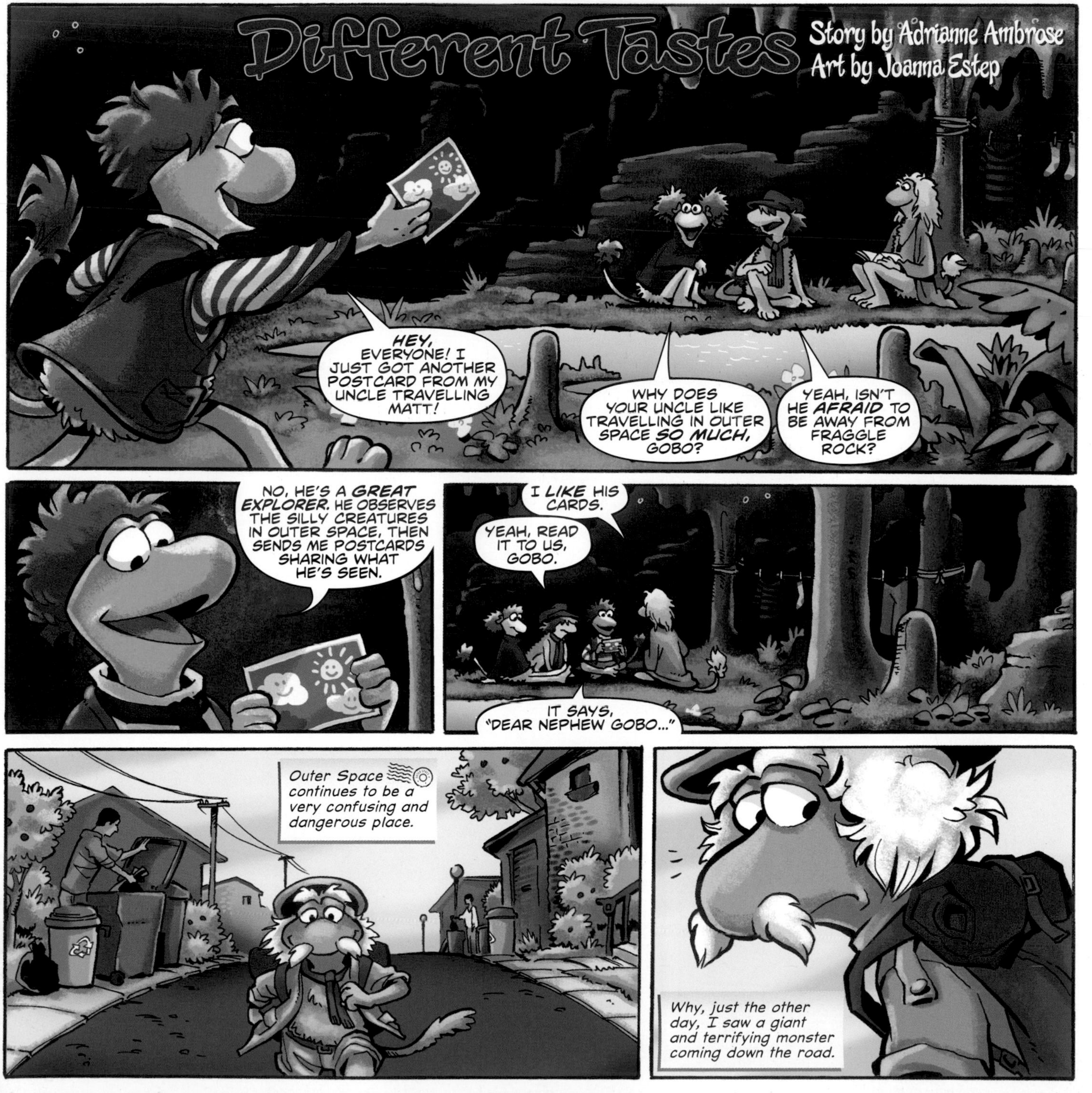

Different Tastes
Story by Adrianne Ambrose
Art by Joanna Estep
HEY, EVERYONE! I JUST GOT ANOTHER POSTCARD FROM MY UNCLE TRAVELLING MATT!
WHY DOES YOUR UNCLE LIKE TRAVELLING IN OUTER SPACE SO MUCH, GOBO?
YEAH, ISN'T HE AFRAID TO BE AWAY FROM FRAGGLE ROCK?
NO, HE'S A GREAT EXPLORER. HE OBSERVES THE SILLY CREATURES IN OUTER SPACE, THEN SENDS ME POSTCARDS SHARING WHAT HE'S SEEN.
I LIKE HIS CARDS.
YEAH, READ IT TO US, GOBO.
IT SAYS, "DEAR NEPHEW GOBO..."
Outer Space continues to be a very confusing and dangerous place.
Why, just the other day, I saw a giant and terrifying monster coming down the road.

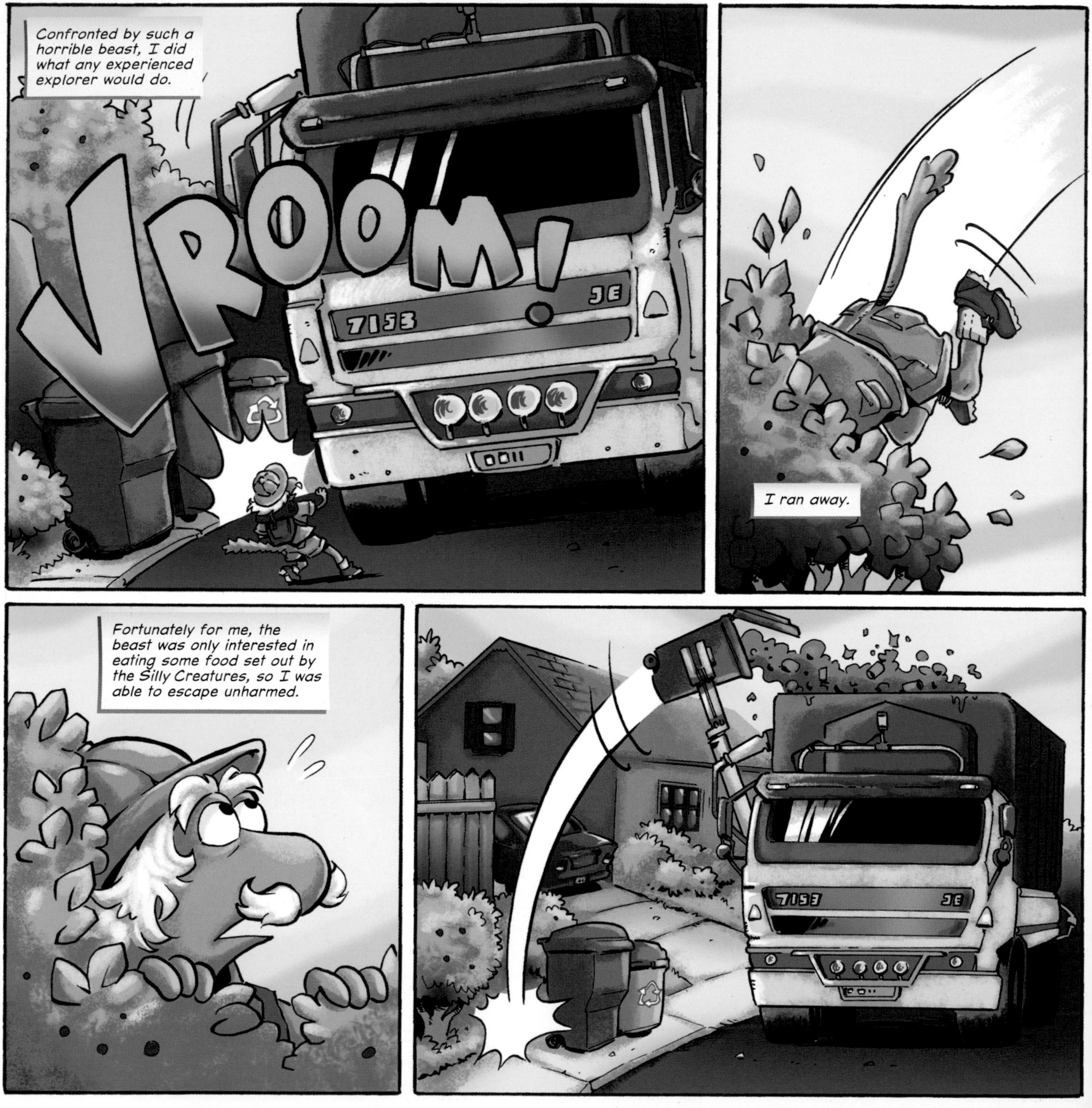
Confronted by such a horrible beast, I did what any experienced explorer would do.
VROOM!
7153
JE
I ran away.
Fortunately for me, the beast was only interested in eating some food set out by the Silly Creatures, so I was able to escape unharmed.
7153
JE

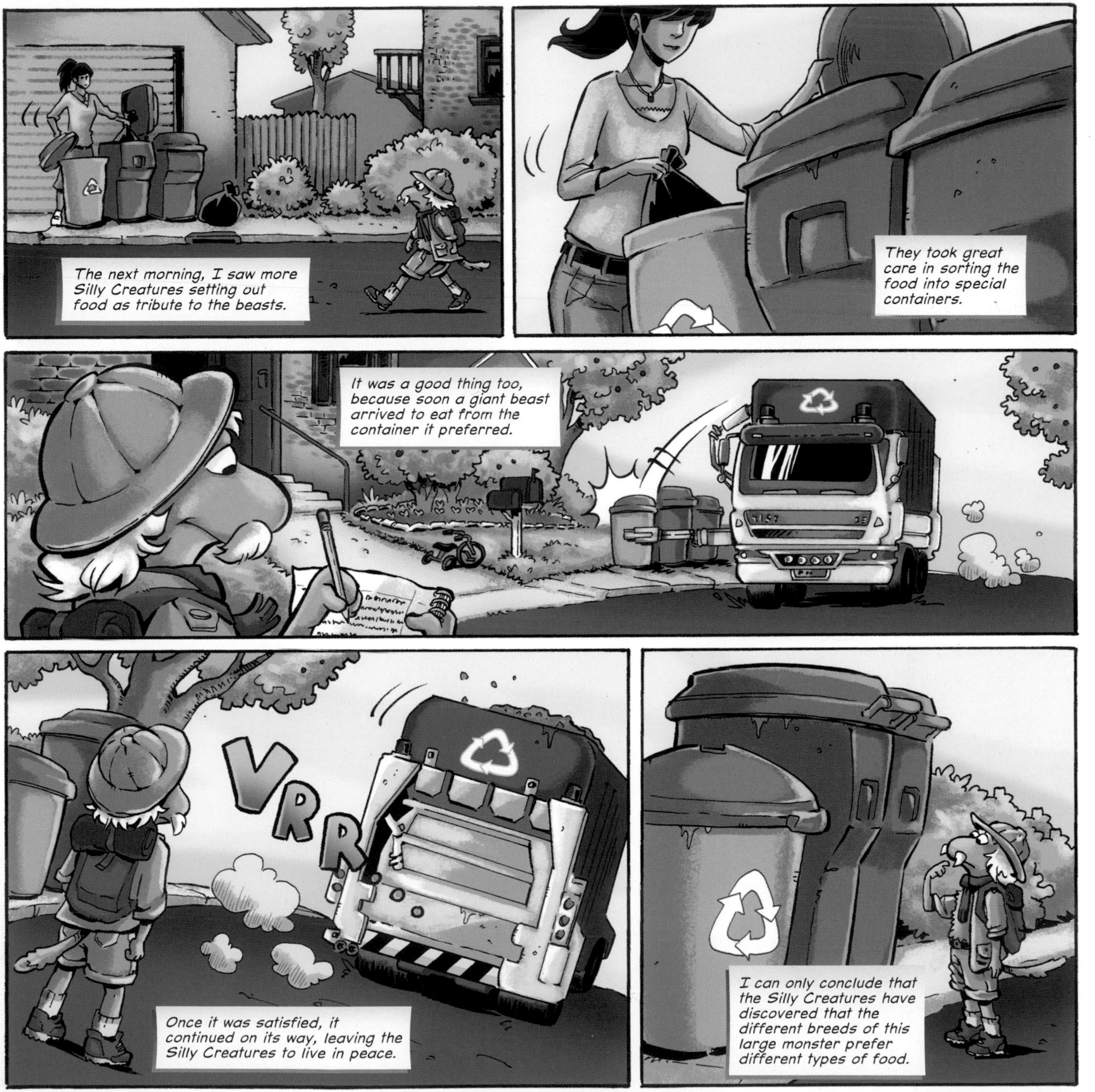
The next morning, I saw more Silly Creatures setting out food as tribute to the beasts.
They took great care in sorting the food into special containers.
It was a good thing too, because soon a giant beast arrived to eat from the container it preferred.
VRR
Once it was satisfied, it continued on its way, leaving the Silly Creatures to live in peace.
I can only conclude that the Silly Creatures have discovered that the different breeds of this large monster prefer different types of food.

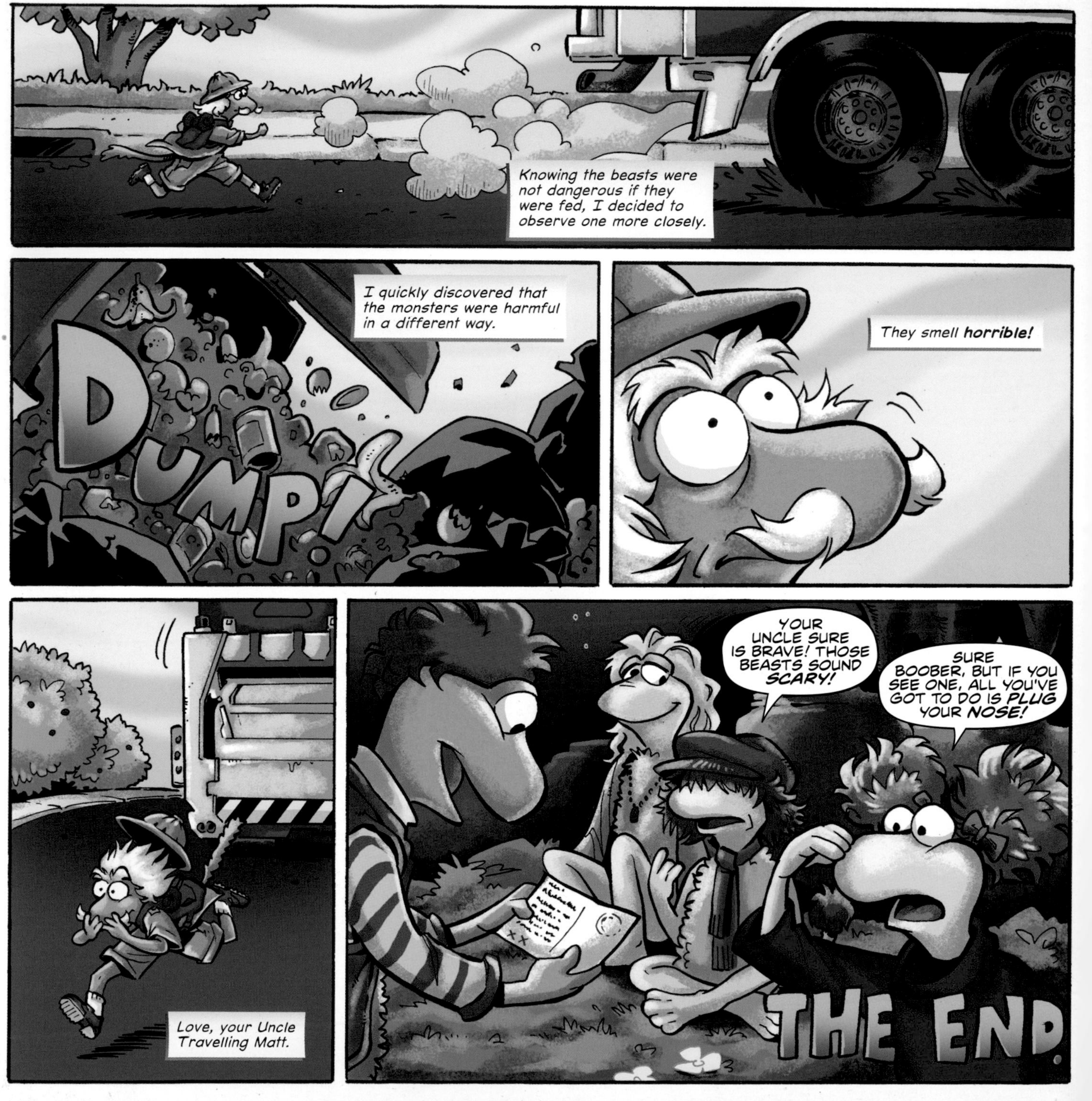
Knowing the beasts were not dangerous if they were fed, I decided to observe one more closely.
I quickly discovered that the monsters were harmful in a different way.
DUMP!
They smell **horrible!**
Love, your Uncle Travelling Matt.
YOUR UNCLE SURE IS BRAVE! THOSE BEASTS SOUND *SCARY!*
SURE BOOBER, BUT IF YOU SEE ONE, ALL YOU'VE GOT TO DO IS *PLUG* YOUR *NOSE!*
THE END.

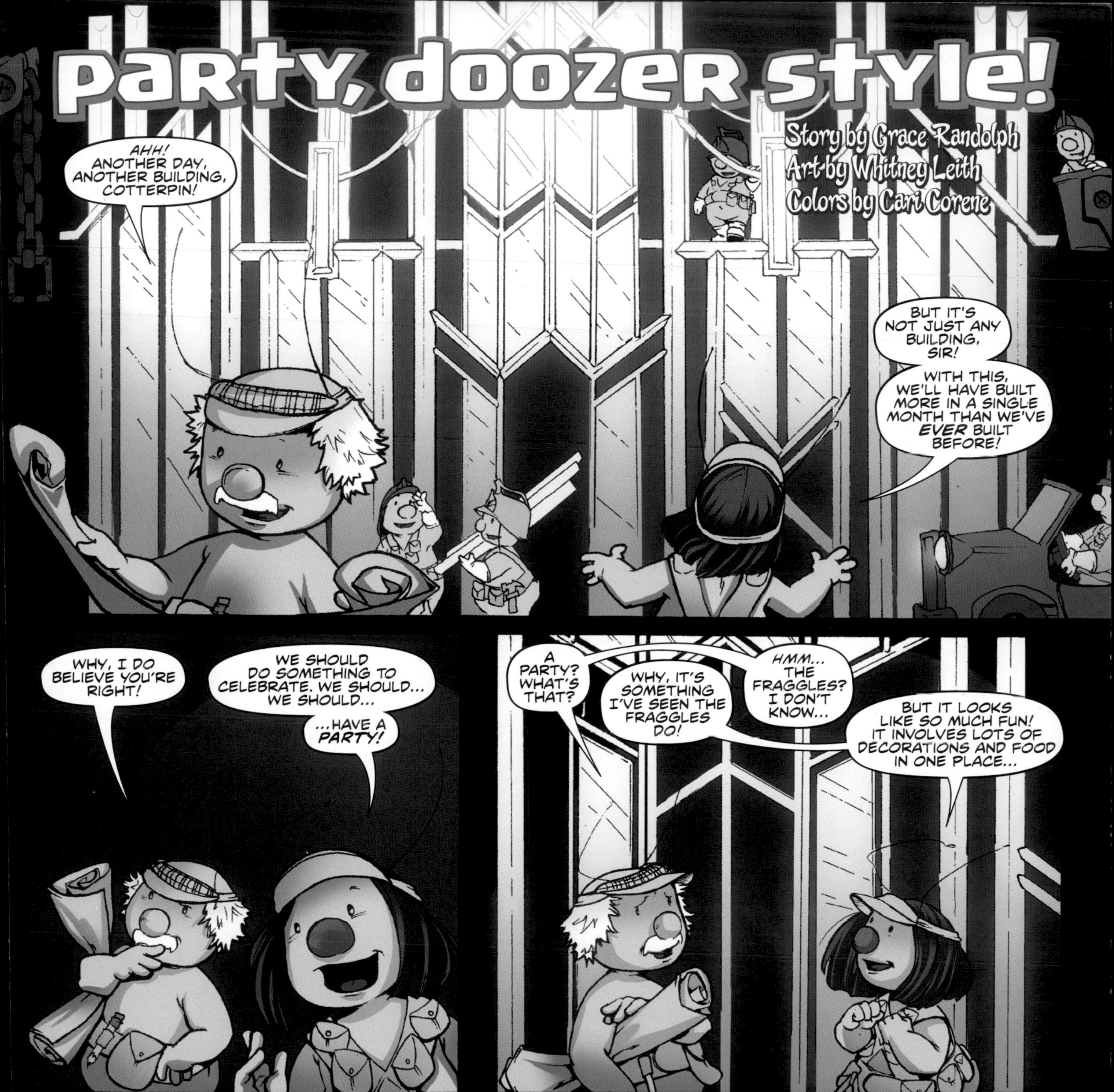
PARTY, DOOZER STYLE!
Story by Grace Randolph
Art by Whitney Leith
Colors by Cari Corene
AHH! ANOTHER DAY, ANOTHER BUILDING, COTTERPIN!
BUT IT'S NOT JUST ANY BUILDING, SIR!
WITH THIS, WE'LL HAVE BUILT MORE IN A SINGLE MONTH THAN WE'VE EVER BUILT BEFORE!
WHY, I DO BELIEVE YOU'RE RIGHT!
WE SHOULD DO SOMETHING TO CELEBRATE. WE SHOULD... WE SHOULD...
...HAVE A PARTY!
A PARTY? WHAT'S THAT?
WHY, IT'S SOMETHING I'VE SEEN THE FRAGGLES DO!
HMM... THE FRAGGLES? I DON'T KNOW...
BUT IT LOOKS LIKE SO MUCH FUN! IT INVOLVES LOTS OF DECORATIONS AND FOOD IN ONE PLACE...

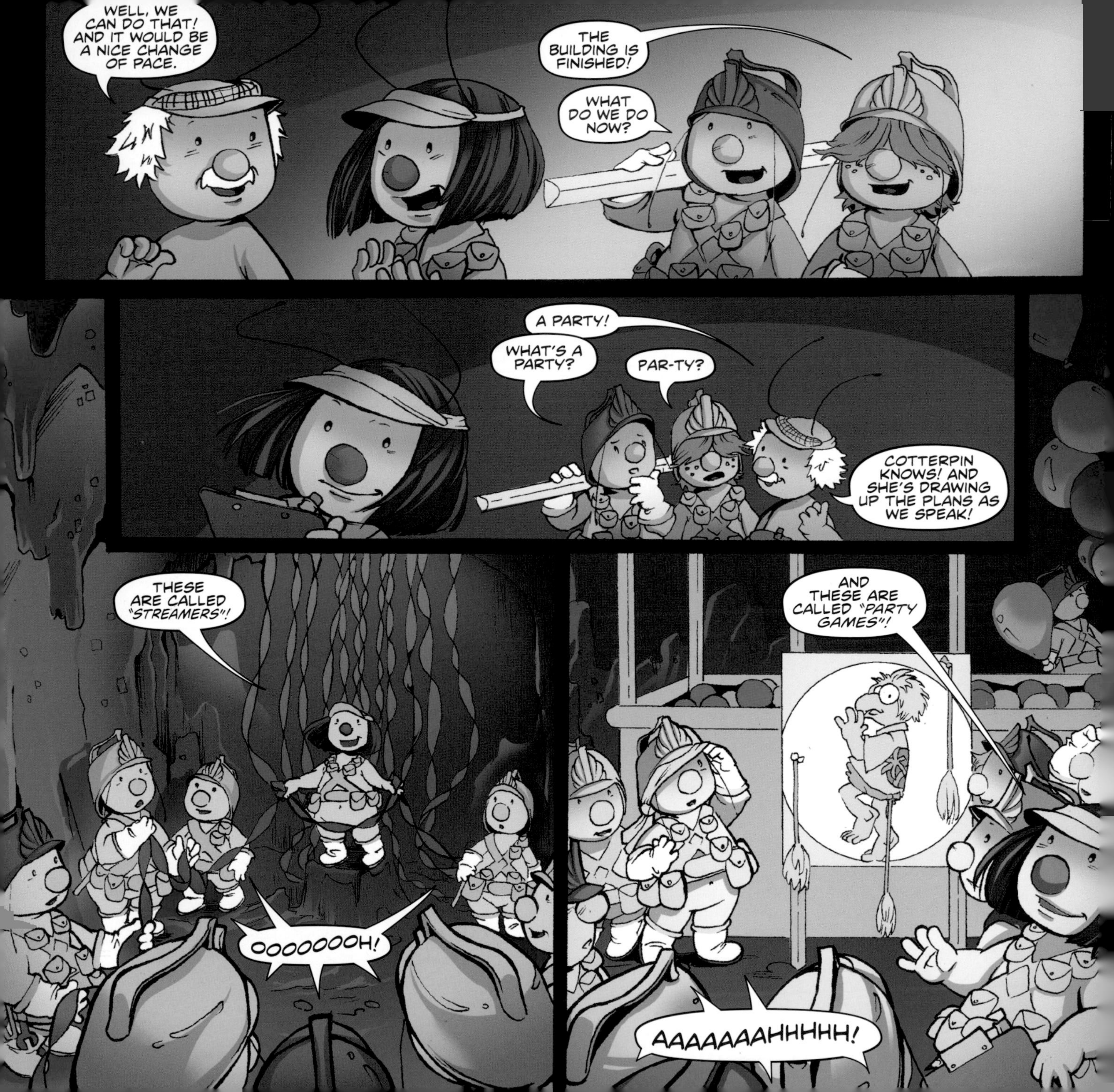
WELL, WE CAN DO THAT! AND IT WOULD BE A NICE CHANGE OF PACE.
THE BUILDING IS FINISHED!
WHAT DO WE DO NOW?
A PARTY!
WHAT'S A PARTY?
PAR-TY?
COTTERPIN KNOWS! AND SHE'S DRAWING UP THE PLANS AS WE SPEAK!
THESE ARE CALLED "STREAMERS"!
OOOOOOOH!
AND THESE ARE CALLED "PARTY GAMES"!
AAAAAAAHHHHH!

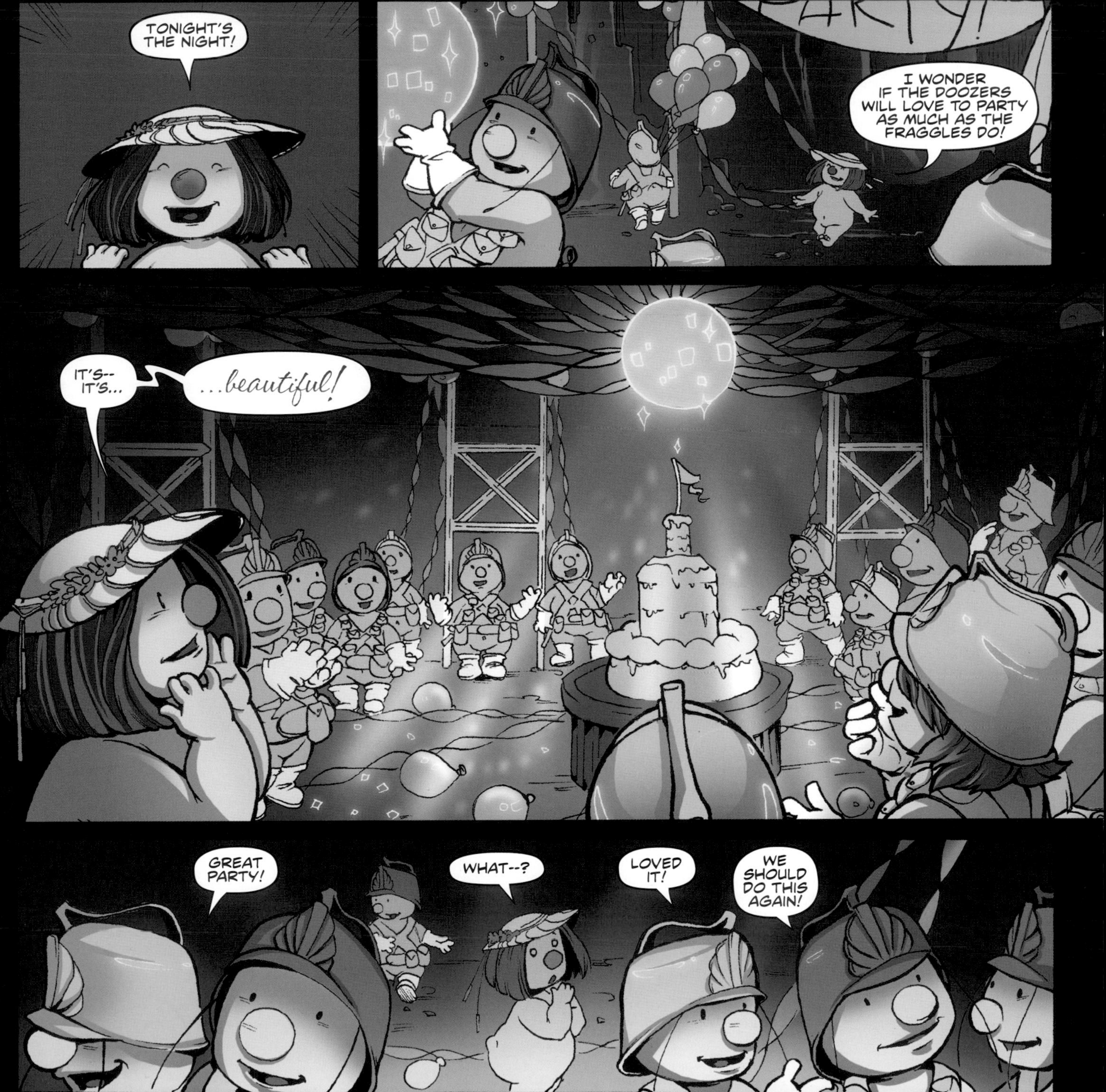
TONIGHT'S THE NIGHT!
I WONDER IF THE DOOZERS WILL LOVE TO PARTY AS MUCH AS THE FRAGGLES DO!
IT'S-- IT'S...
...beautiful!
GREAT PARTY!
WHAT--?
LOVED IT!
WE SHOULD DO THIS AGAIN!

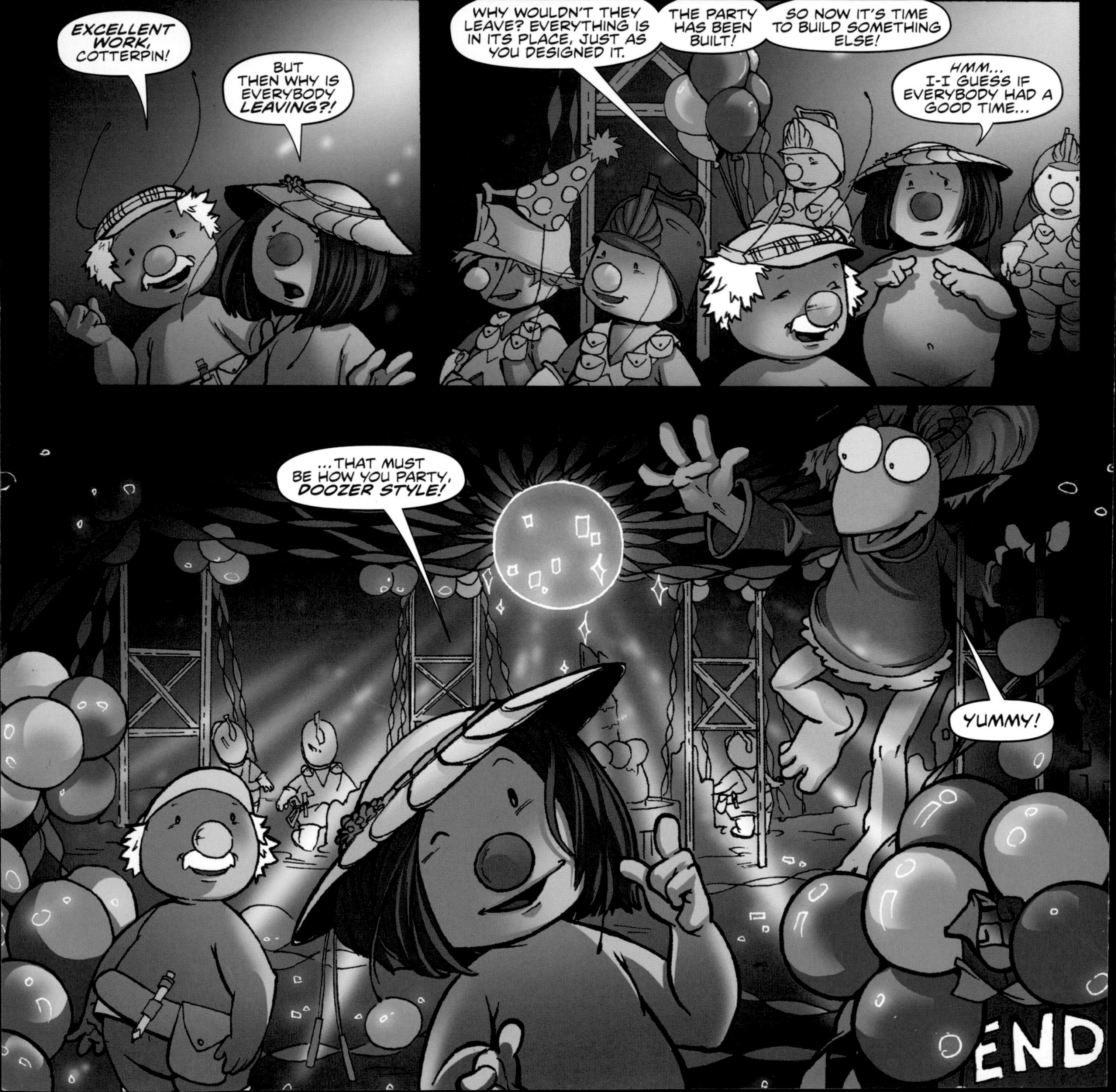
EXCELLENT WORK, COTTERPIN!
BUT THEN WHY IS EVERYBODY LEAVING?!
WHY WOULDN'T THEY LEAVE? EVERYTHING IS IN ITS PLACE, JUST AS YOU DESIGNED IT.
THE PARTY HAS BEEN BUILT!
SO NOW IT'S TIME TO BUILD SOMETHING ELSE!
HMM... I-I GUESS IF EVERYBODY HAD A GOOD TIME...
...THAT MUST BE HOW YOU PARTY, DOOZER STYLE!
YUMMY!
END

A Visitor from Outer Space

Story by Leigh Dragoon Art by Jake Myler

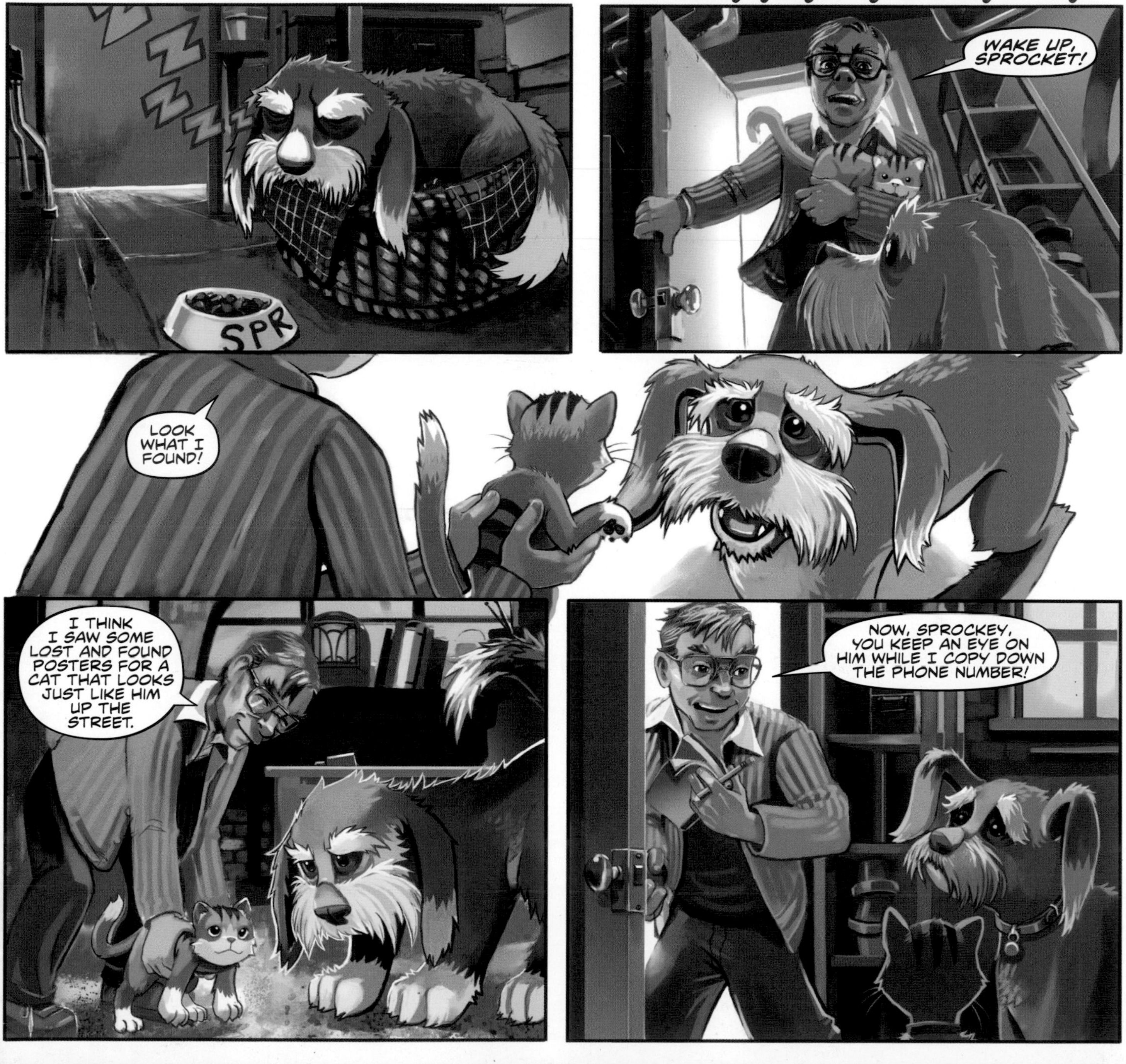
SPR
WAKE UP, SPROCKET!
LOOK WHAT I FOUND!
I THINK I SAW SOME LOST AND FOUND POSTERS FOR A CAT THAT LOOKS JUST LIKE HIM UP THE STREET.
NOW, SPROCKEY, YOU KEEP AN EYE ON HIM WHILE I COPY DOWN THE PHONE NUMBER!

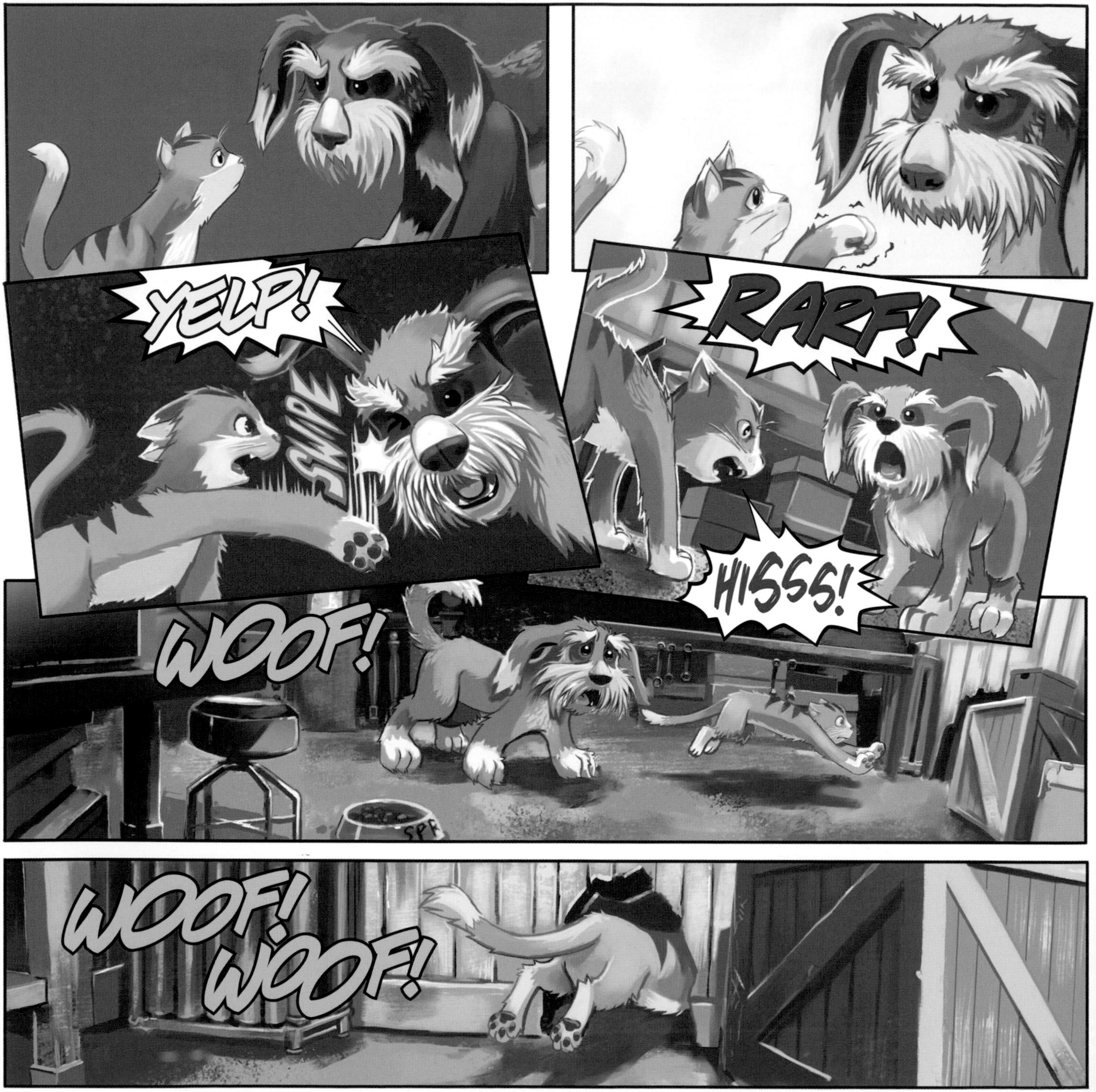
YELP!
SWIPE
RARF!
HISSS!
WOOF!
SPR
WOOF!
WOOF!

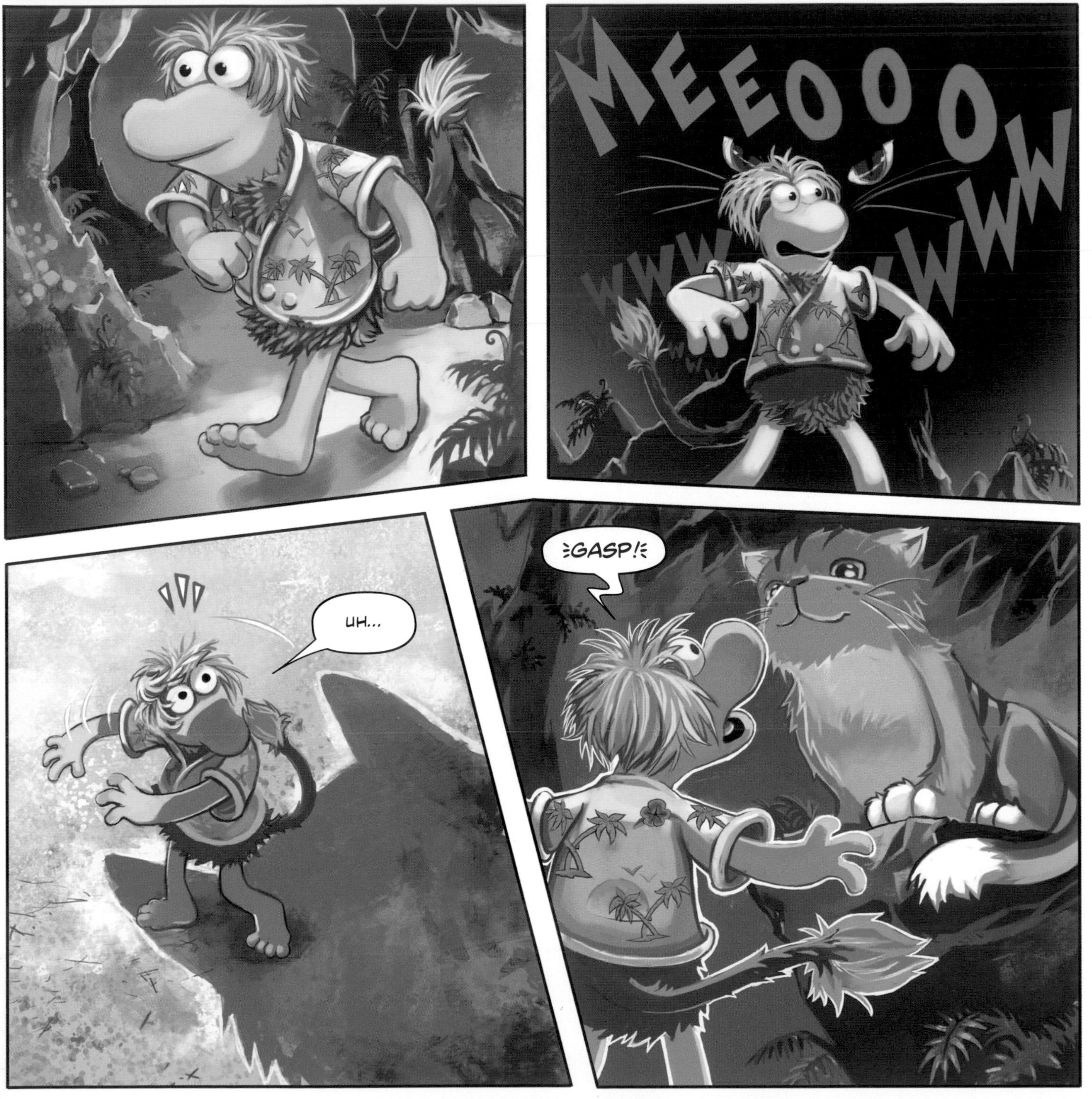
MEEOOOWWWWWWWW
UH...
GASP!

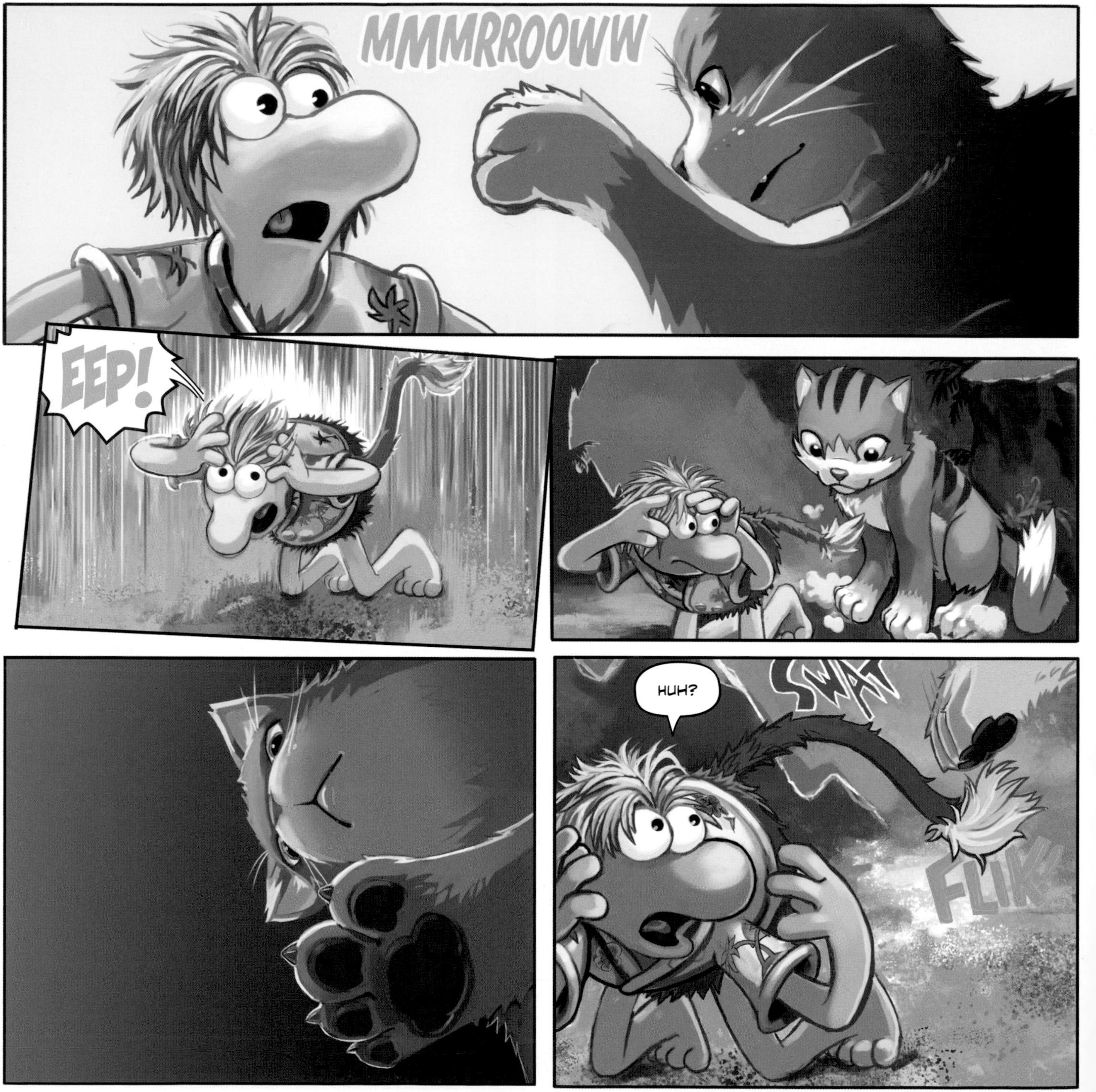
MMMRROOWW
EEP!
HUH?
FLIK

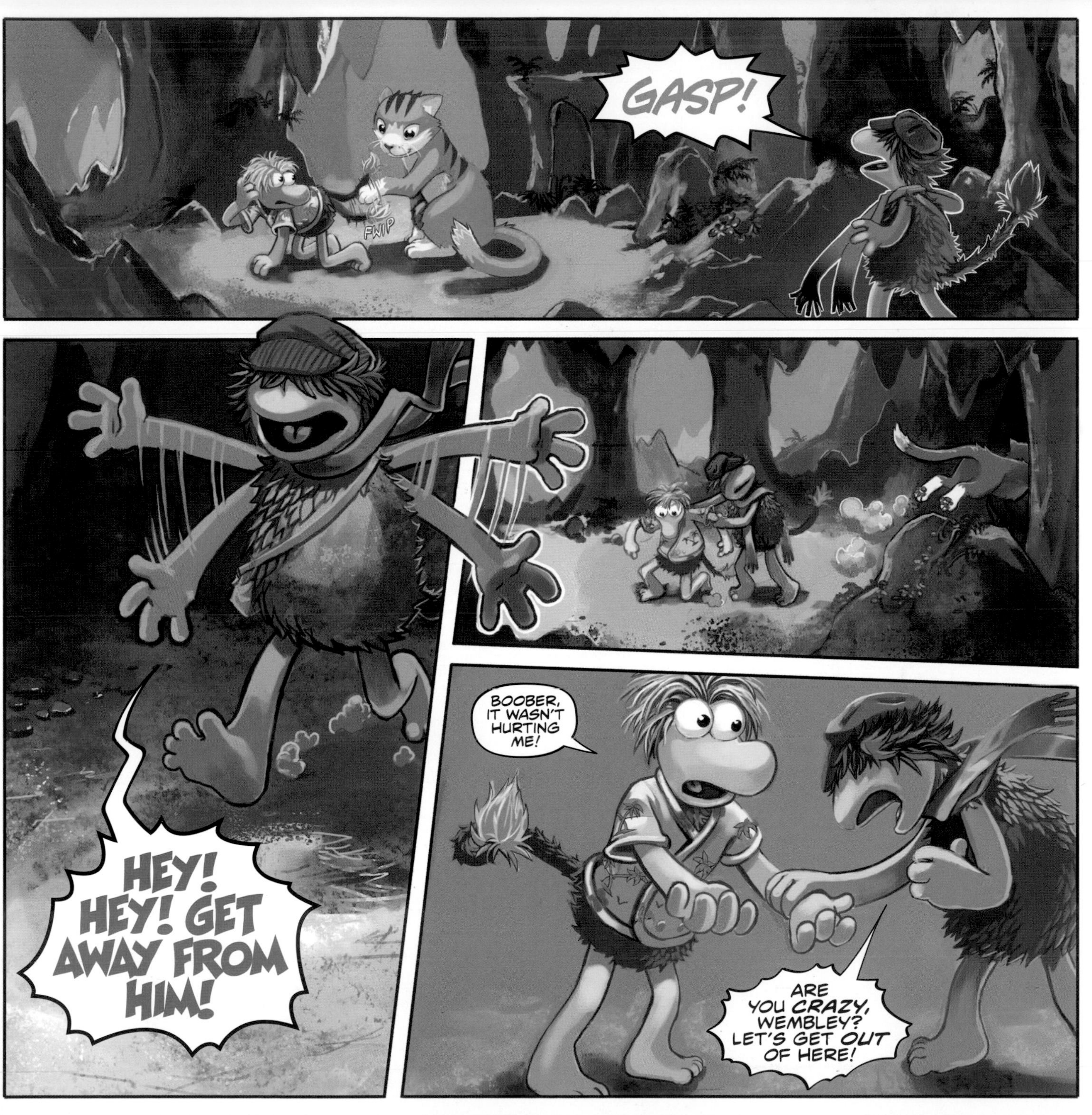
GASP!
FWIP
HEY! HEY! GET AWAY FROM HIM!
BOOBER, IT WASN'T HURTING ME!
ARE YOU CRAZY, WEMBLEY? LET'S GET OUT OF HERE!

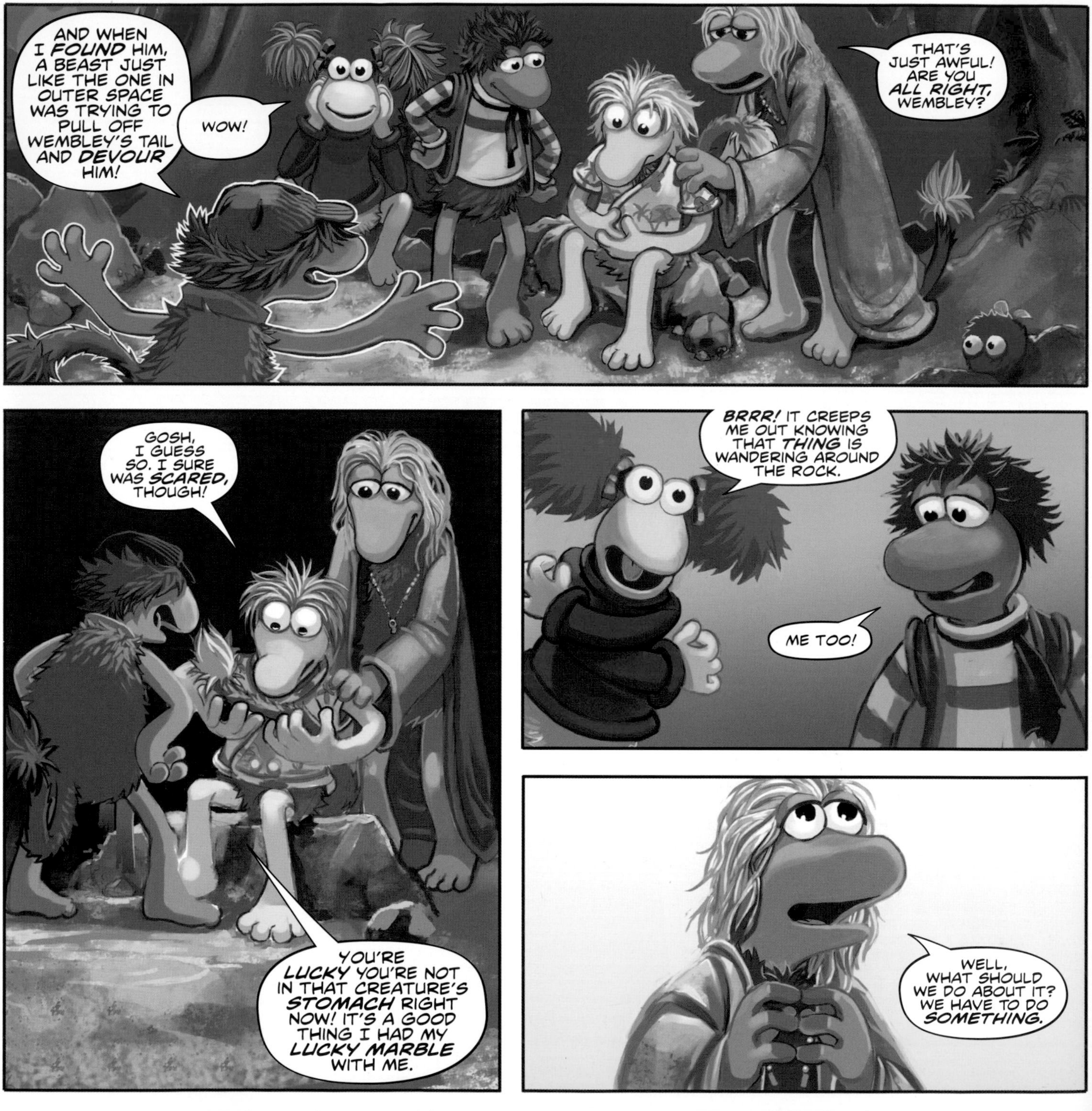
AND WHEN I FOUND HIM, A BEAST JUST LIKE THE ONE IN OUTER SPACE WAS TRYING TO PULL OFF WEMBLEY'S TAIL AND DEVOUR HIM!
WOW!
THAT'S JUST AWFUL! ARE YOU ALL RIGHT, WEMBLEY?
GOSH, I GUESS SO. I SURE WAS SCARED, THOUGH!
YOU'RE LUCKY YOU'RE NOT IN THAT CREATURE'S STOMACH RIGHT NOW! IT'S A GOOD THING I HAD MY LUCKY MARBLE WITH ME.
BRRR! IT CREEPS ME OUT KNOWING THAT THING IS WANDERING AROUND THE ROCK.
ME TOO!
WELL, WHAT SHOULD WE DO ABOUT IT? WE HAVE TO DO SOMETHING.

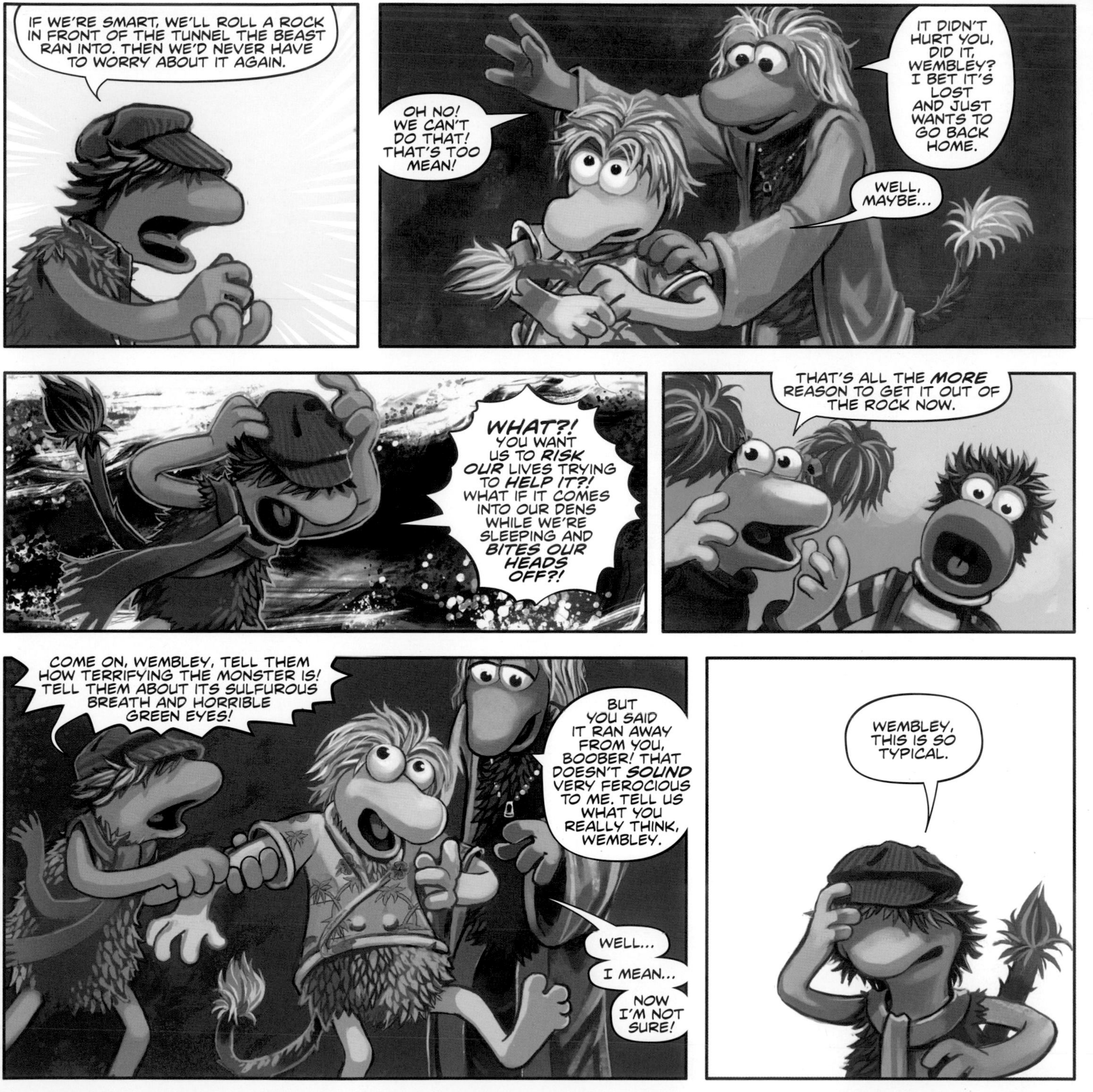
IF WE'RE SMART, WE'LL ROLL A ROCK IN FRONT OF THE TUNNEL THE BEAST RAN INTO. THEN WE'D NEVER HAVE TO WORRY ABOUT IT AGAIN.
OH NO! WE CAN'T DO THAT! THAT'S TOO MEAN!
IT DIDN'T HURT YOU, DID IT, WEMBLEY? I BET IT'S LOST AND JUST WANTS TO GO BACK HOME.
WELL, MAYBE...
WHAT?! YOU WANT US TO RISK OUR LIVES TRYING TO HELP IT?! WHAT IF IT COMES INTO OUR DENS WHILE WE'RE SLEEPING AND BITES OUR HEADS OFF?!
THAT'S ALL THE MORE REASON TO GET IT OUT OF THE ROCK NOW.
COME ON, WEMBLEY, TELL THEM HOW TERRIFYING THE MONSTER IS! TELL THEM ABOUT ITS SULFUROUS BREATH AND HORRIBLE GREEN EYES!
BUT YOU SAID IT RAN AWAY FROM YOU, BOOBER! THAT DOESN'T SOUND VERY FEROCIOUS TO ME. TELL US WHAT YOU REALLY THINK, WEMBLEY.
WELL...
I MEAN...
NOW I'M NOT SURE!
WEMBLEY, THIS IS SO TYPICAL.

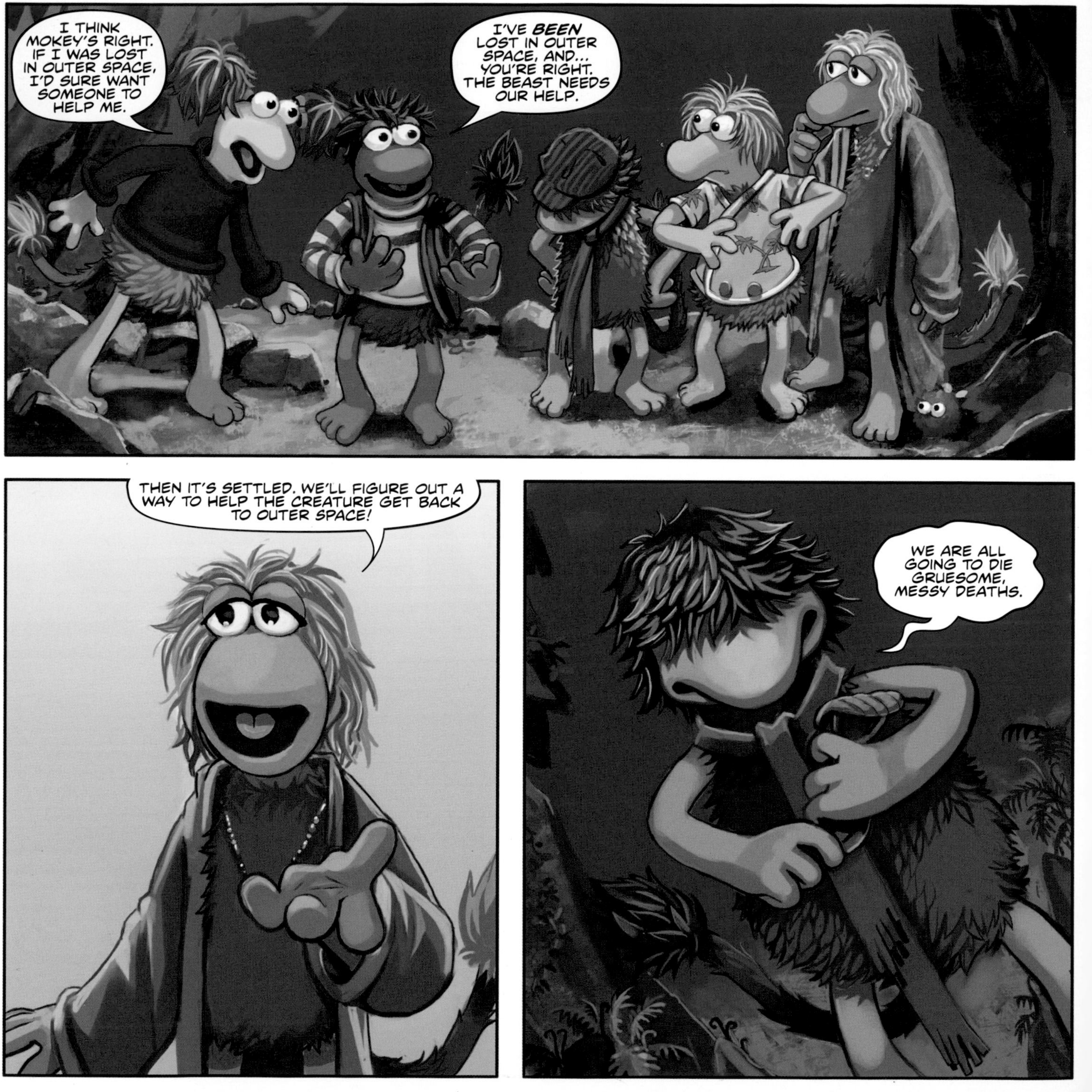
I THINK MOKEY'S RIGHT. IF I WAS LOST IN OUTER SPACE, I'D SURE WANT SOMEONE TO HELP ME.
I'VE BEEN LOST IN OUTER SPACE, AND... YOU'RE RIGHT. THE BEAST NEEDS OUR HELP.
THEN IT'S SETTLED. WE'LL FIGURE OUT A WAY TO HELP THE CREATURE GET BACK TO OUTER SPACE!
WE ARE ALL GOING TO DIE GRUESOME, MESSY DEATHS.

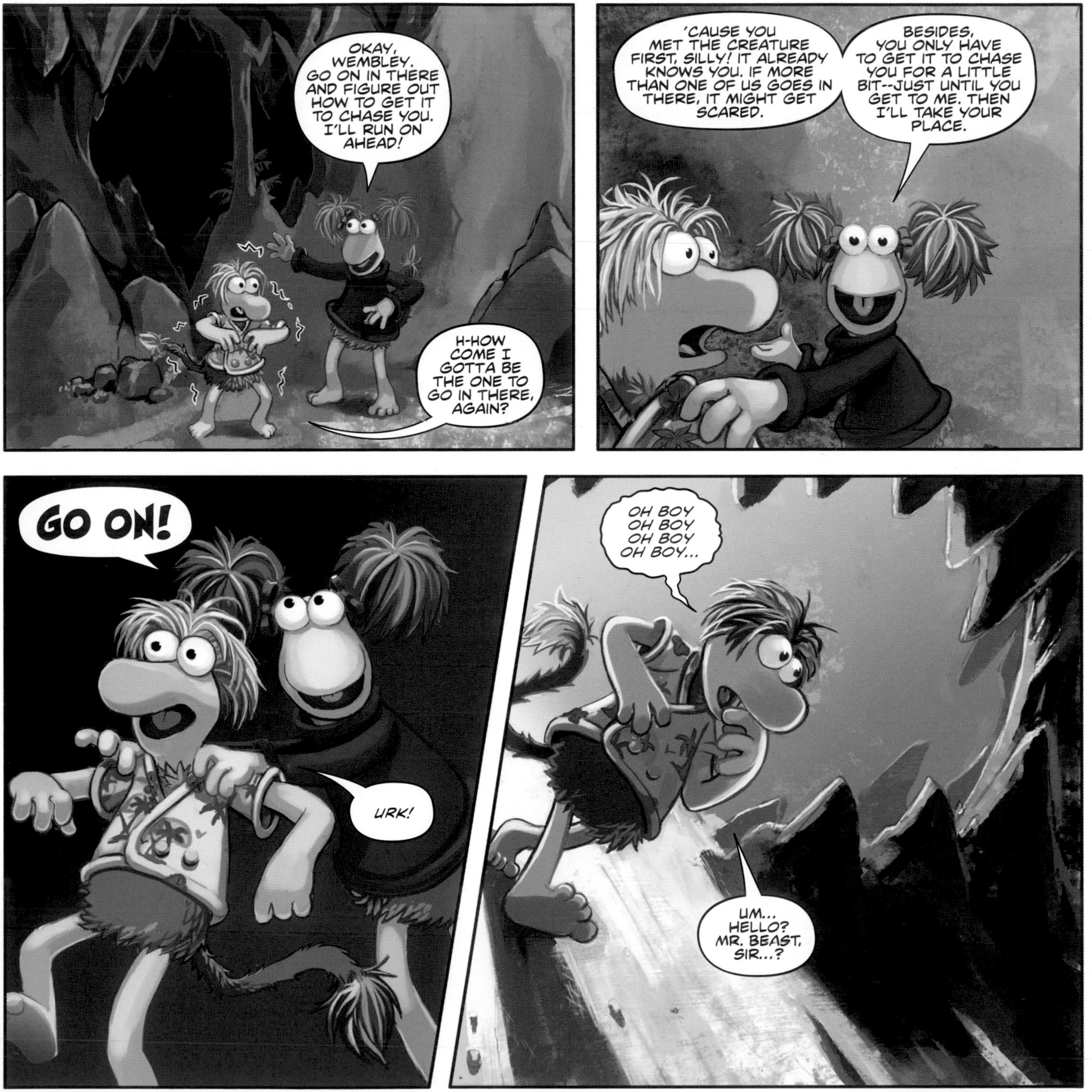
OKAY, WEMBLEY. GO ON IN THERE AND FIGURE OUT HOW TO GET IT TO CHASE YOU. I'LL RUN ON AHEAD!
H-HOW COME I GOTTA BE THE ONE TO GO IN THERE, AGAIN?
'CAUSE YOU MET THE CREATURE FIRST, SILLY! IT ALREADY KNOWS YOU. IF MORE THAN ONE OF US GOES IN THERE, IT MIGHT GET SCARED.
BESIDES, YOU ONLY HAVE TO GET IT TO CHASE YOU FOR A LITTLE BIT--JUST UNTIL YOU GET TO ME. THEN I'LL TAKE YOUR PLACE.
GO ON!
URK!
OH BOY OH BOY OH BOY OH BOY...
UM... HELLO? MR. BEAST, SIR...?

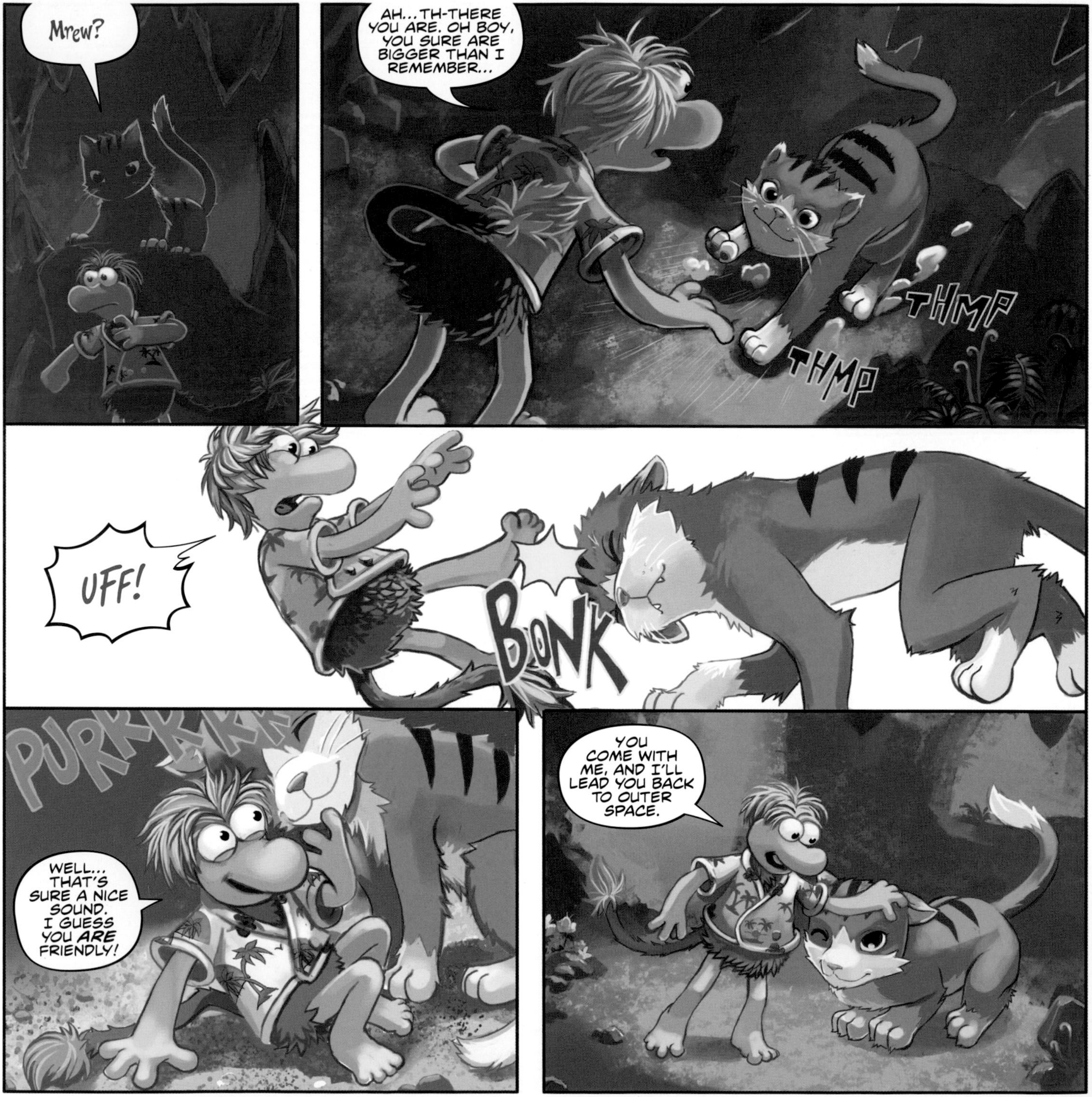

Mrew?
AH...TH-THERE YOU ARE. OH BOY, YOU SURE ARE BIGGER THAN I REMEMBER...
THMP
THMP
UFF!
BONK
PURRRRR
WELL... THAT'S SURE A NICE SOUND. I GUESS YOU *ARE* FRIENDLY!
YOU COME WITH ME, AND I'LL LEAD YOU BACK TO OUTER SPACE.

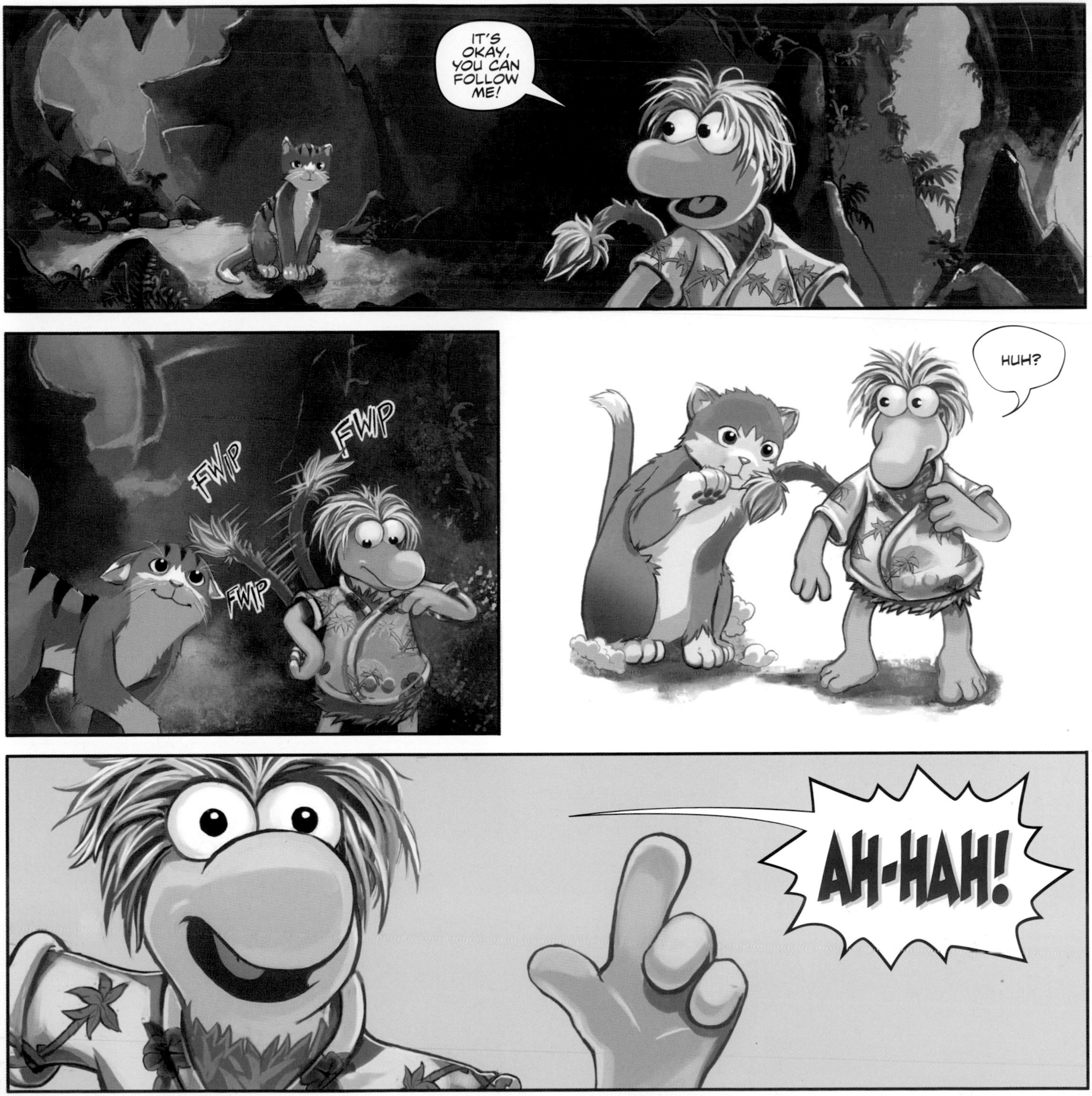
IT'S OKAY, YOU CAN FOLLOW ME!
FWIP
FWIP
FWIP
HUH?
AH-HAH!

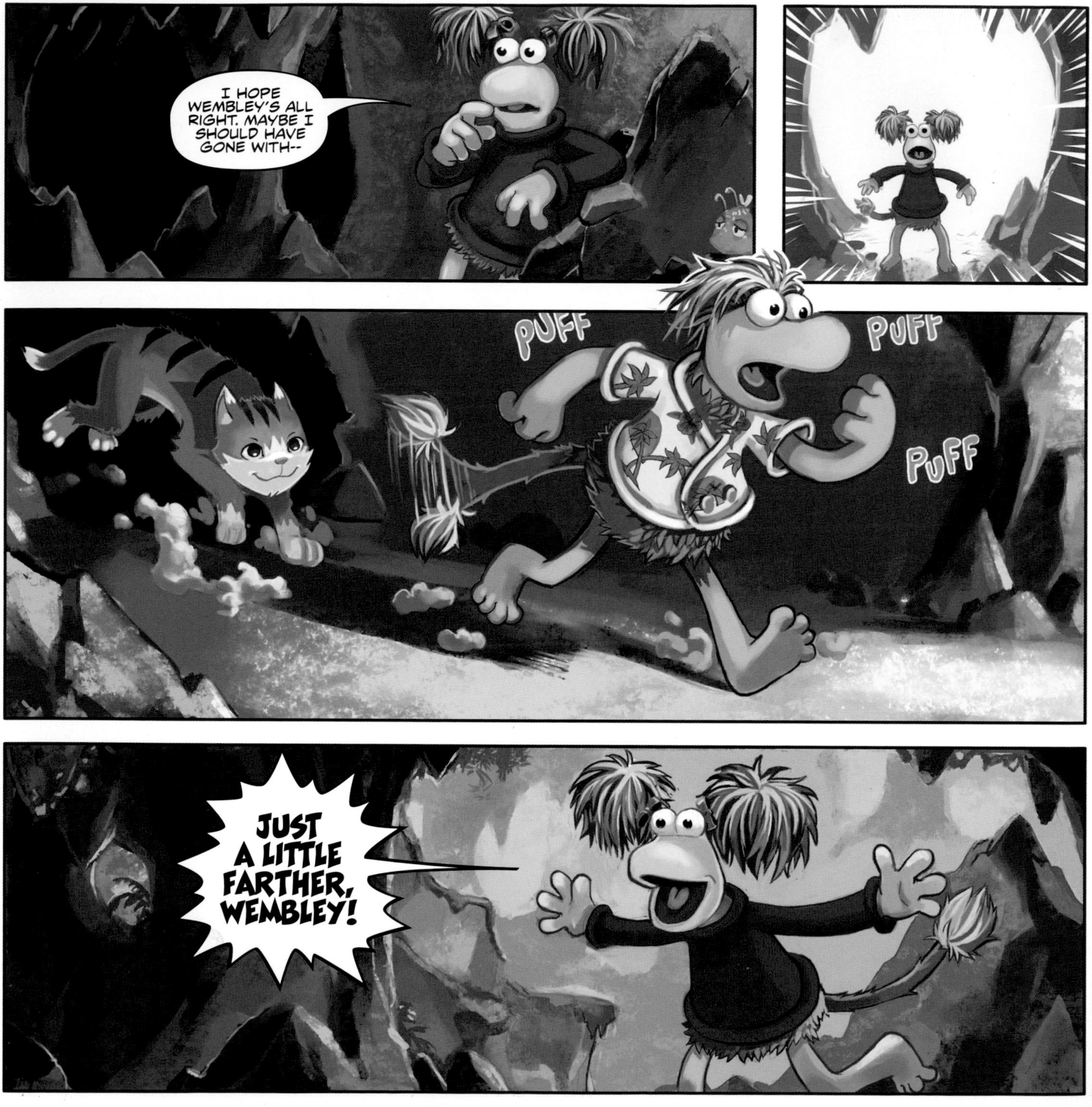
I HOPE WEMBLEY'S ALL RIGHT. MAYBE I SHOULD HAVE GONE WITH--
PUFF
PUFF
PUFF
JUST A LITTLE FARTHER, WEMBLEY!

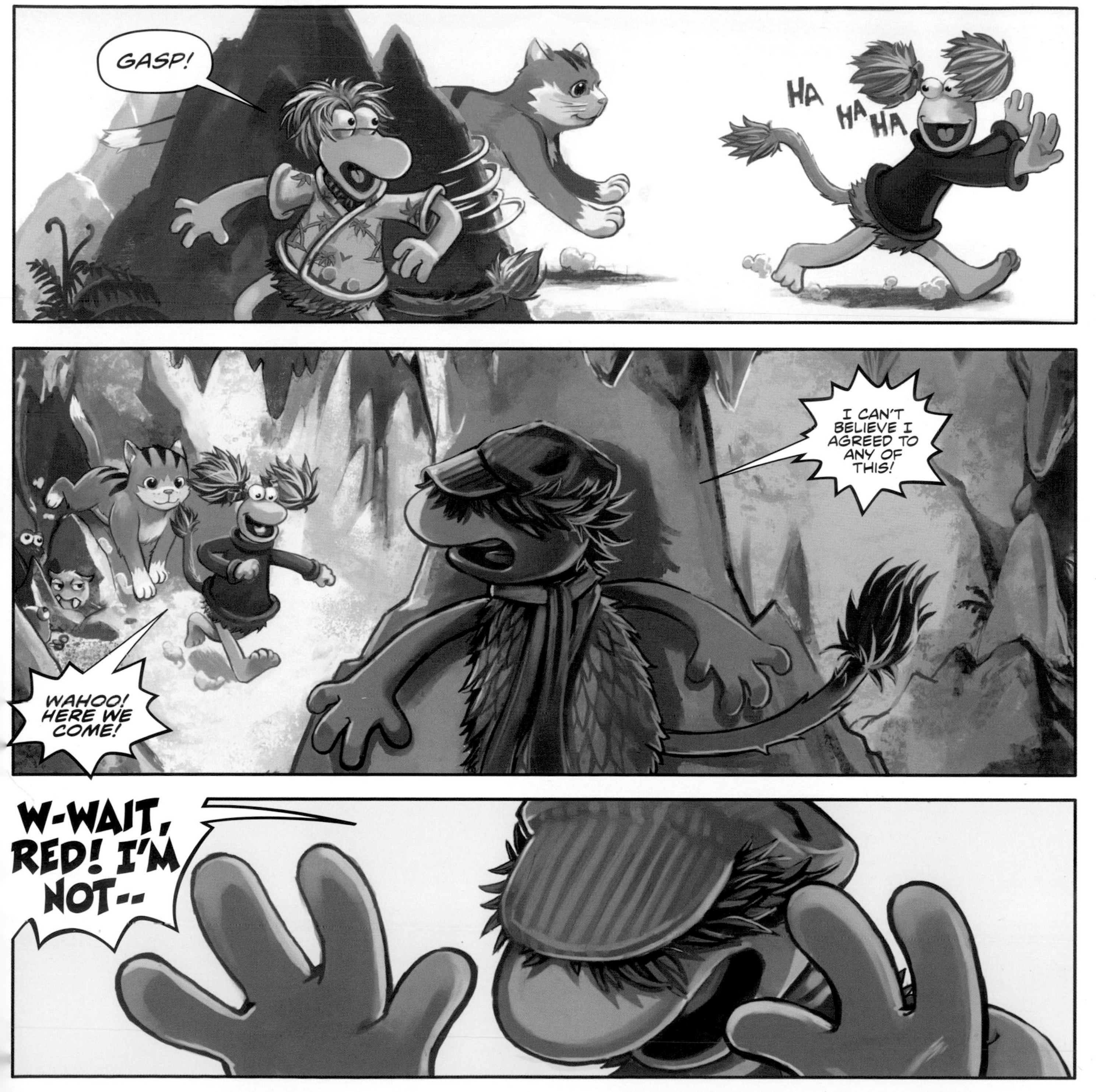
GASP!
HA HA HA
I CAN'T BELIEVE I AGREED TO ANY OF THIS!
WAHOO! HERE WE COME!
W-WAIT, RED! I'M NOT--

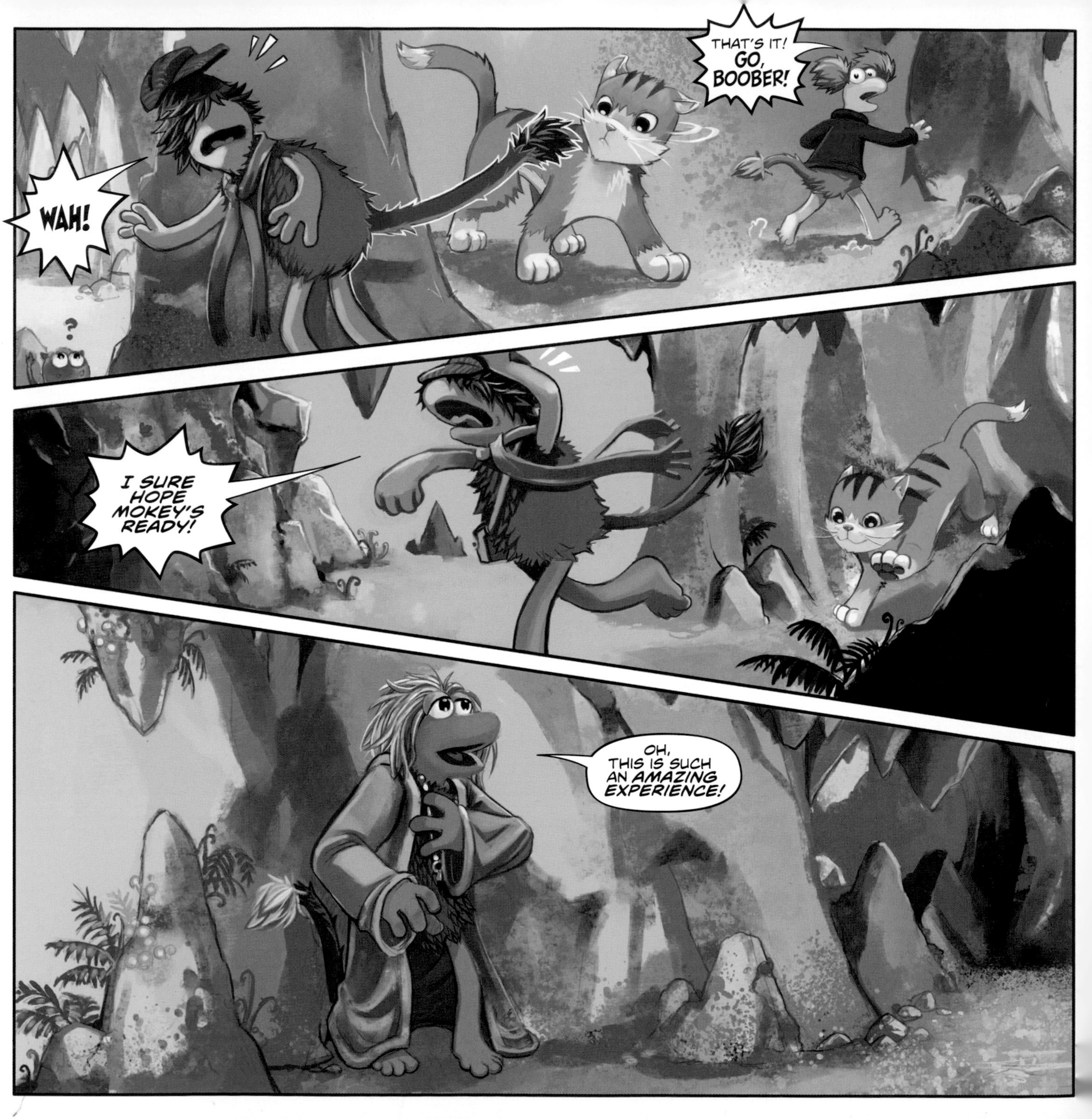
THAT'S IT! GO, BOOBER!
WAH!
I SURE HOPE MOKEY'S READY!
OH, THIS IS SUCH AN AMAZING EXPERIENCE!

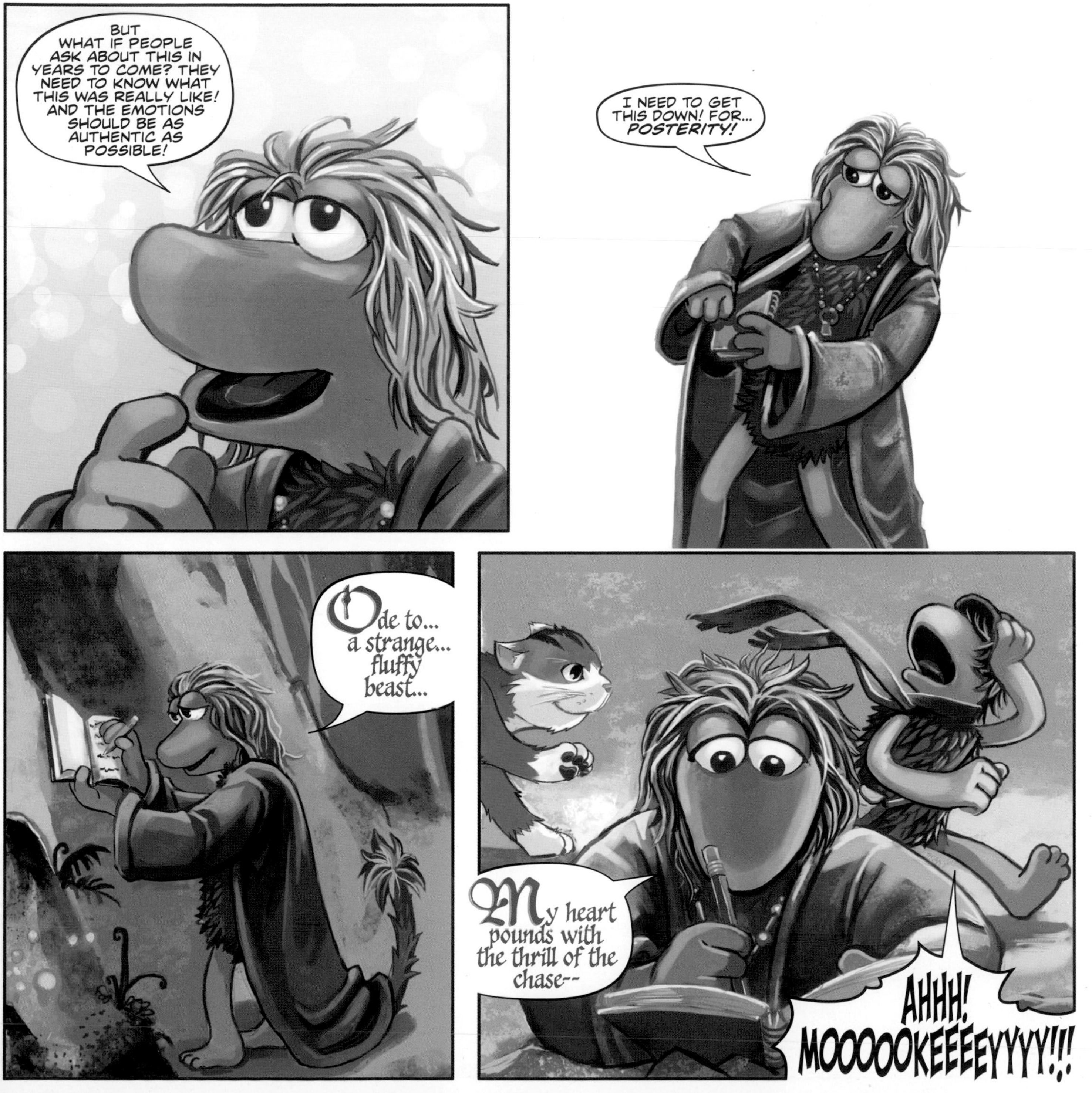
BUT WHAT IF PEOPLE ASK ABOUT THIS IN YEARS TO COME? THEY NEED TO KNOW WHAT THIS WAS REALLY LIKE! AND THE EMOTIONS SHOULD BE AS AUTHENTIC AS POSSIBLE!
I NEED TO GET THIS DOWN! FOR... POSTERITY!
Ode to... a strange... fluffy beast...
My heart pounds with the thrill of the chase--
AHHH! MOOOOOKEEEEYYYY!!!

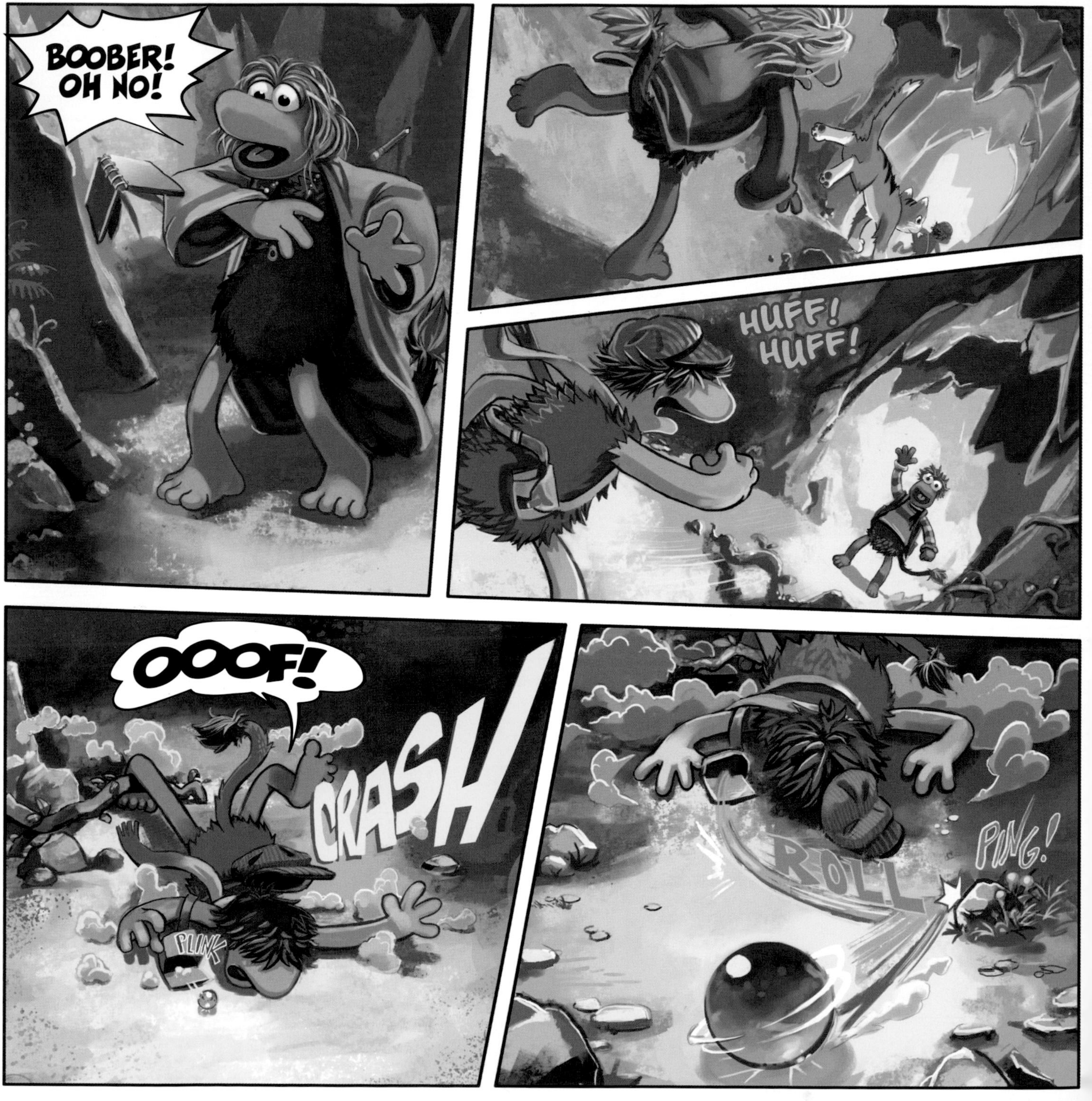
BOOBER! OH NO!
HUFF! HUFF!
OOOF!
CRASH
PLINK
ROLL
PING!

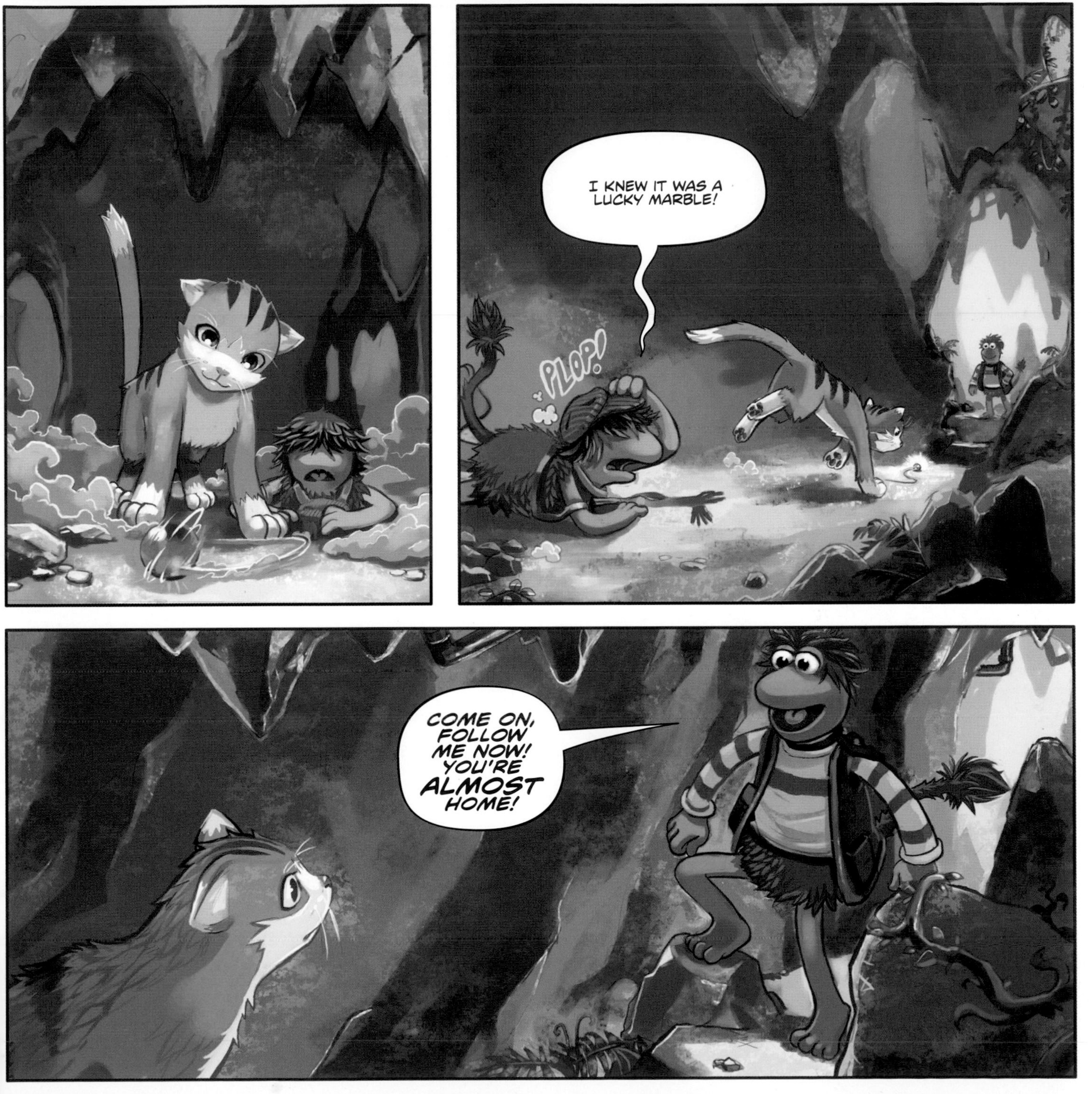

I KNEW IT WAS A LUCKY MARBLE!
PLOP!
COME ON, FOLLOW ME NOW! YOU'RE ALMOST HOME!

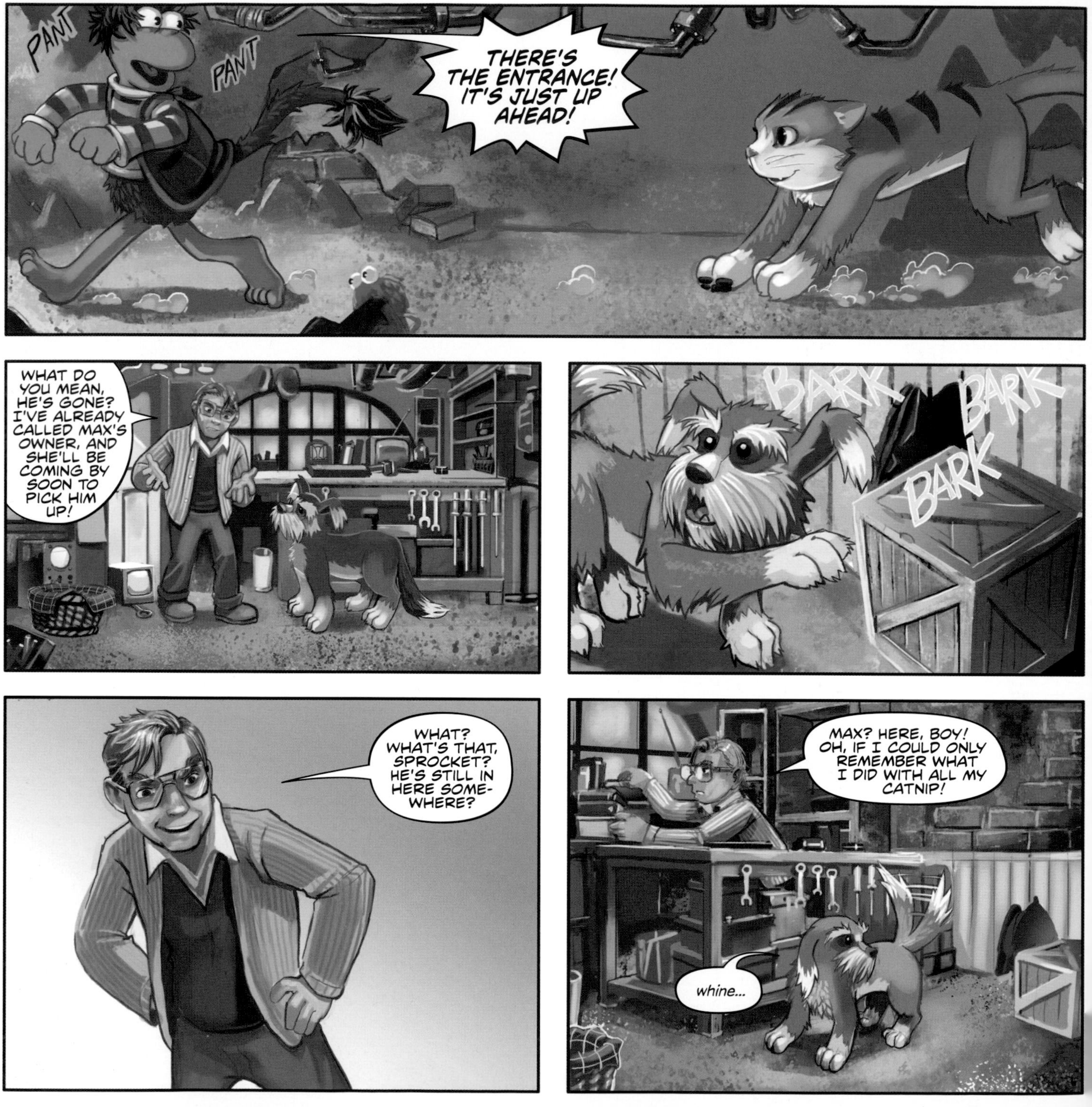
PANT
PANT
THERE'S THE ENTRANCE! IT'S JUST UP AHEAD!
WHAT DO YOU MEAN, HE'S GONE? I'VE ALREADY CALLED MAX'S OWNER, AND SHE'LL BE COMING BY SOON TO PICK HIM UP!
BARK
BARK
BARK
WHAT? WHAT'S THAT, SPROCKET? HE'S STILL IN HERE SOME-WHERE?
MAX? HERE, BOY! OH, IF I COULD ONLY REMEMBER WHAT I DID WITH ALL MY CATNIP!
whine...

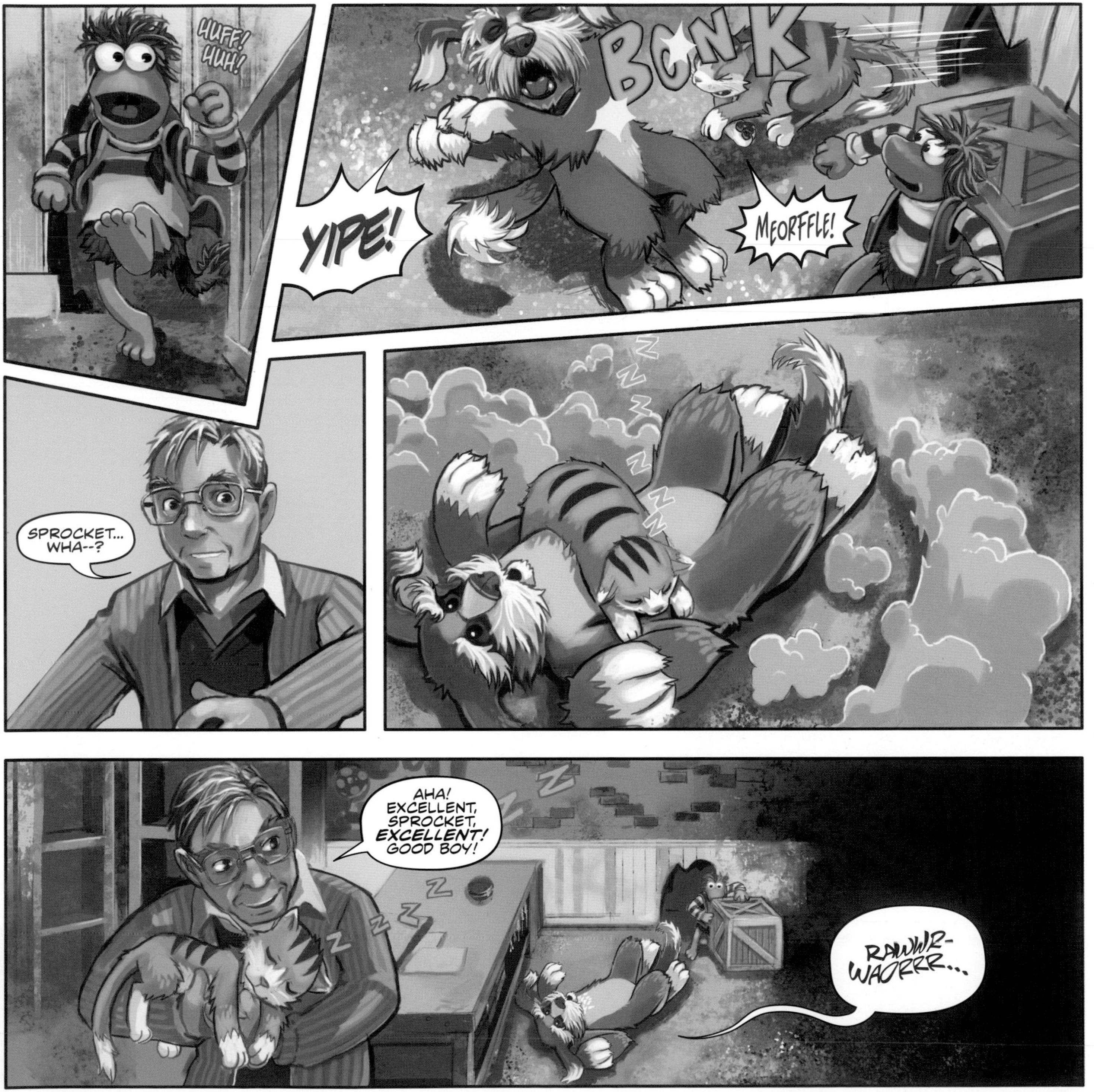
HUFF! HUH!
BONK!
YIPE!
MEORFFLE!
SPROCKET... WHA--?
AHA! EXCELLENT, SPROCKET, *EXCELLENT!* GOOD BOY!
RAWWR-WAORRR...

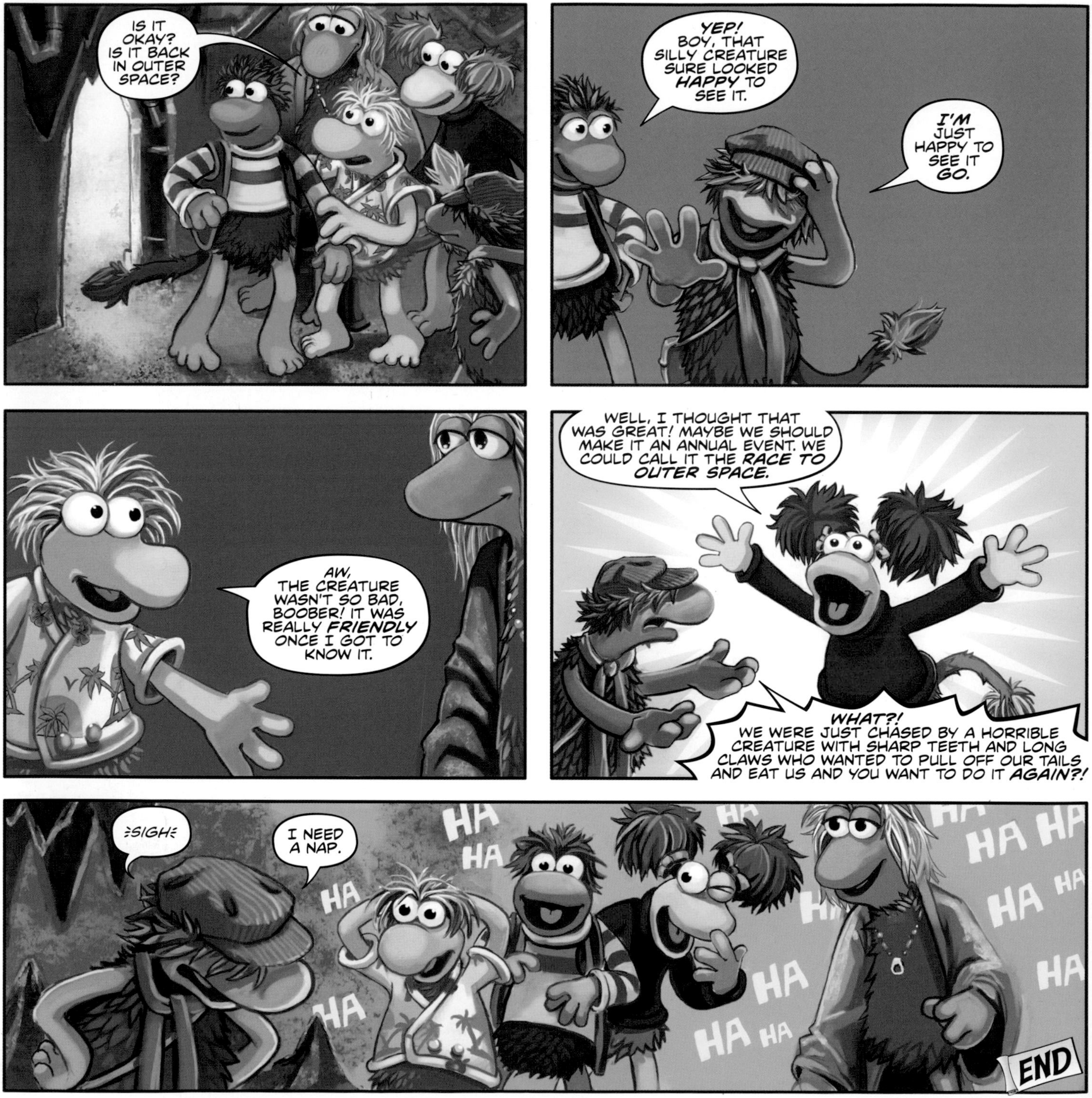
IS IT OKAY? IS IT BACK IN OUTER SPACE?
YEP! BOY, THAT SILLY CREATURE SURE LOOKED HAPPY TO SEE IT.
I'M JUST HAPPY TO SEE IT GO.
AW, THE CREATURE WASN'T SO BAD, BOOBER! IT WAS REALLY FRIENDLY ONCE I GOT TO KNOW IT.
WELL, I THOUGHT THAT WAS GREAT! MAYBE WE SHOULD MAKE IT AN ANNUAL EVENT. WE COULD CALL IT THE RACE TO OUTER SPACE.
WHAT?! WE WERE JUST CHASED BY A HORRIBLE CREATURE WITH SHARP TEETH AND LONG CLAWS WHO WANTED TO PULL OFF OUR TAILS AND EAT US AND YOU WANT TO DO IT AGAIN?!
SIGH
I NEED A NAP.
HA HA HA HA HA HA HA HA HA HA HA HA HA
END

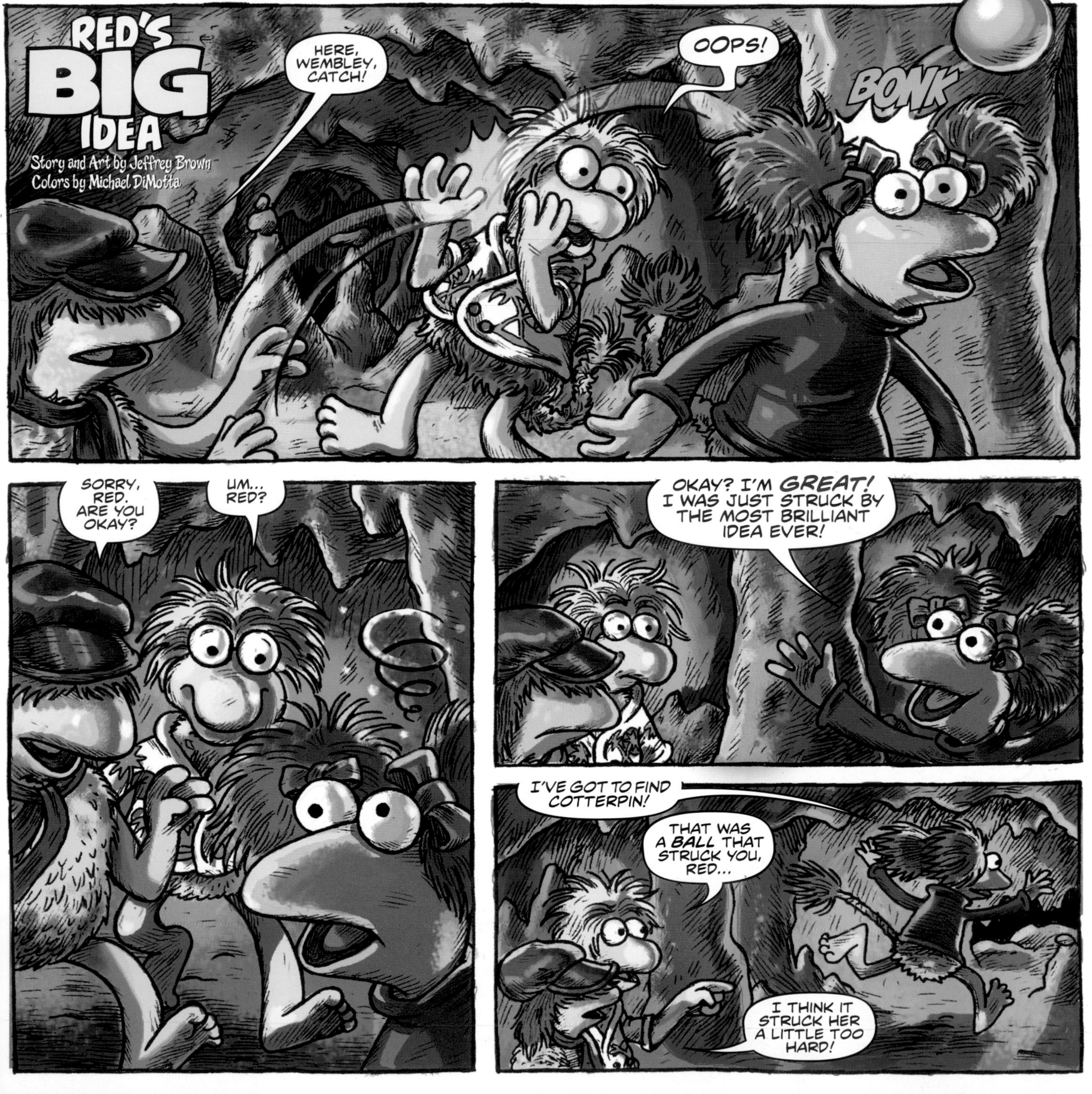

RED'S BIG IDEA
Story and Art by Jeffrey Brown
Colors by Michael DiMotta
HERE, WEMBLEY, CATCH!
OOPS!
BONK
SORRY, RED. ARE YOU OKAY?
UM... RED?
OKAY? I'M GREAT! I WAS JUST STRUCK BY THE MOST BRILLIANT IDEA EVER!
I'VE GOT TO FIND COTTERPIN!
THAT WAS A BALL THAT STRUCK YOU, RED...
I THINK IT STRUCK HER A LITTLE TOO HARD!

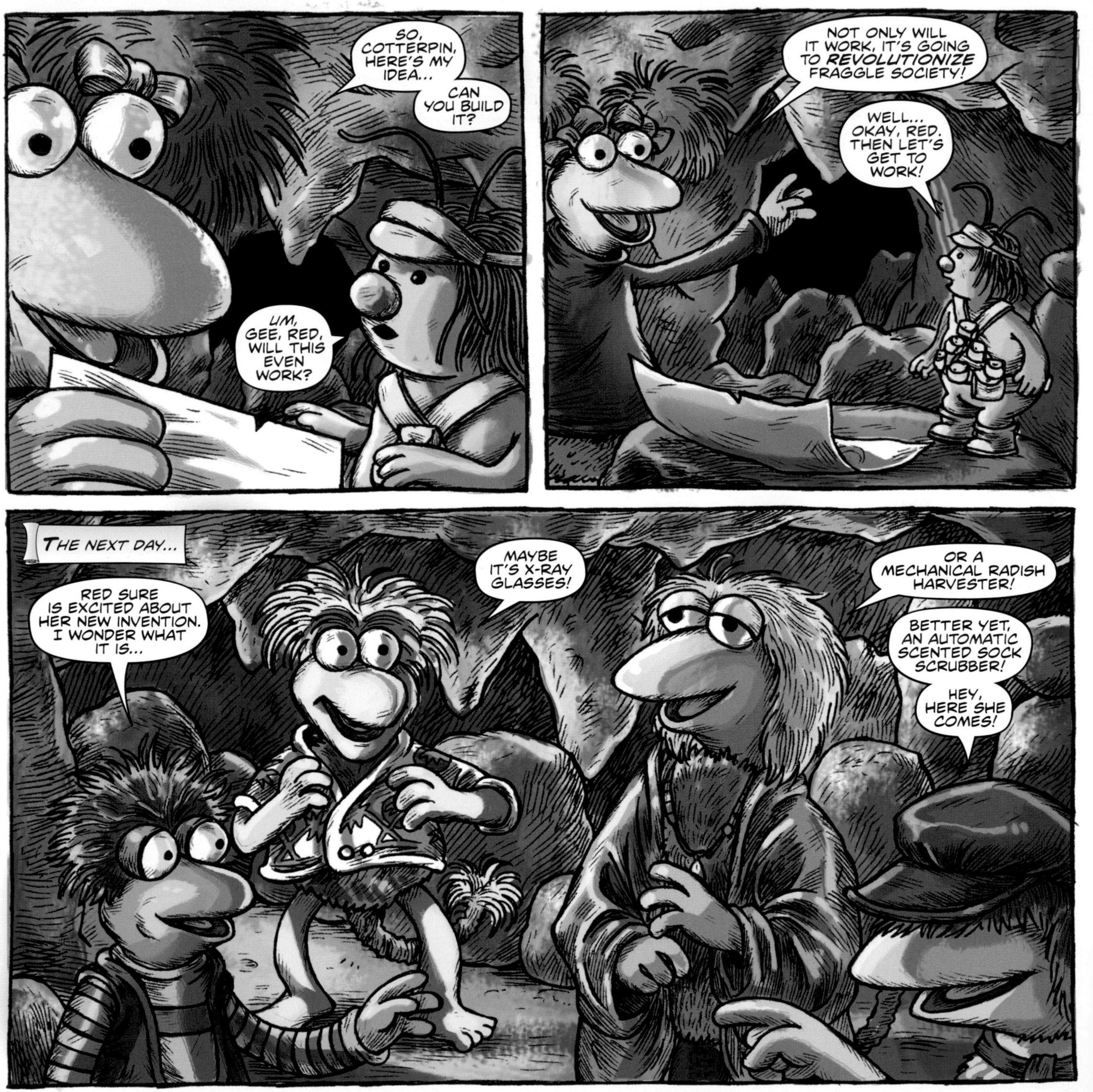
SO, COTTERPIN, HERE'S MY IDEA...
CAN YOU BUILD IT?
UM, GEE, RED, WILL THIS EVEN WORK?
NOT ONLY WILL IT WORK, IT'S GOING TO REVOLUTIONIZE FRAGGLE SOCIETY!
WELL... OKAY, RED. THEN LET'S GET TO WORK!
THE NEXT DAY...
RED SURE IS EXCITED ABOUT HER NEW INVENTION. I WONDER WHAT IT IS...
MAYBE IT'S X-RAY GLASSES!
OR A MECHANICAL RADISH HARVESTER!
BETTER YET, AN AUTOMATIC SCENTED SOCK SCRUBBER!
HEY, HERE SHE COMES!

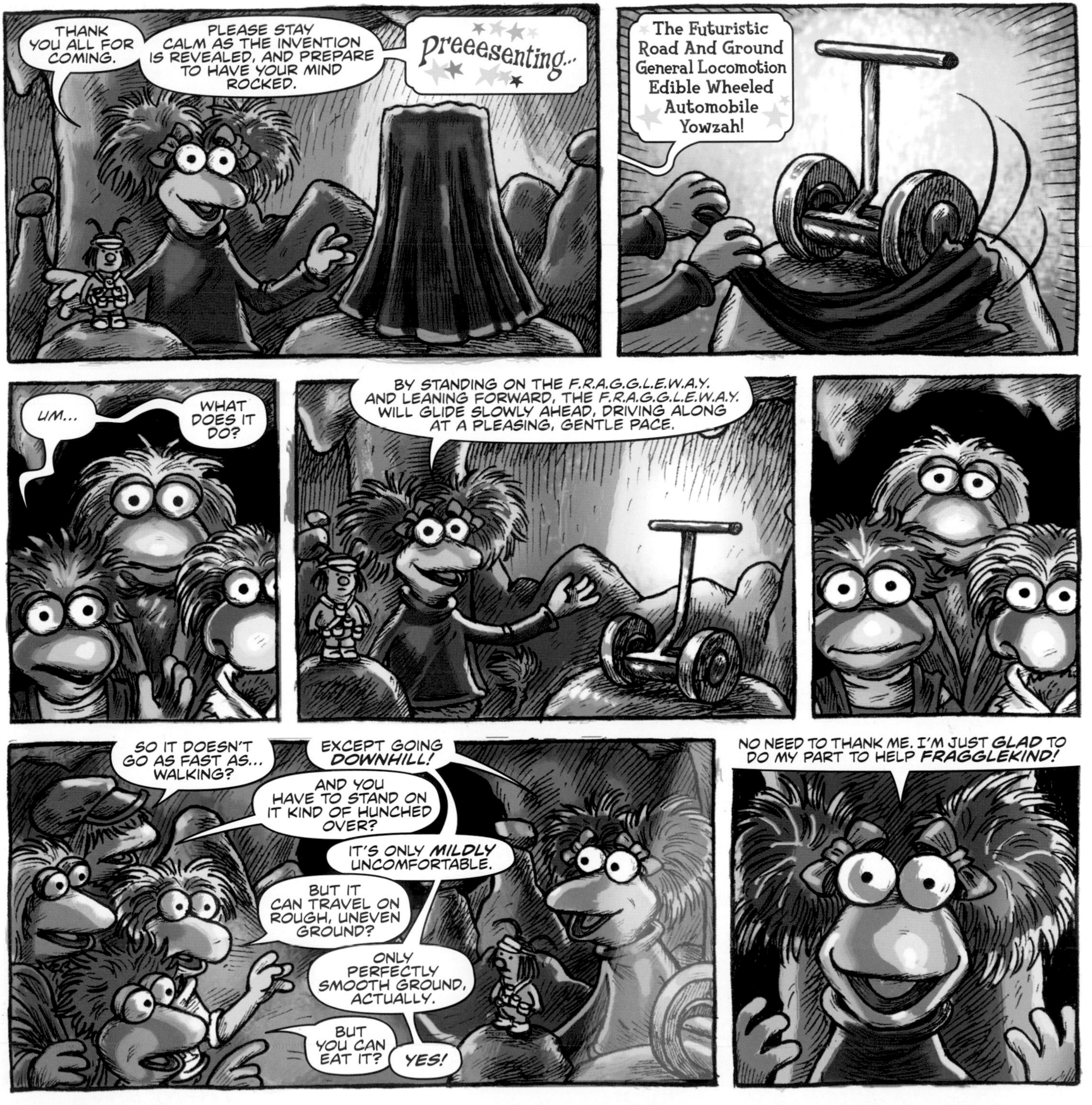

THANK YOU ALL FOR COMING.
PLEASE STAY CALM AS THE INVENTION IS REVEALED, AND PREPARE TO HAVE YOUR MIND ROCKED.
Preeeesenting...
The Futuristic Road And Ground General Locomotion Edible Wheeled Automobile Yowzah!
UM...
WHAT DOES IT DO?
BY STANDING ON THE F.R.A.G.G.L.E.W.A.Y. AND LEANING FORWARD, THE F.R.A.G.G.L.E.W.A.Y. WILL GLIDE SLOWLY AHEAD, DRIVING ALONG AT A PLEASING, GENTLE PACE.
SO IT DOESN'T GO AS FAST AS... WALKING?
EXCEPT GOING DOWNHILL!
AND YOU HAVE TO STAND ON IT KIND OF HUNCHED OVER?
IT'S ONLY MILDLY UNCOMFORTABLE.
BUT IT CAN TRAVEL ON ROUGH, UNEVEN GROUND?
ONLY PERFECTLY SMOOTH GROUND, ACTUALLY.
BUT YOU CAN EAT IT?
YES!
NO NEED TO THANK ME. I'M JUST GLAD TO DO MY PART TO HELP FRAGGLEKIND!

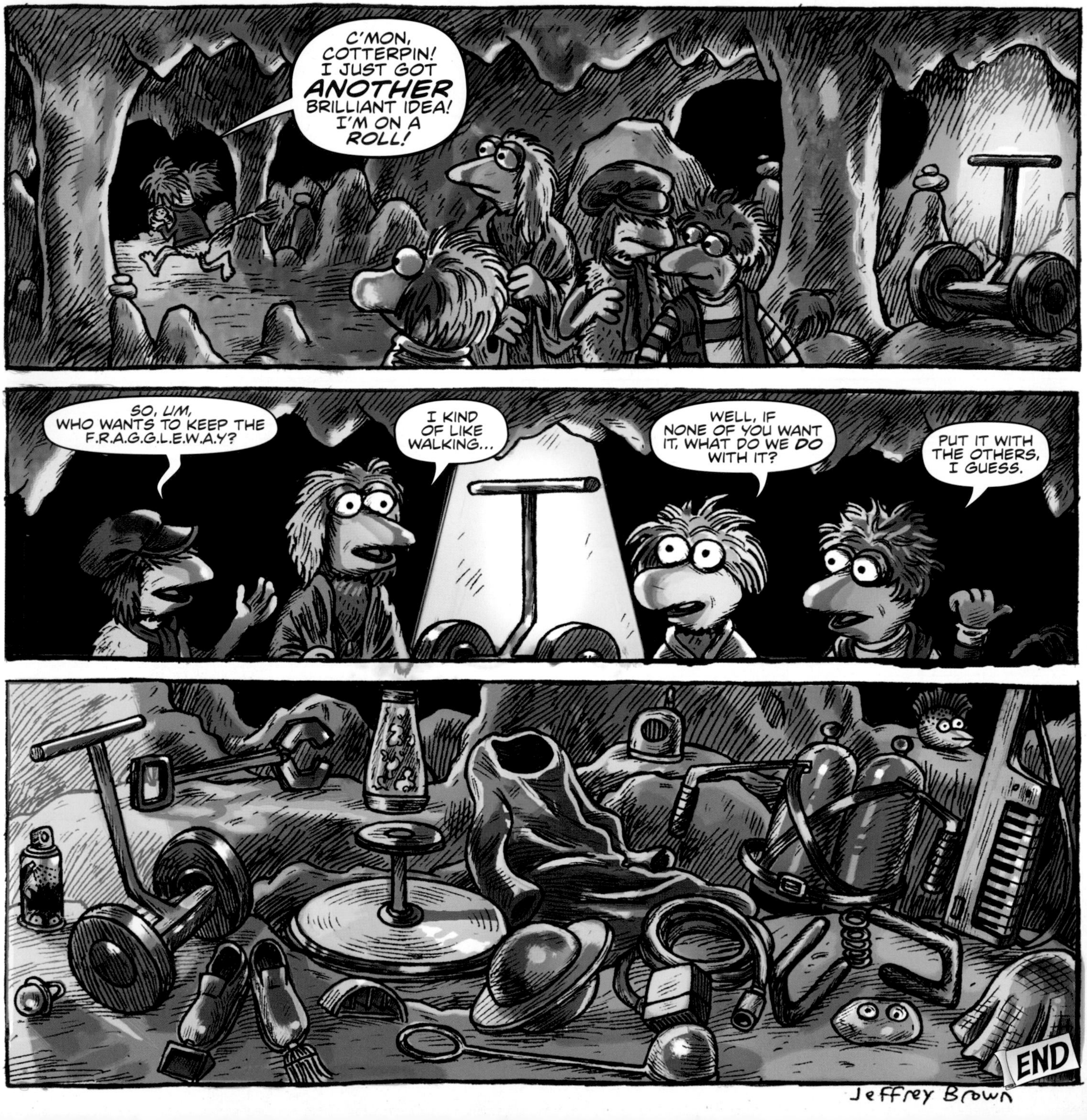

C'MON, COTTERPIN! I JUST GOT **ANOTHER** BRILLIANT IDEA! I'M ON A *ROLL!*
SO, UM, WHO WANTS TO KEEP THE F.R.A.G.G.L.E.W.A.Y?
I KIND OF LIKE WALKING...
WELL, IF NONE OF YOU WANT IT, WHAT DO WE *DO* WITH IT?
PUT IT WITH THE OTHERS, I GUESS.
END
Jeffrey Brown

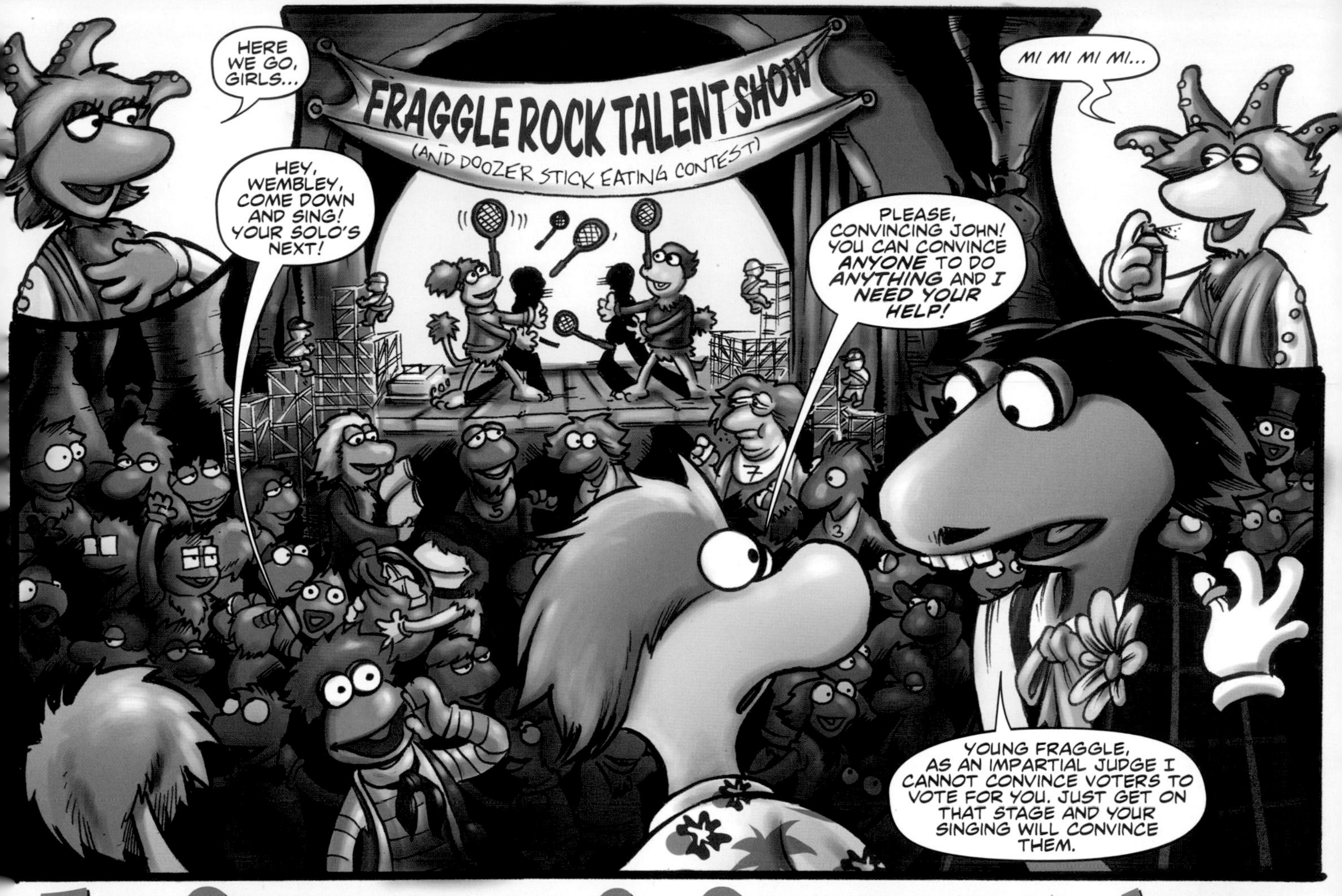
HERE WE GO, GIRLS...
MI MI MI MI...
FRAGGLE ROCK TALENT SHOW
(AND DOOZER STICK EATING CONTEST)
HEY, WEMBLEY, COME DOWN AND SING! YOUR SOLO'S NEXT!
PLEASE, CONVINCING JOHN! YOU CAN CONVINCE *ANYONE* TO DO *ANYTHING* AND I *NEED YOUR HELP!*
YOUNG FRAGGLE, AS AN IMPARTIAL JUDGE I CANNOT CONVINCE VOTERS TO VOTE FOR YOU. JUST GET ON THAT STAGE AND YOUR SINGING WILL CONVINCE THEM.

THE CONVINCING OF CONVINCING JOHN

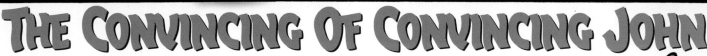

Convincing Lyrics by Neil Kleid   Motivational Artwork by Fernando Pinto

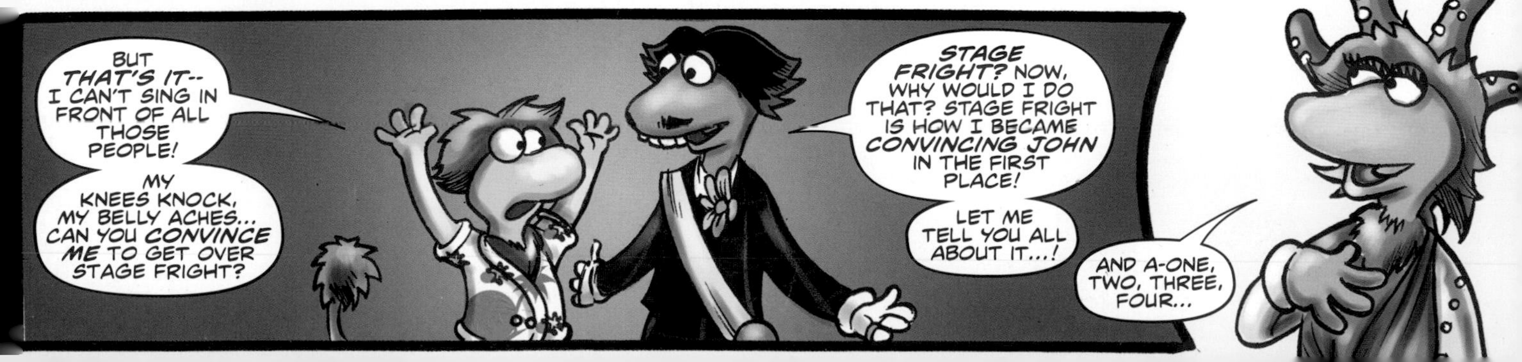
BUT *THAT'S IT*-- I CAN'T SING IN FRONT OF ALL THOSE PEOPLE!
MY KNEES KNOCK, MY BELLY ACHES... CAN YOU *CONVINCE ME* TO GET OVER STAGE FRIGHT?
STAGE FRIGHT? NOW, WHY WOULD I DO THAT? STAGE FRIGHT IS HOW I BECAME *CONVINCING JOHN* IN THE FIRST PLACE!
LET ME TELL YOU ALL ABOUT IT...!
AND A-ONE, TWO, THREE, FOUR...

♪♫ LISTEN TO CONVINCING JOHN, ♫
AND ALL YOUR TROUBLES WILL BE GONE.
HE'S GONNA TELL IT, SELL IT, SPELL IT
♪ JUST FOR YOOOOUUU! ♫♫

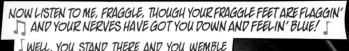

NOW LISTEN TO ME, FRAGGLE, THOUGH YOUR FRAGGLE FEET ARE FLAGGIN'
♪ AND YOUR NERVES HAVE GOT YOU DOWN AND FEELIN' BLUE! ♪

♪ WELL, YOU STAND THERE AND YOU WEMBLE
AND YOU SHAKE AND ALL BUT TREMBLE,
BUT YOUR STAGE FRIGHT MIGHT
♪♪ DO SOME **GOOD** FOR YOU. ♪

SO IF YOU WANT TO SING IT PROUD AND ON A STAGE TO SING OUT LOUD
♪ HEAR THIS STORY AND KNOW THAT EVERY WORD IS TRUE... ♪

♪♫ BECAUSE BEFORE ♪ ♫
I WAS CONVINCING,
THAT OL' STAGE FRIGHT
HAD **ME** WINCING TOO!

♪ LISTEN TO CONVINCING JOHN, ♫
AND ALL YOUR TROUBLES WILL BE GONE.
HE'S GONNA TELL IT, SELL IT, SPELL IT
♪ JUST FOR YOOOOUUU! ♪

♪♫♪ WELL, LET ME TELL YOU, AS A LAD ♪♫♪
I LIVED WITH MINSTREL DEAR OLD DAD
BUT MY PAPA NEVER STAYED IN ONE PLACE FOR LONG!

♪♪ HE TRAVELED HERE AND THERE AND BACK ♪♪♫
WITH A WORLD CLASS MINSTREL PACK,
LEADING THEM BOTH THERE AND HERE AGAIN IN SONG!

THERE
HERE

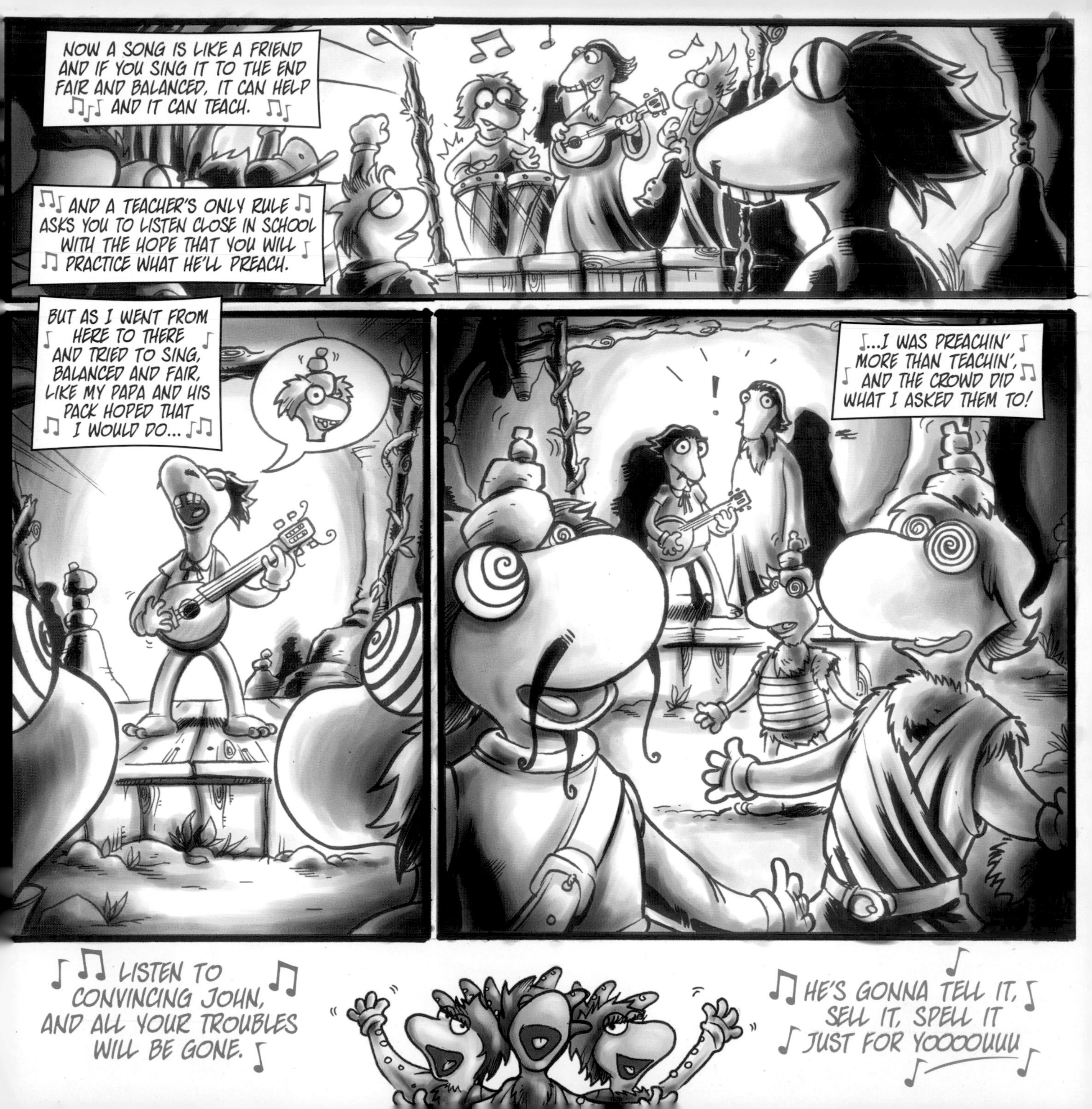

NOW A SONG IS LIKE A FRIEND AND IF YOU SING IT TO THE END FAIR AND BALANCED, IT CAN HELP ♫♪ AND IT CAN TEACH. ♫♪
♫♪ AND A TEACHER'S ONLY RULE ♫ ASKS YOU TO LISTEN CLOSE IN SCHOOL WITH THE HOPE THAT YOU WILL ♪ ♫ PRACTICE WHAT HE'LL PREACH.
BUT AS I WENT FROM ♪ HERE TO THERE ♪ AND TRIED TO SING, BALANCED AND FAIR, LIKE MY PAPA AND HIS PACK HOPED THAT ♫ I WOULD DO... ♪♫
♪...I WAS PREACHIN' ♪ MORE THAN TEACHIN', ♪ AND THE CROWD DID ♫ WHAT I ASKED THEM TO!
!
♪♫ LISTEN TO CONVINCING JOHN, ♫ AND ALL YOUR TROUBLES WILL BE GONE. ♪
♫ HE'S GONNA TELL IT, ♪ SELL IT, SPELL IT ♪ JUST FOR YOOOOUUU ♪

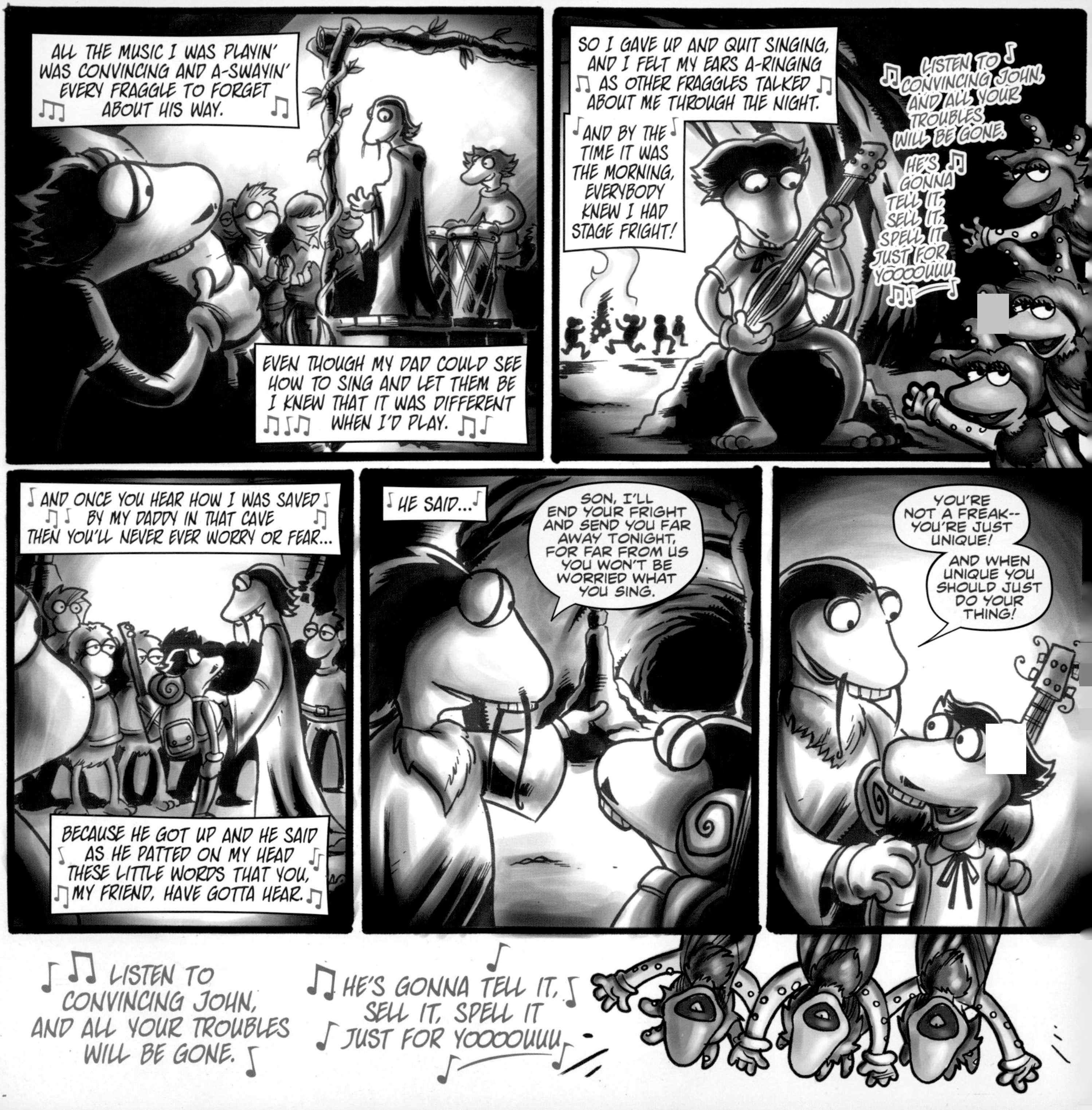
ALL THE MUSIC I WAS PLAYIN' WAS CONVINCING AND A-SWAYIN' EVERY FRAGGLE TO FORGET ABOUT HIS WAY.
EVEN THOUGH MY DAD COULD SEE HOW TO SING AND LET THEM BE I KNEW THAT IT WAS DIFFERENT WHEN I'D PLAY.
SO I GAVE UP AND QUIT SINGING, AND I FELT MY EARS A-RINGING AS OTHER FRAGGLES TALKED ABOUT ME THROUGH THE NIGHT.
AND BY THE TIME IT WAS THE MORNING, EVERYBODY KNEW I HAD STAGE FRIGHT!
LISTEN TO CONVINCING JOHN, AND ALL YOUR TROUBLES WILL BE GONE.
HE'S GONNA TELL IT, SELL IT, SPELL IT JUST FOR YOOOOUUU
AND ONCE YOU HEAR HOW I WAS SAVED BY MY DADDY IN THAT CAVE THEN YOU'LL NEVER EVER WORRY OR FEAR...
BECAUSE HE GOT UP AND HE SAID AS HE PATTED ON MY HEAD THESE LITTLE WORDS THAT YOU, MY FRIEND, HAVE GOTTA HEAR.
HE SAID...
SON, I'LL END YOUR FRIGHT AND SEND YOU FAR AWAY TONIGHT, FOR FAR FROM US YOU WON'T BE WORRIED WHAT YOU SING.
YOU'RE NOT A FREAK-- YOU'RE JUST UNIQUE!
AND WHEN UNIQUE YOU SHOULD JUST DO YOUR THING!
LISTEN TO CONVINCING JOHN, AND ALL YOUR TROUBLES WILL BE GONE.
HE'S GONNA TELL IT, SELL IT, SPELL IT JUST FOR YOOOOUUU

SO, BY NOW YOU KNOW MY STORY-- HOW I FOUND MY FAME AND GLORY, KNOWING NOW WHAT WE BOTH KNOW I SHOULD HAVE KNEW. ♫

♫ 'CAUSE IF YOU WANT TO MAKE YOUR MARK ♫ AND LEAVE YOUR WORRIES IN THE DARK THEN THIS STORY SHOWS **EXACTLY** WHAT TO DO.

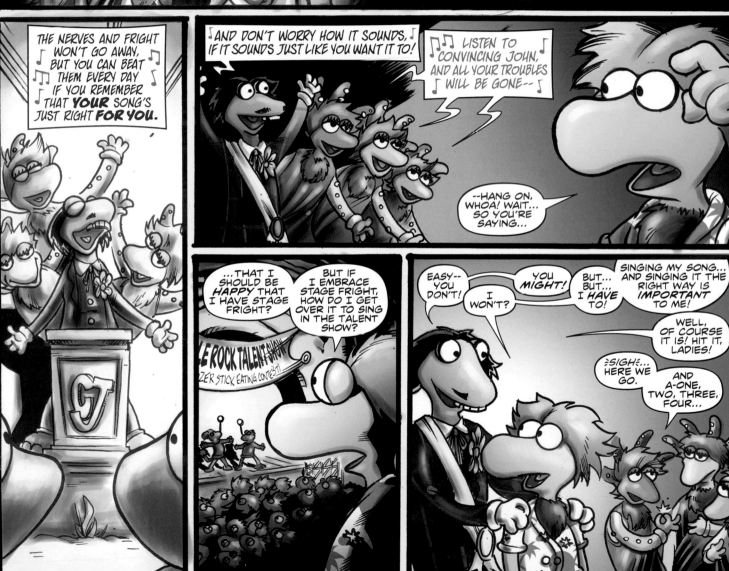

THE NERVES AND FRIGHT ♫ WON'T GO AWAY, ♫ BUT YOU CAN BEAT ♫♫ THEM EVERY DAY IF YOU REMEMBER THAT **YOUR** SONG'S JUST RIGHT **FOR YOU.**

♫ AND DON'T WORRY HOW IT SOUNDS, ♫ IF IT SOUNDS JUST LIKE YOU WANT IT TO!

♫♫ LISTEN TO ♫ CONVINCING JOHN, AND ALL YOUR TROUBLES ♫ WILL BE GONE-- ♫

--HANG ON, WHOA! WAIT... SO YOU'RE SAYING...

...THAT I SHOULD BE **HAPPY** THAT I HAVE STAGE FRIGHT?

BUT IF I EMBRACE STAGE FRIGHT, HOW DO I GET OVER IT TO SING IN THE TALENT SHOW?

LE ROCK TALENT SHOW
ZER STICK EATING CONTEST!

EASY-- YOU DON'T!

I WON'T?

YOU **MIGHT!**

BUT... BUT... I **HAVE** TO!

SINGING MY SONG... AND SINGING IT THE RIGHT WAY IS **IMPORTANT** TO ME!

WELL, OF COURSE IT IS! HIT IT, LADIES!

≋SIGH≋... HERE WE GO.

AND A-ONE, TWO, THREE, FOUR...

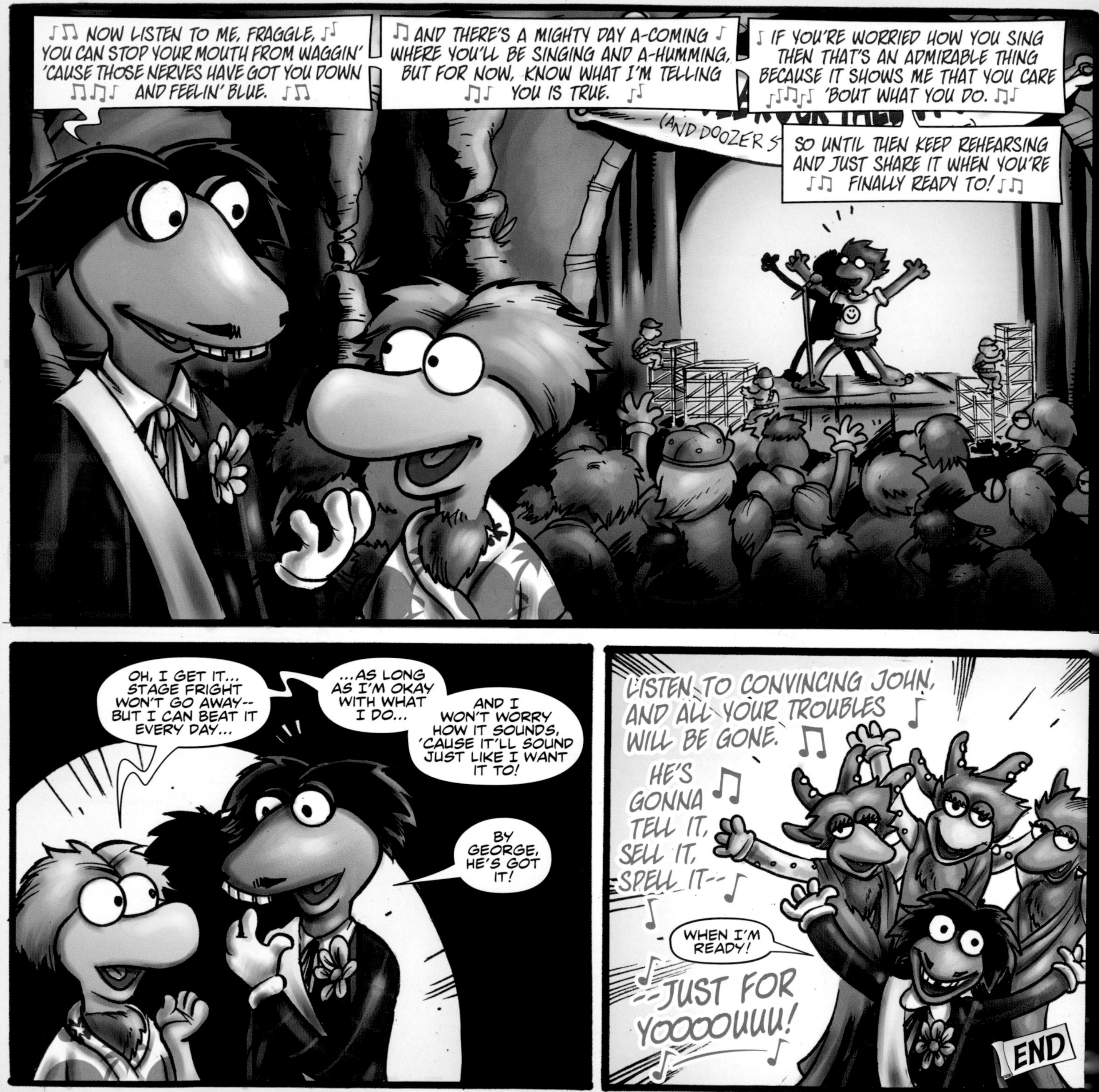
NOW LISTEN TO ME, FRAGGLE, YOU CAN STOP YOUR MOUTH FROM WAGGIN' 'CAUSE THOSE NERVES HAVE GOT YOU DOWN AND FEELIN' BLUE.
AND THERE'S A MIGHTY DAY A-COMING WHERE YOU'LL BE SINGING AND A-HUMMING, BUT FOR NOW, KNOW WHAT I'M TELLING YOU IS TRUE.
IF YOU'RE WORRIED HOW YOU SING THEN THAT'S AN ADMIRABLE THING BECAUSE IT SHOWS ME THAT YOU CARE 'BOUT WHAT YOU DO.
(AND DOOZER S
SO UNTIL THEN KEEP REHEARSING AND JUST SHARE IT WHEN YOU'RE FINALLY READY TO!
OH, I GET IT... STAGE FRIGHT WON'T GO AWAY-- BUT I CAN BEAT IT EVERY DAY...
...AS LONG AS I'M OKAY WITH WHAT I DO...
AND I WON'T WORRY HOW IT SOUNDS, 'CAUSE IT'LL SOUND JUST LIKE I WANT IT TO!
BY GEORGE, HE'S GOT IT!
LISTEN TO CONVINCING JOHN, AND ALL YOUR TROUBLES WILL BE GONE.
HE'S GONNA TELL IT, SELL IT, SPELL IT--
WHEN I'M READY!
--JUST FOR YOOOOUUU!
END

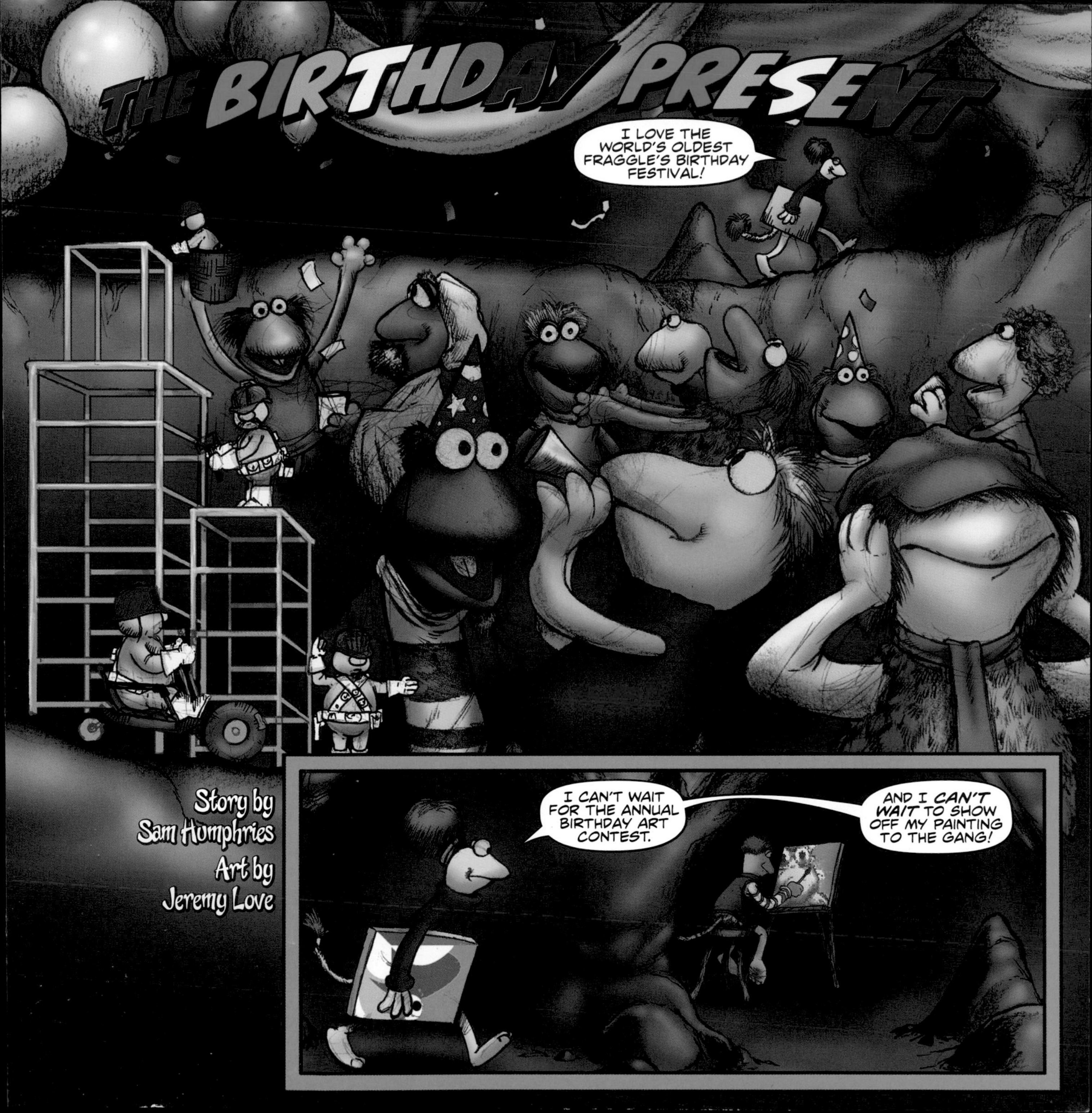
THE BIRTHDAY PRESENT
I LOVE THE WORLD'S OLDEST FRAGGLE'S BIRTHDAY FESTIVAL!
Story by Sam Humphries
Art by Jeremy Love
I CAN'T WAIT FOR THE ANNUAL BIRTHDAY ART CONTEST.
AND I CAN'T WAIT TO SHOW OFF MY PAINTING TO THE GANG!

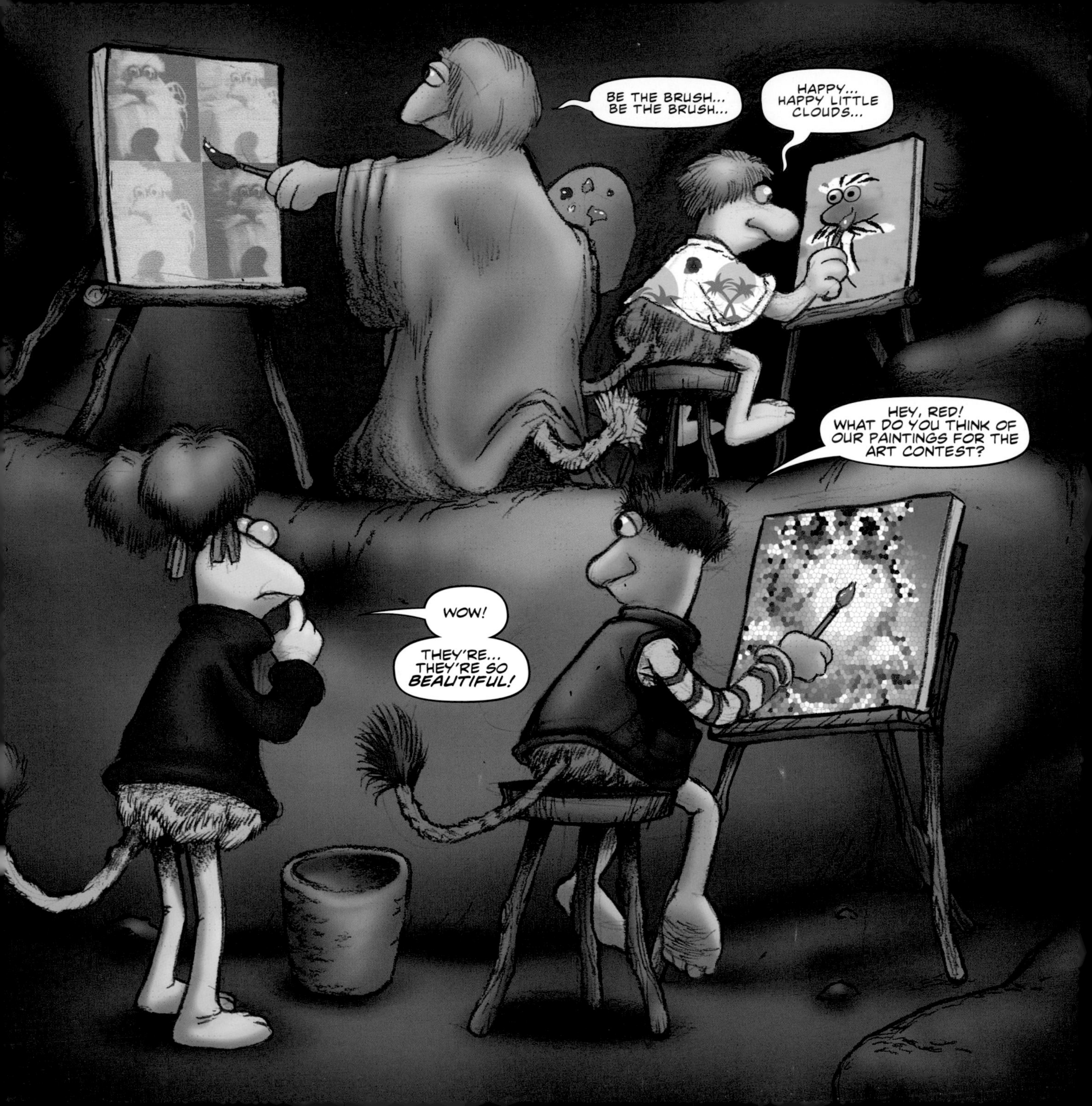
BE THE BRUSH... BE THE BRUSH...
HAPPY... HAPPY LITTLE CLOUDS...
HEY, RED! WHAT DO YOU THINK OF OUR PAINTINGS FOR THE ART CONTEST?
WOW!
THEY'RE... THEY'RE SO *BEAUTIFUL!*

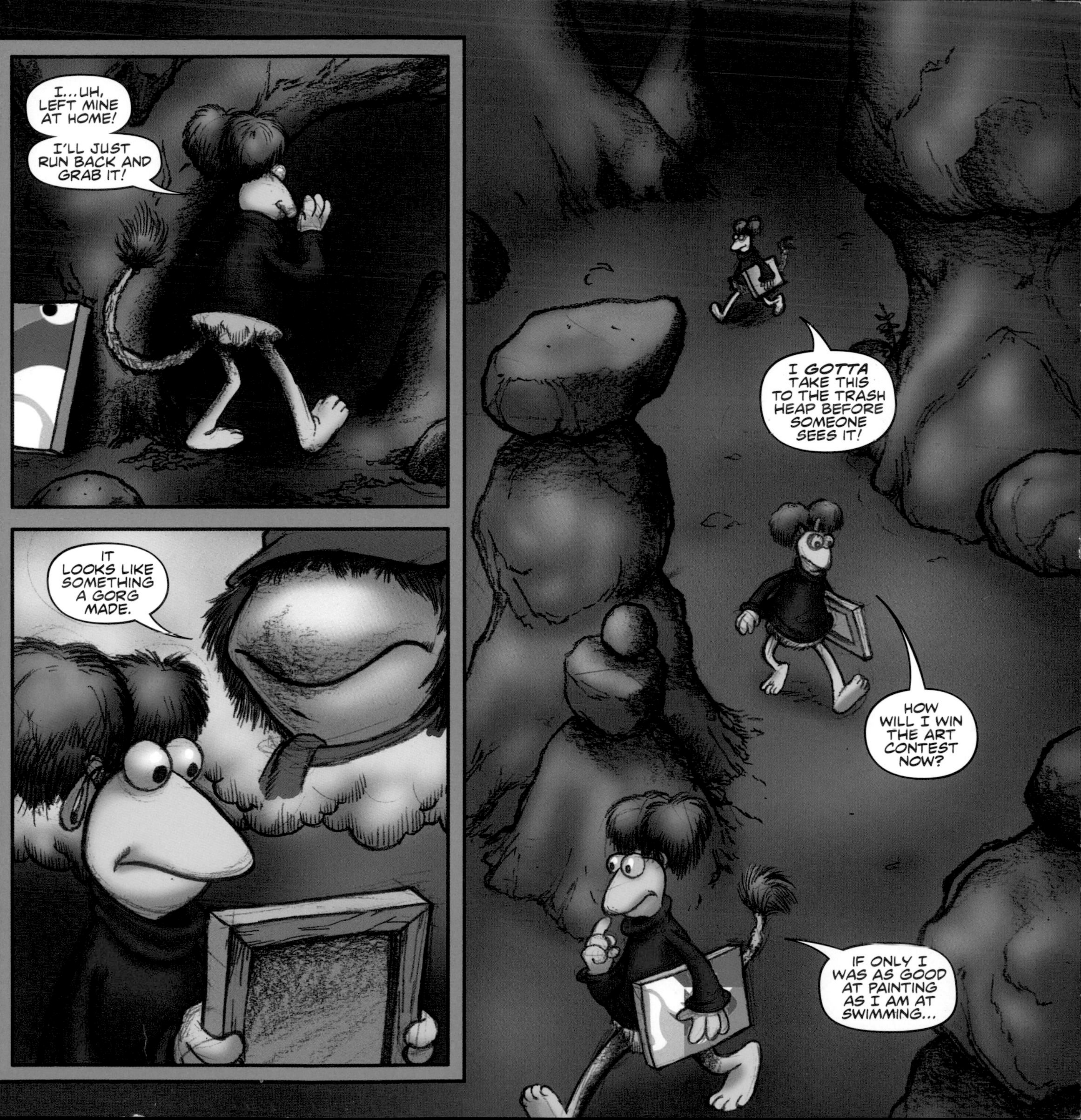
I...UH, LEFT MINE AT HOME!
I'LL JUST RUN BACK AND GRAB IT!
IT LOOKS LIKE SOMETHING A GORG MADE.
I GOTTA TAKE THIS TO THE TRASH HEAP BEFORE SOMEONE SEES IT!
HOW WILL I WIN THE ART CONTEST NOW?
IF ONLY I WAS AS GOOD AT PAINTING AS I AM AT SWIMMING...

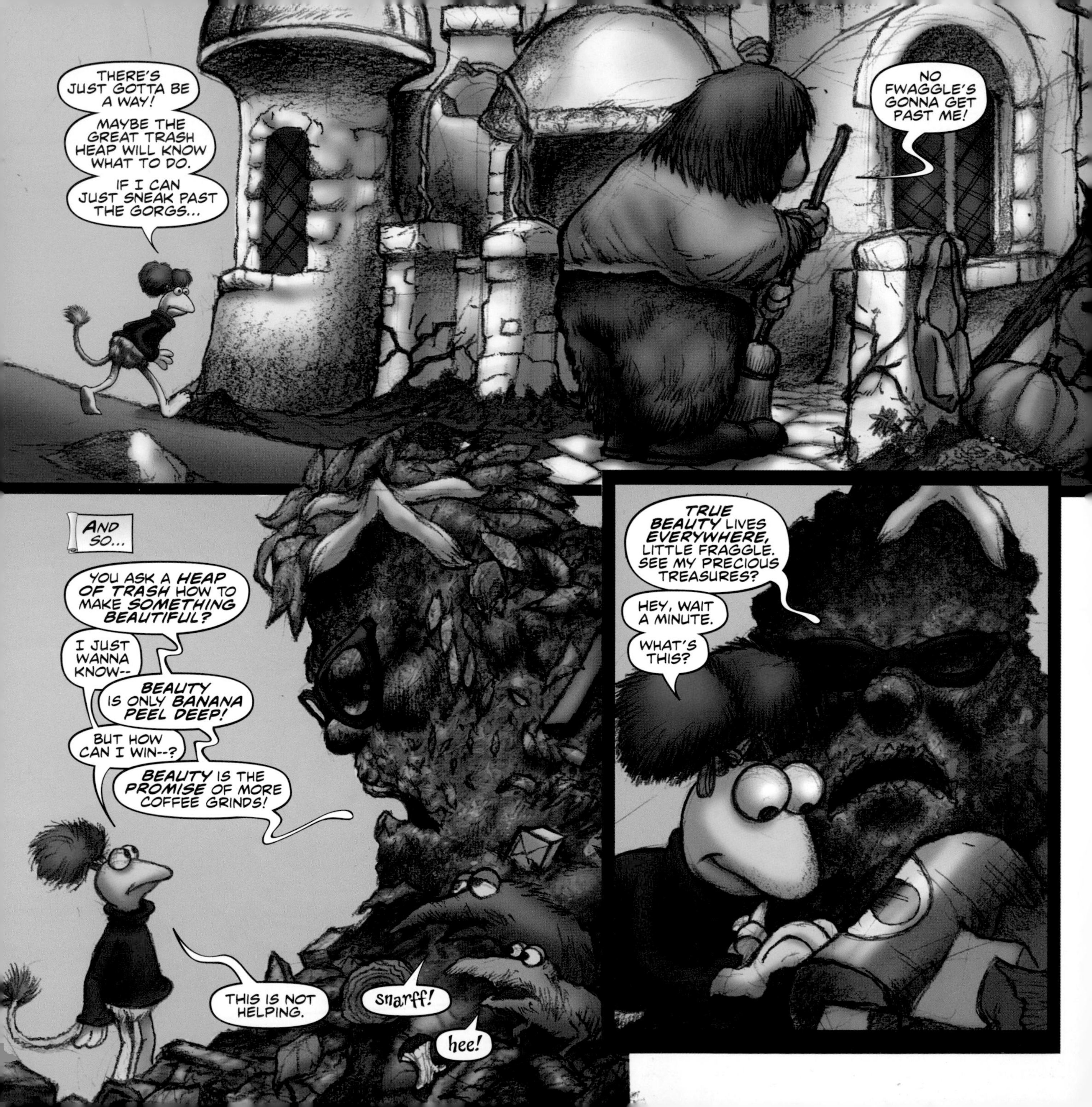
THERE'S JUST GOTTA BE A WAY!
MAYBE THE GREAT TRASH HEAP WILL KNOW WHAT TO DO.
IF I CAN JUST SNEAK PAST THE GORGS...
NO FWAGGLE'S GONNA GET PAST ME!
AND SO...
YOU ASK A HEAP OF TRASH HOW TO MAKE SOMETHING BEAUTIFUL?
I JUST WANNA KNOW--
BEAUTY IS ONLY BANANA PEEL DEEP!
BUT HOW CAN I WIN--?
BEAUTY IS THE PROMISE OF MORE COFFEE GRINDS!
THIS IS NOT HELPING.
snarff!
hee!
TRUE BEAUTY LIVES EVERYWHERE, LITTLE FRAGGLE. SEE MY PRECIOUS TREASURES?
HEY, WAIT A MINUTE.
WHAT'S THIS?

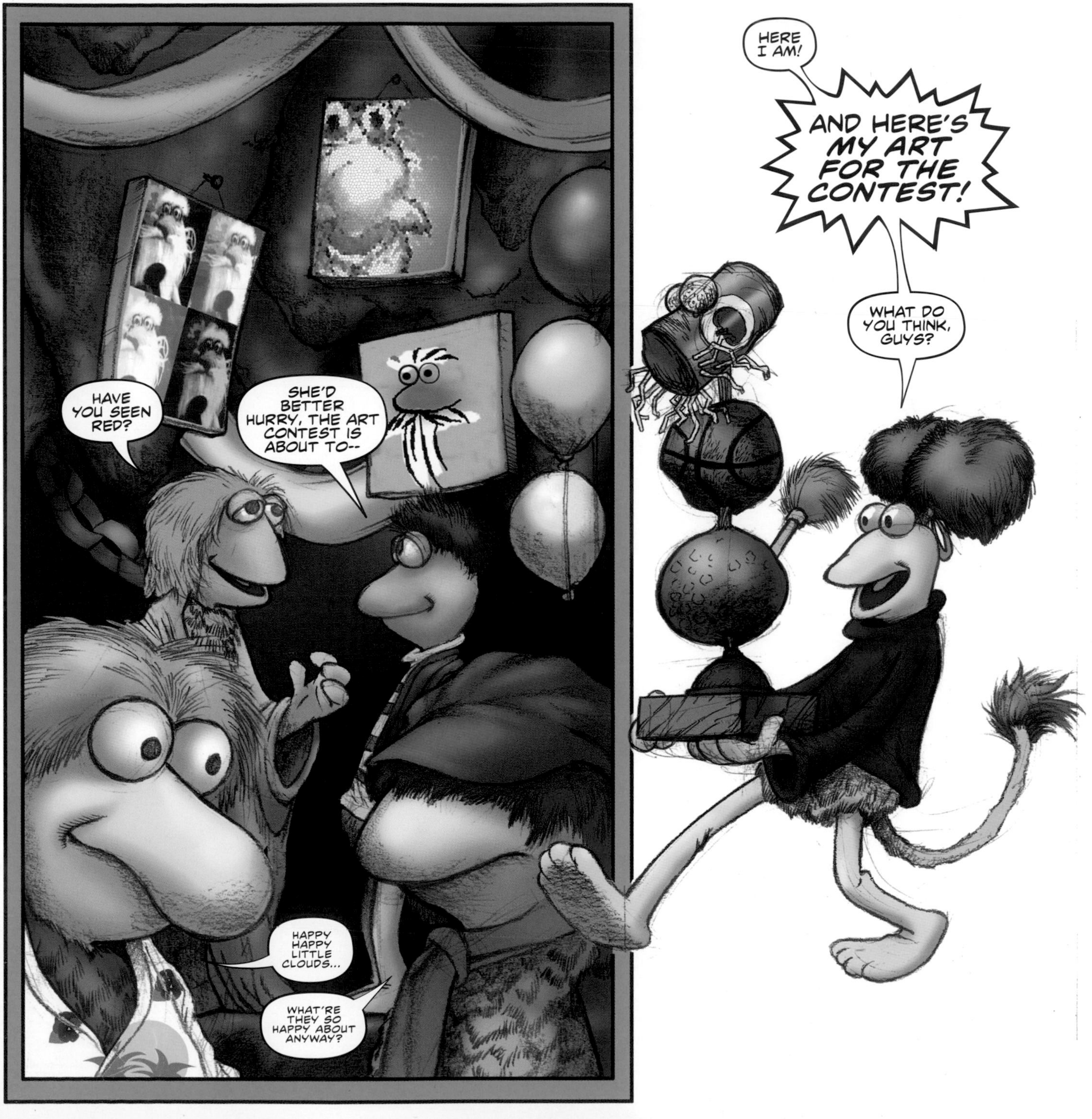
HAVE YOU SEEN RED?
SHE'D BETTER HURRY, THE ART CONTEST IS ABOUT TO--
HAPPY HAPPY LITTLE CLOUDS...
WHAT'RE THEY SO HAPPY ABOUT ANYWAY?
HERE I AM!
AND HERE'S MY ART FOR THE CONTEST!
WHAT DO YOU THINK, GUYS?

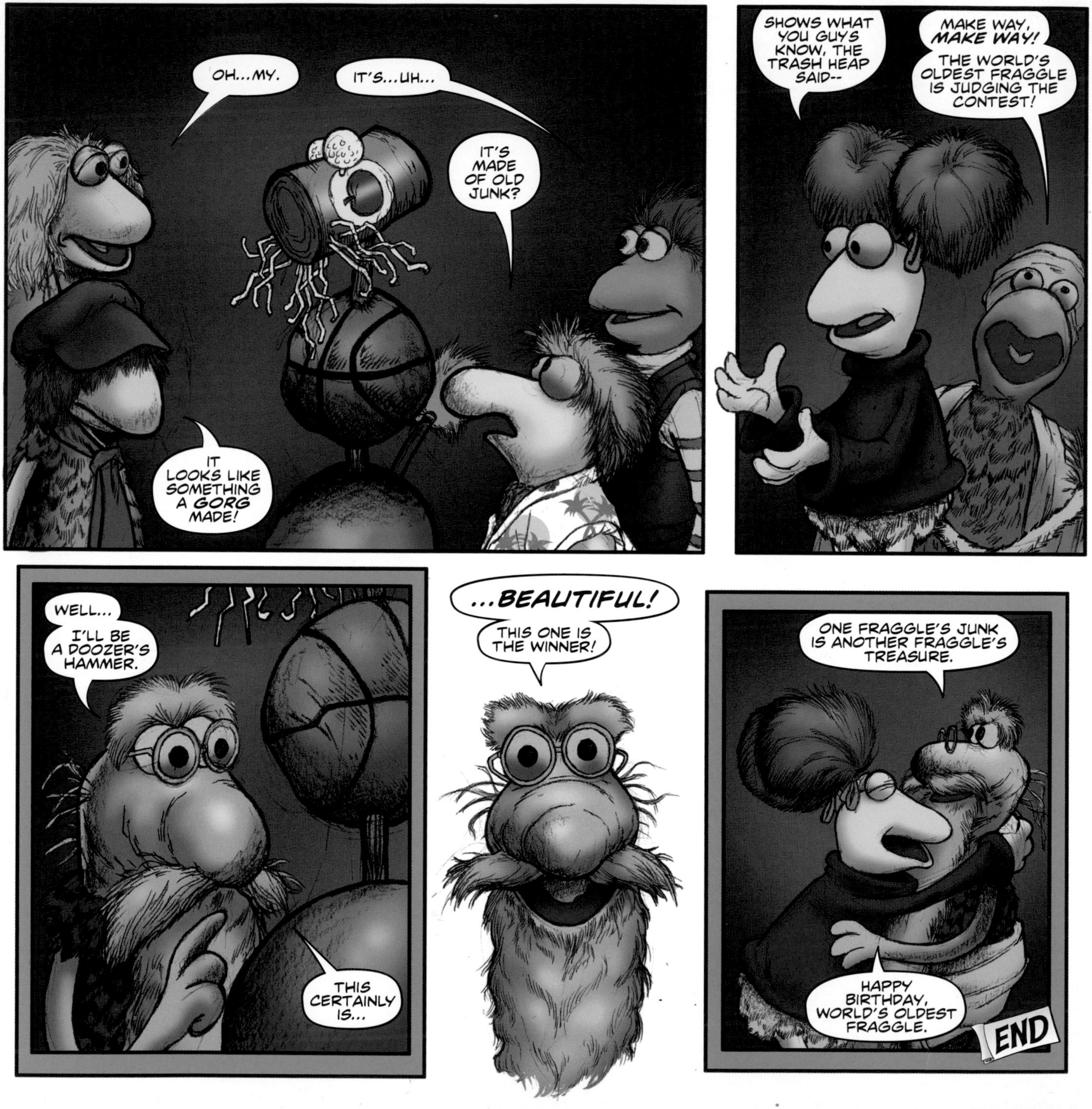
OH...MY.
IT'S...UH...
IT'S MADE OF OLD JUNK?
IT LOOKS LIKE SOMETHING A GORG MADE!
SHOWS WHAT YOU GUYS KNOW, THE TRASH HEAP SAID--
MAKE WAY, MAKE WAY!
THE WORLD'S OLDEST FRAGGLE IS JUDGING THE CONTEST!
WELL... I'LL BE A DOOZER'S HAMMER.
THIS CERTAINLY IS...
...BEAUTIFUL!
THIS ONE IS THE WINNER!
ONE FRAGGLE'S JUNK IS ANOTHER FRAGGLE'S TREASURE.
HAPPY BIRTHDAY, WORLD'S OLDEST FRAGGLE.
END

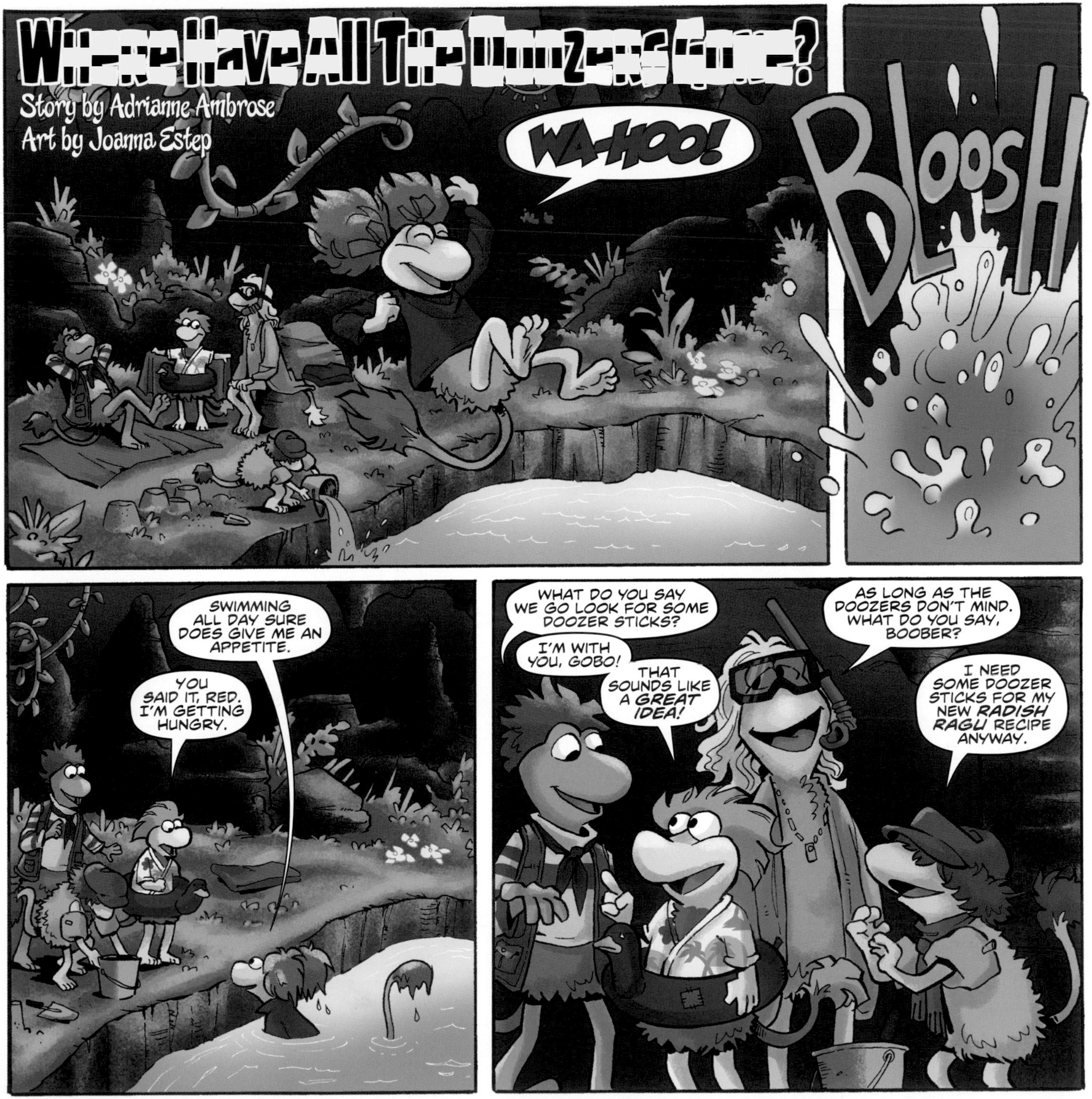
Where Have All The Doozers Gone?
Story by Adrianne Ambrose
Art by Joanna Estep
WA-HOO!
BLOOSH
SWIMMING ALL DAY SURE DOES GIVE ME AN APPETITE.
YOU SAID IT, RED. I'M GETTING HUNGRY.
WHAT DO YOU SAY WE GO LOOK FOR SOME DOOZER STICKS?
I'M WITH YOU, GOBO!
THAT SOUNDS LIKE A *GREAT IDEA!*
AS LONG AS THE DOOZERS DON'T MIND. WHAT DO YOU SAY, BOOBER?
I NEED SOME DOOZER STICKS FOR MY NEW *RADISH RAGU* RECIPE ANYWAY.

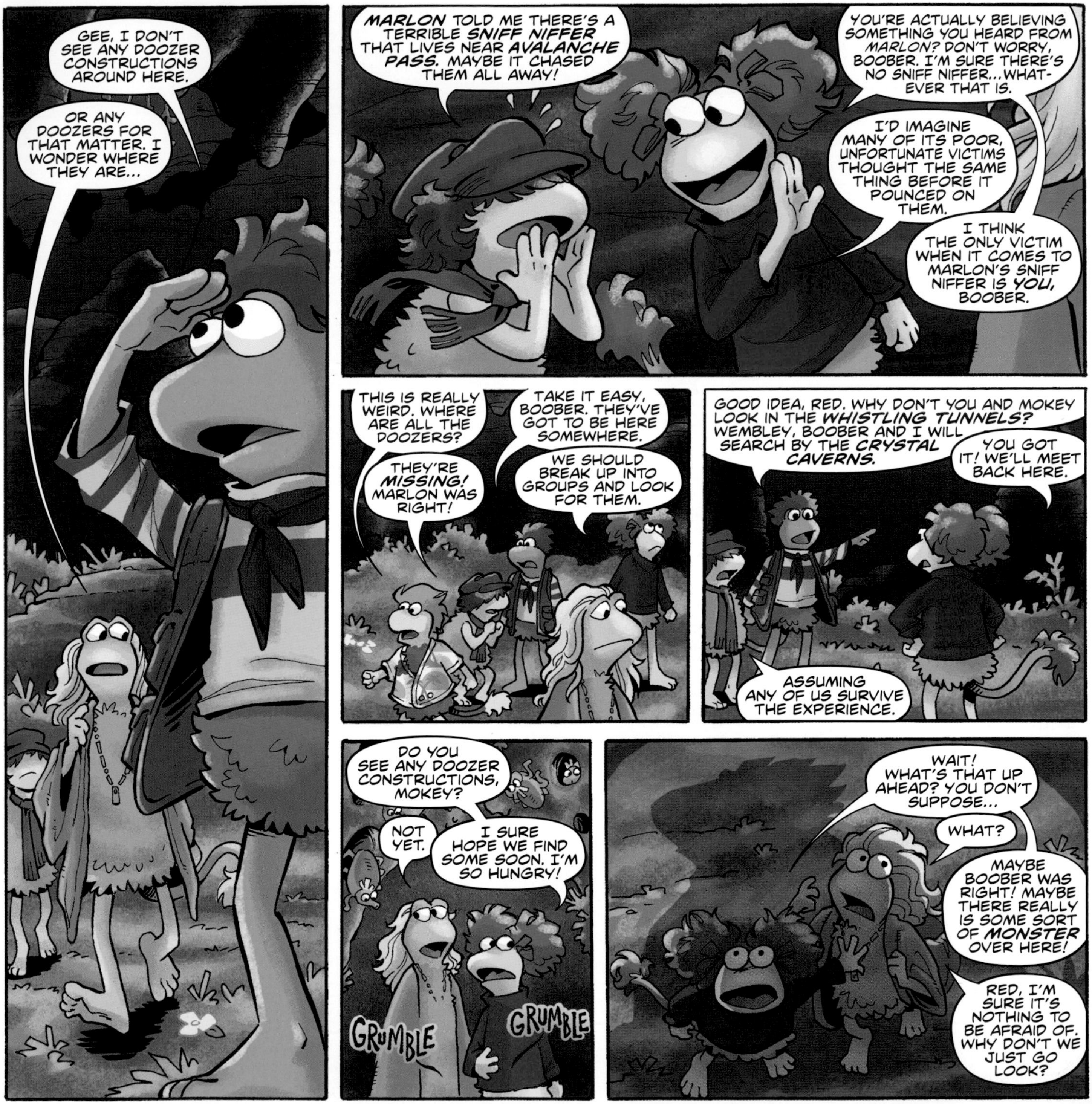
GEE, I DON'T SEE ANY DOOZER CONSTRUCTIONS AROUND HERE.
OR ANY DOOZERS FOR THAT MATTER. I WONDER WHERE THEY ARE...
MARLON TOLD ME THERE'S A TERRIBLE SNIFF NIFFER THAT LIVES NEAR AVALANCHE PASS. MAYBE IT CHASED THEM ALL AWAY!
YOU'RE ACTUALLY BELIEVING SOMETHING YOU HEARD FROM MARLON? DON'T WORRY, BOOBER. I'M SURE THERE'S NO SNIFF NIFFER...WHAT-EVER THAT IS.
I'D IMAGINE MANY OF ITS POOR, UNFORTUNATE VICTIMS THOUGHT THE SAME THING BEFORE IT POUNCED ON THEM.
I THINK THE ONLY VICTIM WHEN IT COMES TO MARLON'S SNIFF NIFFER IS YOU, BOOBER.
THIS IS REALLY WEIRD. WHERE ARE ALL THE DOOZERS?
TAKE IT EASY, BOOBER. THEY'VE GOT TO BE HERE SOMEWHERE.
THEY'RE MISSING! MARLON WAS RIGHT!
WE SHOULD BREAK UP INTO GROUPS AND LOOK FOR THEM.
GOOD IDEA, RED. WHY DON'T YOU AND MOKEY LOOK IN THE WHISTLING TUNNELS? WEMBLEY, BOOBER AND I WILL SEARCH BY THE CRYSTAL CAVERNS.
YOU GOT IT! WE'LL MEET BACK HERE.
ASSUMING ANY OF US SURVIVE THE EXPERIENCE.
DO YOU SEE ANY DOOZER CONSTRUCTIONS, MOKEY?
NOT YET.
I SURE HOPE WE FIND SOME SOON. I'M SO HUNGRY!
GRUMBLE
GRUMBLE
WAIT! WHAT'S THAT UP AHEAD? YOU DON'T SUPPOSE...
WHAT?
MAYBE BOOBER WAS RIGHT! MAYBE THERE REALLY IS SOME SORT OF MONSTER OVER HERE!
RED, I'M SURE IT'S NOTHING TO BE AFRAID OF. WHY DON'T WE JUST GO LOOK?

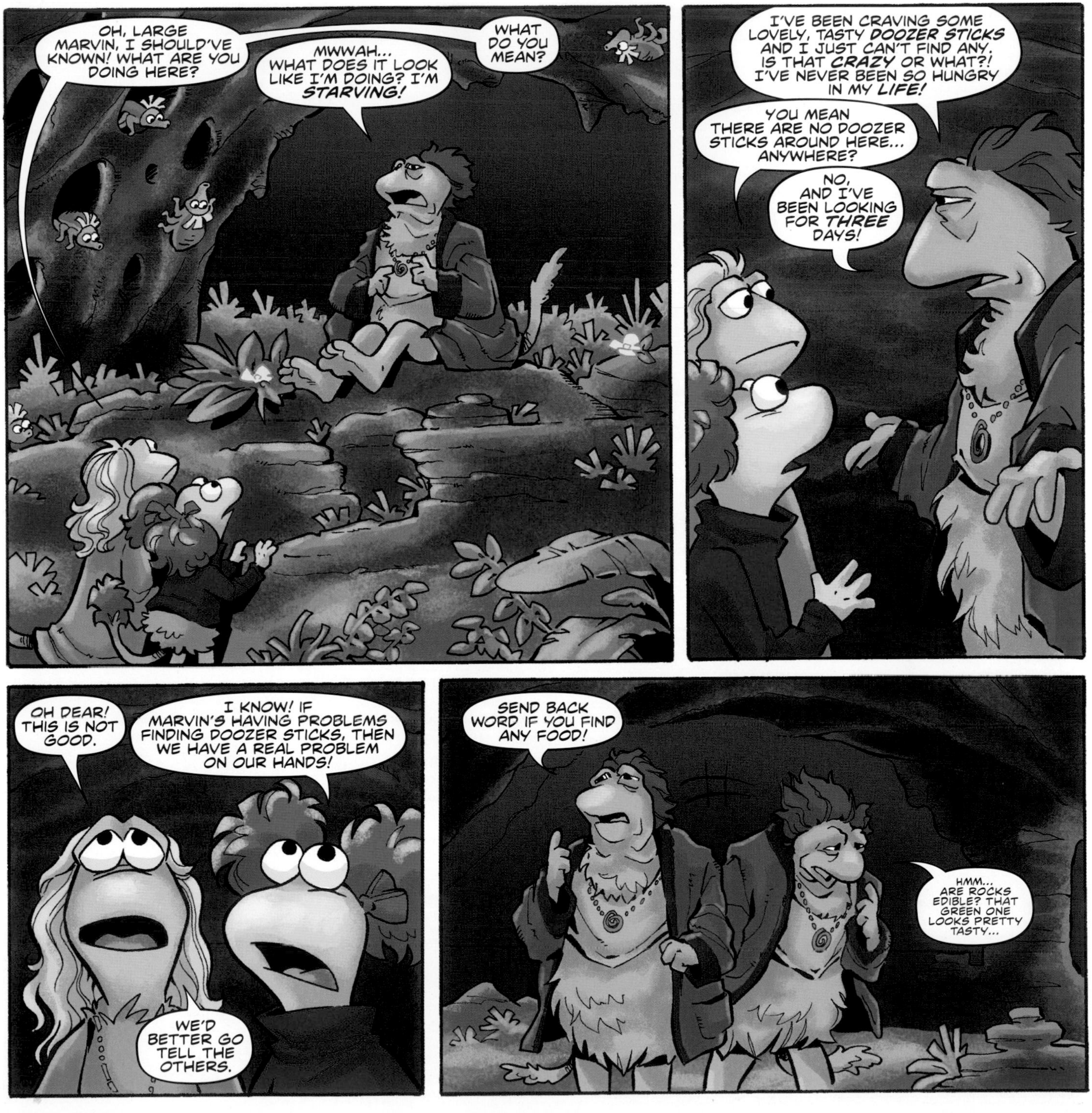
OH, LARGE MARVIN, I SHOULD'VE KNOWN! WHAT ARE YOU DOING HERE?
MWWAH... WHAT DOES IT LOOK LIKE I'M DOING? I'M STARVING!
WHAT DO YOU MEAN?
I'VE BEEN CRAVING SOME LOVELY, TASTY DOOZER STICKS AND I JUST CAN'T FIND ANY. IS THAT CRAZY OR WHAT?! I'VE NEVER BEEN SO HUNGRY IN MY LIFE!
YOU MEAN THERE ARE NO DOOZER STICKS AROUND HERE... ANYWHERE?
NO, AND I'VE BEEN LOOKING FOR THREE DAYS!
OH DEAR! THIS IS NOT GOOD.
I KNOW! IF MARVIN'S HAVING PROBLEMS FINDING DOOZER STICKS, THEN WE HAVE A REAL PROBLEM ON OUR HANDS!
WE'D BETTER GO TELL THE OTHERS.
SEND BACK WORD IF YOU FIND ANY FOOD!
HMM... ARE ROCKS EDIBLE? THAT GREEN ONE LOOKS PRETTY TASTY...

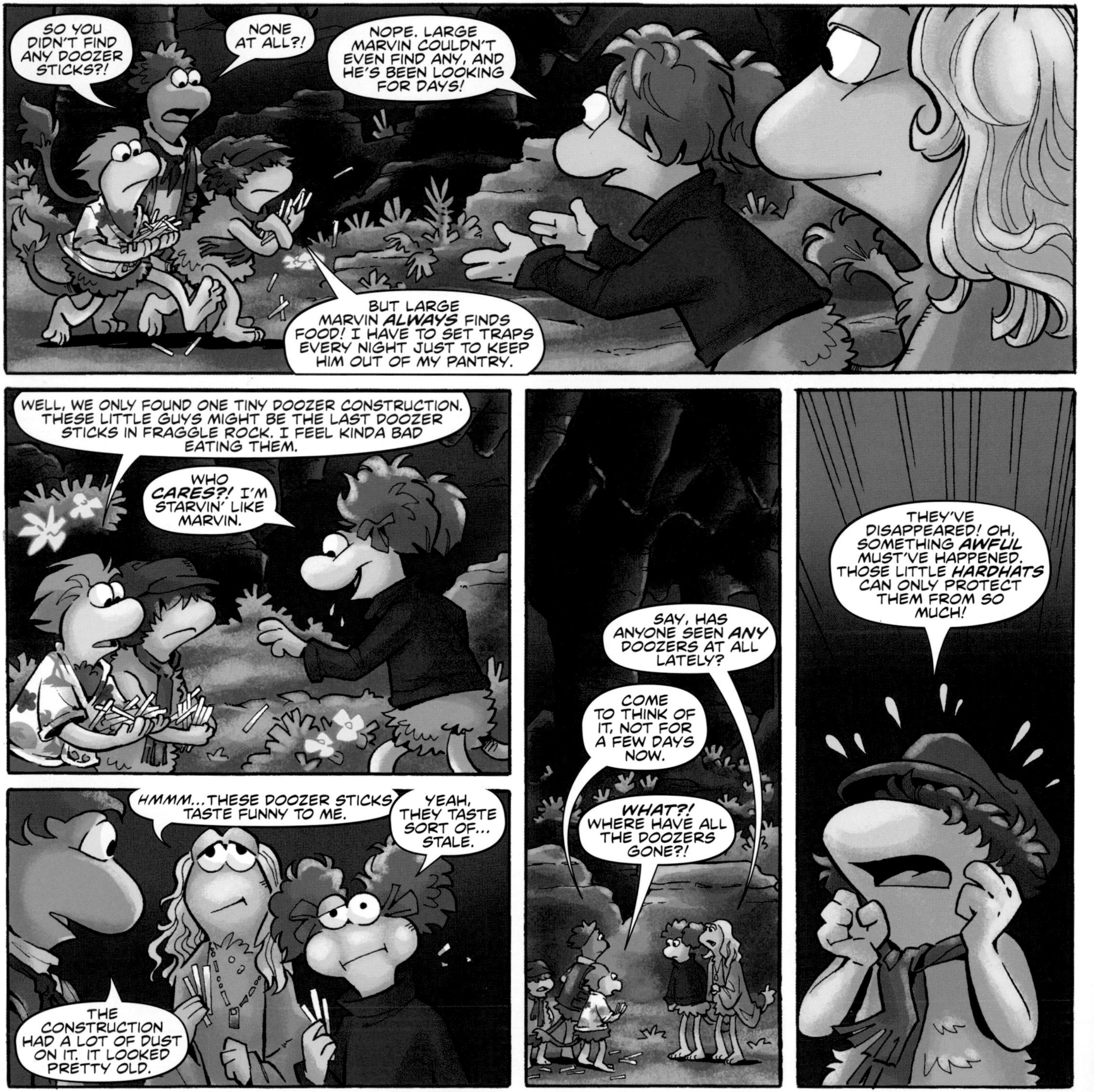
SO YOU DIDN'T FIND ANY DOOZER STICKS?!
NONE AT ALL?!
NOPE. LARGE MARVIN COULDN'T EVEN FIND ANY, AND HE'S BEEN LOOKING FOR DAYS!
BUT LARGE MARVIN ALWAYS FINDS FOOD! I HAVE TO SET TRAPS EVERY NIGHT JUST TO KEEP HIM OUT OF MY PANTRY.
WELL, WE ONLY FOUND ONE TINY DOOZER CONSTRUCTION. THESE LITTLE GUYS MIGHT BE THE LAST DOOZER STICKS IN FRAGGLE ROCK. I FEEL KINDA BAD EATING THEM.
WHO CARES?! I'M STARVIN' LIKE MARVIN.
HMMM... THESE DOOZER STICKS TASTE FUNNY TO ME.
YEAH, THEY TASTE SORT OF... STALE.
THE CONSTRUCTION HAD A LOT OF DUST ON IT. IT LOOKED PRETTY OLD.
SAY, HAS ANYONE SEEN ANY DOOZERS AT ALL LATELY?
COME TO THINK OF IT, NOT FOR A FEW DAYS NOW.
WHAT?! WHERE HAVE ALL THE DOOZERS GONE?!
THEY'VE DISAPPEARED! OH, SOMETHING AWFUL MUST'VE HAPPENED. THOSE LITTLE HARDHATS CAN ONLY PROTECT THEM FROM SO MUCH!

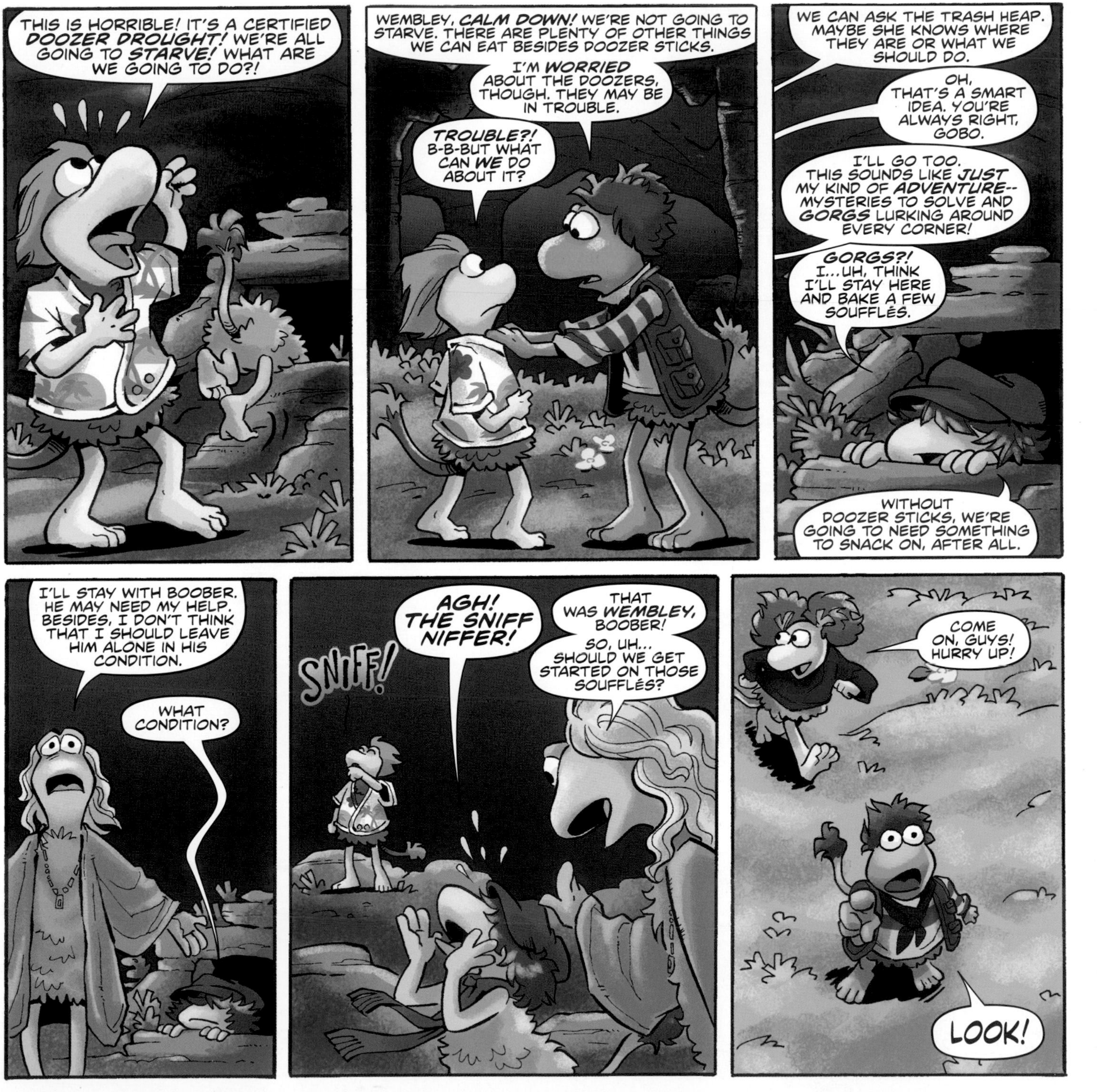
THIS IS HORRIBLE! IT'S A CERTIFIED DOOZER DROUGHT! WE'RE ALL GOING TO STARVE! WHAT ARE WE GOING TO DO?!
WEMBLEY, CALM DOWN! WE'RE NOT GOING TO STARVE. THERE ARE PLENTY OF OTHER THINGS WE CAN EAT BESIDES DOOZER STICKS.
I'M WORRIED ABOUT THE DOOZERS, THOUGH. THEY MAY BE IN TROUBLE.
TROUBLE?! B-B-BUT WHAT CAN WE DO ABOUT IT?
WE CAN ASK THE TRASH HEAP. MAYBE SHE KNOWS WHERE THEY ARE OR WHAT WE SHOULD DO.
OH, THAT'S A SMART IDEA. YOU'RE ALWAYS RIGHT, GOBO.
I'LL GO TOO. THIS SOUNDS LIKE JUST MY KIND OF ADVENTURE-- MYSTERIES TO SOLVE AND GORGS LURKING AROUND EVERY CORNER!
GORGS?! I...UH, THINK I'LL STAY HERE AND BAKE A FEW SOUFFLÉS.
WITHOUT DOOZER STICKS, WE'RE GOING TO NEED SOMETHING TO SNACK ON, AFTER ALL.
I'LL STAY WITH BOOBER. HE MAY NEED MY HELP. BESIDES, I DON'T THINK THAT I SHOULD LEAVE HIM ALONE IN HIS CONDITION.
WHAT CONDITION?
SNIFF!
AGH! THE SNIFF NIFFER!
THAT WAS WEMBLEY, BOOBER!
SO, UH... SHOULD WE GET STARTED ON THOSE SOUFFLÉS?
COME ON, GUYS! HURRY UP!
LOOK!

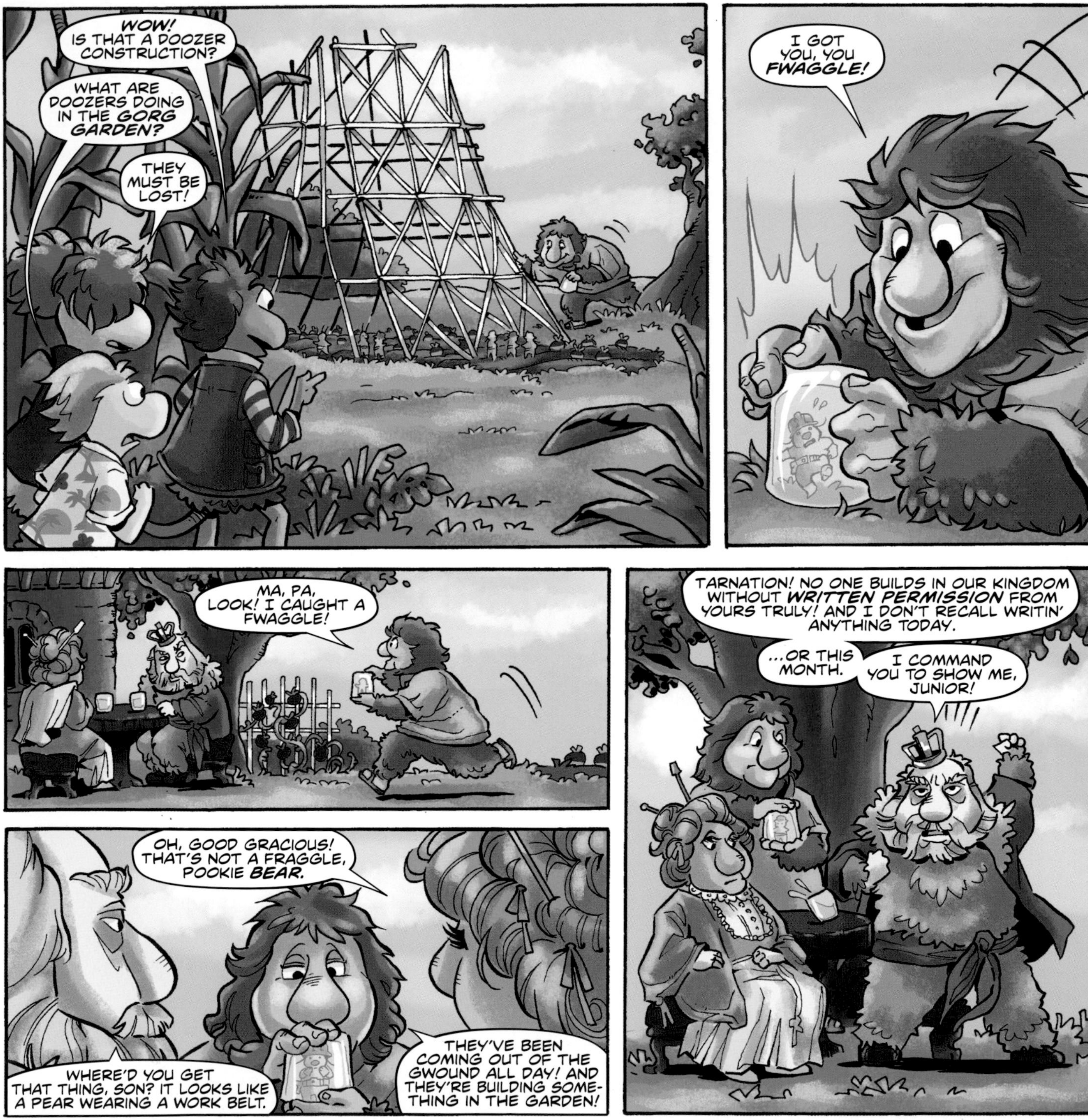
WOW! IS THAT A DOOZER CONSTRUCTION?
WHAT ARE DOOZERS DOING IN THE GORG GARDEN?
THEY MUST BE LOST!
I GOT YOU, YOU FWAGGLE!
MA, PA, LOOK! I CAUGHT A FWAGGLE!
OH, GOOD GRACIOUS! THAT'S NOT A FRAGGLE, POOKIE BEAR.
WHERE'D YOU GET THAT THING, SON? IT LOOKS LIKE A PEAR WEARING A WORK BELT.
THEY'VE BEEN COMING OUT OF THE GWOUND ALL DAY! AND THEY'RE BUILDING SOME-THING IN THE GARDEN!
TARNATION! NO ONE BUILDS IN OUR KINGDOM WITHOUT WRITTEN PERMISSION FROM YOURS TRULY! AND I DON'T RECALL WRITIN' ANYTHING TODAY.
...OR THIS MONTH.
I COMMAND YOU TO SHOW ME, JUNIOR!

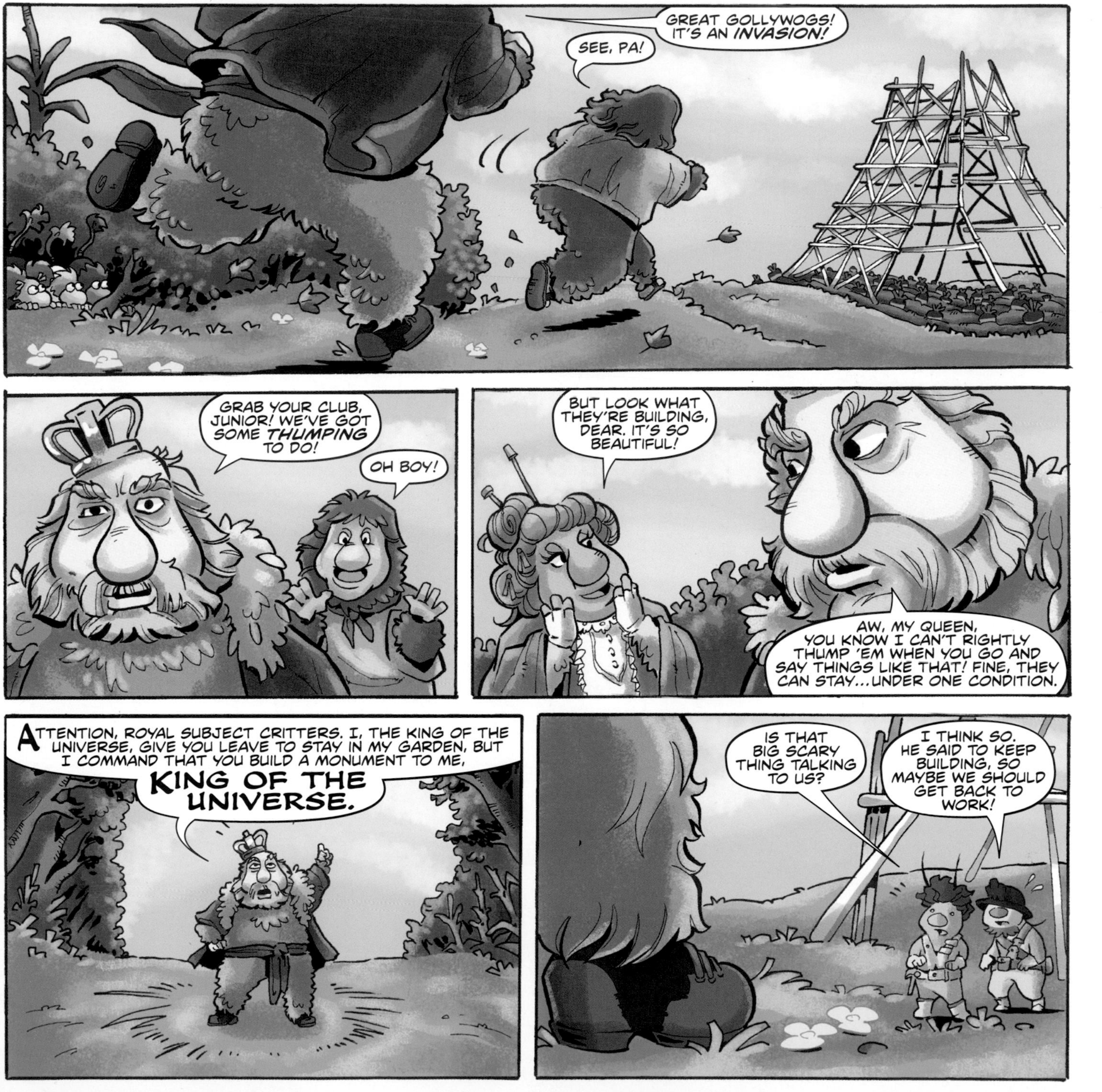
SEE, PA!
GREAT GOLLYWOGS! IT'S AN *INVASION!*
GRAB YOUR CLUB, JUNIOR! WE'VE GOT SOME *THUMPING* TO DO!
OH BOY!
BUT LOOK WHAT THEY'RE BUILDING, DEAR. IT'S SO BEAUTIFUL!
AW, MY QUEEN, YOU KNOW I CAN'T RIGHTLY THUMP 'EM WHEN YOU GO AND SAY THINGS LIKE THAT! FINE, THEY CAN STAY...UNDER ONE CONDITION.
ATTENTION, ROYAL SUBJECT CRITTERS. I, THE KING OF THE UNIVERSE, GIVE YOU LEAVE TO STAY IN MY GARDEN, BUT I COMMAND THAT YOU BUILD A MONUMENT TO ME, **KING OF THE UNIVERSE.**
IS THAT BIG SCARY THING TALKING TO US?
I THINK SO. HE SAID TO KEEP BUILDING, SO MAYBE WE SHOULD GET BACK TO WORK!

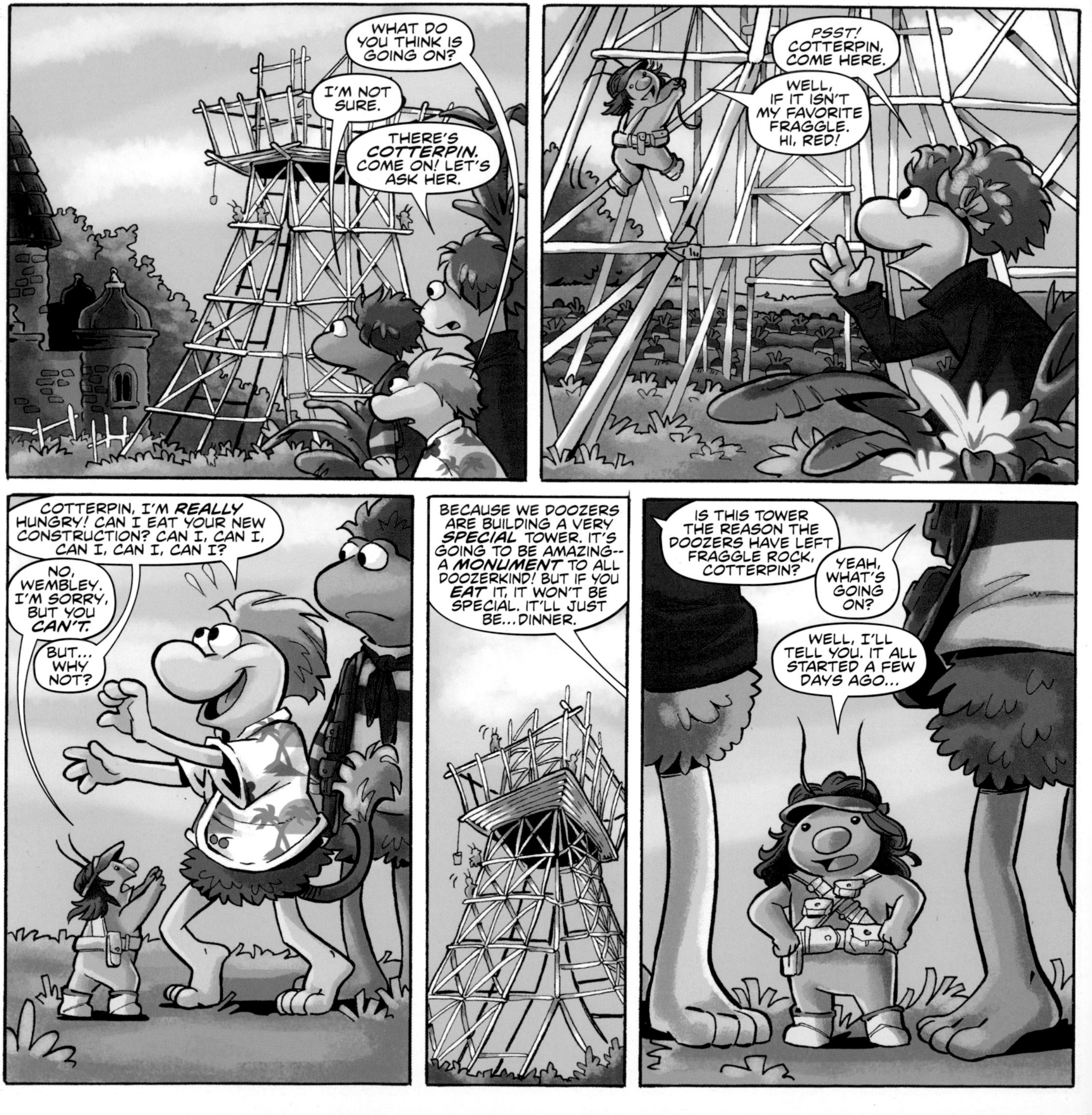
WHAT DO YOU THINK IS GOING ON?
I'M NOT SURE.
THERE'S COTTERPIN. COME ON! LET'S ASK HER.
PSST! COTTERPIN, COME HERE.
WELL, IF IT ISN'T MY FAVORITE FRAGGLE. HI, RED!
COTTERPIN, I'M REALLY HUNGRY! CAN I EAT YOUR NEW CONSTRUCTION? CAN I, CAN I, CAN I, CAN I, CAN I?
NO, WEMBLEY. I'M SORRY, BUT YOU CAN'T.
BUT... WHY NOT?
BECAUSE WE DOOZERS ARE BUILDING A VERY SPECIAL TOWER. IT'S GOING TO BE AMAZING-- A MONUMENT TO ALL DOOZERKIND! BUT IF YOU EAT IT, IT WON'T BE SPECIAL. IT'LL JUST BE... DINNER.
IS THIS TOWER THE REASON THE DOOZERS HAVE LEFT FRAGGLE ROCK, COTTERPIN?
YEAH, WHAT'S GOING ON?
WELL, I'LL TELL YOU. IT ALL STARTED A FEW DAYS AGO...

TOMORROW, WE'LL START WORK ON A NEW TOWER.

ANOTHER ONE? GEE, THAT'LL BE THE *THIRD* TOWER THIS WEEK. CAN'T WE EVER DO ANYTHING *NEW*?

BUILDING TOWERS IS A MIGHTY FINE THING, AND THIS ONE WILL BE PARTICULARLY FINE.

WHY? WHAT MAKES THIS ONE SO SPECIAL?

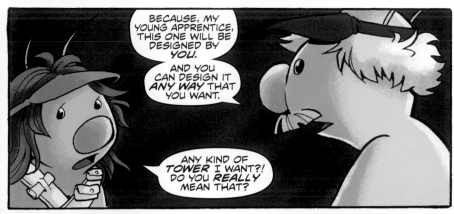

BECAUSE, MY YOUNG APPRENTICE, THIS ONE WILL BE DESIGNED BY *YOU*.

AND YOU CAN DESIGN IT *ANY WAY* THAT YOU WANT.

ANY KIND OF *TOWER* I WANT?! DO YOU *REALLY* MEAN THAT?

WELL, THEN I'M GOING TO DESIGN THE *BIGGEST, TALLEST* TOWER FRAGGLE ROCK HAS *EVER* SEEN! I WANT TO SHOW THE WORLD HOW *SPECTACULAR* OUR CONSTRUCTIONS CAN BE WHEN WE LET OUR *IMAGINATIONS* RUN WILD! AND I WANT--

SLOW DOWN, COTTERPIN. YOU KNOW THAT AS *SOON* AS THAT TOWER GETS MORE THAN A *FEW STORIES* TALL, THE FRAGGLES ARE GOING TO EAT IT.

WELL, WE WON'T LET THEM! NOT THIS TOWER!

HEH HEH...IF ANYONE COULD KEEP THEM FROM DINING ON OUR WORK, I HAVE *NO* DOUBT IT WOULD BE *YOU*. BUT WHY WOULD WE DO THAT?

THE FRAGGLES ENJOY EATING OUR CONSTRUCTIONS, AND WE ENJOY BUILDING FOR THEM. IT'S A GOOD ARRANGEMENT! WITHOUT IT, WE WOULD HAVE RUN OUT OF *ROOM* TO BUILD AGES AGO.

I KNOW, BUT FOR ONCE I'D LIKE TO SEE WHAT WE CAN CREATE WHEN WE'RE BUILDING SOMETHING ENTIRELY FOR OURSELVES. HAVEN'T YOU EVER WONDERED ABOUT THAT?

MAYBE WHEN I WAS A BIT YOUNGER...BACK WHEN I HAD TIME FOR THINKING SUCH THINGS.

≷SIGH≷...WELL, I'M SURE THE FRAGGLES WON'T MIND LEAVING ONE OF OUR TOWERS ALONE IF WE ASKED THEM TO.

BUT THERE'S ONLY SO MUCH ROOM IN FRAGGLE ROCK. WHERE DO YOU INTEND TO BUILD IT?

I DON'T KNOW, BUT I'M GOING TO START LOOKING *RIGHT NOW*!

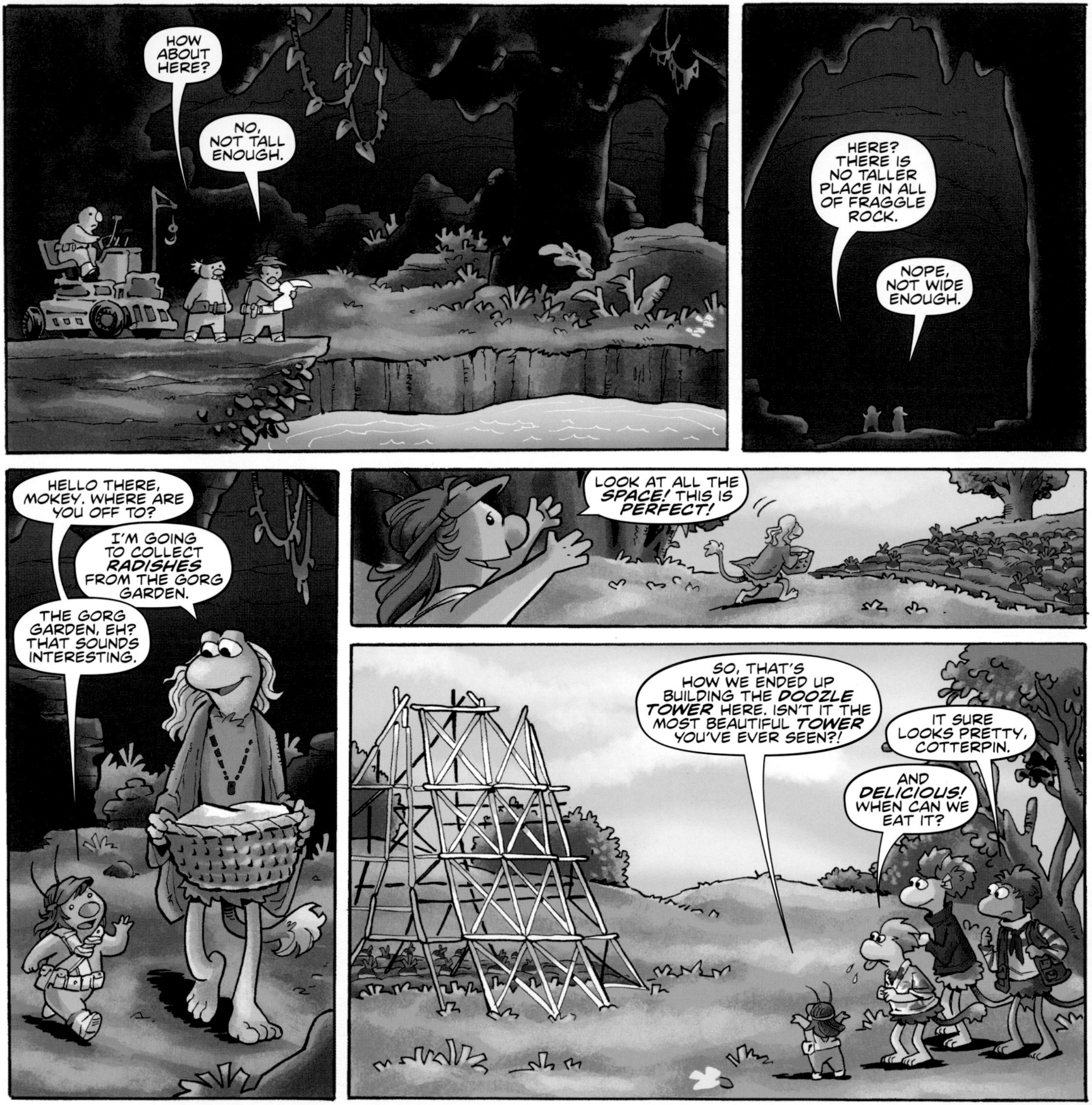
HOW ABOUT HERE?
NO, NOT TALL ENOUGH.
HERE? THERE IS NO TALLER PLACE IN ALL OF FRAGGLE ROCK.
NOPE, NOT WIDE ENOUGH.
HELLO THERE, MOKEY. WHERE ARE YOU OFF TO?
I'M GOING TO COLLECT RADISHES FROM THE GORG GARDEN.
THE GORG GARDEN, EH? THAT SOUNDS INTERESTING.
LOOK AT ALL THE SPACE! THIS IS PERFECT!
SO, THAT'S HOW WE ENDED UP BUILDING THE DOOZLE TOWER HERE. ISN'T IT THE MOST BEAUTIFUL TOWER YOU'VE EVER SEEN?!
IT SURE LOOKS PRETTY, COTTERPIN.
AND DELICIOUS! WHEN CAN WE EAT IT?

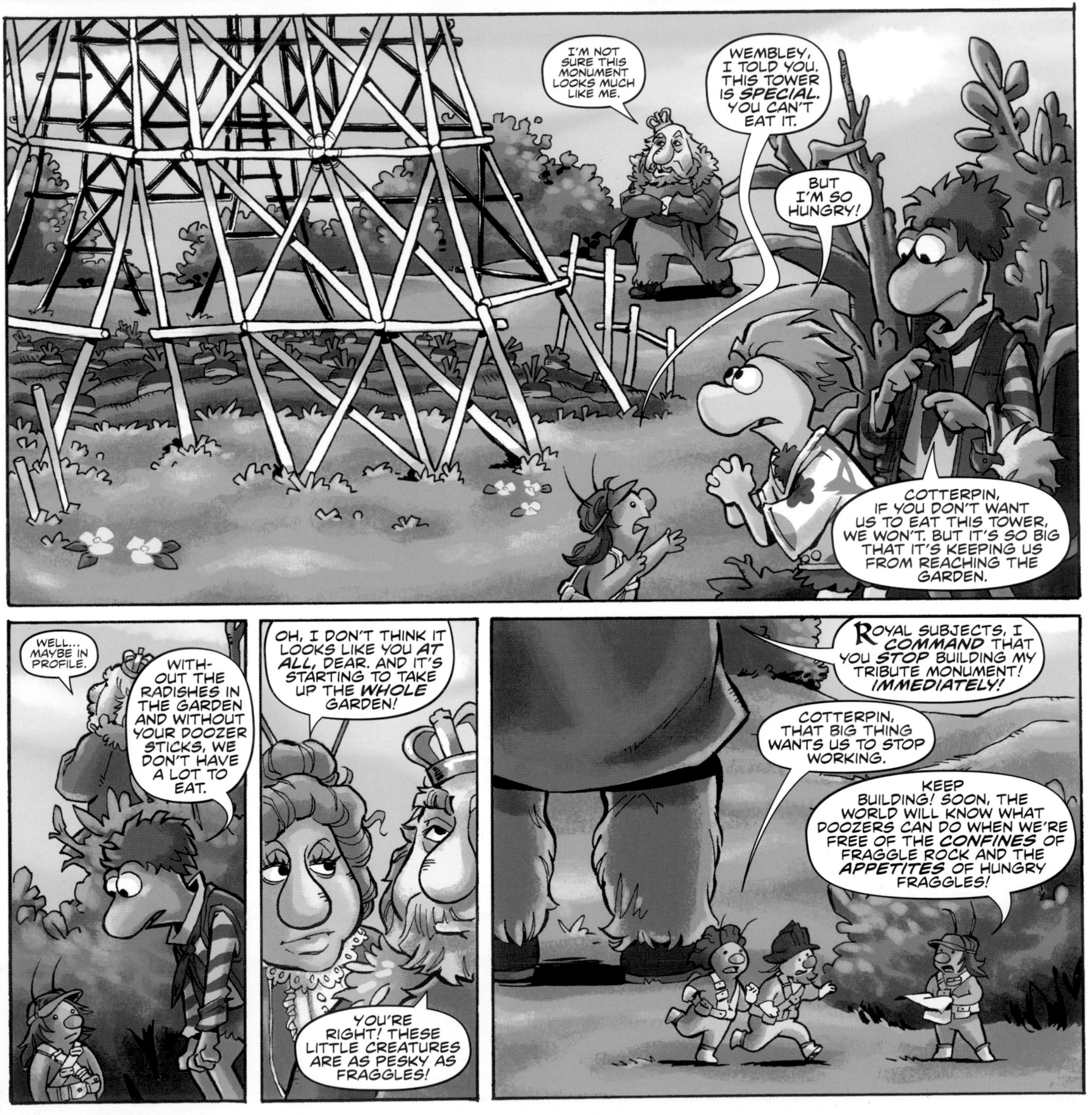
I'M NOT SURE THIS MONUMENT LOOKS MUCH LIKE ME.
WEMBLEY, I TOLD YOU. THIS TOWER IS SPECIAL. YOU CAN'T EAT IT.
BUT I'M SO HUNGRY!
COTTERPIN, IF YOU DON'T WANT US TO EAT THIS TOWER, WE WON'T. BUT IT'S SO BIG THAT IT'S KEEPING US FROM REACHING THE GARDEN.
WELL... MAYBE IN PROFILE.
WITH-OUT THE RADISHES IN THE GARDEN AND WITHOUT YOUR DOOZER STICKS, WE DON'T HAVE A LOT TO EAT.
OH, I DON'T THINK IT LOOKS LIKE YOU AT ALL, DEAR. AND IT'S STARTING TO TAKE UP THE WHOLE GARDEN!
YOU'RE RIGHT! THESE LITTLE CREATURES ARE AS PESKY AS FRAGGLES!
ROYAL SUBJECTS, I COMMAND THAT YOU STOP BUILDING MY TRIBUTE MONUMENT! IMMEDIATELY!
COTTERPIN, THAT BIG THING WANTS US TO STOP WORKING.
KEEP BUILDING! SOON, THE WORLD WILL KNOW WHAT DOOZERS CAN DO WHEN WE'RE FREE OF THE CONFINES OF FRAGGLE ROCK AND THE APPETITES OF HUNGRY FRAGGLES!

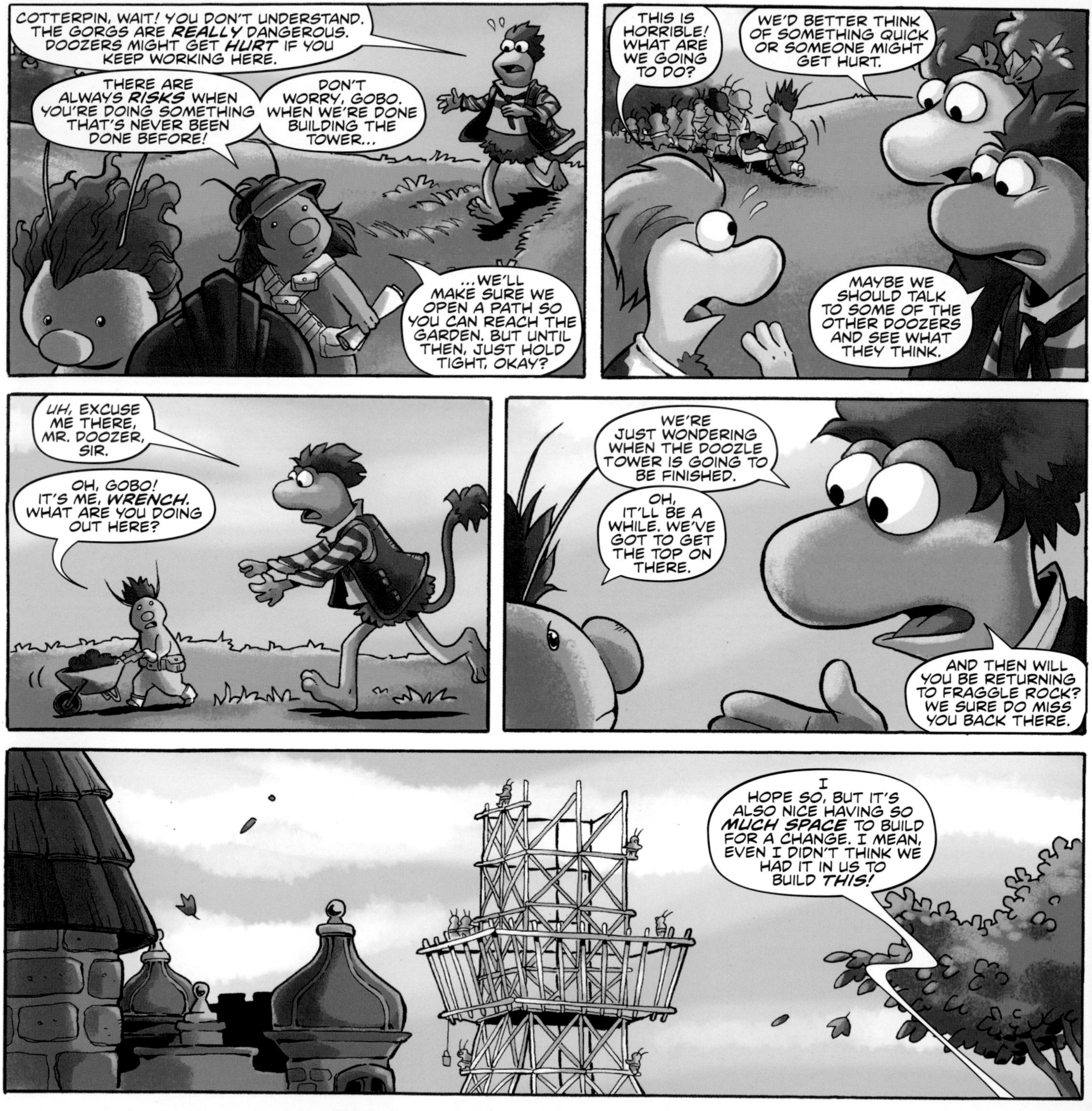

COTTERPIN, WAIT! YOU DON'T UNDERSTAND. THE GORGS ARE REALLY DANGEROUS. DOOZERS MIGHT GET HURT IF YOU KEEP WORKING HERE.
THERE ARE ALWAYS RISKS WHEN YOU'RE DOING SOMETHING THAT'S NEVER BEEN DONE BEFORE!
DON'T WORRY, GOBO. WHEN WE'RE DONE BUILDING THE TOWER...
...WE'LL MAKE SURE WE OPEN A PATH SO YOU CAN REACH THE GARDEN. BUT UNTIL THEN, JUST HOLD TIGHT, OKAY?
THIS IS HORRIBLE! WHAT ARE WE GOING TO DO?
WE'D BETTER THINK OF SOMETHING QUICK OR SOMEONE MIGHT GET HURT.
MAYBE WE SHOULD TALK TO SOME OF THE OTHER DOOZERS AND SEE WHAT THEY THINK.
UH, EXCUSE ME THERE, MR. DOOZER, SIR.
OH, GOBO! IT'S ME, WRENCH. WHAT ARE YOU DOING OUT HERE?
WE'RE JUST WONDERING WHEN THE DOOZLE TOWER IS GOING TO BE FINISHED.
OH, IT'LL BE A WHILE. WE'VE GOT TO GET THE TOP ON THERE.
AND THEN WILL YOU BE RETURNING TO FRAGGLE ROCK? WE SURE DO MISS YOU BACK THERE.
I HOPE SO, BUT IT'S ALSO NICE HAVING SO MUCH SPACE TO BUILD FOR A CHANGE. I MEAN, EVEN I DIDN'T THINK WE HAD IT IN US TO BUILD THIS!

KEEP BUILDING! WE'RE SO CLOSE TO FINISHING, I CAN ALMOST *TASTE* IT!

I THINK WE USED MORE DOOZER STICKS IN THIS SINGLE WALL THAN WE DID IN OUR ENTIRE LAST CONSTRUCTION.

YEAH, BUT WHO'S COUNTING?

UH... YOU *HAVEN'T* BEEN COUNTING, RIGHT?

WHOA! FROM DOWN HERE IT LOOKS LIKE IT GOES ON FOREVER!

IT'S IMPRESSIVE, BUT I HAVE TO SAY, I WISH THERE WERE MORE FRAGGLES HERE TO APPRECIATE IT.

OH... I'M SO HUNGRY. ARE YOU *SURE* WE CAN'T EAT THE TOWER?

COTTERPIN ASKED US NOT TO, WEMBLEY, AND WE DON'T EAT DOOZER CONSTRUCTIONS WITHOUT THEIR PERMISSION.

YOU SOUND LIKE MOKEY.

RUMBLE RUMBLE.

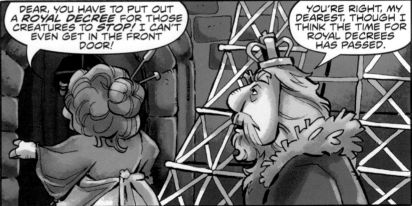

DEAR, YOU HAVE TO PUT OUT A *ROYAL DECREE* FOR THOSE CREATURES TO *STOP!* I CAN'T EVEN GET IN THE FRONT DOOR!

YOU'RE RIGHT, MY DEAREST, THOUGH I THINK THE TIME FOR ROYAL DECREES HAS PASSED.

JUNIOR! IT'S *THUMPING TIME!*

THUMPING TIME, NOT THUMPING TIME, NOW IT'S THUMPING TIME AGAIN. *SHEESH!* KING DADDY SURE CAN BE INDECISIVE.

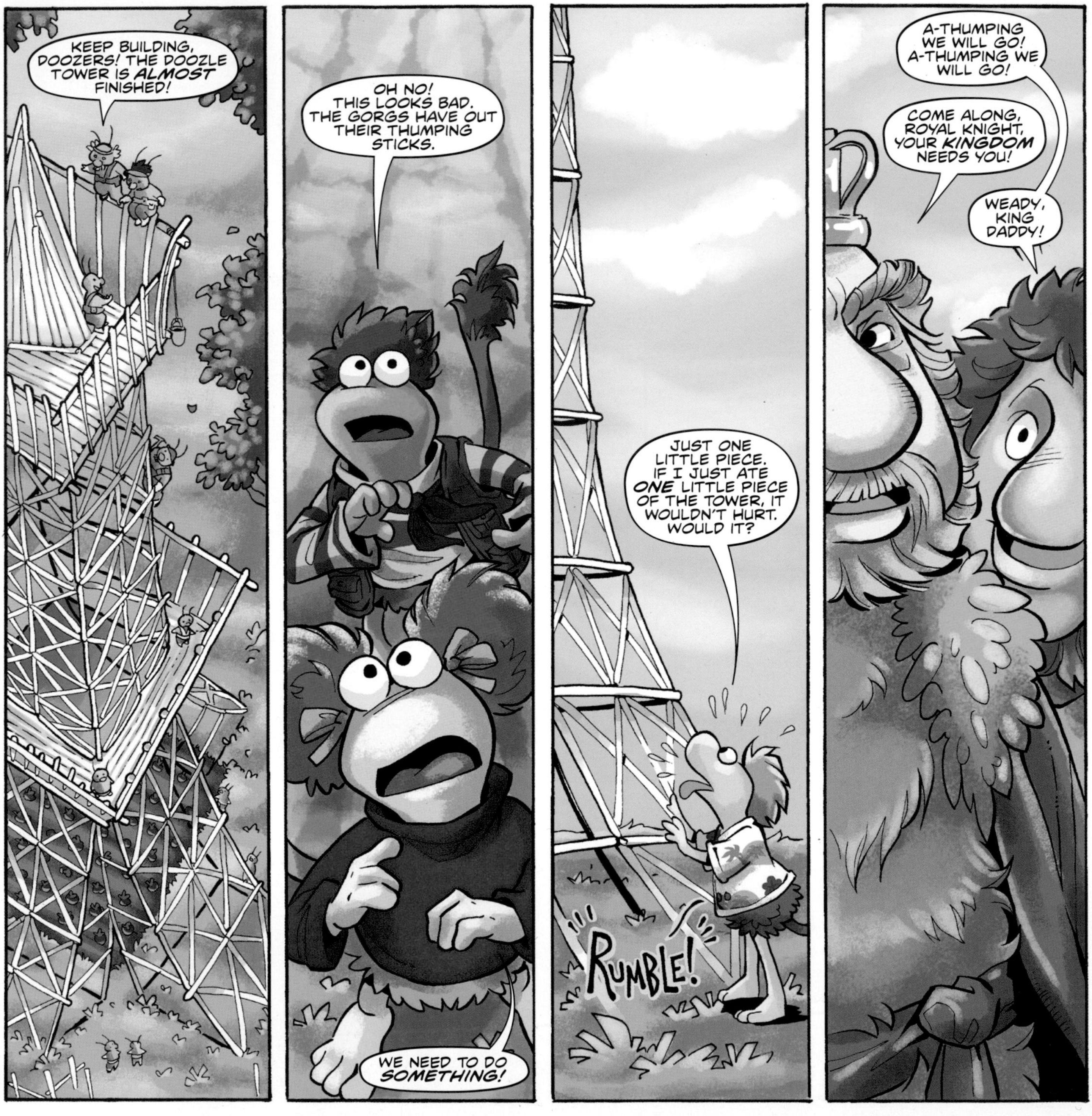
KEEP BUILDING, DOOZERS! THE DOOZLE TOWER IS ALMOST FINISHED!
OH NO! THIS LOOKS BAD. THE GORGS HAVE OUT THEIR THUMPING STICKS.
WE NEED TO DO SOMETHING!
JUST ONE LITTLE PIECE. IF I JUST ATE ONE LITTLE PIECE OF THE TOWER, IT WOULDN'T HURT. WOULD IT?
RUMBLE!
A-THUMPING WE WILL GO! A-THUMPING WE WILL GO!
COME ALONG, ROYAL KNIGHT, YOUR KINGDOM NEEDS YOU!
WEADY, KING DADDY!

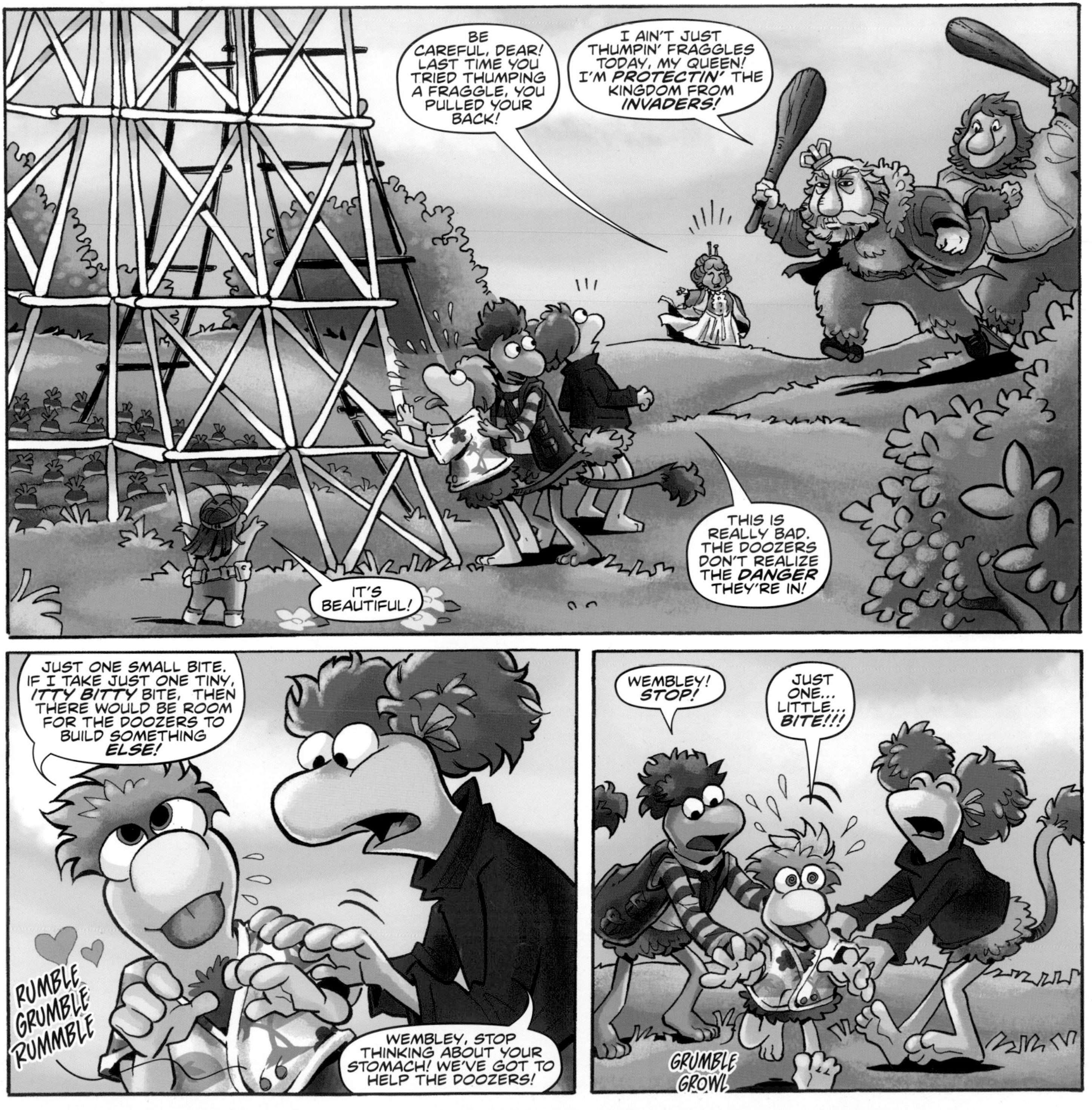
BE CAREFUL, DEAR! LAST TIME YOU TRIED THUMPING A FRAGGLE, YOU PULLED YOUR BACK!
I AIN'T JUST THUMPIN' FRAGGLES TODAY, MY QUEEN! I'M PROTECTIN' THE KINGDOM FROM INVADERS!
IT'S BEAUTIFUL!
THIS IS REALLY BAD. THE DOOZERS DON'T REALIZE THE DANGER THEY'RE IN!
JUST ONE SMALL BITE. IF I TAKE JUST ONE TINY, ITTY BITTY BITE, THEN THERE WOULD BE ROOM FOR THE DOOZERS TO BUILD SOMETHING ELSE!
RUMBLE GRUMBLE RUMMBLE
WEMBLEY, STOP THINKING ABOUT YOUR STOMACH! WE'VE GOT TO HELP THE DOOZERS!
WEMBLEY! STOP!
JUST ONE... LITTLE... BITE!!!
GRUMBLE GROWL

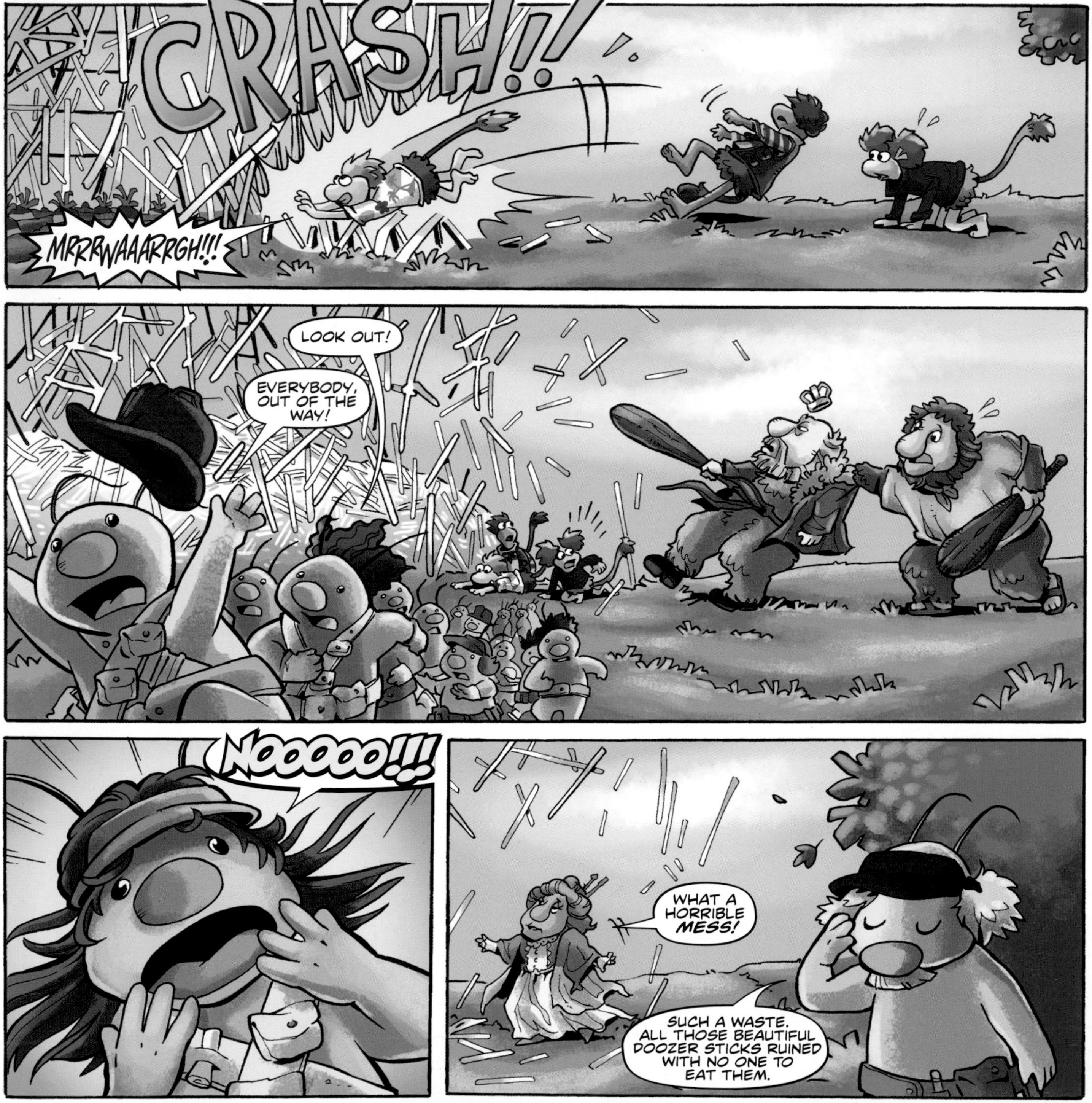
CRASH!!
MRRRWAAARRGH!!!
LOOK OUT!
EVERYBODY, OUT OF THE WAY!
NOOOOO!!!
WHAT A HORRIBLE MESS!
SUCH A WASTE. ALL THOSE BEAUTIFUL DOOZER STICKS RUINED WITH NO ONE TO EAT THEM.

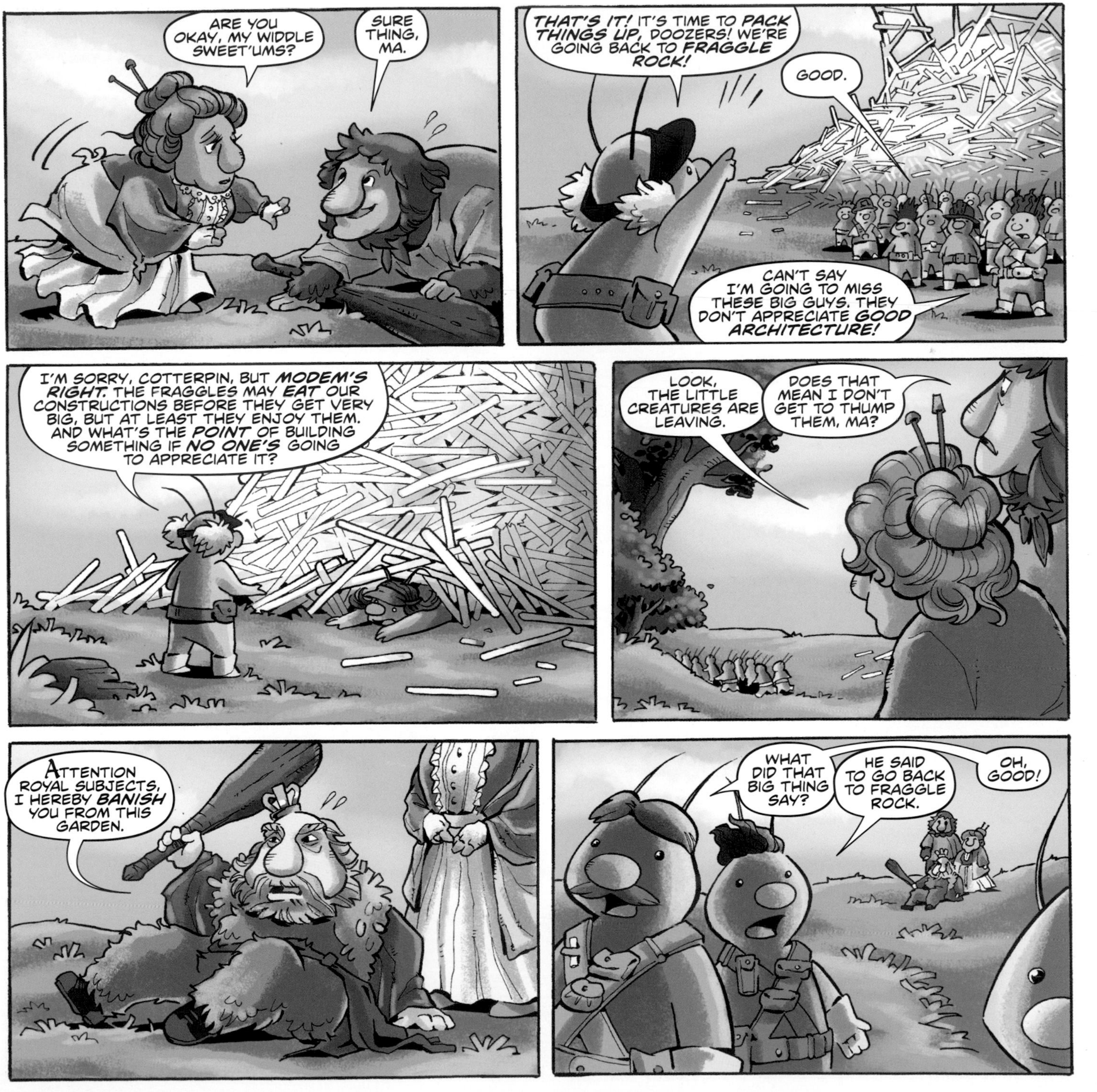
ARE YOU OKAY, MY WIDDLE SWEET'UMS?
SURE THING, MA.
THAT'S IT! IT'S TIME TO PACK THINGS UP, DOOZERS! WE'RE GOING BACK TO FRAGGLE ROCK!
GOOD.
CAN'T SAY I'M GOING TO MISS THESE BIG GUYS. THEY DON'T APPRECIATE GOOD ARCHITECTURE!
I'M SORRY, COTTERPIN, BUT MODEM'S RIGHT. THE FRAGGLES MAY EAT OUR CONSTRUCTIONS BEFORE THEY GET VERY BIG, BUT AT LEAST THEY ENJOY THEM. AND WHAT'S THE POINT OF BUILDING SOMETHING IF NO ONE'S GOING TO APPRECIATE IT?
LOOK, THE LITTLE CREATURES ARE LEAVING.
DOES THAT MEAN I DON'T GET TO THUMP THEM, MA?
ATTENTION ROYAL SUBJECTS, I HEREBY BANISH YOU FROM THIS GARDEN.
WHAT DID THAT BIG THING SAY?
HE SAID TO GO BACK TO FRAGGLE ROCK.
OH, GOOD!

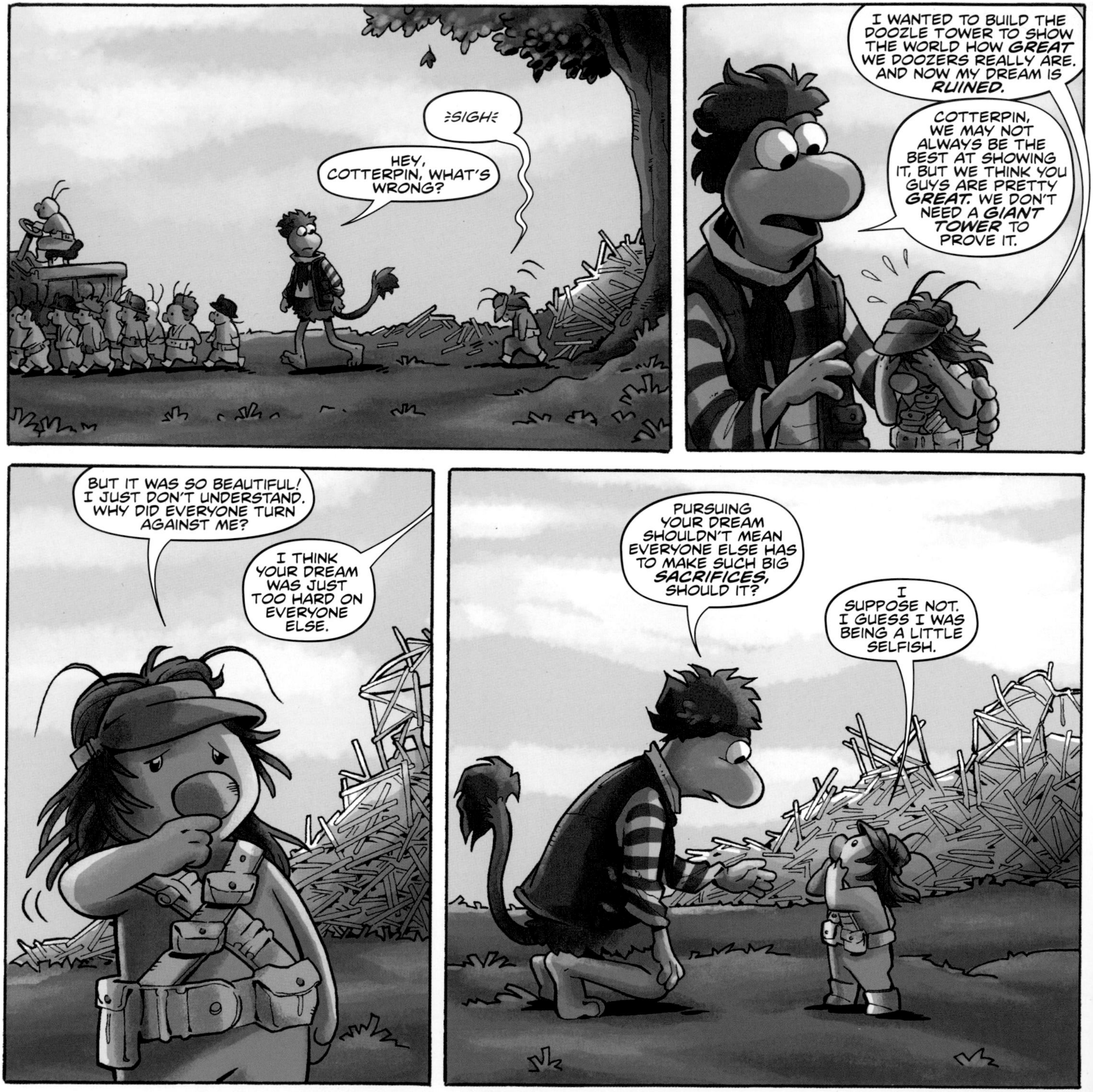

=SIGH=
HEY, COTTERPIN, WHAT'S WRONG?
I WANTED TO BUILD THE DOOZLE TOWER TO SHOW THE WORLD HOW GREAT WE DOOZERS REALLY ARE. AND NOW MY DREAM IS RUINED.
COTTERPIN, WE MAY NOT ALWAYS BE THE BEST AT SHOWING IT, BUT WE THINK YOU GUYS ARE PRETTY GREAT. WE DON'T NEED A GIANT TOWER TO PROVE IT.
BUT IT WAS SO BEAUTIFUL! I JUST DON'T UNDERSTAND. WHY DID EVERYONE TURN AGAINST ME?
I THINK YOUR DREAM WAS JUST TOO HARD ON EVERYONE ELSE.
PURSUING YOUR DREAM SHOULDN'T MEAN EVERYONE ELSE HAS TO MAKE SUCH BIG SACRIFICES, SHOULD IT?
I SUPPOSE NOT. I GUESS I WAS BEING A LITTLE SELFISH.

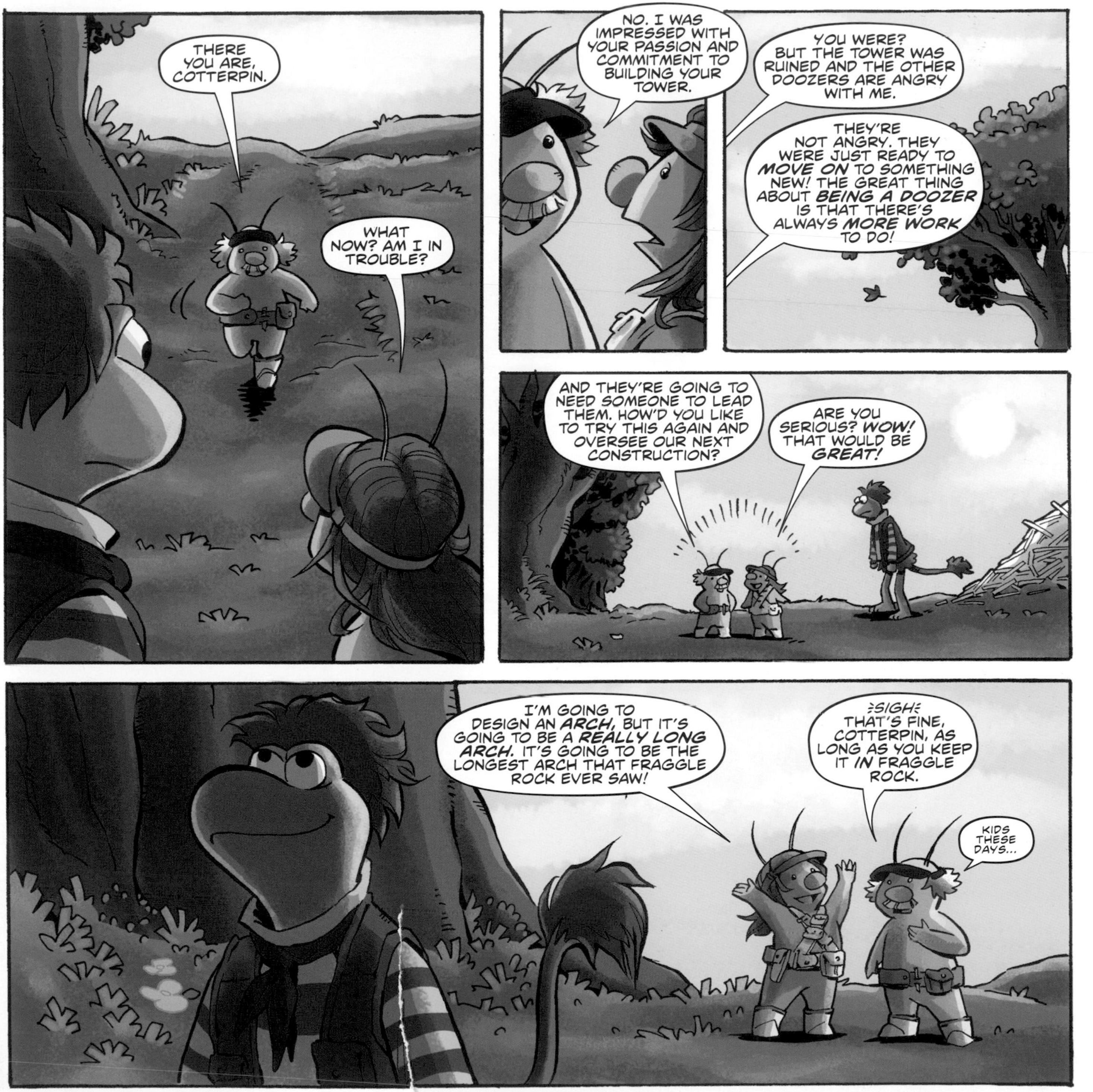
THERE YOU ARE, COTTERPIN.
WHAT NOW? AM I IN TROUBLE?
NO. I WAS IMPRESSED WITH YOUR PASSION AND COMMITMENT TO BUILDING YOUR TOWER.
YOU WERE? BUT THE TOWER WAS RUINED AND THE OTHER DOOZERS ARE ANGRY WITH ME.
THEY'RE NOT ANGRY. THEY WERE JUST READY TO MOVE ON TO SOMETHING NEW! THE GREAT THING ABOUT BEING A DOOZER IS THAT THERE'S ALWAYS MORE WORK TO DO!
AND THEY'RE GOING TO NEED SOMEONE TO LEAD THEM. HOW'D YOU LIKE TO TRY THIS AGAIN AND OVERSEE OUR NEXT CONSTRUCTION?
ARE YOU SERIOUS? WOW! THAT WOULD BE GREAT!
I'M GOING TO DESIGN AN ARCH, BUT IT'S GOING TO BE A REALLY LONG ARCH. IT'S GOING TO BE THE LONGEST ARCH THAT FRAGGLE ROCK EVER SAW!
SIGH THAT'S FINE, COTTERPIN, AS LONG AS YOU KEEP IT IN FRAGGLE ROCK.
KIDS THESE DAYS...

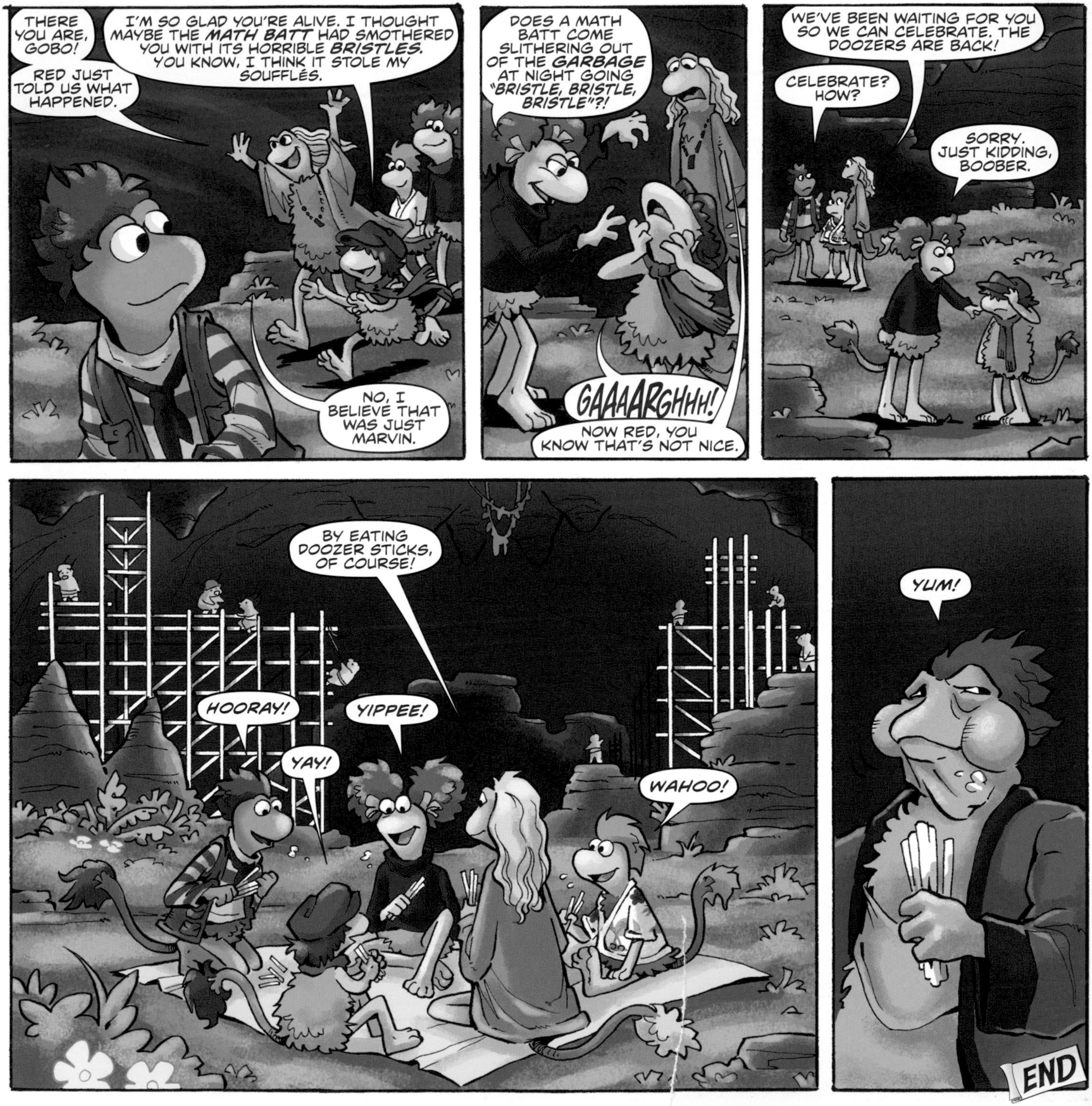
THERE YOU ARE, GOBO!
RED JUST TOLD US WHAT HAPPENED.
I'M SO GLAD YOU'RE ALIVE. I THOUGHT MAYBE THE MATH BATT HAD SMOTHERED YOU WITH ITS HORRIBLE BRISTLES. YOU KNOW, I THINK IT STOLE MY SOUFFLÉS.
NO, I BELIEVE THAT WAS JUST MARVIN.
DOES A MATH BATT COME SLITHERING OUT OF THE GARBAGE AT NIGHT GOING "BRISTLE, BRISTLE, BRISTLE"?!
GAAAARGHHH!
NOW RED, YOU KNOW THAT'S NOT NICE.
WE'VE BEEN WAITING FOR YOU SO WE CAN CELEBRATE. THE DOOZERS ARE BACK!
CELEBRATE? HOW?
SORRY. JUST KIDDING, BOOBER.
BY EATING DOOZER STICKS, OF COURSE!
HOORAY!
YIPPEE!
YAY!
WAHOO!
YUM!
END

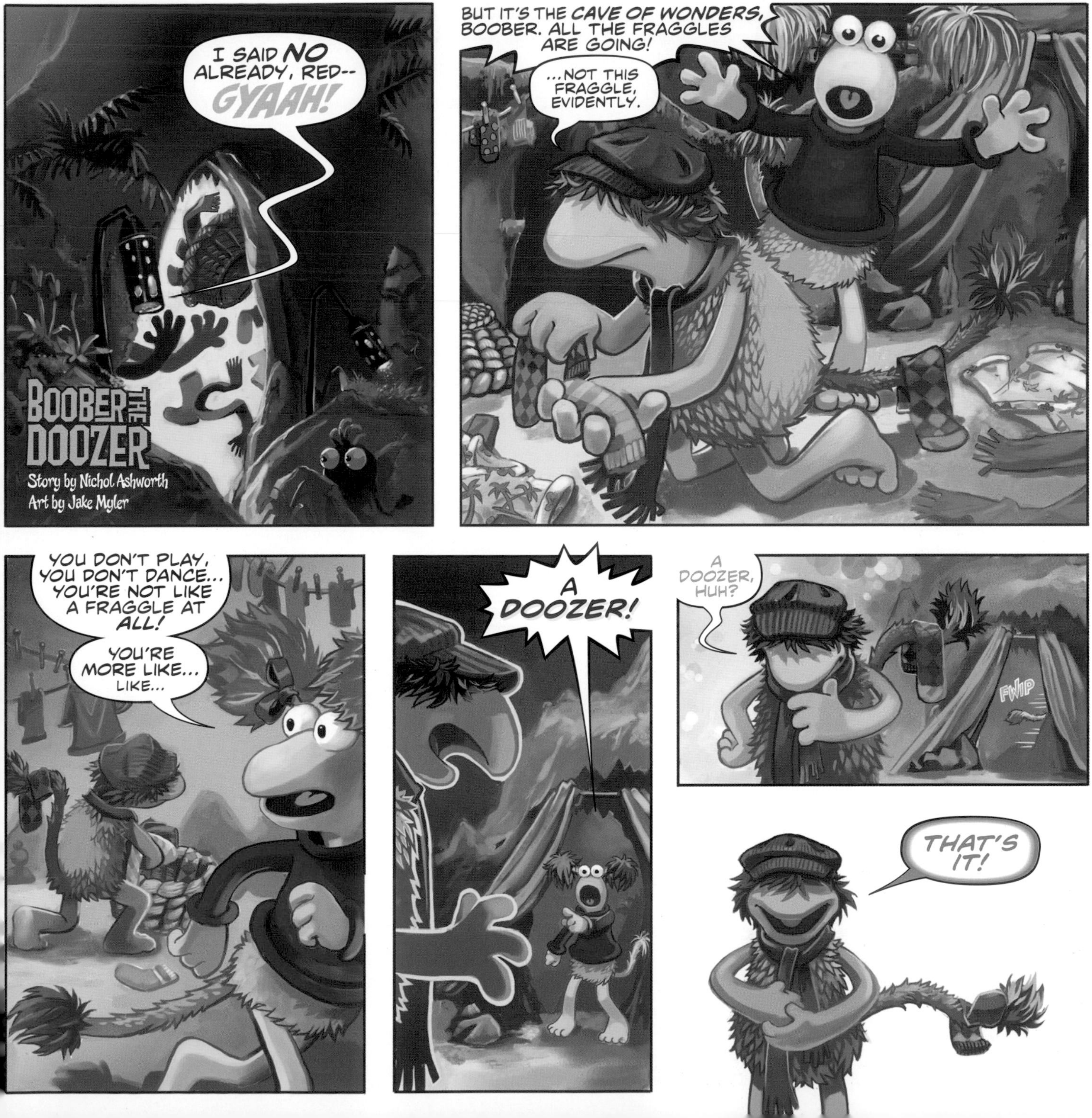
I SAID NO ALREADY, RED-- GYAAH!
BOOBER THE DOOZER
Story by Nichol Ashworth
Art by Jake Myler
BUT IT'S THE CAVE OF WONDERS, BOOBER. ALL THE FRAGGLES ARE GOING!
...NOT THIS FRAGGLE, EVIDENTLY.
YOU DON'T PLAY, YOU DON'T DANCE... YOU'RE NOT LIKE A FRAGGLE AT ALL!
YOU'RE MORE LIKE... LIKE...
A DOOZER!
A DOOZER, HUH?
FWIP
THAT'S IT!

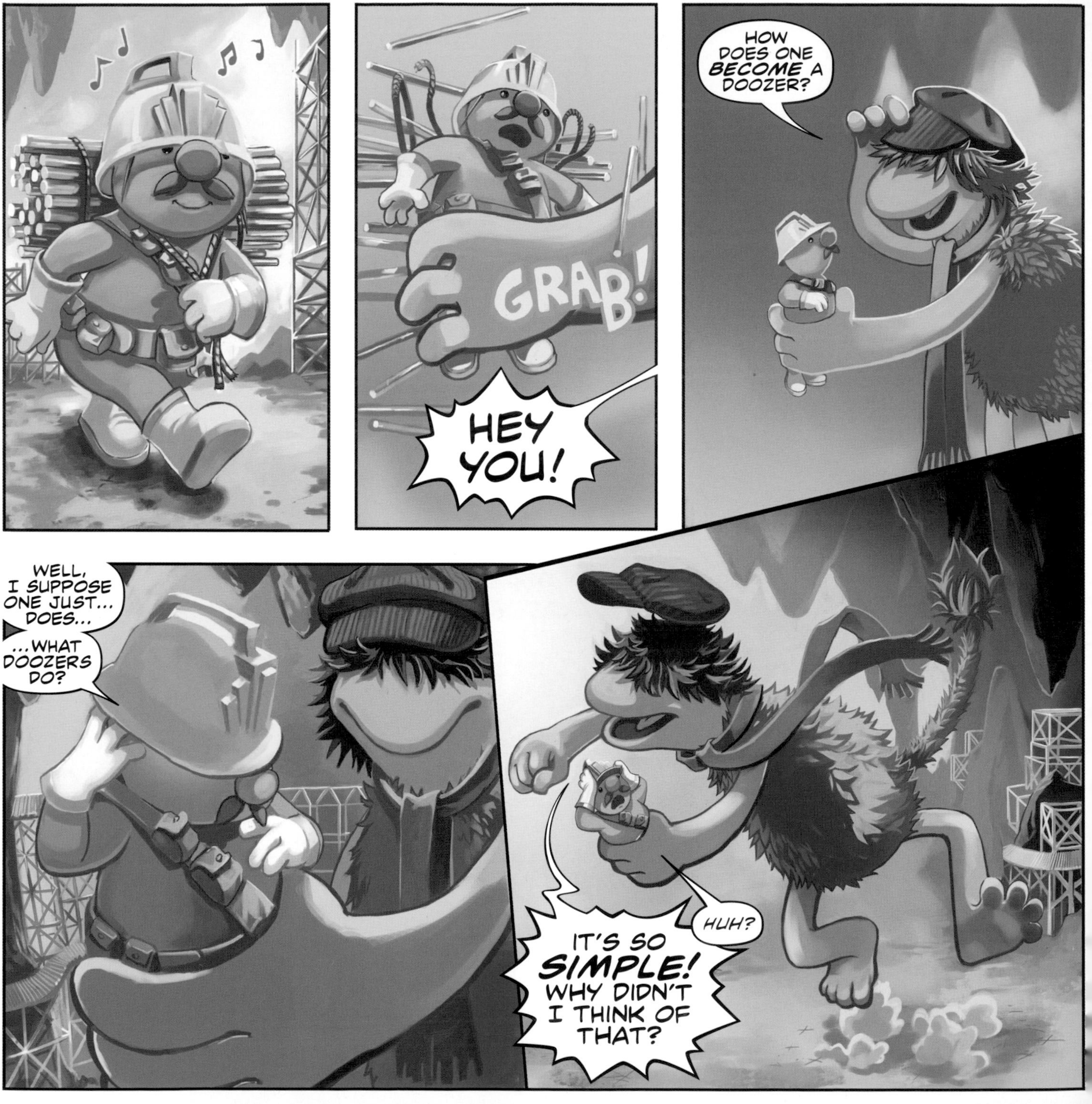
GRAB!
HEY YOU!
HOW DOES ONE BECOME A DOOZER?
WELL, I SUPPOSE ONE JUST... DOES...
...WHAT DOOZERS DO?
HUH?
IT'S SO SIMPLE! WHY DIDN'T I THINK OF THAT?

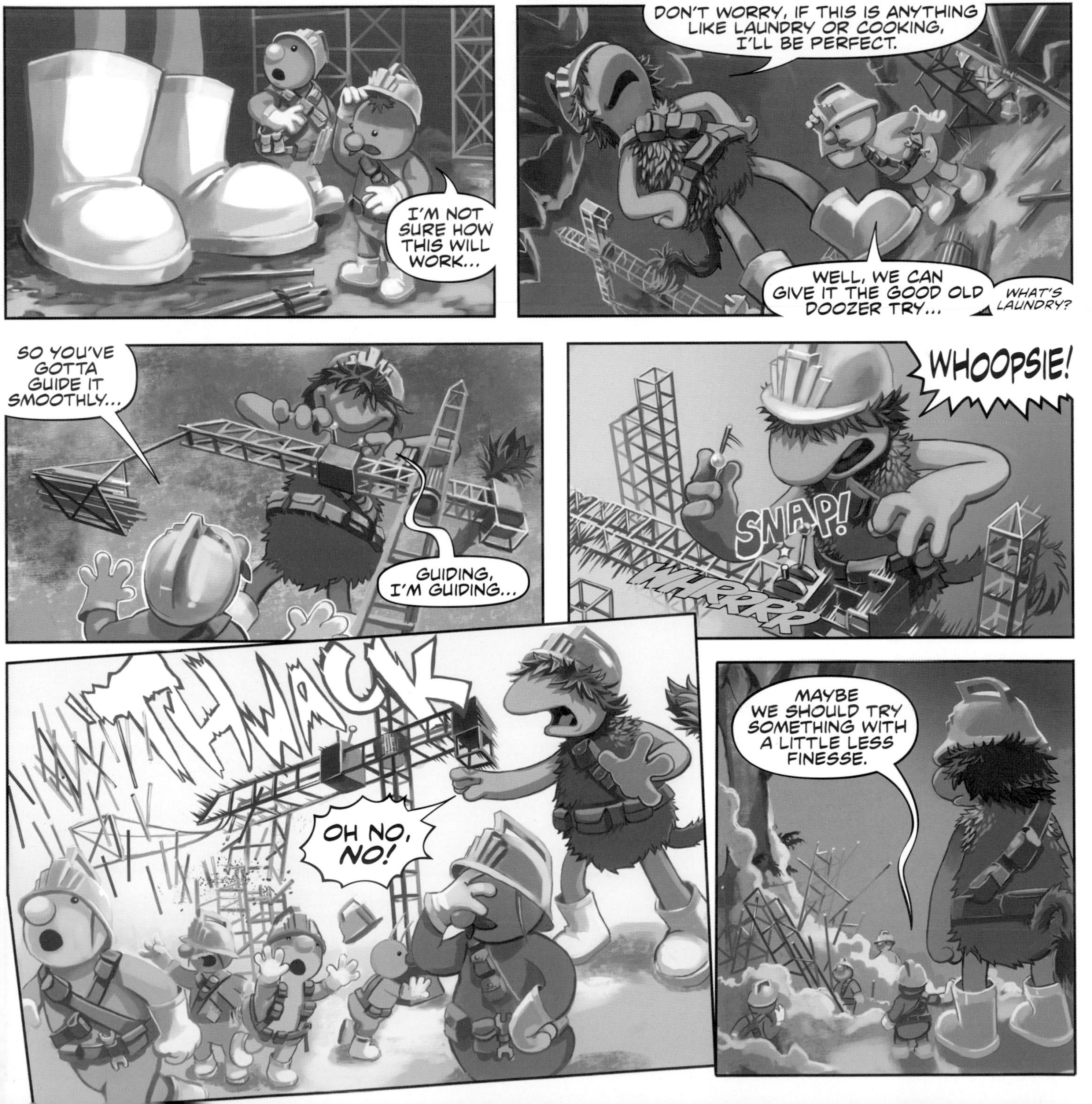
I'M NOT SURE HOW THIS WILL WORK...
DON'T WORRY, IF THIS IS ANYTHING LIKE LAUNDRY OR COOKING, I'LL BE PERFECT.
WELL, WE CAN GIVE IT THE GOOD OLD DOOZER TRY...
WHAT'S LAUNDRY?
SO YOU'VE GOTTA GUIDE IT SMOOTHLY...
GUIDING, I'M GUIDING...
WHOOPSIE!
SNAP!
WHRRRR
THWACK
OH NO, NO!
MAYBE WE SHOULD TRY SOMETHING WITH A LITTLE LESS FINESSE.

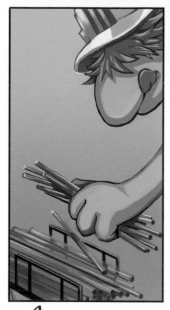

WHAT ON EARTH IS THAT FRAGGLE DOING?

HE SAYS HE WANTS TO BE A DOOZER!

WELL, I CAN UNDERSTAND THAT-- WHO WANTS TO BE A FRAGGLE?

CRUMBLE

NOOOOOO OOOOOO!

CRRASH

IT'S ALL RIGHT. THE COEFFICIENT WAS WRONG... BUT IT HAPPENS SOMETIMES.

I MEAN, WE DOOZERS DON'T MAKE THOSE KINDS OF MISTAKES, BUT...

...YOU'RE ONLY A DOOZER-IN-TRAINING, SO IT'S OKAY TO MAKE *SOME* MISTAKES, I GUESS.

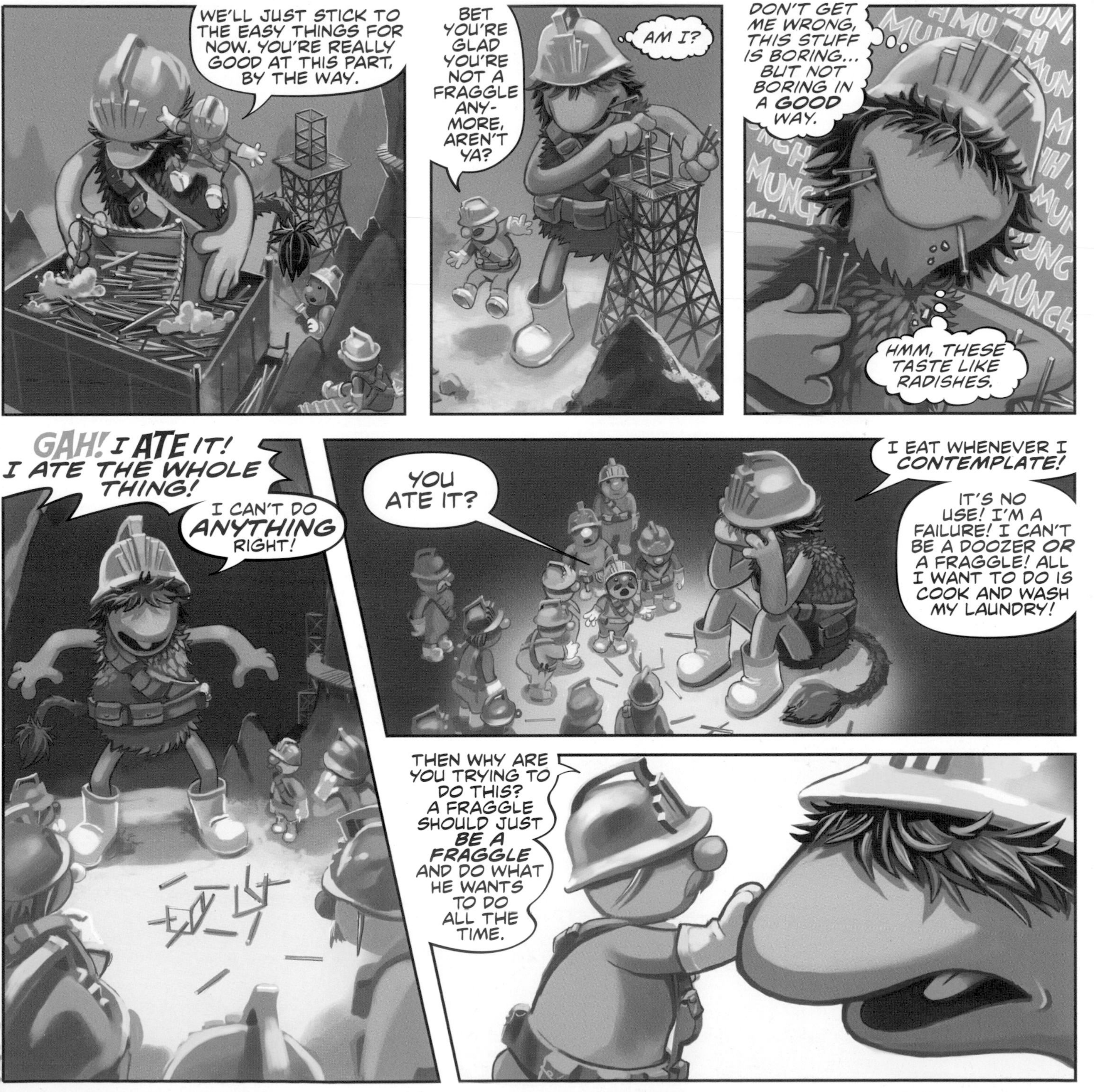
WE'LL JUST STICK TO THE EASY THINGS FOR NOW. YOU'RE REALLY GOOD AT THIS PART, BY THE WAY.
BET YOU'RE GLAD YOU'RE NOT A FRAGGLE ANY-MORE, AREN'T YA?
AM I?
DON'T GET ME WRONG, THIS STUFF IS BORING... BUT NOT BORING IN A GOOD WAY.
MUNCH MUNCH MUNCH
HMM, THESE TASTE LIKE RADISHES.
GAH! I ATE IT! I ATE THE WHOLE THING!
I CAN'T DO ANYTHING RIGHT!
YOU ATE IT?
I EAT WHENEVER I CONTEMPLATE!
IT'S NO USE! I'M A FAILURE! I CAN'T BE A DOOZER OR A FRAGGLE! ALL I WANT TO DO IS COOK AND WASH MY LAUNDRY!
THEN WHY ARE YOU TRYING TO DO THIS? A FRAGGLE SHOULD JUST BE A FRAGGLE AND DO WHAT HE WANTS TO DO ALL THE TIME.

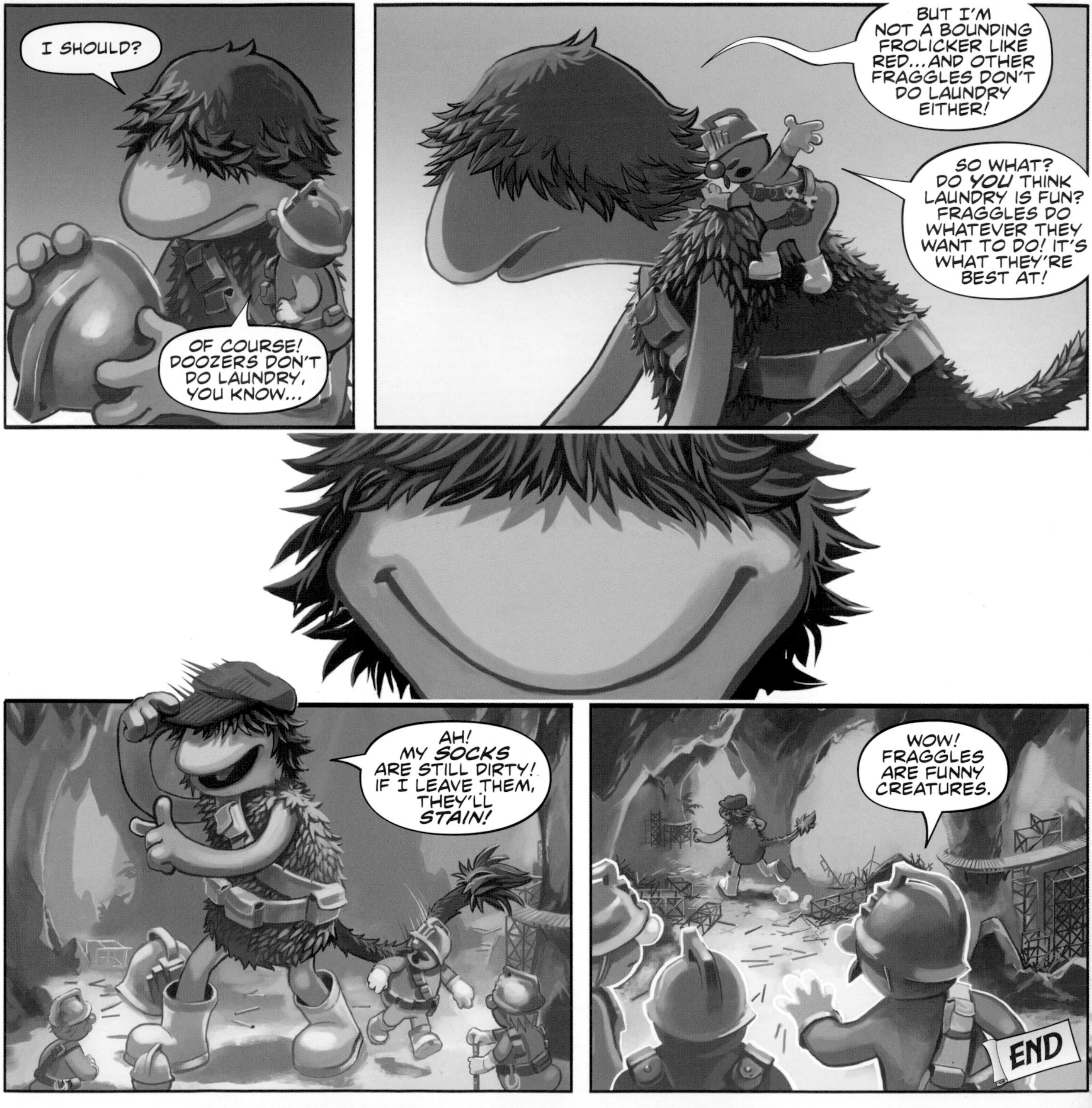
I SHOULD?
OF COURSE! DOOZERS DON'T DO LAUNDRY, YOU KNOW...
BUT I'M NOT A BOUNDING FROLICKER LIKE RED...AND OTHER FRAGGLES DON'T DO LAUNDRY EITHER!
SO WHAT? DO *YOU* THINK LAUNDRY IS FUN? FRAGGLES DO WHATEVER THEY WANT TO DO! IT'S WHAT THEY'RE BEST AT!
AH! MY *SOCKS* ARE STILL DIRTY! IF I LEAVE THEM, THEY'LL *STAIN!*
WOW! FRAGGLES ARE FUNNY CREATURES.
END

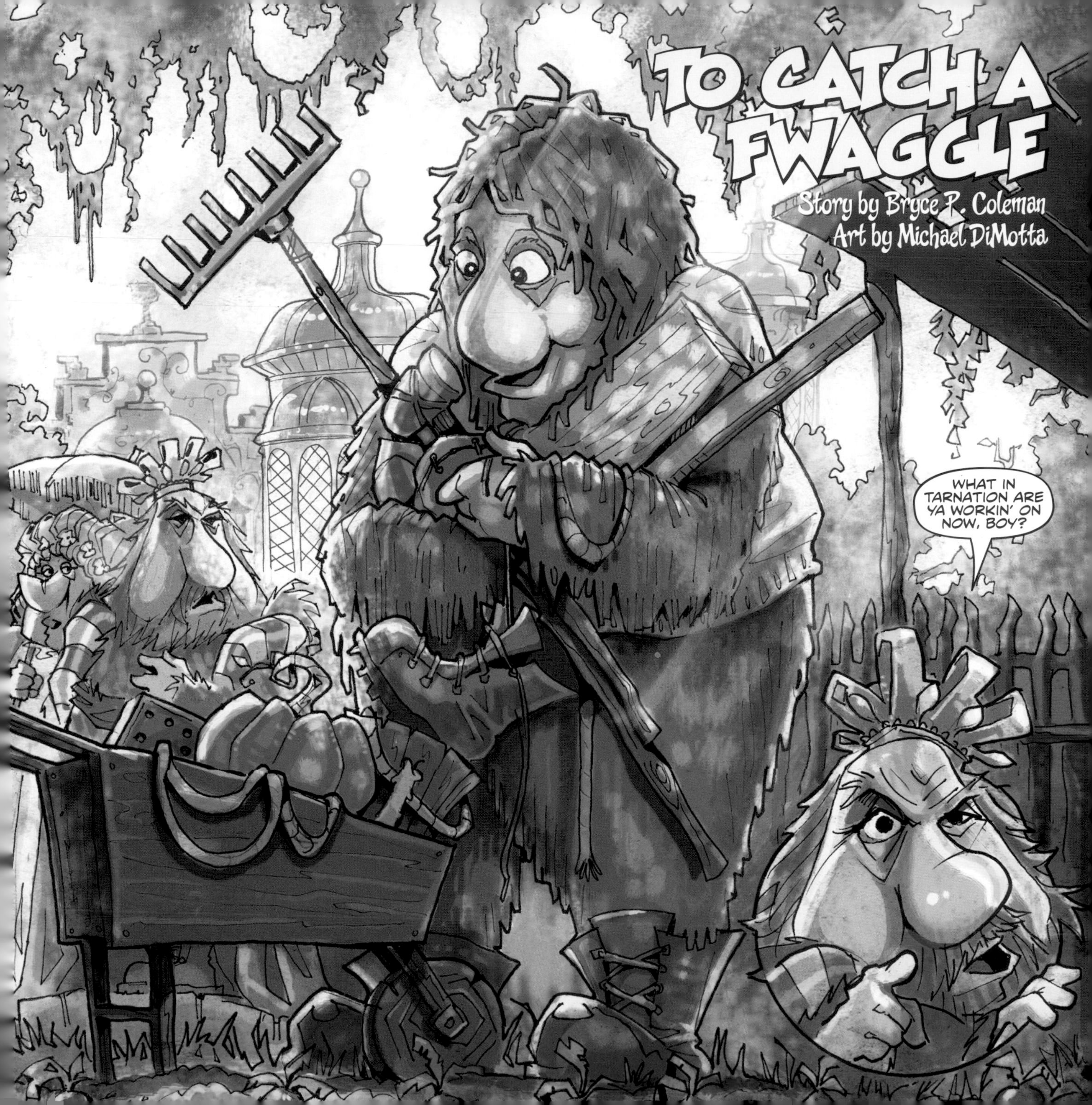
TO CATCH A FWAGGLE
Story by Bryce P. Coleman
Art by Michael DiMotta
WHAT IN TARNATION ARE YA WORKIN' ON NOW, BOY?

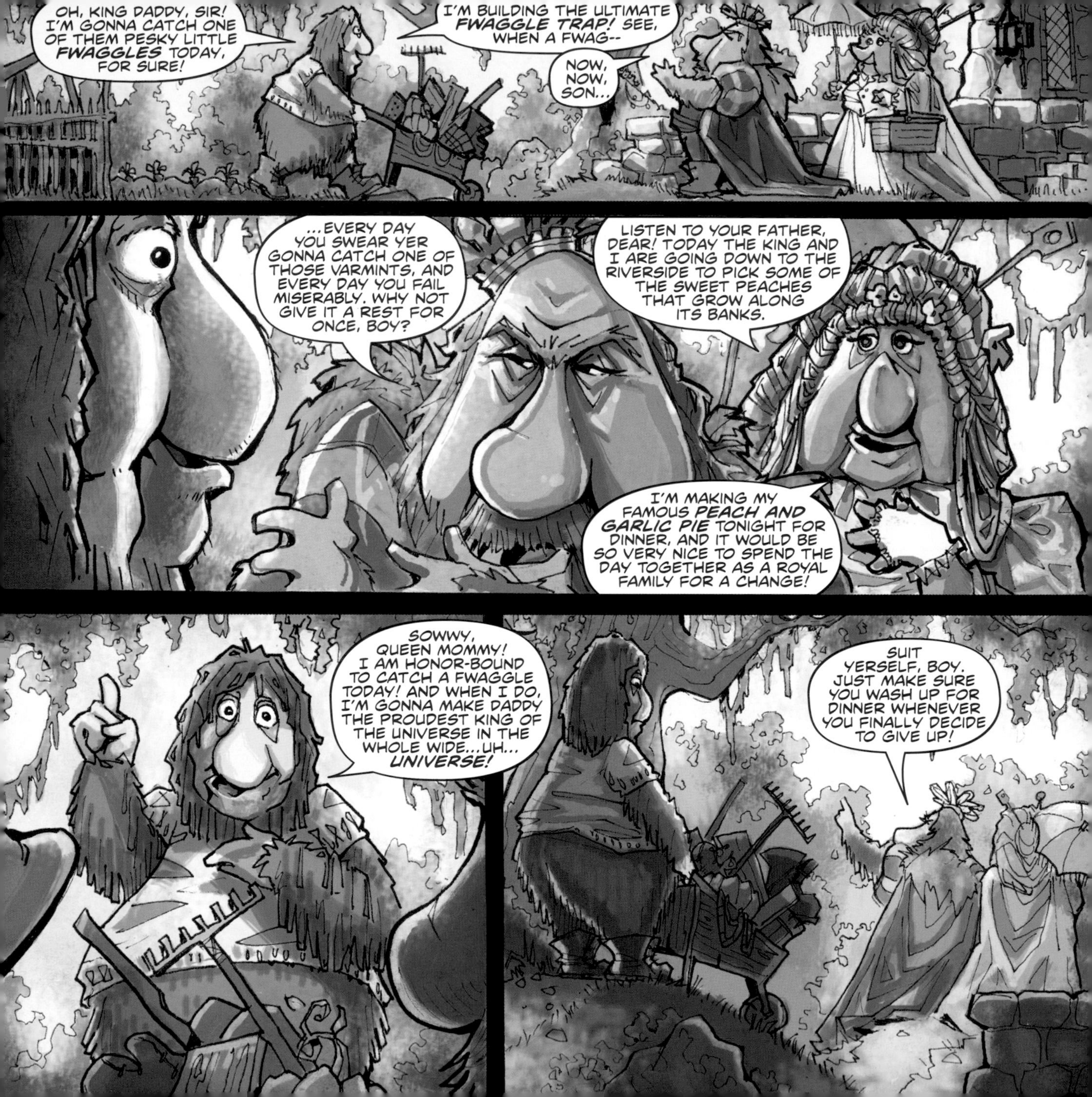
OH, KING DADDY, SIR! I'M GONNA CATCH ONE OF THEM PESKY LITTLE FWAGGLES TODAY, FOR SURE!
I'M BUILDING THE ULTIMATE FWAGGLE TRAP! SEE, WHEN A FWAG--
NOW, NOW, SON...
...EVERY DAY YOU SWEAR YER GONNA CATCH ONE OF THOSE VARMINTS, AND EVERY DAY YOU FAIL MISERABLY. WHY NOT GIVE IT A REST FOR ONCE, BOY?
LISTEN TO YOUR FATHER, DEAR! TODAY THE KING AND I ARE GOING DOWN TO THE RIVERSIDE TO PICK SOME OF THE SWEET PEACHES THAT GROW ALONG ITS BANKS.
I'M MAKING MY FAMOUS PEACH AND GARLIC PIE TONIGHT FOR DINNER, AND IT WOULD BE SO VERY NICE TO SPEND THE DAY TOGETHER AS A ROYAL FAMILY FOR A CHANGE!
SOWWY, QUEEN MOMMY! I AM HONOR-BOUND TO CATCH A FWAGGLE TODAY! AND WHEN I DO, I'M GONNA MAKE DADDY THE PROUDEST KING OF THE UNIVERSE IN THE WHOLE WIDE...UH... UNIVERSE!
SUIT YERSELF, BOY. JUST MAKE SURE YOU WASH UP FOR DINNER WHENEVER YOU FINALLY DECIDE TO GIVE UP!

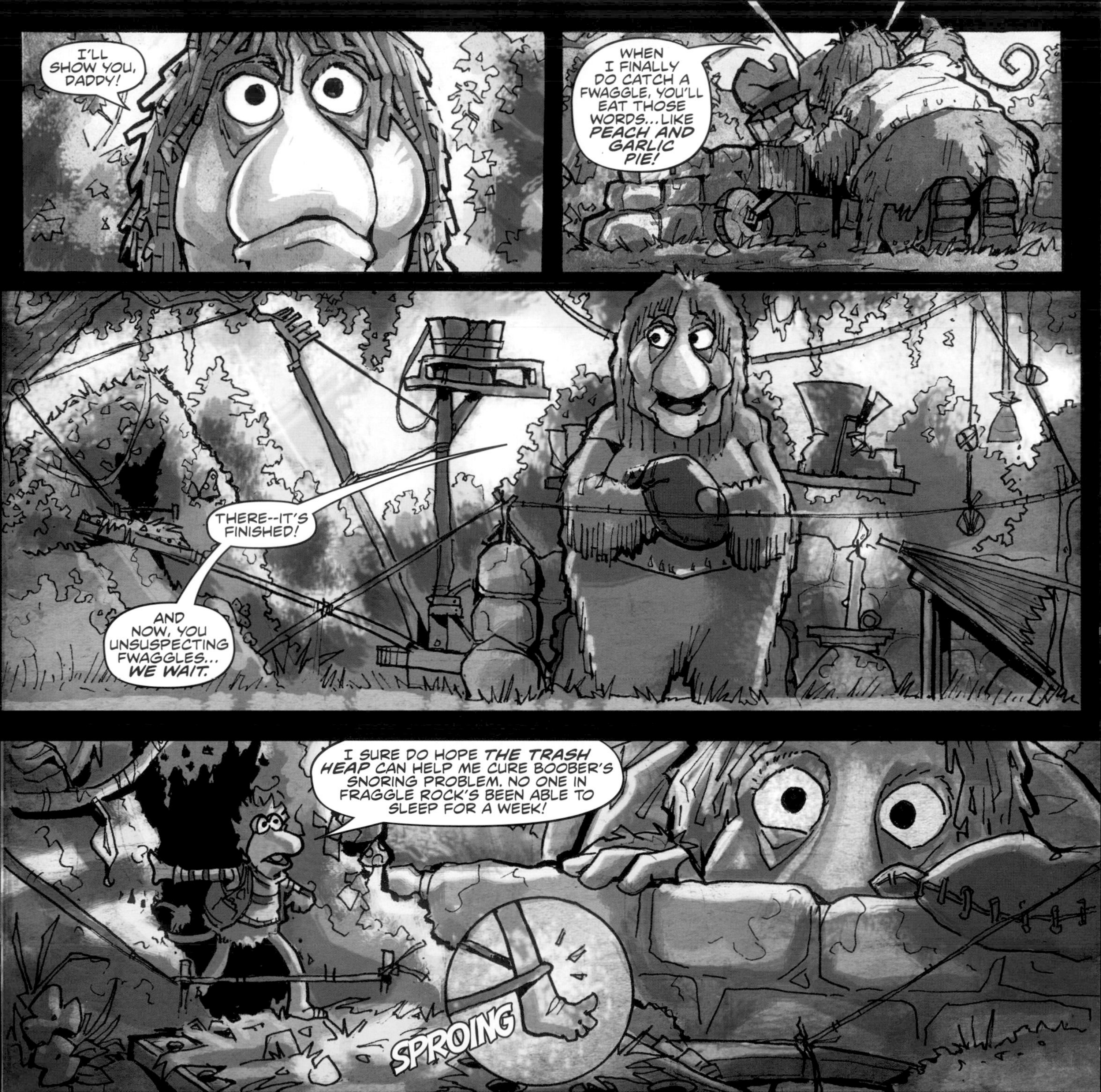
I'LL SHOW YOU, DADDY!
WHEN I FINALLY DO CATCH A FWAGGLE, YOU'LL EAT THOSE WORDS...LIKE PEACH AND GARLIC PIE!
THERE--IT'S FINISHED!
AND NOW, YOU UNSUSPECTING FWAGGLES... WE WAIT.
I SURE DO HOPE THE TRASH HEAP CAN HELP ME CURE BOOBER'S SNORING PROBLEM. NO ONE IN FRAGGLE ROCK'S BEEN ABLE TO SLEEP FOR A WEEK!
SPROING

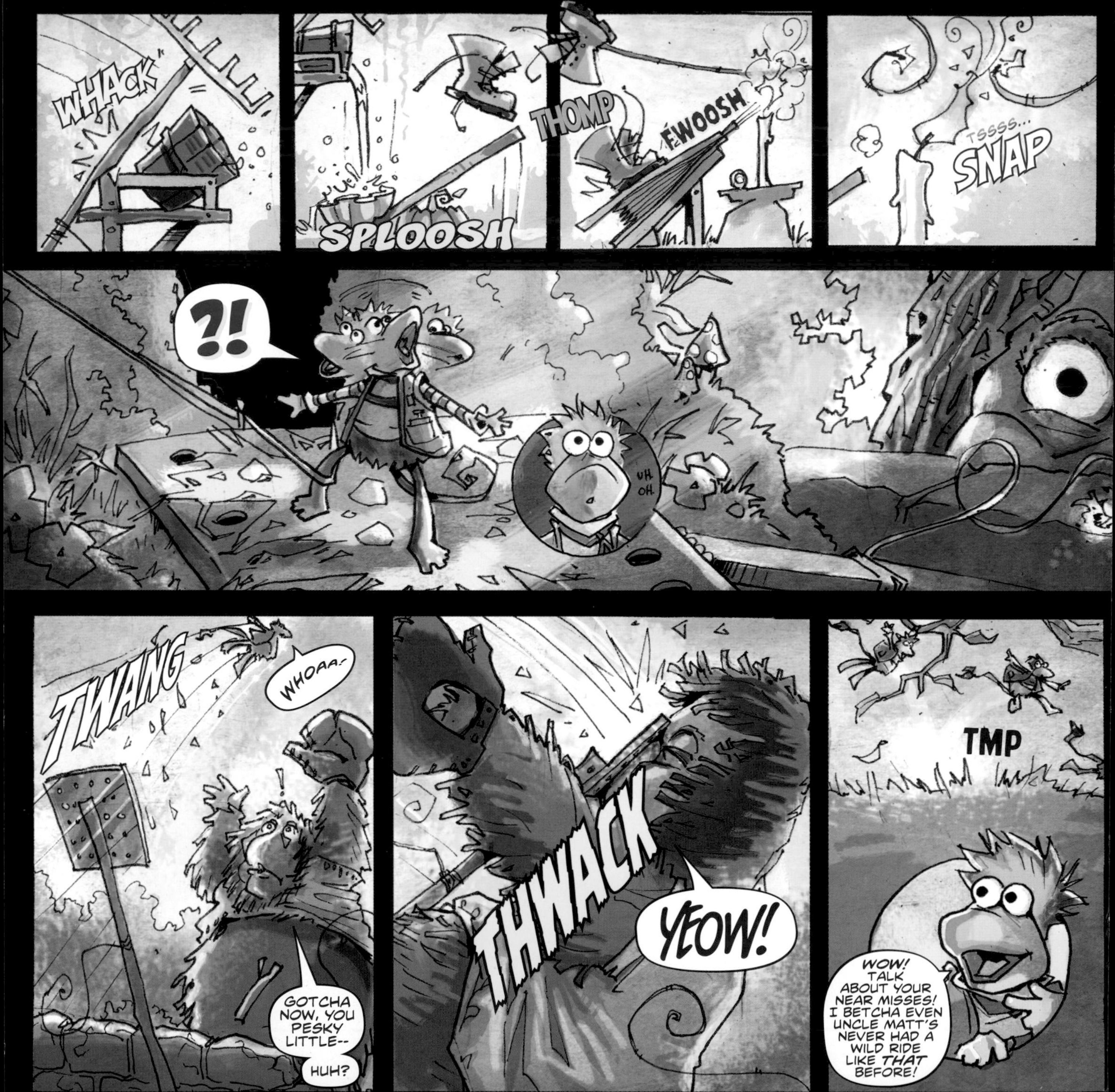
WHACK
SPLOOSH
THOMP
FWOOSH
TSSSS...
SNAP
?!
UH. OH.
TWANG
WHOAA-
!
GOTCHA NOW, YOU PESKY LITTLE--
HUH?
THWACK
YEOW!
TMP
WOW! TALK ABOUT YOUR NEAR MISSES! I BETCHA EVEN UNCLE MATT'S NEVER HAD A WILD RIDE LIKE *THAT* BEFORE!

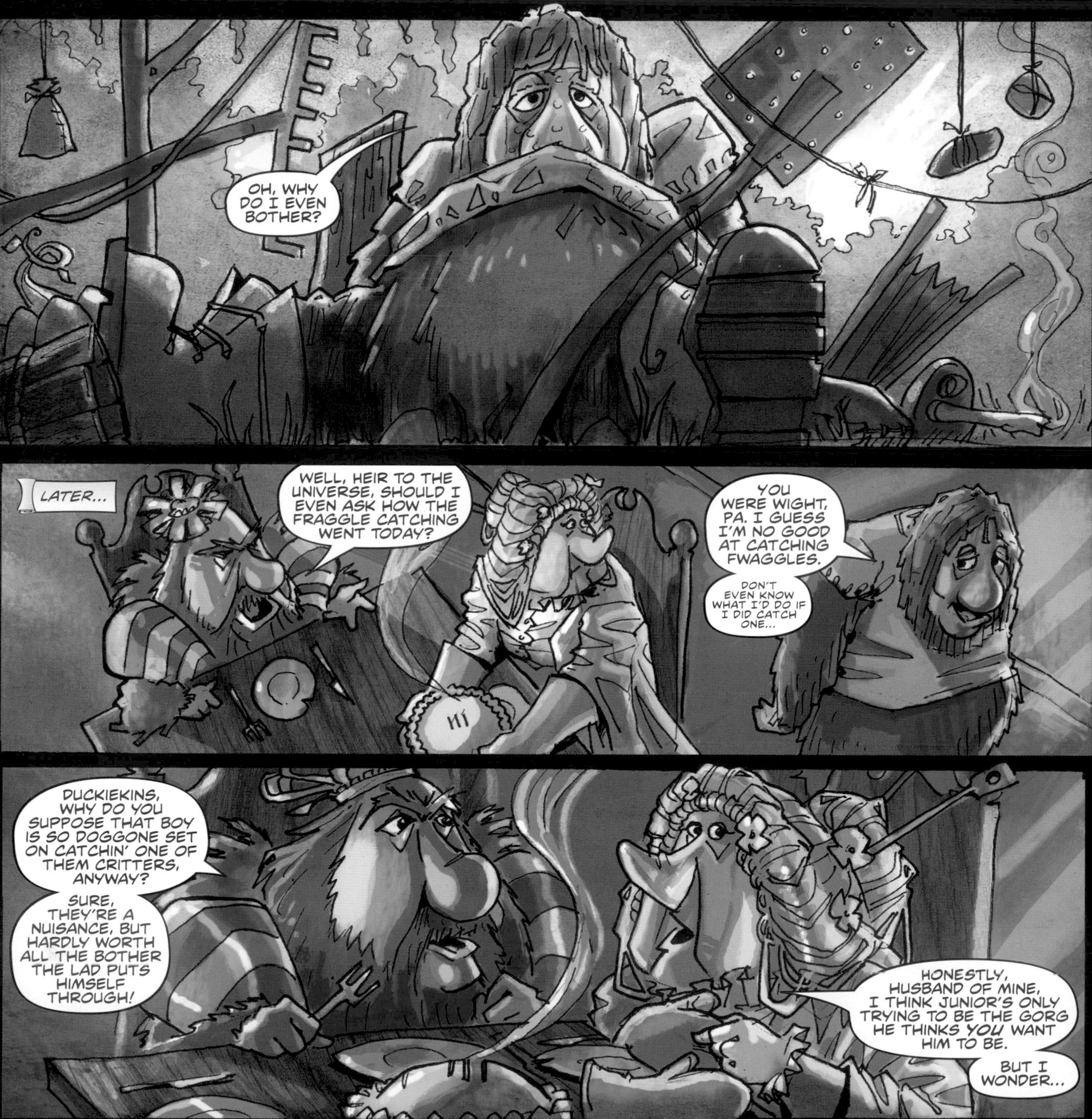
OH, WHY DO I EVEN BOTHER?
LATER...
WELL, HEIR TO THE UNIVERSE, SHOULD I EVEN ASK HOW THE FRAGGLE CATCHING WENT TODAY?
YOU WERE WIGHT, PA. I GUESS I'M NO GOOD AT CATCHING FWAGGLES.
DON'T EVEN KNOW WHAT I'D DO IF I DID CATCH ONE...
DUCKIEKINS, WHY DO YOU SUPPOSE THAT BOY IS SO DOGGONE SET ON CATCHIN' ONE OF THEM CRITTERS, ANYWAY?
SURE, THEY'RE A NUISANCE, BUT HARDLY WORTH ALL THE BOTHER THE LAD PUTS HIMSELF THROUGH!
HONESTLY, HUSBAND OF MINE, I THINK JUNIOR'S ONLY TRYING TO BE THE GORG HE THINKS YOU WANT HIM TO BE.
BUT I WONDER...

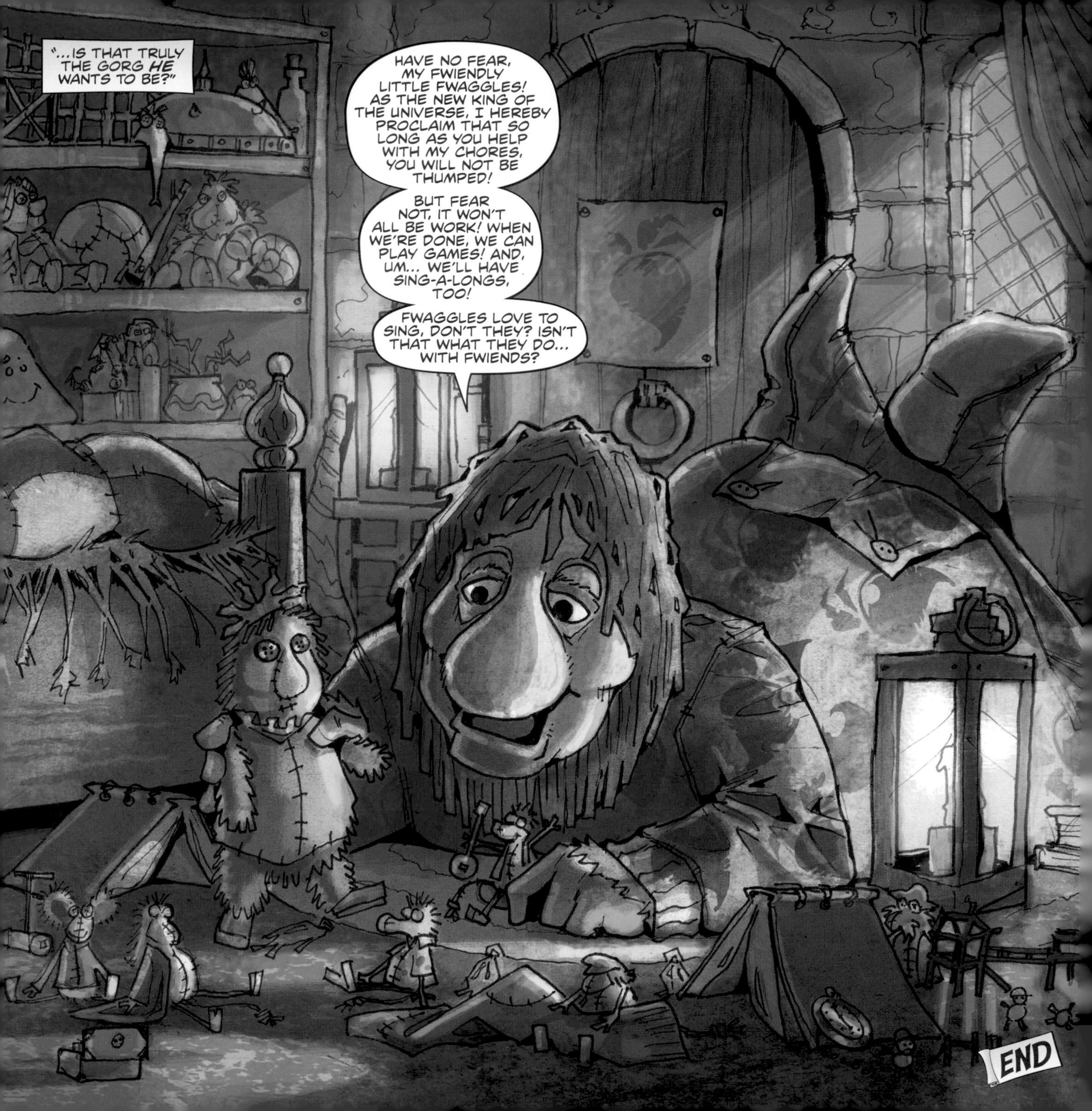
"...IS THAT TRULY THE GORG *HE* WANTS TO BE?"
HAVE NO FEAR, MY FWIENDLY LITTLE FWAGGLES! AS THE NEW KING OF THE UNIVERSE, I HEREBY PROCLAIM THAT SO LONG AS YOU HELP WITH MY CHORES, YOU WILL NOT BE THUMPED!
BUT FEAR NOT, IT WON'T ALL BE WORK! WHEN WE'RE DONE, WE CAN PLAY GAMES! AND, UM... WE'LL HAVE SING-A-LONGS, TOO!
FWAGGLES LOVE TO SING, DON'T THEY? ISN'T THAT WHAT THEY DO... WITH FWIENDS?
END

Cover Gallery

Issue One

Issue Two

Issue Three

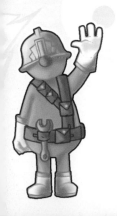

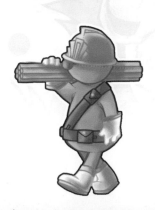

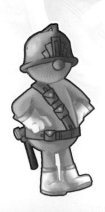

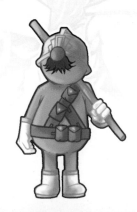

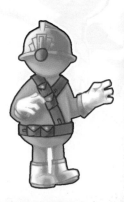

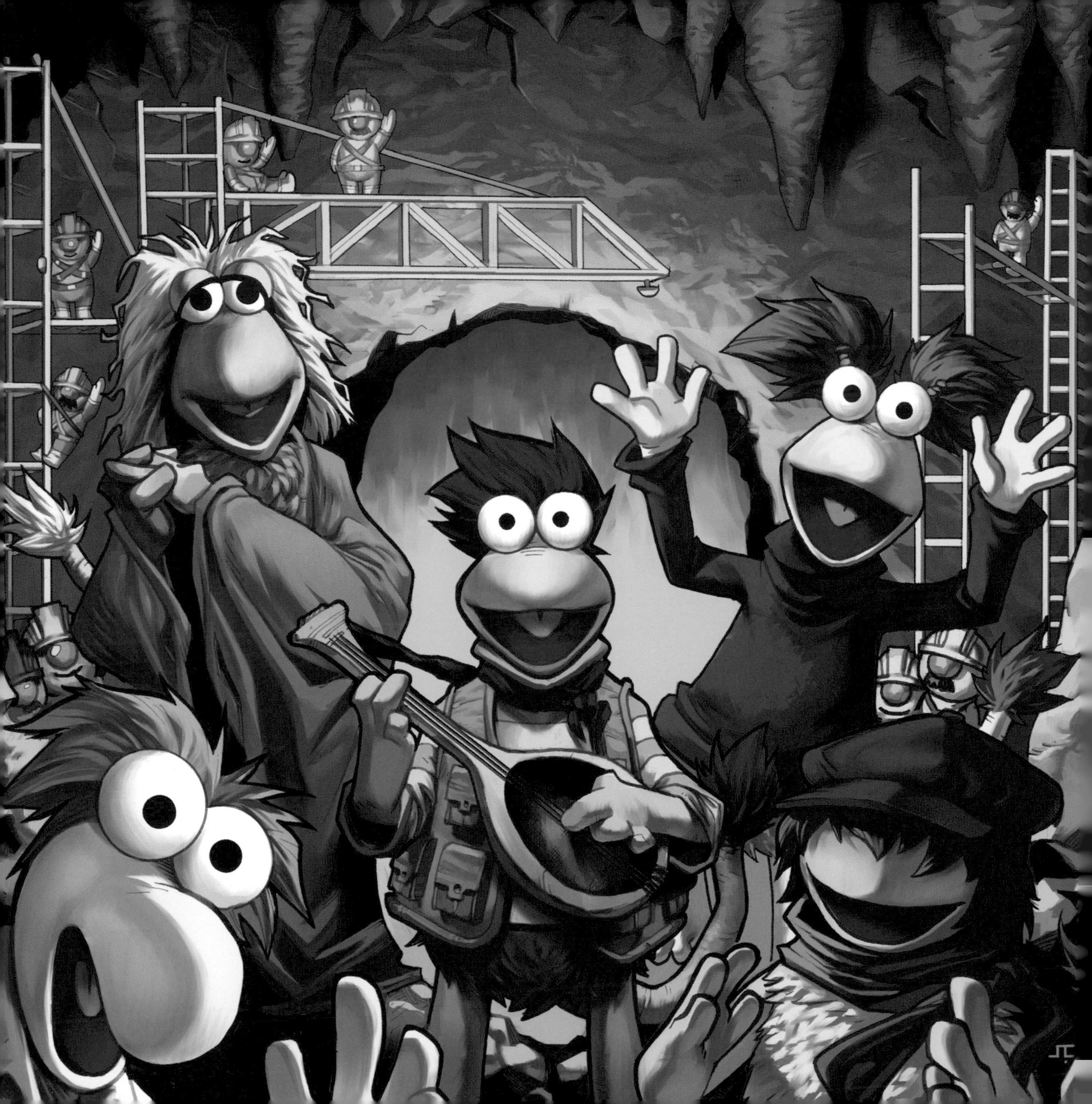

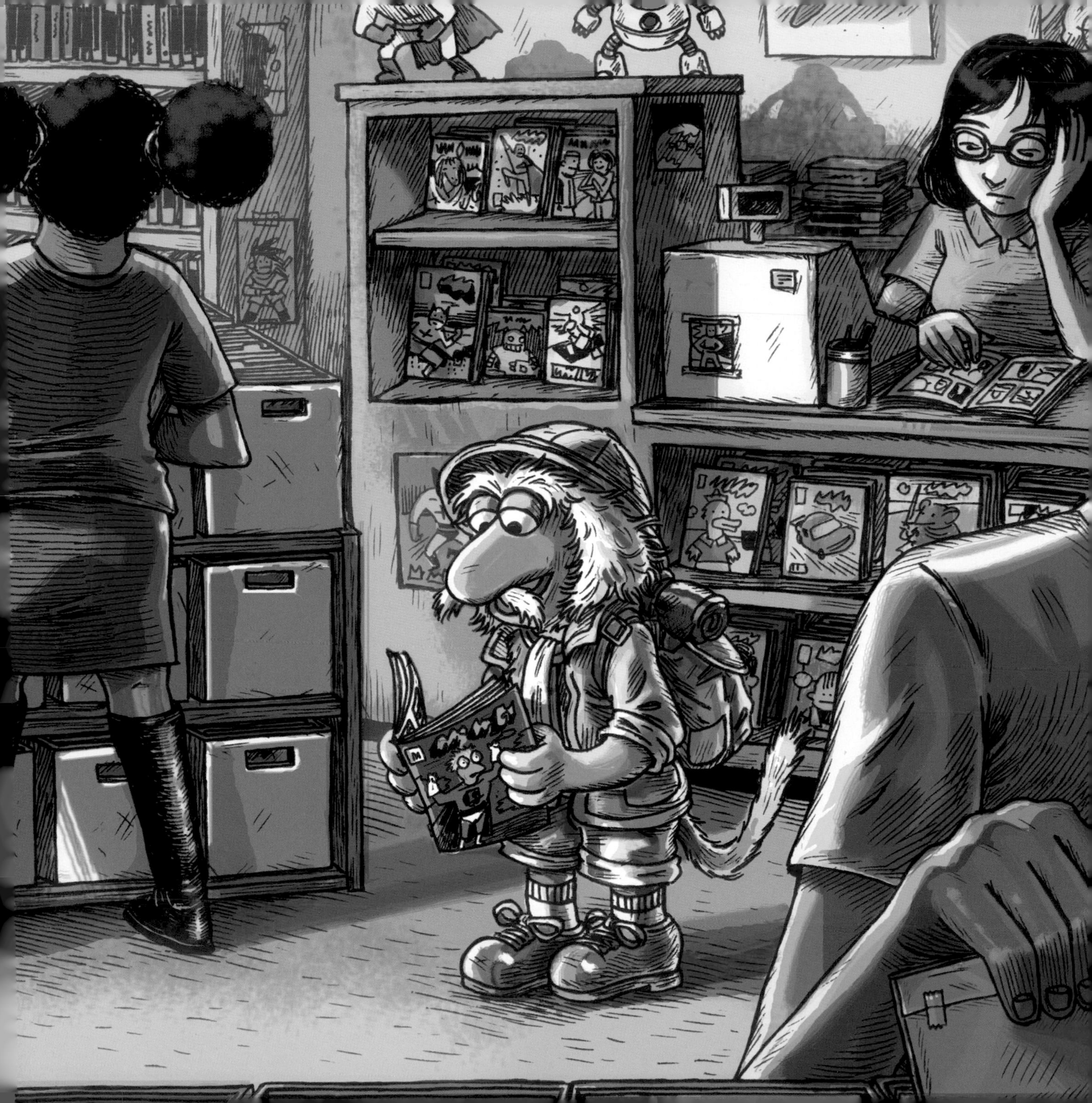

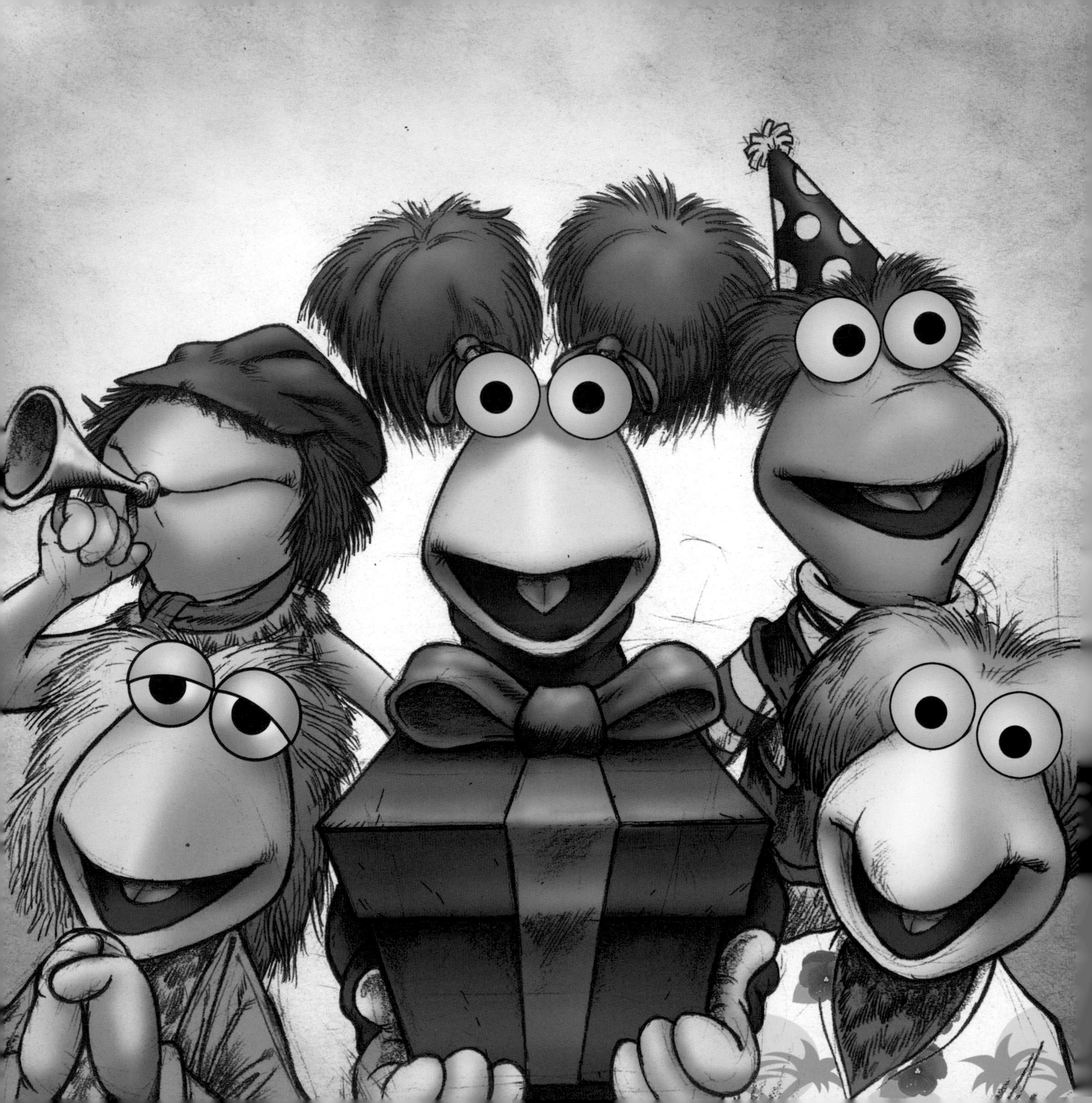

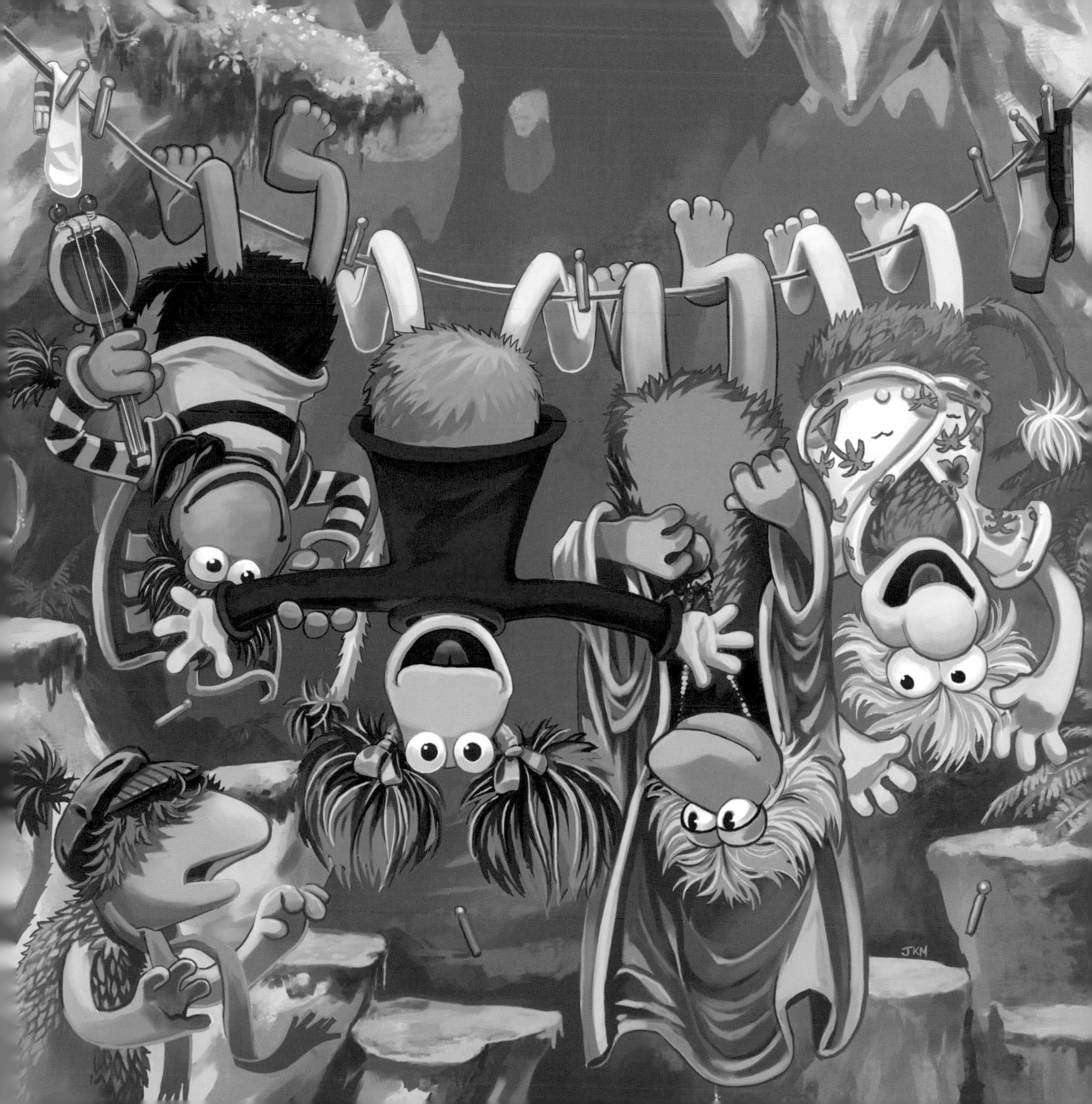
JKM

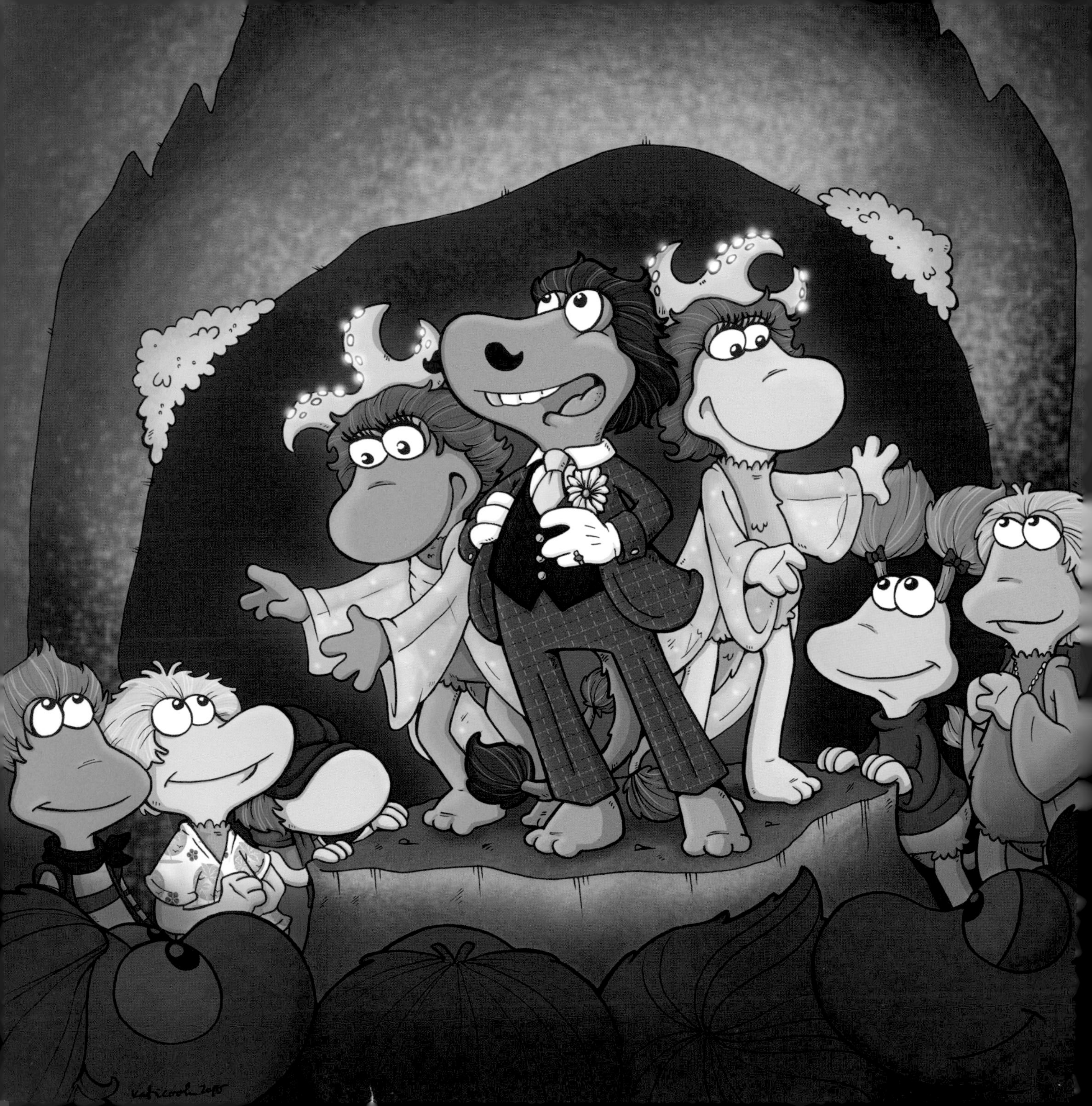

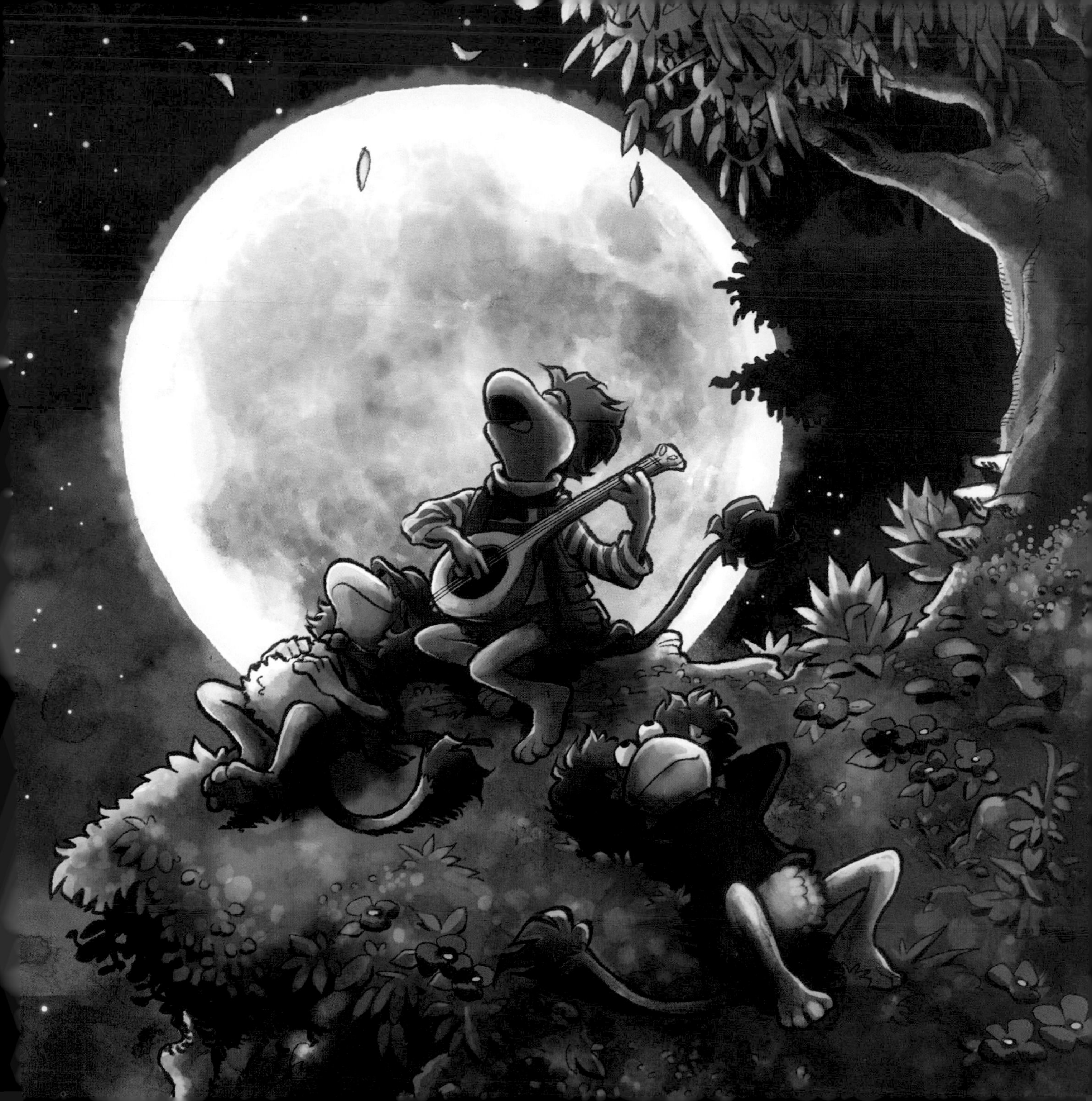

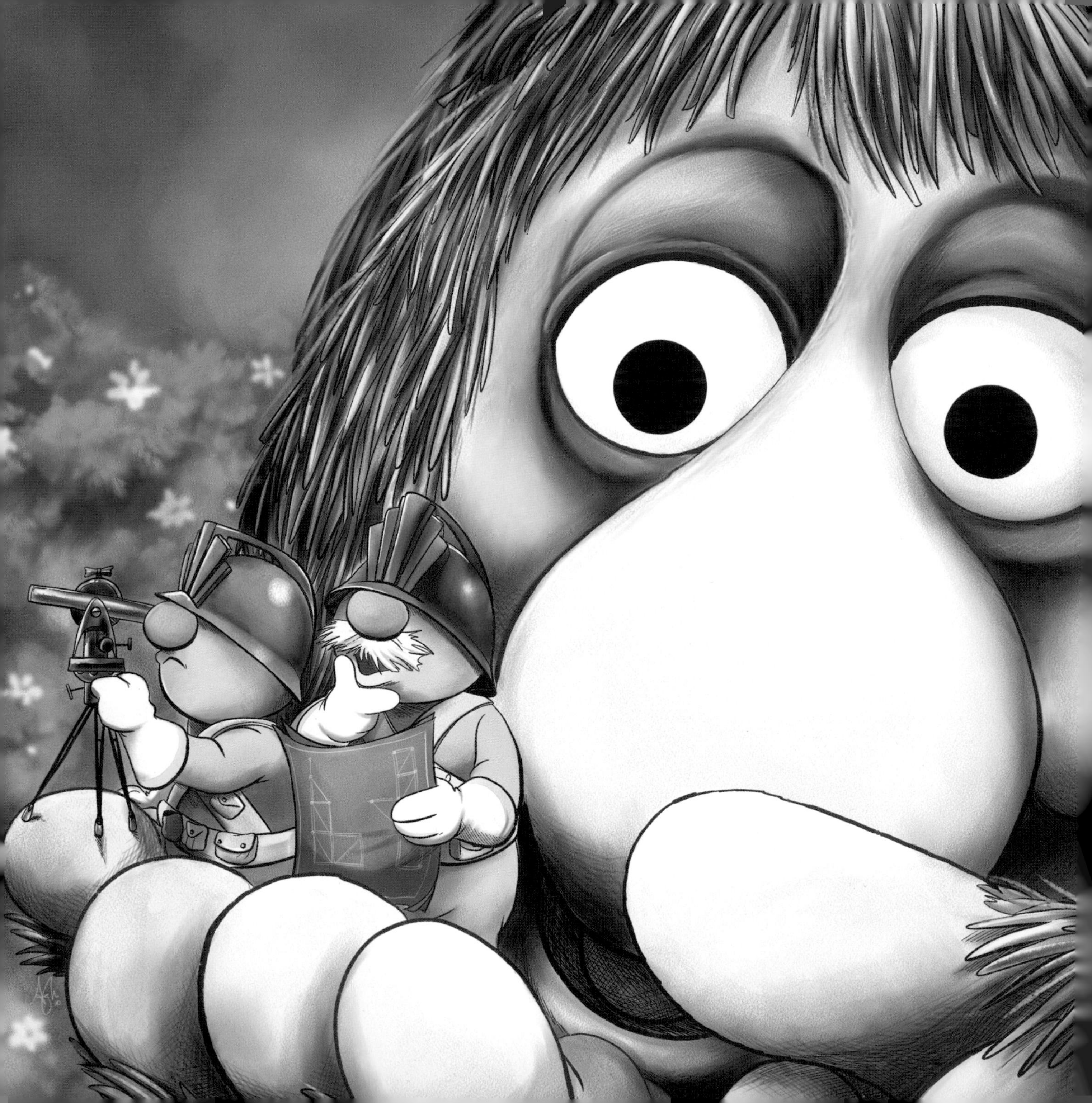

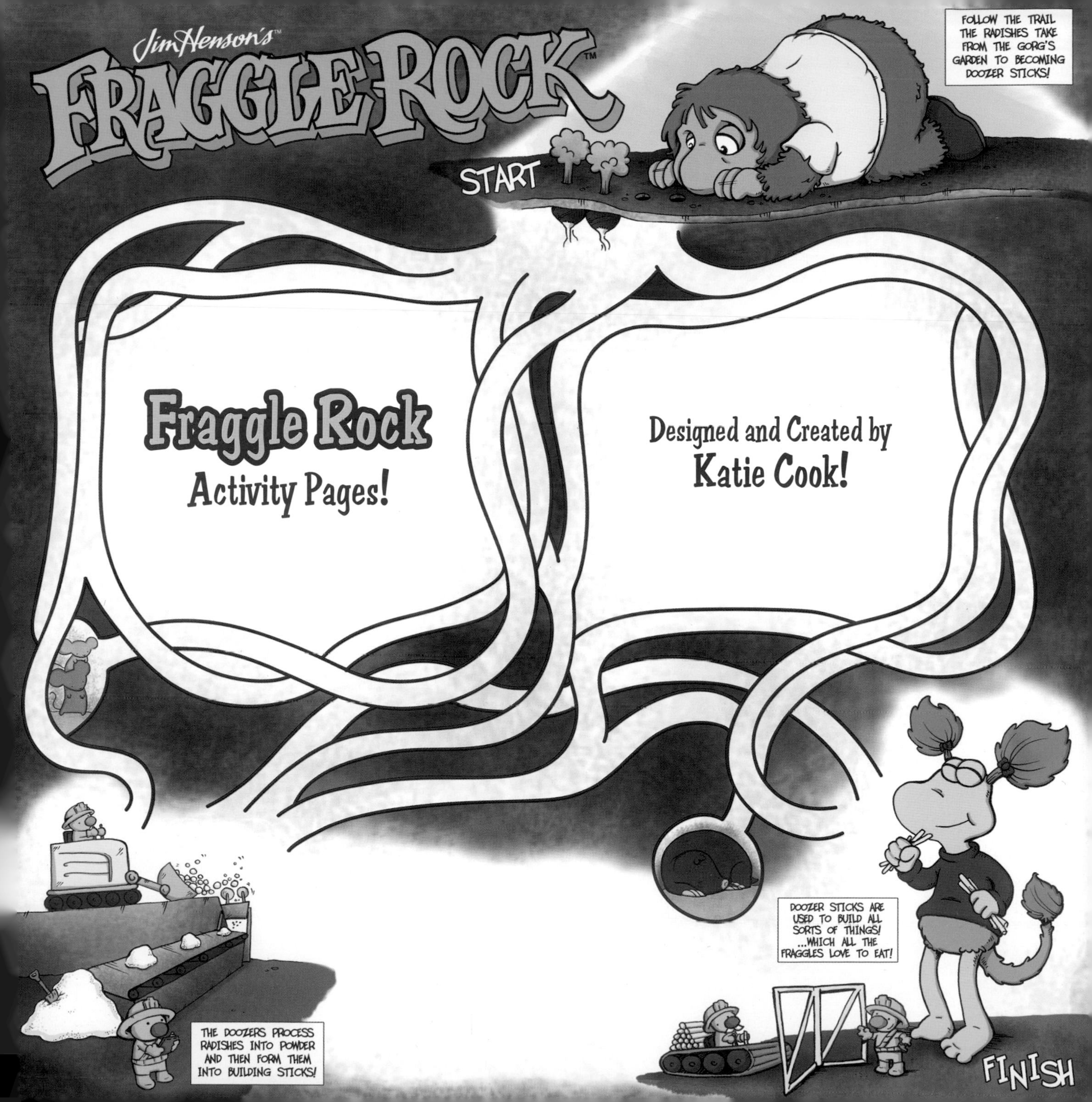

Jim Henson's™
FRAGGLE ROCK™
FOLLOW THE TRAIL THE RADISHES TAKE FROM THE GORG'S GARDEN TO BECOMING DOOZER STICKS!
START
Fraggle Rock
Activity Pages!
Designed and Created by
Katie Cook!
DOOZER STICKS ARE USED TO BUILD ALL SORTS OF THINGS! ...WHICH ALL THE FRAGGLES LOVE TO EAT!
THE DOOZERS PROCESS RADISHES INTO POWDER AND THEN FORM THEM INTO BUILDING STICKS!
FINISH

"how to draw a doozer"

a lesson in artistic interpretation by

MOKEY FRAGGLE

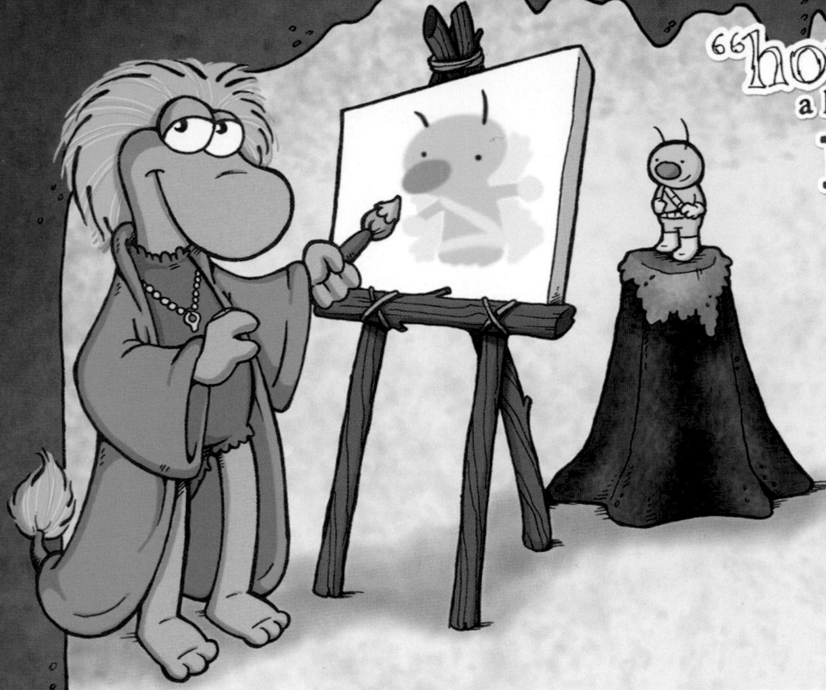

Step 1:
First, in PENCIL, lightly rough in the basic shape of the head and the body of our little Doozer friend!

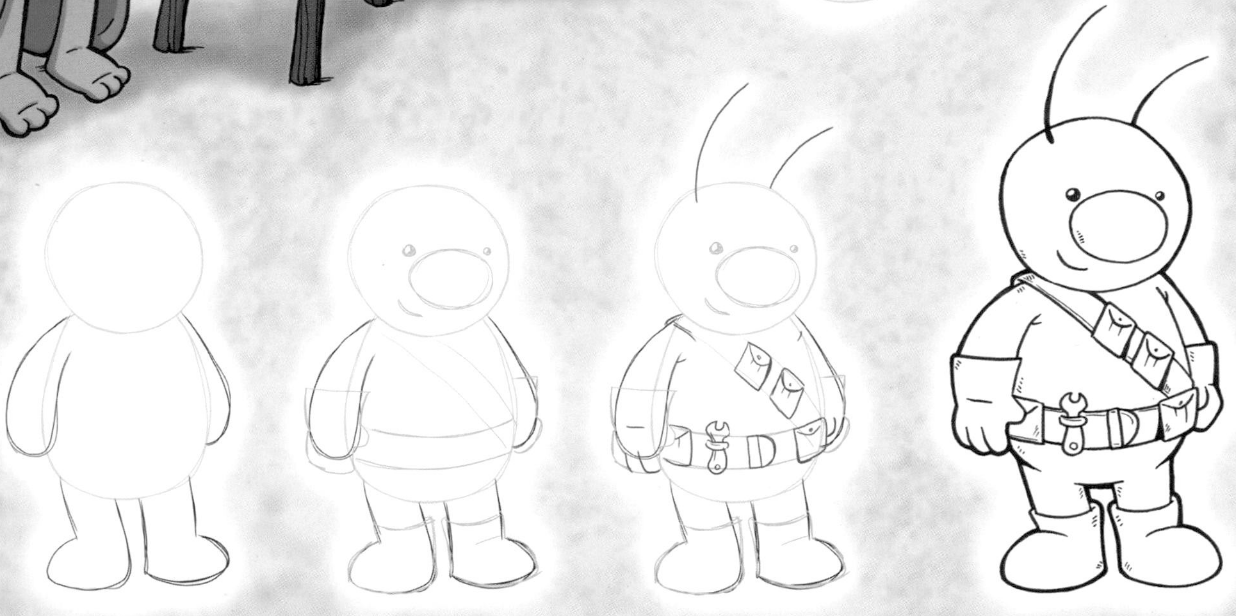

Step 2:
Next, still in pencil, we can add the details of his arms and legs... He's starting to take shape!

Step 3:
On to some more details. Pencil in his facial features and the shape of his boots, gloves and belts.

Step 4:
Details, details! More details! Now it's time to pencil in the pockets on his belts, his tools and his antennae!

Step 5:
Now, with a black pen or marker, trace over your pencil drawing. Erase your pencil lines and you're done!

"how to build a doozer structure"

a lesson in artistic interpretation by
MOKEY FRAGGLE

Things you will need:
- 1/2 cup salt
- 1/2 cup water
- 1 cup flour
- mixing bowl
- toothpicks
- newspaper

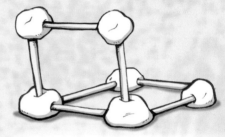

Step 3:
Shape the dough into 1/2" inch round balls. Use them to hold the toothpicks in place so you can create cube structures.

Step 1:
Making homemade play dough! Mix the flour, salt and water in a bowl. When the dough stiffens, knead it with your hands. (Add food coloring if you want to make it colorful!)

Step 2:
Lay down newspaper to protect the surface of the tabletop you'll be working on.

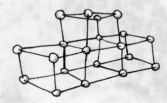

Step 4:
Create your masterpiece! (How tall can you make it without it toppling? How many shapes can you use to make your building unique?)

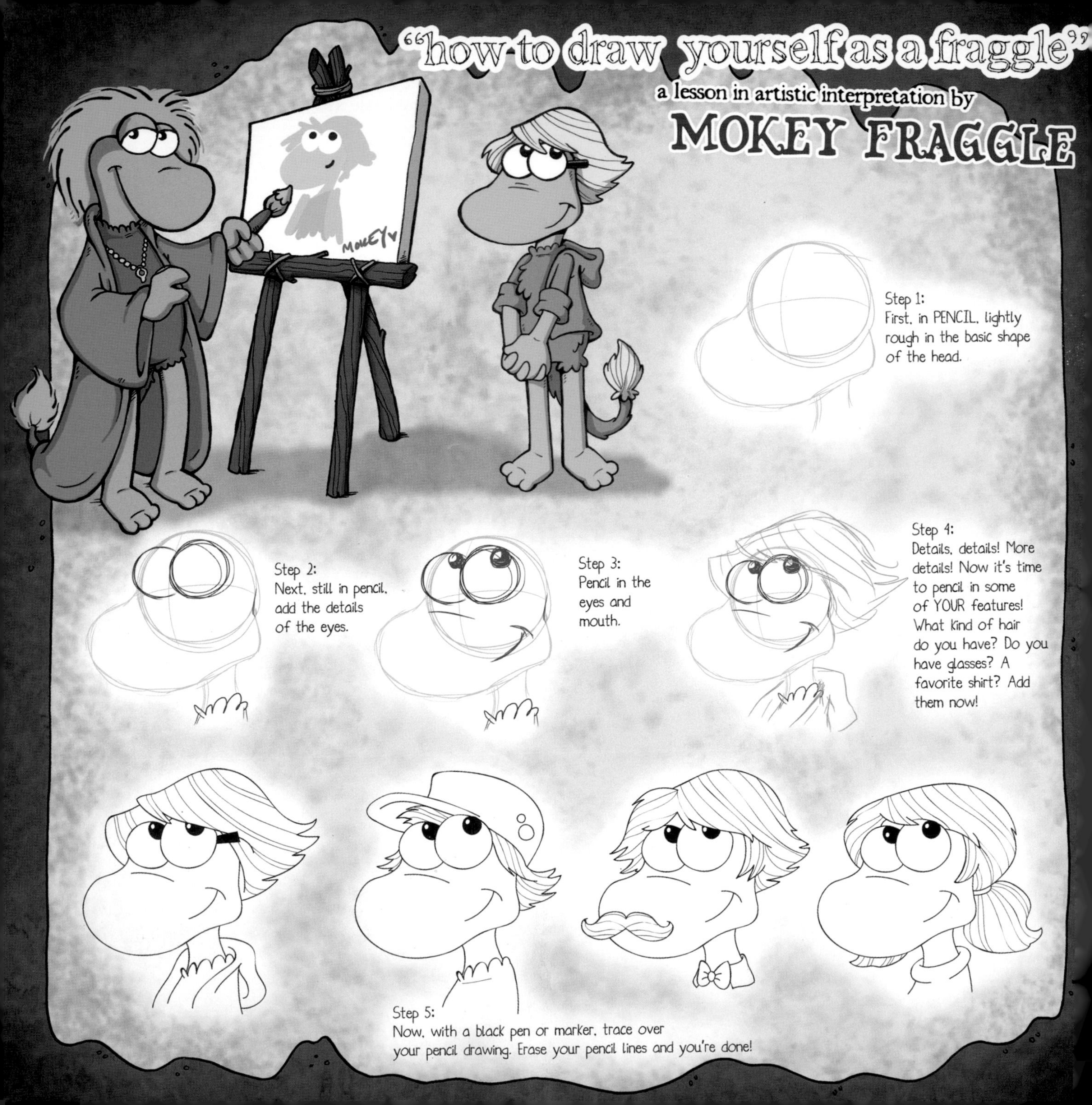
"how to draw yourself as a fraggle"
a lesson in artistic interpretation by
MOKEY FRAGGLE
MOKEY
Step 1:
First, in PENCIL, lightly rough in the basic shape of the head.
Step 2:
Next, still in pencil, add the details of the eyes.
Step 3:
Pencil in the eyes and mouth.
Step 4:
Details, details! More details! Now it's time to pencil in some of YOUR features! What kind of hair do you have? Do you have glasses? A favorite shirt? Add them now!
Step 5:
Now, with a black pen or marker, trace over your pencil drawing. Erase your pencil lines and you're done!

"how to make a radish stamp" with GOBO FRAGGLE

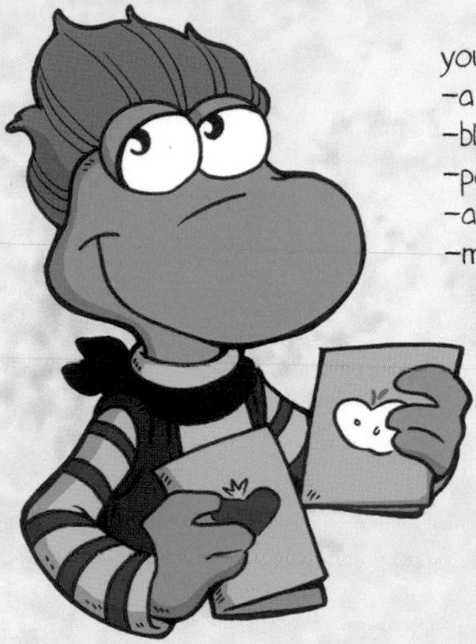

you will need:
- a radish or apple
- blank paper
- paint
- a knife
- markers

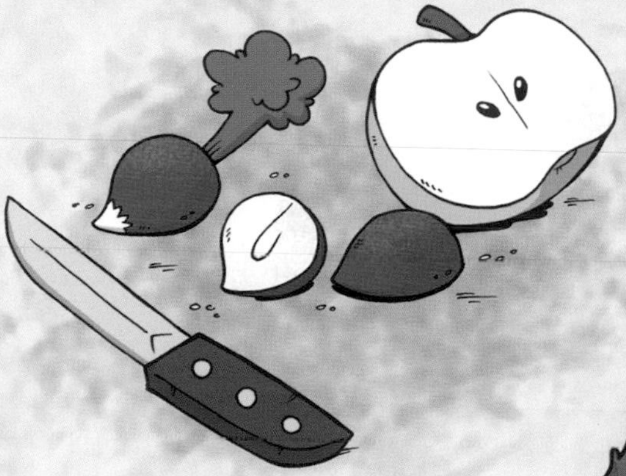

Step 1:
First, get an adult to help. Then, cut the radish (or apple!) in half.

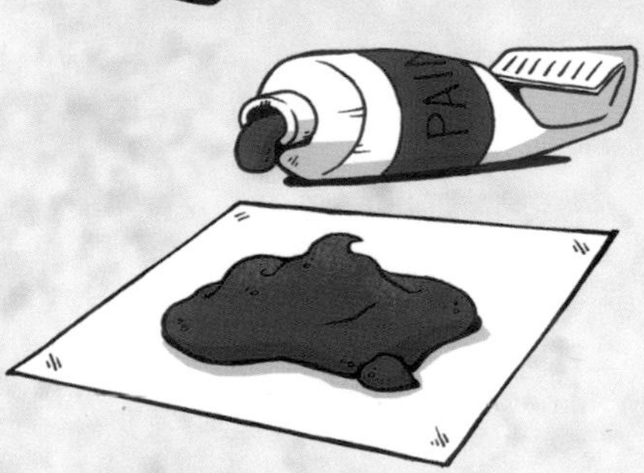
PAINT

Step 2:
On a piece of scrap paper, squeeze out a healthy portion of paint.

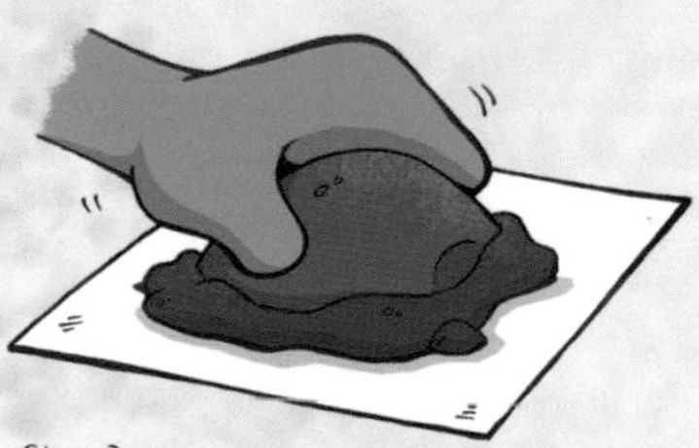

Step 3:
Next, dip one half of the radish or apple into the paint, making sure to coat the whole surface.

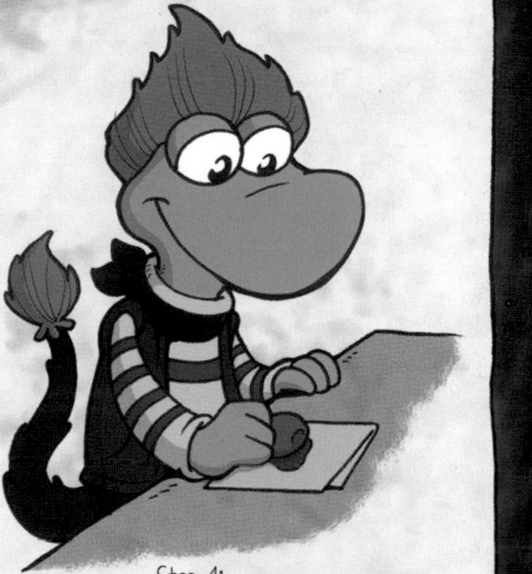

Step 4:
Use the radish or apple to stamp onto your blank sheet of paper.

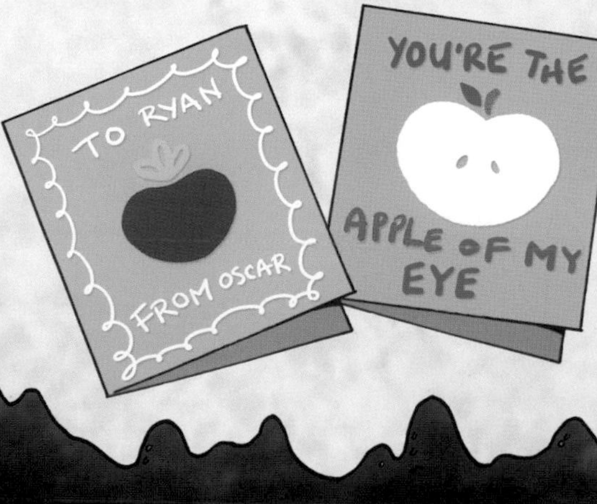
TO RYAN
FROM OSCAR
YOU'RE THE
APPLE OF MY EYE

Step 5:
Decorate around the stamped art using markers, paint and glitter. You can make someone a card or create a fun piece of artwork... What else can you make? What else can you use as a stamp?

About the Creators

Adrianne Ambrose has written about cheerleaders, barbarians, gangsters and dangerous high school girls. She was nominated for a 2008 Writers Guild of America award for video game writing. Her humorous tween diary, *What I Learned From Being a Cheerleader*, is available through Belle Bridge Books.

On top of Fraggle Rock-ing, **Nichol Ashworth** has provided artwork for the self-help book *Perform Like a Rock Star (and Still Have Time for Lunch)*, drawn a monthly comic series for Kaspersky Lab called "Tech-Time Monthly," and recently published *Cog*, a pilot comic with Tokyopop.

Jeffrey Brown is the author of more graphic novels and comics than are necessary, including *Clumsy*, *Incredible Change-Bots* and *Cat Getting Out Of A Bag*. He lives in Chicago with his wife and son.

Bryce P. Coleman is the editor of the latest volumes of *Return to Labyrinth* and *Legends of The Dark Crystal* from Tokyopop, as well as the trade editions of *Hercules: The Knives of Kush* and *FVZA: Federal Vampire and Zombie Agency* from Radical Books.

Katie Cook is an illustrator and comic book artist currently best known for her work in the Star Wars Universe. Her work on many popular licensed properties and her own artwork can be found at **www.katiecandraw.com**.

Cari Corene's current cake in the sky is the webcomic *Toilet Genie*, a fairly epic tale of a pug and a toilet that can be read at **storyofthedoor.com**. Previous sky cakes include Tokyopop's *Rising Stars of Manga Vol. 8*.

Michael DiMotta may or may not be a real life Fraggle. Michael is currently adding a dash of color to comics and dreaming up new children's books that spread love and creativity. His versatility is highlighted by his diverse portfolio which can be viewed at **www.michaeldimotta.com**.

Leigh Dragoon is the creator of the award-winning webseries *By The Wayside*. She also scripted the *The Faerie Path: Lamia's Revenge* graphic novels for HarperCollins/Tokyopop, and contributed artwork to Sam Kieth's *My Inner Bimbo*. She is currently working on a forthcoming Sam Kieth book and several as-yet unannounced projects.

Joanna Estep is an artist, writer, and accomplished whateverist. She has illustrated such titles as *Roadsong*, The S.P.A.C.E. Prize-winning *Reflection*, and her self-penned story *Happy Birthday, Michael Mitchell*.

Sam Humphries is a comic book writer and photographer living in Los Angeles. You can find him online at **samhumphries.com**.

Lizzy John lives in Brooklyn and spends most of her days there drawing pretty pictures. Sometimes she gets paid for it.

Xeric Award-winning cartoonist **Neil Kleid** authored the critically acclaimed graphic novels *Brownsville* and *The Big Kahn* and has written for Marvel, Image, Dark Horse, DC and Random House. Neil lives in New Jersey and is working on three graphic novels, several comic books, a big boy novel and no sleep.

Whitney Leith is an aspiring artist with a love of naps and a talent for daydreaming. She was published in the third *Rising Stars of Manga* anthology for her story "Cupid's Folly" and is currently working on whatever tickles her fancy.

Jeremy Love is a prolific animator, illustrator and writer. He is one third of the Love brothers, founders of Gettosake Entertainment, an illustration and animation studio. His critically acclaimed serialized graphic novel, *Bayou* is an Eisner Award Nominee and Glyph Award winner.

Hopelessly addicted to coffee, it makes perfect sense that **Jake Myle**r settled down with his wife in Seattle, WA. Jake illustrated the graphic novel *Undertown*, which was syndicated in newspapers worldwide, provided covers for many Disney, Pixar and Henson properties and interiors for a series of *Finding Nemo* comics.

Fernando Pinto has drawn comics for Mirage (*TMNT*), SLG (*Ursa Minors*) and DDP (*Hack/Slash*). He also teaches drawing, plays bass, and really likes noodles. You can check his online GN at www.warpedcomic.wordpress.com and his art at www.fernandopintoart.com. He's never heard of himself either, so don't worry.

Grace Randolph has written for Marvel, DC, BOOM! Studios, and Tokyopop. She is also the host and creator of the web show *Beyond The Trailer*. To get a full rundown of her work, visit www.gracerandolph.com. Grace thanks you for taking the time to read her bio.

Jeff Stokely is a newcomer to the comic book scene. *Fraggle Rock* #1 was his first published title and will remain that way indefinitely. Jeff currently resides in Manhattan Beach, CA with his smelly roommate and their empty refrigerator.

Heather White lives and writes in Berkeley, California. When she isn't writing, she's usually practicing telepathic communication with her dog or knitting absurdly difficult things.

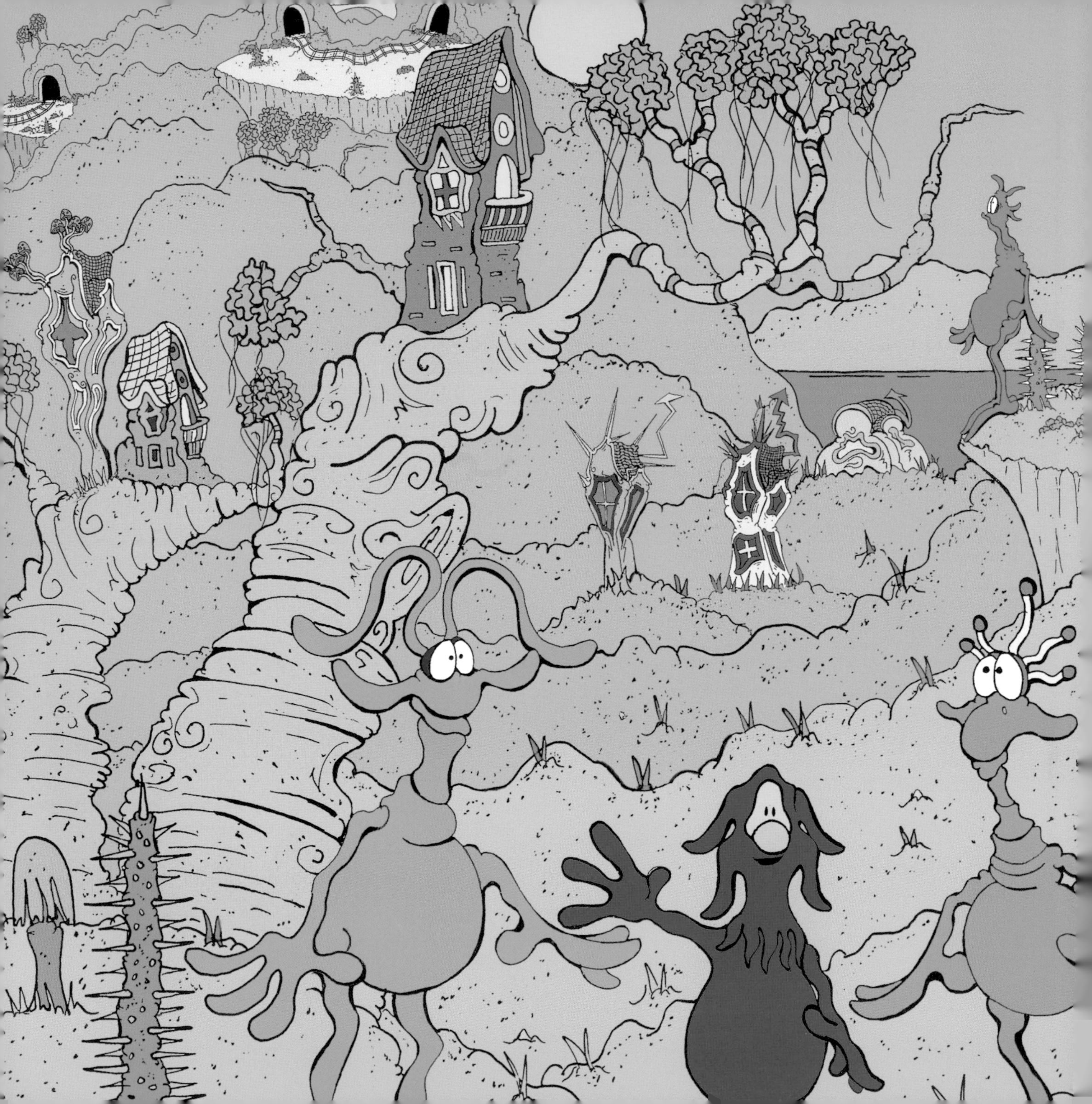

Jim Henson™
THE JIM HENSON COMPANY

presents

THE SKRUMPS™

The Skrumps. I had been writing and illustrating many comics and storybooks, and sculpting the characters that I created. In 1995, I completed a book called *The Wonderful World of Skrumpkinville*. My original story focused on creatures I called Skrumpkins that inhabited the pumpkin patch of a place called Skrumpland. From these origins, I created *The Skrumps* and expanded their universe to include innumerable, quirky, fun, colorful characters and fantastical environments.

From here, I developed the concept for my first line of vinyl toys with storybooks. In 2004, I made Series 1 featuring Skrumpy, The Mooch, Worried Willie, Skraps Baxter, Lazy Louie and The Bathtub Bandit and they were released in toy stores and comic book shops. Since The Jim Henson Company discovered them, we have been working together to bring *The Skrumps* to all new levels in entertainment, including animation, video games, publishing and everything cool.

The Bathtub Bandit. For my new 8-page segment for Archaia, I wanted to revisit the story of The Bathtub Bandit, enhance it, and keep it simple at the same time. This new story raises many questions for the reader. Is there more than meets the eye happening here? Is the Bathtub Bandit stealing baths simply because he loves the bubbles? Is he a nuisance, a menace or some kind of guardian angel? It's up to the reader to decide, but the truth is, we can never know. The Bandit, no matter what kind of ridicule he may face, will never tell. He'll just smile, say, "Bubble, bubble, bubble…" and continue on in his quest for the ultimate bubble bath!

John Chandler
Creator of The Skrumps
June 2010

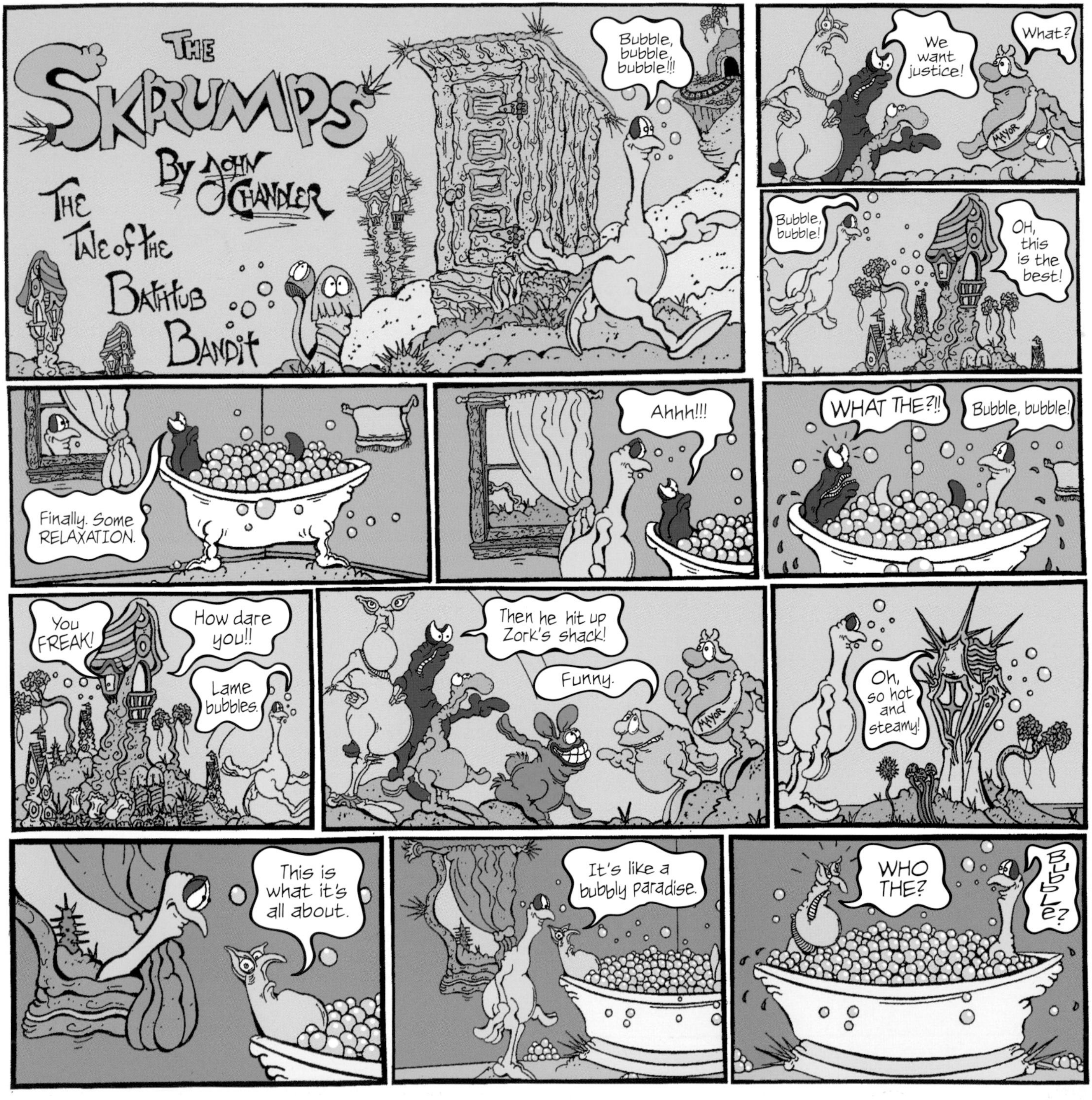

THE SKRUMPS
By John Chandler
The Tale of the Bathtub Bandit
Bubble, bubble, bubble!!!
We want justice!
What?
MAYOR
Bubble, bubble!
OH, this is the best!
Finally. Some RELAXATION.
Ahhh!!!
WHAT THE?!!
Bubble, bubble!
You FREAK!
How dare you!!
Lame bubbles.
Then he hit up Zork's shack!
Funny.
MAYOR
Oh, so hot and steamy!
This is what it's all about.
It's like a bubbly paradise.
WHO THE?
Bubble?

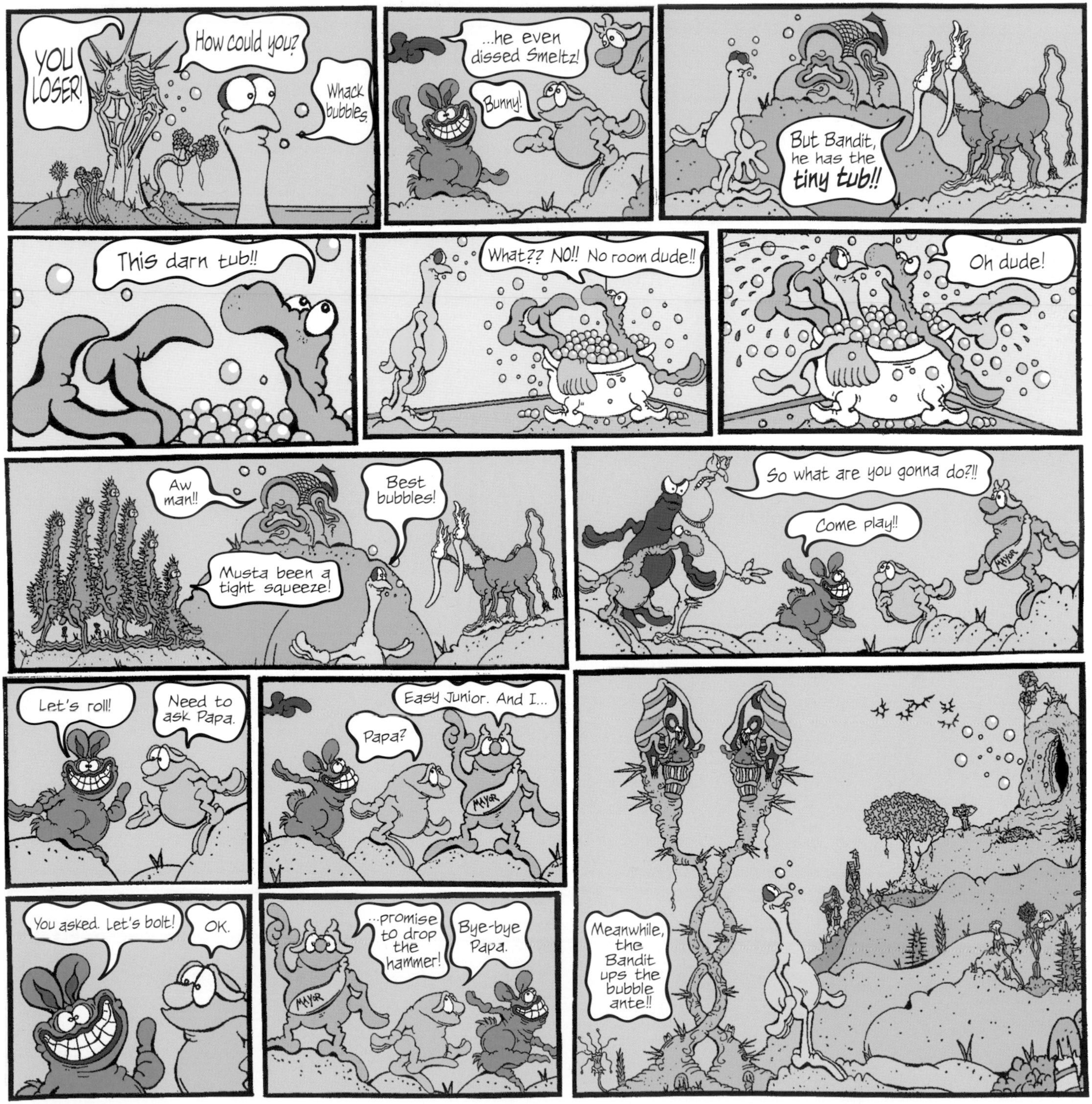
YOU LOSER!
How could you?
Whack bubbles.
...he even dissed Smeltz!
Bunny!
But Bandit, he has the tiny tub!!
This darn tub!!
What?? NO!! No room dude!!
Oh dude!
Aw man!!
Best bubbles!
Musta been a tight squeeze!
So what are you gonna do?!!
Come play!!
MAYOR
Let's roll!
Need to ask Papa.
Easy Junior. And I...
Papa?
MAYOR
You asked. Let's bolt!
OK.
...promise to drop the hammer!
Bye-bye Papa.
MAYOR
Meanwhile, the Bandit ups the bubble ante!!

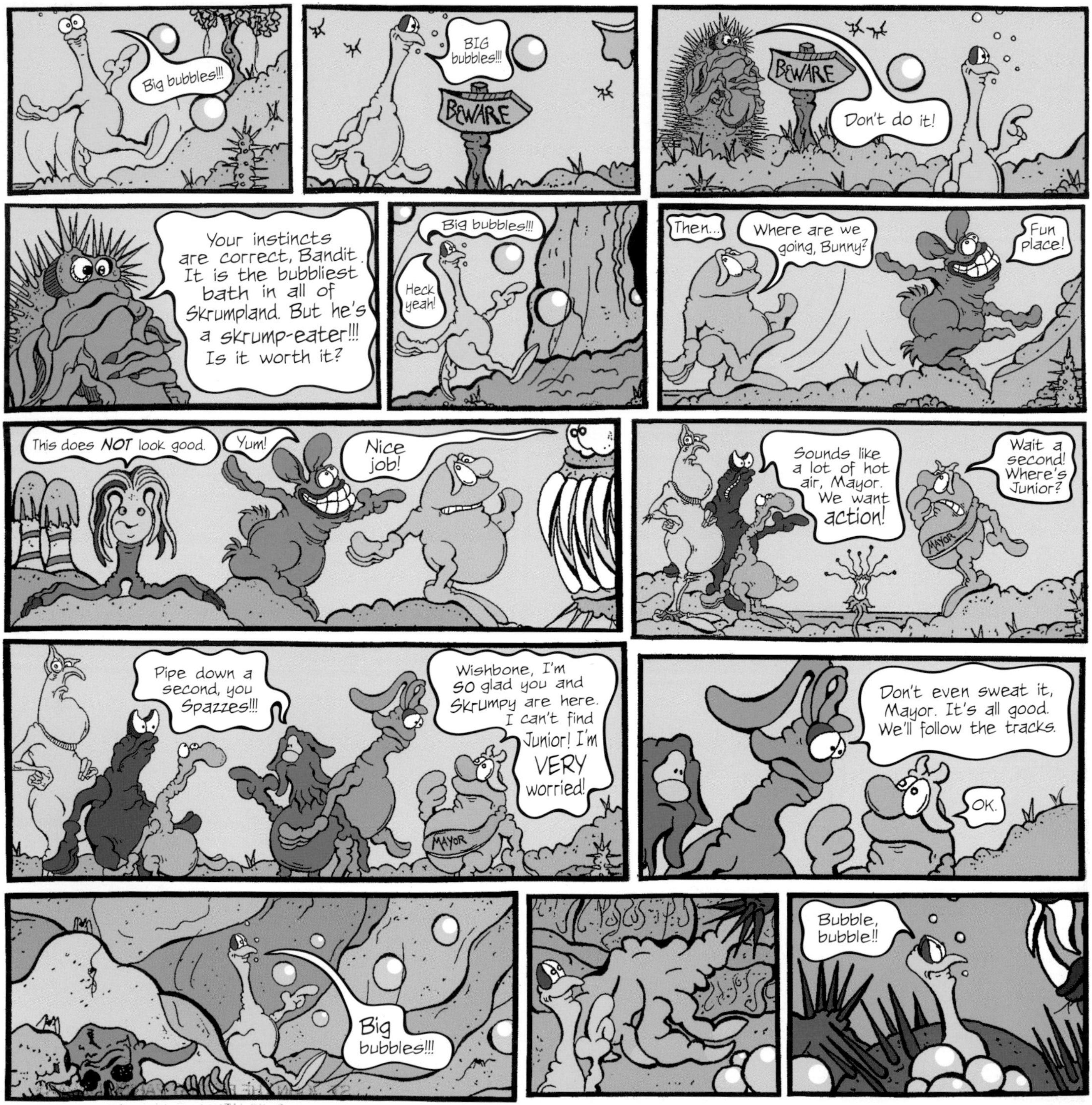
Big bubbles!!!
BIG bubbles!!!
BEWARE
BEWARE
Don't do it!
Your instincts are correct, Bandit. It is the bubbliest bath in all of Skrumpland. But he's a skrump-eater!!! Is it worth it?
Big bubbles!!!
Heck yeah!
Then...
Where are we going, Bunny?
Fun place!
This does NOT look good.
Yum!
Nice job!
Sounds like a lot of hot air, Mayor. We want action!
Wait a second! Where's Junior?
MAYOR
Pipe down a second, you Spazzes!!!
Wishbone, I'm SO glad you and Skrumpy are here. I can't find Junior! I'm VERY worried!
MAYOR
Don't even sweat it, Mayor. It's all good. We'll follow the tracks.
OK.
Big bubbles!!!
Bubble, bubble!!

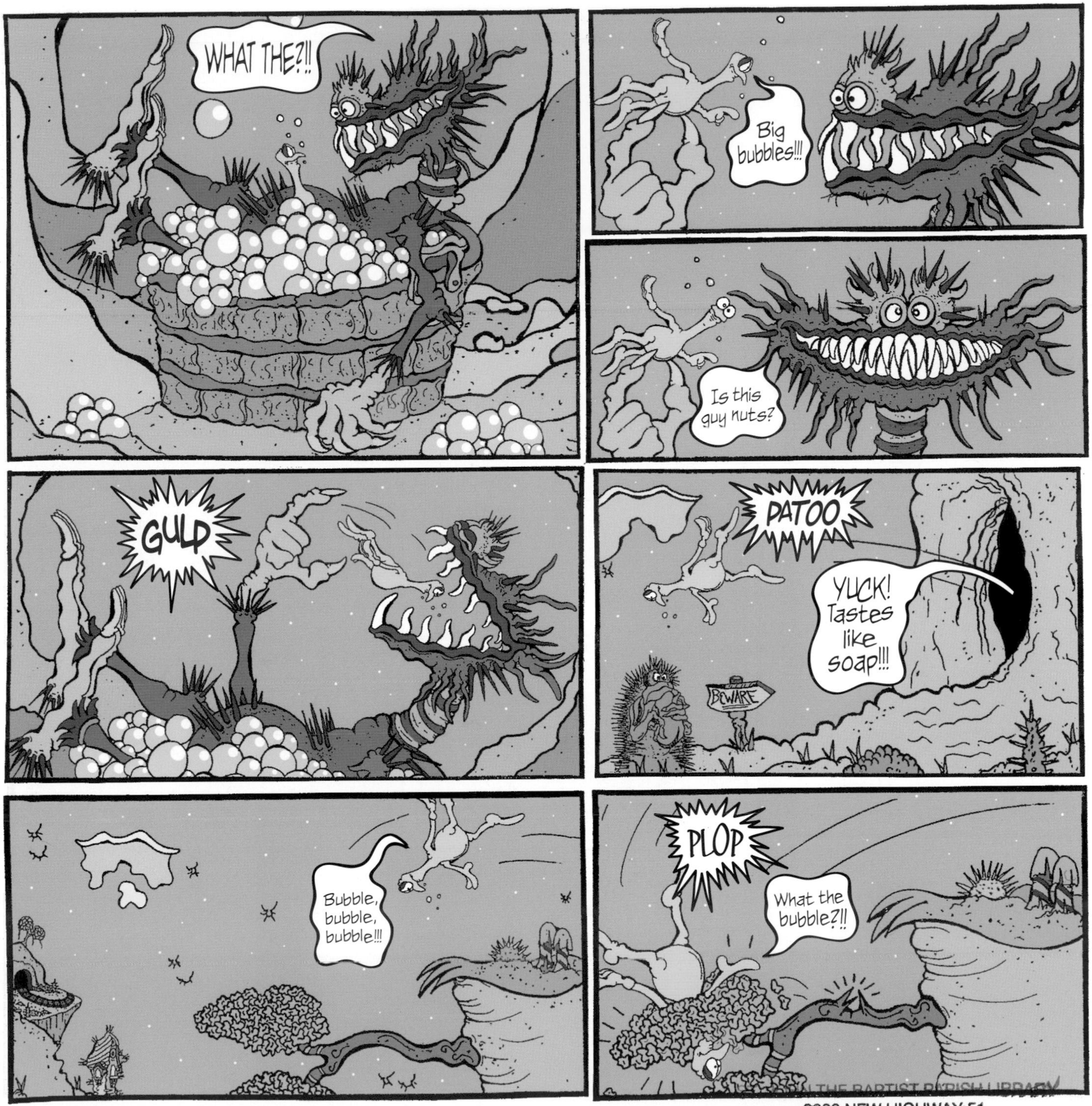
WHAT THE?!!
Big bubbles!!!
Is this guy nuts?
GULP
PATOO
YUCK! Tastes like soap!!!
BEWARE
Bubble, bubble, bubble!!!
PLOP
What the bubble?!!

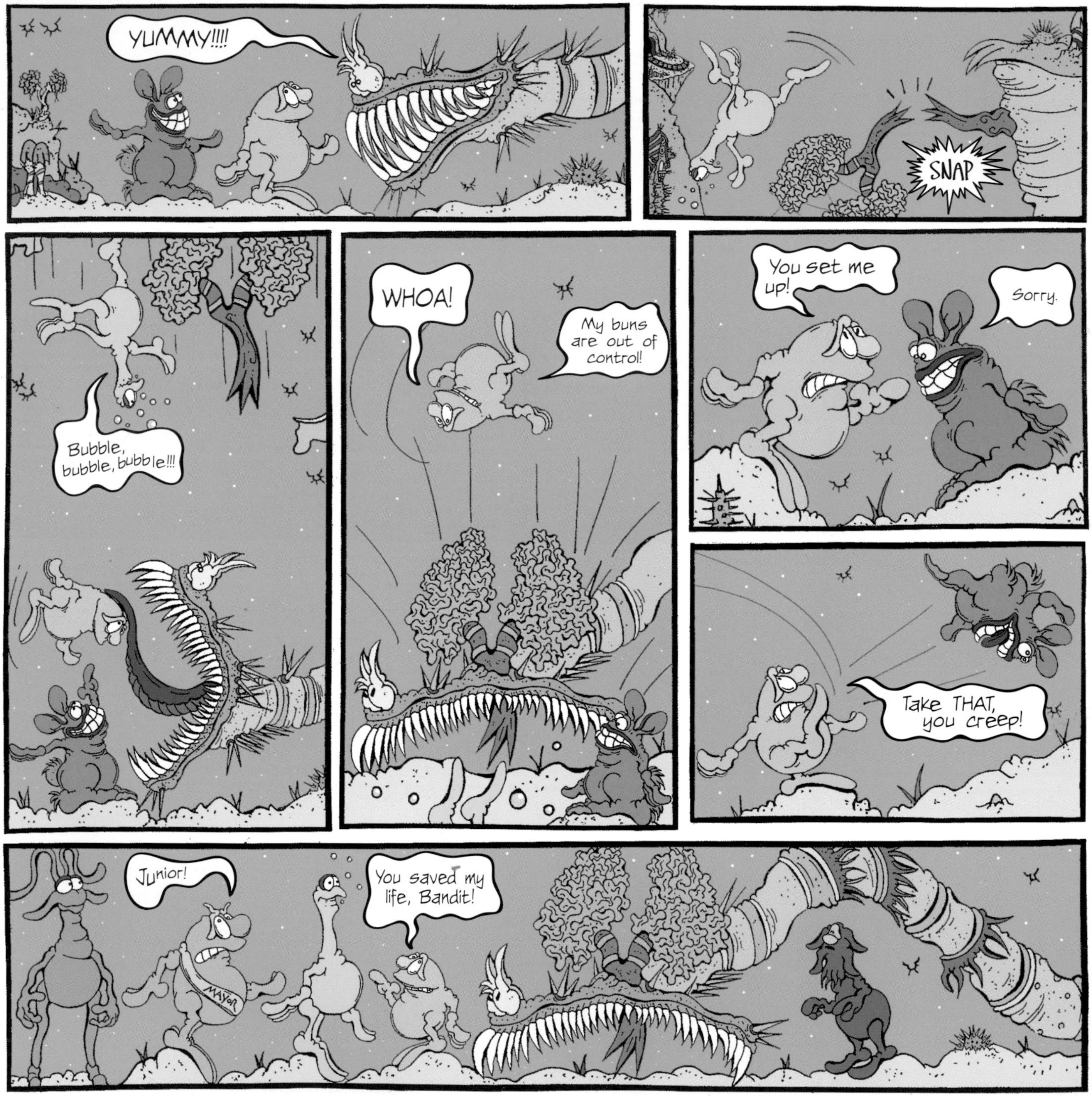
YUMMY!!!!
SNAP
Bubble, bubble, bubble!!!
WHOA!
My buns are out of control!
You set me up!
Sorry.
Take THAT, you creep!
Junior!
You saved my life, Bandit!
MAYOR

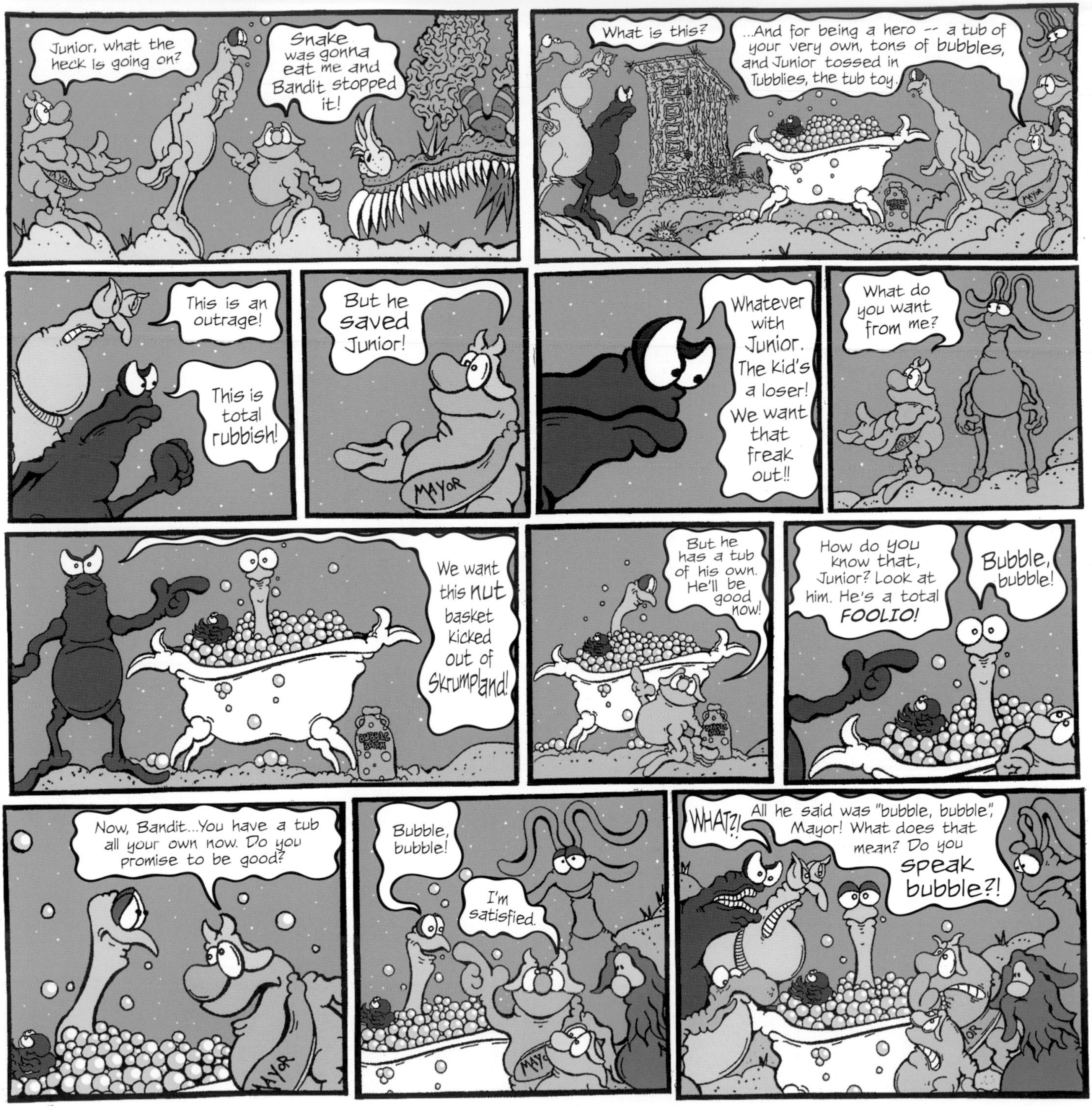
Junior, what the heck is going on?
Snake was gonna eat me and Bandit stopped it!
What is this?
...And for being a hero -- a tub of your very own, tons of bubbles, and Junior tossed in Tubblies, the tub toy.
MAYOR
This is an outrage!
This is total rubbish!
But he saved Junior!
MAYOR
Whatever with Junior. The kid's a loser! We want that freak out!!
What do you want from me?
We want this nut basket kicked out of Skrumpland!
BUBBLE BATH
But he has a tub of his own. He'll be good now!
How do you know that, Junior? Look at him. He's a total FOOLIO!
Bubble, bubble!
Now, Bandit...You have a tub all your own now. Do you promise to be good?
MAYOR
Bubble, bubble!
I'm satisfied.
WHAT?!
All he said was "bubble, bubble," Mayor! What does that mean? Do you speak bubble?!

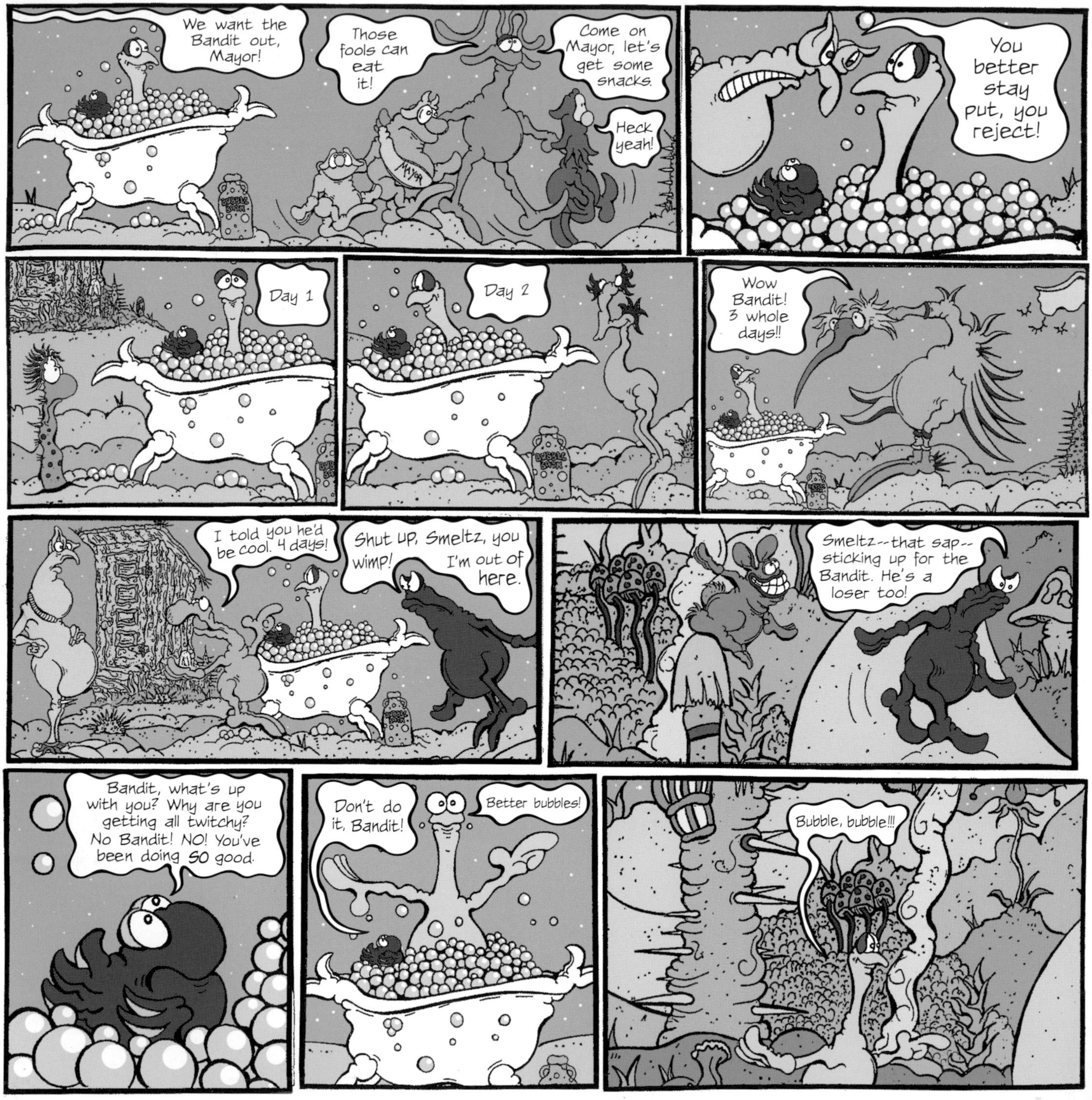
We want the Bandit out, Mayor!
Those fools can eat it!
Come on Mayor, let's get some snacks.
Heck yeah!
MAYOR
BUBBLE BATH
You better stay put, you reject!
Day 1
Day 2
Wow Bandit! 3 whole days!!
I told you he'd be cool. 4 days!
Shut up, Smeltz, you wimp! I'm out of here.
Smeltz--that sap--sticking up for the Bandit. He's a loser too!
Bandit, what's up with you? Why are you getting all twitchy? No Bandit! NO! You've been doing SO good.
Don't do it, Bandit!
Better bubbles!
Bubble, bubble!!!

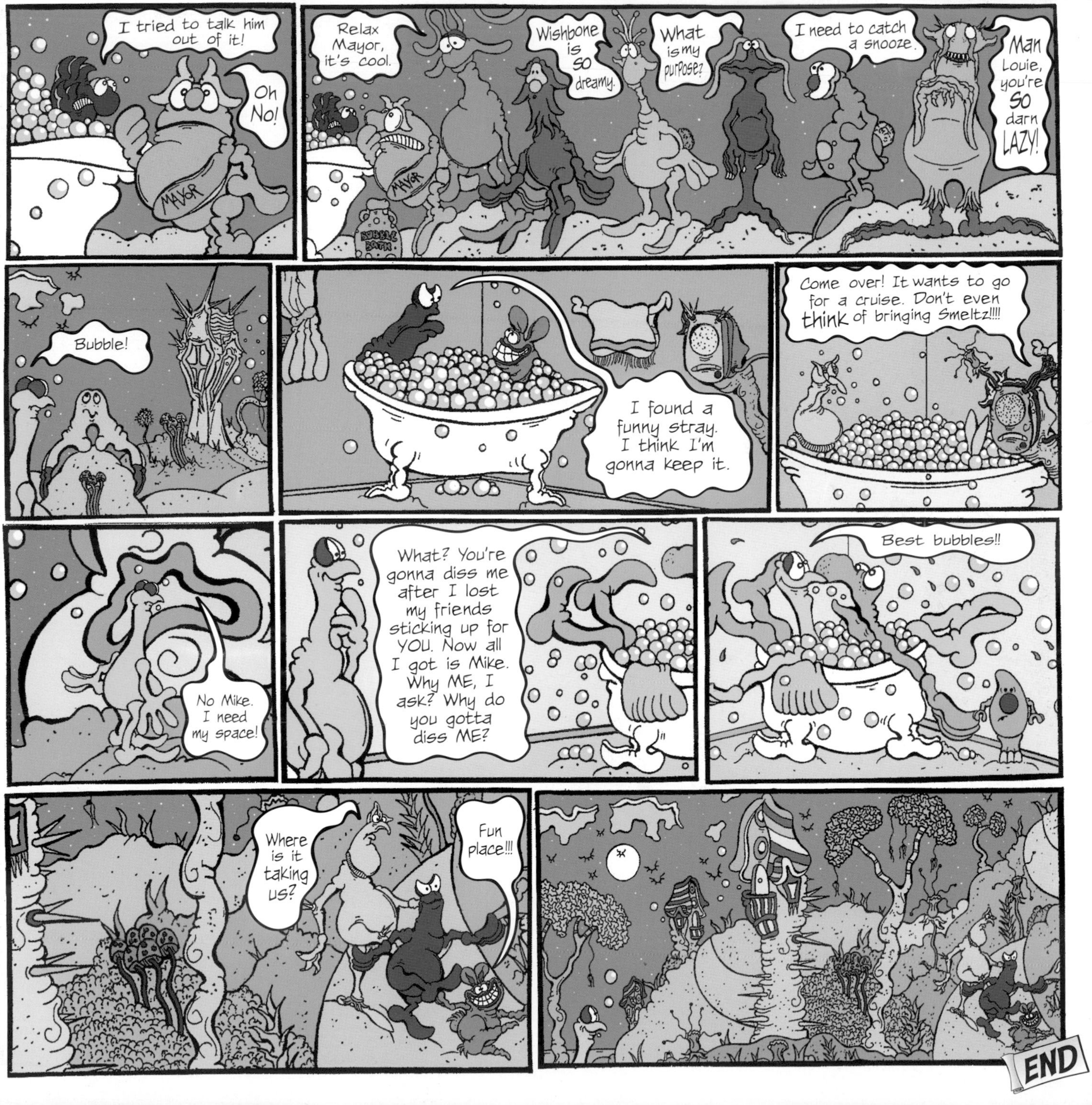
I tried to talk him out of it!
Oh No!
Relax Mayor, it's cool.
Wishbone is SO dreamy.
What is my purpose?
I need to catch a snooze.
Man Louie, you're SO darn LAZY!
MAYOR
BUBBLE BATH
Bubble!
I found a funny stray. I think I'm gonna keep it.
Come over! It wants to go for a cruise. Don't even think of bringing Smeltz!!!!
No Mike. I need my space!
What? You're gonna diss me after I lost my friends sticking up for YOU. Now all I got is Mike. Why ME, I ask? Why do you gotta diss ME?
Best bubbles!!
Where is it taking us?
Fun place!!!
END

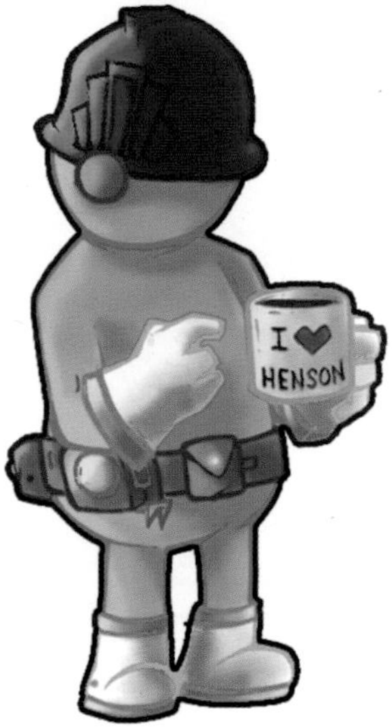
I
HENSON

"Dance your cares away,
Worry's for another day.
Let the music play,
Down at *Fraggle Rock.*"

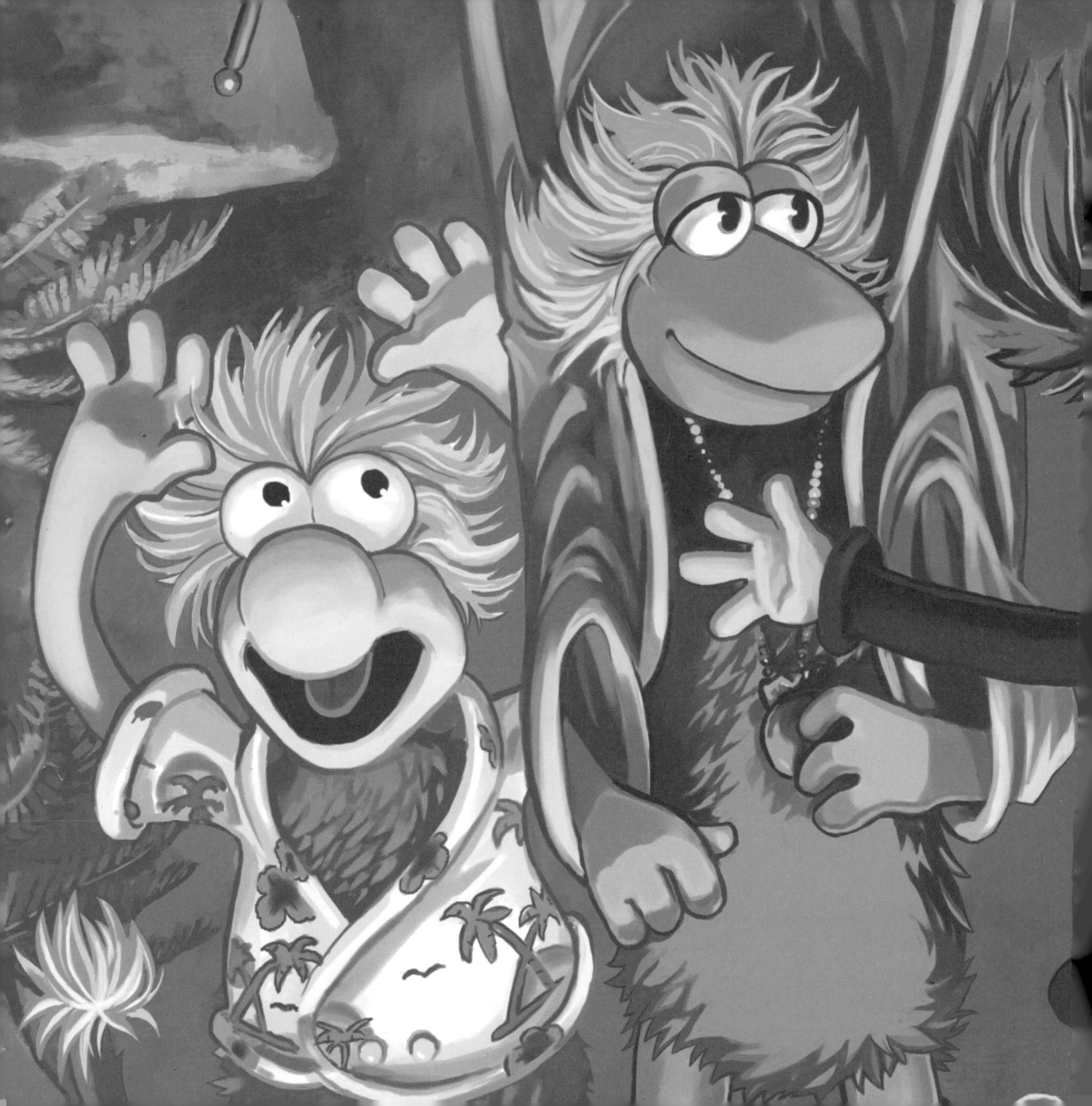